"[A] MOVING EXPLORATION OF MOTHERS AND DAUGHTERS AND THE TIES THAT BIND . . .

This resonant story of three generations of Swedish women, a bestseller in Europe, should also appeal to American readers with its universal truths about women's lives and the constraints of society, family, and love."

—*Library Journal*

"With uncommon wisdom, Marianne Fredriksson spins a generational tale about the inner lives of women and the ties that bind. This is story born of pain and perseverance, inspired by the dignity afforded to those who are courageous enough to retrace the steps of their foremothers in the arduous search for truth, communion, and self-discovery. *Hanna's Daughters* is a generous, consuming, and deeply satisfying novel."

—CONNIE MAY FOWLER
Author of *Before Women Had Wings*

"*Hanna's Daughters* takes you into the whole wide world of mothers and daughters and all the tragedy and triumph therein. Not only does this book entertain, but it teaches its readers big lessons about what matters most. You'll close its covers and think about your own life."

—LORNA LANDVIK
Author of *Patty Jane's House of Curl* and *The Tall Pine Polka*

"Fredriksson's unsentimental, unsparing writing heightens the emotional impact of the women's lives. This fresh look at spiritual and emotional isolation demands a second reading to capture the myriad subtleties missed in the first run-through."

—*Rocky Mountain News*

"This Scandinavian story of a century of sweeping changes believably characterizes three generations of a family while keeping the drama intimate enough for readers to empathize."

—*Booklist*

"A chronicle of emotional and psychological exploration . . . An unerringly perceptive portrait of women in the flux of Scandinavian history."

—*Publishers Weekly*

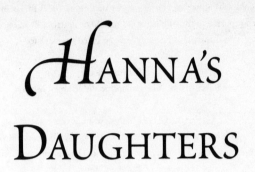

HANNA'S
DAUGHTERS

MARIANNE
FREDRIKSSON

Ballantine Books

New York

A Ballantine Book
Published by The Ballantine Publishing Group

Copyright © 1994 by Marianne Fredriksson
English translation copyright © 1996, 1998 by Joan Tate
Reader's Guide copyright © 1999 by Joan Tate and The Ballantine Publishing Group, a division of Random House, Inc.
Excerpt from *Simon's Family* copyright © 1985 by Marianne Fredriksson
English translation copyright © 1997, 1999 by Joan Tate

http://www.randomhouse.com/BB/

Library of Congress Catalog Card Number: 99-90235

ISBN: 0-345-43349-1

This edition published by agreement with Bengt Nordin Agency, Värdmö, Sweden.

Cover design by Ruth Ross
Cover photo © Lilo Raymond

Manufactured in the United States of America

First American Hardcover Edition: September 1998
First American Trade Paperback Edition: August 1999

20   19   18   17   16

The sins of the fathers are inflicted on the children into the third and fourth generation. We learned that at school when Bible reading was still a subject. I remember thinking that terribly unjust, primitive, and ridiculous. For we were the first generation brought up to be "independent" people, people who were to take their destinies into their own hands.

Gradually, as knowledge of the importance of our social and psychological inheritance increased, the words of the Bible acquired weight. We inherit patterns, behavior, and ways of reacting to a much greater extent than we like to admit. It has not been easy to take this on; so much was "forgotten," disappearing into the subconscious when grandparents left farms and countryside where the family had lived for generations.

There are no biblical words for the deeds of mothers, despite the fact that they are probably of greater importance than those of fathers. Ancient patterns are passed on from mothers to daughters, who have daughters, who then . . .

Perhaps this is an explanation for why women have found it so difficult to stick up for themselves and make use of the rights an equal society has to offer.

I am greatly indebted to Lisbeth Andréasson, superintendent of Bengtsfors Gammalgård, who has scrutinized the book about Hanna from a cultural-historical point of view, provided me with literature on Dalsland, and last but not least translated dialogue from high Swedish to Dalsland borderland dialect. I would also like to thank Anders Söderberg at Wahlström & Widstrand for his criticism, encouragement, and enthusiasm for the project. My thanks also go to my friends Siv and Johnny Hansson, who have come every time I managed to confuse my new computer. That became many times.

* * *

Finally I would like to thank my husband for enduring. I should add that there are no autobiographical elements in this book. Anna, Hanna, and Johanna bear no resemblance to me, my mother, or my grandmother. They are imaginary characters and bear no relation to what is called reality. That is just what makes them real. To me. I hope also to you, the reader, and that you will begin to wonder who your grandmother was and in what way she has shaped your life.

ANNA

INTRODUCTION

*H*er mind was as clear as a winter's day, a day as quiet and shadowless as if snow had just fallen. Harsh sounds penetrated, the clatter of dropped enamel bowls and cries. It frightened her. Like the weeping from the next bed slicing into the whiteness.

There were many who cried where she was.

She had lost her memory four years ago, then only a few months later her words had disappeared. She could see and hear, but could name neither objects nor people, so they lost all meaning.

That was when she came to this white country where time was nonexistent. She didn't know where her bed was or how old she was, but she had found a new way of being and appealed for compassion with humble smiles. Like a child. And like a child, she was wide open to emotions, everything vibrating between people without words.

She was aware she was going to die. That was knowledge, not an idea.

Her family were those who kept her going.

Her husband came every day. He also was wordless but for different reasons: He was over ninety, so he, too, was near the borderline, but he had no wish either to die or to know about it. Just as he had always controlled his life and hers, he put up a fierce struggle against the inevitable. He massaged her back, bent and stretched her knees, and read aloud to her from the daily paper. She had no means of opposing him. They had had a long and complicated relationship.

Most difficult of all was when their daughter, who lived in another town, came to visit. The old woman knew nothing of time or distance, and was always uneasy before she came, as if the moment she woke at dawn, she had already sensed the car making its way through the country, at the wheel the woman with all her unreasonable hopes.

*A*nna realized she was being as demanding as a child. That was no help, and as soon as she gave in, her thoughts slid away: just for once, perhaps, an answer to one of the questions I never had time to ask. After almost five hours of driving, as she turned into the nursing home parking lot, she had accepted that her mother would not recognize her this time, either.

Yet she would ask the questions.

I do it for my own sake, she thought. It makes no difference what I talk about to her.

She was wrong. Johanna did not understand the words, but she was aware of her daughter's torment and her own powerlessness. She did not remember it was her task to console the child who had always asked unreasonable questions. Still, the demand remained as well as the guilt over her inadequacy.

Her desire was to escape into silence, to close her eyes, but she couldn't, her heart thumping, the darkness behind her eyelids scarlet and painful. She started crying. Embarrassed, Anna tried to console her, there, there, wiping the old woman's cheeks.

When she was unable to halt Johanna's despair, Anna became frightened and rang for help. As usual, there was a delay, then the fair girl was standing in the doorway, a girl with young eyes but no depth in them. Anna saw contempt in those blue eyes, and for a moment Anna could see what the girl saw: an older woman, anxious and clumsy, by the side of the really old one.

"There, there," she said, too, but her voice was hard, as hard as the hand that ran over the old woman's head. And yet she succeeded. Johanna fell asleep so suddenly, it seemed unreal.

"We mustn't upset the patients," said the girl. "You must sit there quietly for a while. We'll come and change her and remake the bed in about ten minutes."

Anna slipped out to the terrace like a shamefaced dog, found her cigarettes, and drew the smoke deep down into her lungs. It calmed her and she could think. At first angry thoughts about the girl: damned bitch, hard as nails. Pretty, of course, and horribly young. Had Mother obeyed her out of fear? Was there a discipline here that the helpless old people sensed and gave in to?

Then came the self-reproach. The girl was only doing *her* job, everything she, Anna, ought to be doing, according to the laws of nature. But she couldn't, couldn't bring herself to, even if the time and place had existed.

Last of all came the astonishing realization that Mother had somehow been touched by the questions she'd asked.

She stubbed out her cigarette in the rusty tray at the far end of the table. God, how tired she was. Mother, she thought, dear wonderful Mother, why can't you show pity and die?

Frightened, she glanced out over the nursing home grounds where the Norway maples were in flower and smelling of honey. She drew in the scent with deep breaths, as if seeking consolation in the spring, but her senses were dulled. I'm as if dead, too, she thought as she turned on her heel and walked determinedly to the ward sister's door. She knocked and just had time to think, please let it be Märta.

It was Sister Märta, the only one she knew here. They greeted each other like old friends, then the daughter sat in the visitor's chair and was just about to start asking when she was overwhelmed by emotion.

"I don't want to start crying," she said, then did.

"It's not easy," said the sister, pushing the box of tissues across.

"I want to know how much she understands," said the daughter, adding her hope of being recognized and the questions she'd asked her mother, who didn't understand, yet did.

Sister Märta listened with no surprise.

"I think the old understand in a way we find difficult to grasp. Like newborn infants. You've had two babies yourself, so you know they take everything in, anxieties and joys. Well, you must remember?"

No, she didn't remember. She remembered nothing but her own overwhelming feeling of tenderness and inadequacy, though she knew what the nurse was talking about. She had learned a great deal from her grandchildren.

Then Sister Märta talked about the old woman's general condition in consoling terms. They had gotten rid of her bedsores, so she was in no physical pain.

"But she's rather uneasy at night," she said. "She seems to have nightmares. She wakes up screaming."

"She dreams?"

"But of course she dreams, everyone does. The pity is we can never find out what they're dreaming, our patients."

Anna thought about the cat they'd had at home, a lovely creature leaping up out of its sleep, hissing, its claws extended. Then she was ashamed of the thought. But Sister Märta didn't notice her embarrassment.

"Considering Johanna's poor condition, we prefer not to give her tranquilizers. I also think perhaps she needs her dreams."

"Needs?"

Sister Märta pretended to ignore the surprise in the other woman's voice.

"We're thinking of giving her a room of her own," she went on. "As things are, she's disturbing the others in the ward."

"A room of her own? Is that possible?"

"We're waiting out Emil in number seven," said the nurse, lowering her eyes.

Not until the daughter was backing the car out of the parking lot did she take in what had been said about Emil, the old priest whose hymns she'd heard over the years. She hadn't thought about it today, that there'd been no sound from his room. For years, she'd heard him singing about life in the valley of the shadow of death, and the Lord waiting with his terrible judgments.

$\mathcal{J}$ohanna's secret world followed the clock. It opened at three in the morning and closed again at dawn.

Her world contained a wealth of images, filled with colors, scents, and voices. Other sounds, too. The roar of the falls, the wind singing in the tops of the maples, and the forest rejoicing with birdsong.

On this night the pictures she sees tremble with excitement. It is summer and early morning, with slanting rays of the sun and long shadows.

"You must be mad," shouts the voice she knows best, her father's. He's red in the face and frightening in his agitation. She's afraid and flings her arms around his leg. He lifts her up, runs his hand over her head.

"Don't you think, girl?" he says.

But her eldest brother is standing in the middle of the room, handsome, with shiny buttons and high boots, and he's shouting, too.

"To the cave, all of you, and today, too. They might already be here tomorrow."

Then another voice, resourceful.

"Listen now, lad. Would Axel and Ole come here from Moss and would Astrid's lad come here from Fredrikshald to shoot us?"

"Yes, Mother."

"I think you've gone mad," says the voice, but now it's uncertain. And her father looks at the soldier, eye meets eye, and the old man can't mistake the gravity in the young man's eyes.

"Then we'll do as you say."

Then the pictures change, start moving. Feet stomp, burdens are lifted. She sees the earth cellar and store emptied. The great barrel of salt pork is carried out, the herring barrel, the potato bin, the cloudberry jar, the butter in its wooden tub, the hard round slabs of crispbread, all out on the ground, then carried down toward the boat. Sacks filled with blankets and clothes, all the wool in the cottage going the same way, down the slope toward the lake. She sees the brothers rowing. It's heavy going toward the promontory, easier back.

"The oil lamps!" It's her mother calling out on her way indoors.

But the soldier stops her, calling, too, "No, Mother, we'll have to do without light."

The child is wide-eyed and anxious. But then a brimstone butterfly lands on her hand.

The picture changes again; the daylight is miserly, and she's perched on her father's back. As so often, she's being carried up the slopes to the mountain lakes, so secretive and introverted they are, quite different from the great lake with its light and blue glitter. But just above the mill, the largest of the dark lakes breaks the stillness and looks as if it would hurtle down the falls with all its strength were the dam not there.

Father checks the floodgate as always in the evenings.

"Norwegian water," he says, with weight in his voice. "Remember that, Johanna, that the water that gives us bread comes from Norway. Water," he says, "is much wiser than people, it doesn't give a damn about borders."

He's enraged. But she's not afraid as long as she's on his back.

Dusk is falling. Laboriously, heavily, he makes his way down the slopes, goes to the mill, feels the locks. The girl hears him muttering wicked curses before he goes on along the path down toward the boat. It's quiet in the cave. Her brothers have fallen asleep, but her mother is moving uneasily on her hard bed.

The girl is allowed to sleep curled inside her father's arm, as close as she can get. It's cold.

Later, new pictures. She's bigger, she can see that from her feet running toward the mouth of the cave, in clogs, for it's slippery on the slopes now.

"Father!" she calls. "Father!"

But he doesn't reply. It's autumn and it'll soon be dark. Then she sees the light in the cave and grows anxious. Someone's shouting in the cave, and Rudolf is there, the blacksmith she's afraid of. She sees them staggering about, he and Father.

"Get on home, brat!" he yells, and she runs, crying, running and falling, hurting herself, but the pain from her grazed knees is nothing to the hurt in her breast.

"Father!" she screams. "Father!"

Then the night sister is there, worried.

"There, there, Johanna. It was only a dream, sleep now, go to sleep."

She obeys, as she usually does, and is allowed to sleep for an hour or two before the voices of the day shift explode in her body and race like ice through her veins. She's shaking with cold but no one sees it. The windows are flung open, they change her, and she's no longer cold or feels any shame.

She's back in the white emptiness.

*A*nna had a night of difficult and clarifying thoughts. They started with the feeling that had come over her when Sister Märta had asked her about her own babies. Tenderness and inadequacy. It had always been like that for her; when her emotions were strong, her strength ebbed away.

She hadn't fallen asleep until three in the morning. She dreamed about Mother and the mill and the falls hurtling down into the bright lake. In her dream the great waters had been gleaming and still.

The dream had consoled her.

Oh, what stories Mother had told. About elves dancing over the lake in the moonlight, and the witch who was married to the blacksmith and could conjure the minds out of people and beasts. When Anna was older, the stories grew into long tales of the lives and deaths of the people in that magical border country. Then when she was eleven and more critical, she considered it all lies, that that amazing country existed only in her mother's imagination.

One day when she was grown up and had her driver's license, she put her mother into the car and drove her home to the falls by the long lake. It was only 150 miles. She could still remember how angry she was with her father when she measured the distance on the map. He had had a car for many years and could well have driven Johanna and the girl those few hours, the girl who had heard so many stories about this country of her childhood. If the will had been there. And the compassion.

But when she and her mother reached their goal, that sunny summer's day thirty years ago, her anger had blown away. Solemnly and with surprise, she stood there and looked. Here it was, the land of fairy tales with the long lake at the bottom, the water falling twenty meters, and the still Norwegian lakes up in the mountains.

The mill had been pulled down and a power station built, in disuse now that nuclear power had taken over. But the lovely little red mill house was still there, long ago turned into a summer place for some unknown person.

The moment was too great for words, so they said little. Mother wept and apologized for doing so. "I'm so stupid." Not until they had taken the picnic basket out of the car and sat down with coffee and sandwiches on a smooth flat rock by the lake did Johanna begin to speak, and her words came just as they used to when Anna was small. She chose the story of the war that never happened.

"I was only three when the Union crisis came and we moved into the cave. Over there, behind the promontory. Perhaps I think I can remember because I'd been told the story so many times as I grew up. But I seem to have such a clear picture of it. Ragnar came home. He was so handsome as he stood there in his blue uniform with its shiny buttons and told us there was going to be a war. Between us and the Norwegians!"

The surprise was still there in her voice, a child's amazement when faced with what is incomprehensible. The three-year-old, like everyone in the borderlands, had relatives on the other side of the Norwegian lakes, where her mother's sister had married a fish merchant in Halden, which was called Fredrikshald in those days. The cousins had spent many summer weeks in the mill house, and Johanna had gone with her mother to spend a month or two in that town with its great fortress. She remembered how the fish merchant smelled and what he had said as they stood there looking at the walls of the fortress.

"We shot 'im there, the damned Swede."

"Who?"

"The Swedish king."

The girl had been afraid, but her aunt, a gentler person than her mother, had lifted her up and consoled her.

"That was long ago. And people in those days had no sense."

But perhaps there had been something in her uncle's voice that had stuck in her mind, for some time after her visit to Norway, Johanna asked her father about it. He laughed and said much what her aunt had said, that that was a long time ago when people let themselves be ruled by kings and mad officers.

"But it weren't no Norwegian what shot him. It was a Swede, an unknown hero in history."

Johanna hadn't understood, but she remembered the words. A long time later, at school in Göteborg, she had thought he was right. It had been a blessed shot, the one that had been the end of King Karl XII.

They sat for a long time on that rock that day, Johanna and Anna. Then they walked slowly around the bay, through the forest to the school, which was still there but much smaller than Johanna remembered. In the middle of the forest was a large boulder, thrown there by a giant, thought Anna. Mother stopped by the boulder in surprise. "How small it is." Anna herself had charged her own childhood mountain with magic, so she didn't laugh.

Despite her poor sleep, Anna managed to remain a good daughter for the whole of that long Saturday. She cooked her father's favorite dishes, listened with no apparent impatience to his endless stories, and drove him to the jetty where his boat was, then sat there freezing slightly as he checked the fenders and hoods, tried out the engine, and fed the ducks with bread crumbs.

"Shall we take a trip around?"

"No, it's too cold. And I have to go see Mother."

He looked scornful. Anna had never learned to sail or start an outboard engine. Probably because he . . . but she'd better be careful.

"You've never done anything in your life," he said, "but stick your nose in books."

He had intended to hurt and succeeded.

"I've made a good living out of it," she said.

"Money," he said, scorn now dripping in the corners of his mouth. "Money's not everything in this world."

"That's true. But quite a lot to you, the way you complain about your pension and watch every öre."

The mask of the good daughter cracked then, she thought, cursing her vulnerability and hunching up against the inevitable quarrel. But he was as unpredictable as ever. That's what makes him so difficult, she thought.

"You'll never know what it is to be hungry and poor," he said. "I had to learn early to watch every öre."

She managed to smile, saying, "I was only joking, Dad," and the cloud passed as she helped him ashore and into the car.

He has only two sides, anger and sentimentality, she thought. When one's let off steam, it's time for the other. Then she thought she was being unfair. He was right, anyhow; she had never gone hungry.

Things also went better at the nursing home that day. Anna did as she ought to, chattering away to her mother, holding her hand, feeding her when lunch came. One spoon for Pappa, one spoon for Mamma, then she stopped in the middle, embarrassed. It was degrading.

The old woman fell asleep after the meal. Anna stayed where she was, watching the calm face. When her mother was asleep, she was almost the same as she'd been before, and Anna, almost bursting with tenderness and helplessness, went out to the terrace for a while for a smoke. Cigarette in hand, she tried to think about the difficult sides of her mother, her self-obliteration and burden of guilt. A stay-at-home housewife with one child and all the time in the world to worship it.

That was silly and no help. Nothing hurts so much as love, she thought. What's wrong with me is that I've had too much, that's why I can't control myself, neither when it comes to Mother nor to Rickard. And never when it comes to the children.

The thought of her two daughters also hurt. For no reason; there was no cause for her to worry about them. But they had had an inadequate mother, too. And nothing done can be undone.

When she got back to the sickroom, her mother woke and looked at her, trying to smile. It was only for a moment, and perhaps it never happened at all. And yet Anna was as pleased as if she'd met an angel.

"Hello, Mother dear," she said. "Do you know what I dreamed last night? I dreamed about the Norwegian waters, about everything you told me.

"It reminded me of when we were there for the first time, you and I. You remember, I'm sure. It was a lovely summer's day, and I was surprised that everything was just as you'd told me. We sat on that big rock down by the lake, do you remember? You talked about the cave you fled to when you thought there was going to be war with Norway, how you lived there and how cold you all were. Except you, who was allowed to sleep curled up in your father's arm."

Perhaps it was wishful thinking, but Anna thought she could see some life come into the old face as it shifted from surprise to joy. She smiled.

I'm imagining things. It's not possible. But I can see it's possible. Keep it there, Mother, keep it.

She went on talking about the waterfall and the forest, then the face vanished again. But Anna went on.

"I've often wondered what it felt like sleeping in that cave. When it was so damp and you couldn't light a fire and had only cold food."

This time there was no doubt about it, her face shifted again, this time toward amusement.

She was trying to smile at Anna. It was a great effort and she didn't manage it, so it became a grimace. But then the miracle happened again. The brown eyes looked straight into Anna's, steadily and meaningfully.

The next moment she was asleep. Anna stayed where she was for a long time. Half an hour later, the door opened and the blue-eyed girl said, "Time to change the patients now."

Anna got up and whispered "thank you" into her mother's ear. As she left the room, the old woman in the next bed cried out.

*A*nna made a detour by the shore and sat in the car for a while, looking out over at the promontory where she'd learned to swim. There was a boatyard where hawkweed and sea campion, cranesbill and bird's-foot trefoil grew among the coarse grass, and the once simple cottages were scarcely recognizable now, smartened up as they were with Mexican tiles and other flashy additions. Over toward the mountains where her childhood meadows had been, with their wild strawberries, cornflowers, and cows, were now rows of ter-raced houses like horizontal high-rises.

Only the lake beyond was unchanged; and the islands, their low profiles outlined against the gray horizon.

Lost country, lost childhood.

We once walked hand in hand across that shore meadow with towels and food, sandwiches, coffee for you, soft drinks for me. I'm growing old, she thought with grief and anger. Why does it have to be so ugly, so barbaric?

Once upon a time her mother had been as beautiful as the land-scape here. Now she's falling apart. I'm trying to learn to accept it. About time, for I'm old, too, or soon will be.

I must go home.

But she needn't have hurried. Her father was asleep.

Silently, like a thief, she roamed through the house and finally found what she was looking for. The photo album. But the photo-graphs aroused no memories and were largely an external confirma-tion. Yes, that's what we looked like.

Cautiously, she opened the drawer to put back the old album. It got wedged, and it took a moment for her to see why. Under the floral pa-per her mother had for years used to line the drawers was yet another photograph, this time in a frame. Grandmother. Her mother's mother.

She took it out and looked in surprise at the wall where it had always hung beside those of her paternal grandfather and grandmother,
children and grandchildren. It was true, the photograph was gone and
the unfaded patch on the wallpaper showed where it had been.

How strange. Why had he taken Grandmother away? Hadn't he
liked her? But he had, hadn't he?

What do I know? What can anyone know about parents? About
children?

Why was it so important? Why does it seem a loss not to remember, not to understand? In me, it's like a hole that has to be
filled. As if I hadn't had a childhood, only a story about it, about
what happened, or perhaps didn't happen.

They were good storytellers, Mother most of all with her talent
for making pictures of everything.

Gilded pictures?

She had known since childhood that Dad embroidered, adding
things for effect and avoiding anything complicated. She'd excused
that because the drama was exciting and the point fun.

She crept slowly up the stairs to her old room and went to bed,
feeling how tired she was. On the edge of sleep, she made an important discovery. Perhaps she had so few memories of childhood because she had been living in a description, a story in which she
never really recognized herself.

Was that how a sense of alienation was born?

She was woken by the old man clattering about in the kitchen
with the kettle. She hurried out of bed, guilty conscience sending
her racing downstairs.

"Oh, there you are," he said, smiling. "I thought I'd dreamed
you'd come to see me."

"You'd forgotten?"

"I forget so easily these days."

She took the kettle from him.

"You sit there on the kitchen sofa and I'll fix the coffee."

She found cinnamon buns in the freezer, put them in the oven,
watched the hot water bubbling through the filter paper, smelled

the aroma of coffee, not listening to the old man, now far into some account of how he met a whale one day when sailing from Skagen. An old, old story she'd heard many times—with pleasure.

He'd lost the art of maintaining the tension, though, and of keeping the threads together. His story crawled on, made detours, got lost. "Where did I get to?"

"Outside Varberg."

"Yes, that's right," he said gratefully, but the thread from Varberg soon became part of another story about a girl and a dance in the courtyard of the old fortress. He broke off in confusion in the middle of it, saying it was probably Kungälv fortress where he'd been dancing one light summer night and gotten involved in a fight with the girl's fiancé.

As he described his exceptional victory over the fiancé, he was quite clear and distinct, and the story lifted and glowed, only to collapse into a muddle of other memories of fighting and winning, stopping a bolting horse, and saving the life of a child who'd fallen into a harbor somewhere.

She took the cinnamon buns out of the oven, her despair unendurable. It was terrible, all this foolish boasting, a decayed mind blurting out jumbled memories.

Memories? Perhaps they were just tall tales that had simply become enlarged over the years.

I don't want to grow old, she thought. As she poured the coffee, she thought, how can I ever be truthful? But aloud, she said, "Your tablecloth's beginning to wear out. We must go and buy another tomorrow."

When he'd finished his coffee, the old man went over to the television, the blessed, loathsome television. There, in a sagging armchair, he fell asleep, as usual. She was able to prepare dinner and even managed a short walk through the oaks between the mountains and the house.

They plowed through dinner, beef burgers with cream sauce and cranberries.

"I only get food like this when you're here," he said. "The girls who keep coming don't have time to cook real food."

There was reproach in his words. When she didn't appear to understand, he emphasized it again.

"You could just as well do your writing here."

"I have a husband and children."

"They could come and see you," he said, and she thought, actually he was quite right. She could perfectly well finish her book up there in her old room. Truth, she thought, smiling in all her misery, how do I tell the truth? Suppose I said that I don't get a moment's peace in your house, Dad. I just don't know how I'll stand two more days without going mad.

"I wouldn't disturb you," he said.

There was an appeal in his words and she felt tears coming. But she started talking about the computers she needed for her work, machines that couldn't be moved.

Truth, she thought as she sat there, lying to her father's face. When he got up and thanked her for the meal, his voice was frosty. I don't like him, she thought. I'm afraid of him. I can't stand him. I loathe him. The problem is that I love him.

She did the dishes. A neighbor came in, a man she liked, an amiable man. He was cheerful as usual, stroked her cheek, and said, "It's not easy, I know." She felt an incomprehensible fear as her eyes met his, as if a shadow had flitted through the kitchen.

"You go on in to Dad," she said, hearing the unsteadiness in her voice, "and I'll fix a drink."

With fumbling hands, she laid a tray with the gin bottle she'd brought with her, tonic, a bowl of peanuts. Premonitions? No. I'm tired and an idiot. She said it several times half aloud, tired and idiotic. He's still young, healthy and happy, the kind of person who lives long. As she served the drinks, she said as if in passing, "And how are you, Birgir?"

He looked at her in surprise and said he was well, as always. She nodded but didn't dare meet his eyes all evening.

They went to bed early, at about nine, when the old man suddenly became tired. She helped him to bed, as gently and compliantly as she could. His dignity was vulnerable.

She took a cup of tea up to her room. That was a tradition. Her mother had insisted on it, a cup of tea with honey before they went to bed. As she drank the sweet liquid, her childhood came to life, memories in her senses. The smell of honey in tea, a blue flowery cup, and the shriek of gulls falling from the sky in insolent joie de vivre outside.

She flung open the window and watched the screaming flock as it headed out to sea, above Asper Island and Köpstad Island. The next moment she heard the blackbird singing from the oaks where the may was in bloom.

It was too much; a melancholy of that kind was unbearable. She determinedly took a sleeping pill.

*T*he golden light woke her early. Perhaps not just the light, for in her dreams she'd heard birdsong from the garden, as lovely and strong as the spring itself. For a moment she lay still, trying to distinguish the voices, the chaffinch's joy, the cheerful signals of blue tits, and the whirr of swallows as they flew low in toward the eaves.

The swallows have arrived and are building their nests under the eaves, she thought, for a moment able to feel that everything was as it should be.

She slipped down to the kitchen, and as soundlessly as a ghost she got herself a cup of coffee, stole a cinnamon bun, and crept silently back upstairs, remembered that the sixth stair creaked and successfully stepped over it. The old man snored in the bedroom.

She meditated, the birdsong assisting her into her own silence and the knowledge that nothing is fatal even if all is suffering. For a while, she even succeeded in thinking things weren't too bad for her mother, that she had gone beyond pain. And that her father's memory was so short, he couldn't keep up his bitterness.

Then she took out the photograph of her grandmother and gazed at it for a long time.

Hanna Broman. Who are you? I knew you, oddly enough, almost completely from hearsay. You were a legend, magnificent and questionable. So amazingly strong, Mother said.

I must have images of my own. You lived until I was an adult, a wife, and a mother. But the photograph bears no resemblance to my memories of you. That's understandable. The photo was taken when you were young, a women in her best years. I saw you only as old, a stranger, tremendously large, enveloped in huge pleated black dresses.

So this is what you looked like in the days of your strength, when you walked six miles with a fifty-kilo sack of flour from the mill to the village on the border. There you bartered with it for coffee, paraffin, salt, and other necessities.

Can it be true? You carried the heavy sack on your back, Mother said. But only in spring and autumn. In the summer you rowed, and in winter you pulled a sled across the ice.

We were born into different worlds, you and I. But I can see now we are alike, the same forehead and the same jagged hairline. The same broad mouth and short nose. But you don't have my chin, no, yours is strong and obstinate. Your gaze is steady, your eyes keeping their distance. I remember they were brown.

Anna looked into Hanna's eyes for a long time. She thought, we're looking at each other for the first time ever.

Who were you? Why did we never get to know each other? Why were you so uninterested in me?

Suddenly Anna heard a question, the child who said, "Why isn't she a proper gran? Whose lap you can sit on and who tells stories?"

And her mother's voice. "She's old and tired, Anna. She's had enough of children. And there was never any time for stories in her life."

Was there bitterness in that voice?

I must go to what I myself remember.

When Anna was small and Grandmother was still able to walk the long way from the bus stop to the house by the sea where Anna's family lived, Grandmother sometimes came to see them in the mornings. She sat on the kitchen sofa in the aroma of cakes and newly baked bread, and the table was laid with a fine cloth and the best cups. She brought comfort with her, like a cat settling in the corner of a sofa and purring. She purred, too, Anna remembered, creaking like a corncrake at night. When she wasn't talking.

Even her talk brought pleasure, a strange language, half Norwegian, easygoing, sometimes incomprehensible.

"Us here," she said. "Indeed, that's it." She always succeeded in surprising herself and others because her words flew out of her mouth before she had time to think. Then she looked surprised and stopped abruptly, shamefaced or laughing.

What had they talked about?

Their neighbors in the block. About children it had gone badly for, about men who drank and women who were ill. But also about weddings and new children born and parties and food and however could people afford it.

For the child, Anna, it was like lifting the roof off a dollhouse and seeing crowds of people. Like a game. But for the two women, it was reality, and serious. They had a living interest in the Höglunds' delicate children, and Johansson the master painter's boozing. Not to mention Mrs. Niklasson's peculiar illness.

Gossip. Not malicious, nor kindly. For the first time, Anna thought now that the endless talk was an orgy of emotions. They wallowed in the misfortunes of others, tut-tutted and lived out their personal needs without ever becoming personal. Talking about yourself was impossible. Shameful.

Grandmother flushed easily.

"Don't you ever cry, Gran?"

"No. No point," she said, flushing scarlet.

Mother was also embarrassed and scolded the child. There was a lot you couldn't ask Grandmother, who probably thought impertinent children should be reprimanded and that Johanna's spoiled daughter had no manners.

"You were so damned practical," Anna said to the photograph.

Perhaps I'm wrong, she thought as she turned her eyes away from the photo to look beyond the window, past all those small houses where anonymous people lived wall to wall and scarcely even knew each other by name. Perhaps you both had a sorrowful longing back to the village you came from. And you were trying to restore the connection and the village feeling when you came to the big city.

Anna could hear her grandmother snorting at that explanation. She liked the city, the electric light and running water, the nearby shops, and the right to close your own door.

Grandmother would come for Sunday dinner. Dad fetched her in the car, and she wore long black jet necklaces and white ruffles at her throat. She said nothing at the table until addressed, and was always submissive to her son-in-law.

Anna suddenly remembered, a perfectly clear memory, she thought with surprise. All around the dinner table were amazed voices turning over and over the schoolmistress's words about Anna being gifted.

Gifted? That was an unusual word. The teacher had talked about high school. Grandmother flushed and snorted, finding the talk indecent. She took a long look at the girl and said, "What use'd that be? She ain't nothing but a girl. She'd get superior and it'd come to nothing."

Perhaps those were the words that settled Anna's future. "Nothing but a girl" had aroused her father's anger. He, who would otherwise never admit to his grief over his only child being a girl.

"Anna'll have to decide for herself," he said. "If she wants to go on at school, she's to do so."

How had I forgotten that Sunday, that conversation, Anna thought, going back to bed and looking at the photograph again. You were wrong, you old witch, she thought. I went on at school, I took exams, I was successful and moved in worlds you couldn't even dream of.

I became superior, too, just as you said, as everyone said. And as far as you're concerned, you became a fossil, a primitive leftover from a vanished time. I excluded you from my life. You were a painful reminder of origins I was ashamed of.

That's why I never got to know you and have no memory of you. But it's also why your photograph speaks so strongly to me. For it says quite clearly that you were a gifted girl, too.

Your prejudices were different from mine, that's true. But you were right sometimes, especially when you said that I wouldn't get away, either. For me, too, a woman's life awaited me.

I didn't carry sacks of flour from the mill to the village, Grandmother. And yet I did.

HANNA

BORN 1871, DIED 1964

*H*anna's mother had two batches of children. The first four died in the famine in the late 1860s. Maja-Lisa marked time, daring to believe she would have no more.

But in 1870, spring came with rain, just as it should, the baked soil drank, and once again there was bread on the table. There was no talk of surplus, but by autumn they had turnips and potatoes in the earth cellar and cows that had grazed enough to give milk once again.

And Maja-Lisa was with child.

She cursed her fate, but August, her husband, said they should be grateful. The bad years hadn't driven them from the farm and they hadn't had to wander the roads as vagrants in gypsy carts like so many other farmers in Dalsland.

Hanna was the eldest child in the new batch, then along came another girl and three boys. Her mother had learned from the famine never to get fond of a new child. And to fear dirt and bad air.

The latter she'd learned in church.

In the days before the famine years, they'd had a young gentle-eyed priest who did his best to live in the imitation of Christ. He shared his bread with the old, and wherever he went, he had milk with him for the children, although the parsonage itself was also short of food. In the daytime, he buried children and the old and signed papers for all those fleeing west to Norway and America. At night he prayed for his poor people.

As his prayers had no visible effect, he instead more and more frequently took to writings he had been given by his brother, a doctor in Karlstad. That was how his sermons came to be about the importance of cleanliness. The consumption thrived in dirt, and rickets in the darkness, he told them. All children should be out in the daylight. They didn't die of cold, but of darkness and filth, he thundered. And they had to have milk.

It was a message his congregation would have scorned if times had been ordinary. But now the mothers listened with anxiety, and Maja-Lisa took his talk about cleanliness seriously.

There was trouble at home as she persuaded her husband not to spit on the rag rugs. But she was relentless, for she found the priest was right. Her new children were unusually strong and healthy.

But the gentle-eyed priest left and was replaced by one given to drink. With the change of priest, as with most things in the district, worse was to come after the famine years. Fear had settled in, and joy was in short supply, but there was plenty of envy. Distances between houses also grew, as the forest took over the fields and meadows around abandoned farms.

And in winter, the procession of beggars straggled through the villages, reminding them all.

When Hanna was ten, the new priest came to Bråten to hear their catechism and told them they ought to thank God for being allowed to live in such a beautiful place. Hanna looked with surprise over the lake and the high mountains. She didn't understand what the priest was talking about. Even less did she grasp what he meant when he assured her God took care of his children. God helped only those with hard hands, those who learned to save every crumb.

At twelve, the girl was sent into service at the farm on the river mouth. She had been at school long enough to be able to write and do sums. That was enough, her father said.

Lyckan, as the farm was called, was ruled by Lovisa, a mean woman, known for her harshness and arrogance. The farm was considered rich in these poverty-stricken areas. Elsewhere, it would have been a pitifully small farm. Lovisa was unlucky with her children, two infant daughters crushed to death, and a son who also died, shrunken and crippled with rickets. Now only one was left, a handsome boy, used to having his own way. He was not like ordinary folk, even in appearance; he was dark and black-eyed.

Malicious tongues talked about the gypsy tribe that had come through the district the summer before he was born. But sensible people reminded themselves that Lovisa's grandfather was Spanish, a shipwrecked sailor rescued off the coast.

The farms were related. Joel Eriksson at Lyckan was Maja-Lisa's brother. Hanna's maternal grandfather, Erik Eriksson, still lived at the main farm, Framgården, but had shared his outlying farms between the children. Joel, the son, was given the large farm of Lyckan. Maja-Lisa and her husband had to be tenants at Bråten, a poorer and smaller farm.

As if nonetheless there was some justice in life after all, Maja-Lisa had a good and hardworking husband in August Olsson, born and bred in Norway, while the son Joel was stuck with the difficult Lovisa from Bohuslän.

Lovisa was pious. Like many of that kind, she delighted in keeping her fellow human beings in the good graces of the Lord and with good conscience was able to indulge daily in being cruel.

By now, Hanna was used to long days, hard work, and much abuse. So she didn't complain and never knew the neighbors pitied her, saying Lovisa worked her like a beast of burden. The girl had enough to eat and once a month she was happy. That was when she went home to her mother with a bushel of flour.

When the darkness closed in, in October, she menstruated. It hurt. She bled a great deal and was frightened, but didn't dare go to Lovisa. She took her most worn shift, tore it into strips, and squeezed her legs together to keep the bloody rag in place.

Lovisa looked suspiciously at her, and shouted, "You moves like a knock-kneed heifer. Get a move on, girl."

Not until Hanna got back home to her mother on Saturday could she cry, and then only slightly, for her mother as usual said crying never did any good. But she got help with proper crocheted towels and a ribbon for around her waist. Two expensive safety pins were found in her mother's sewing box. She felt wealthy.

Then Maja-Lisa said, "Now you has to know it's dangerous. Never let no man closer than two ells from you."

Then came the evening at Lyckan when she fell asleep in the hay. She had her sleeping place in the kitchen, but there was no peace there with all the quarrels in the evenings, usually about the son the mother spoiled and the father wanted to make something of. Hanna was always so tired she was usually able to sleep despite the fearful words flying over the straw mattress in the servant's box-bed. But that evening, her master and mistress were fighting in the bedroom, and the sound of heavy blows and screams penetrated through to the kitchen. Hanna thought, now he's killing her, that Joel. But then she heard dark Rickard calling, a terrible agitated cry like a bellow from the underworld.

They've woken him, God help us.

She slipped out into the barn then, deathly frightened the boy would begin to pinch her the moment his mother's eyes were elsewhere.

She slept in the hay like an exhausted animal and didn't wake up until he was pulling at her skirt. She tried screaming, but he gripped her by the throat and she knew she was going to die. Faced with that, she lay still. He was as heavy as a bull as he hurled himself onto her, and when he thrust inside her and she broke, in all that hideous pain, she prayed to God to take her.

Then she died and was surprised when she woke an hour or so later, bloody and torn. She could move, first her hands, then her arms, and lastly her legs. Finally, she was able to make a decision, or at least shape a thought: home to Mother.

She walked slowly through the forest, leaving a bloodstained trail behind her. She crawled the last bit on all fours, but when she called out outside their door, her voice was loud enough to wake her mother.

For the first and only time in her life, Hanna saw her mother weep. The girl was put on the kitchen table, and her mother washed and washed, but was unable to stop the bleeding.

"Dear Lord," said Maja-Lisa, over and over again, before pulling herself together and sending her eldest boy for Anna, the midwife who had helped Maja-Lisa through her many deliveries. She was also good at stemming bleeding.

"Hurry, hurry!" she yelled at the boy.

Then when she was about to take off the girl's ripped clothing, she stopped. In her wild fury, she had remembered only that Anna was the midwife, but not that she was also the one who went from cottage to cottage with all the wicked secrets of the village.

Hanna was asleep, or unconscious; Maja-Lisa couldn't make out which. The kitchen looked like a slaughtering shed, and more and more vociferously she called upon God to show mercy, while the children around her put their hands over their ears and eyes.

Then Anna came at last, sturdy and calm. She had brought finely grated wild parsley and mixed rubella into it, then she greased the girl's loins with the ointment. The treatment woke Hanna, and slowly she began to weep.

The midwife leaned over the child and said, "Who?"

"Black Rickard," the girl whispered.

"Might've known," said Anna harshly. Then she gave the child a concoction of mistletoe and white deadnettle. "That should stop the bleeding and make you sleep like the dead," she said. "But God knows if you'll ever be able to have babes. And you won't never get married."

Maja-Lisa didn't look upset, nor had she any idea that Anna's two predictions would come to nothing. She sent the child off to bed in the other room, put on the coffee, cleaned up the kitchen, then noticed the shotgun had gone from the wall and August had vanished.

She screamed again. The children came racing out of the other room, but Anna had seen what Maja-Lisa had seen, and just snorted.

"Men! Calm down, woman. There ain't nothing we can do."

"He'll end up in the fortress," cried Maja-Lisa.

"I don't think he'll succeed."

She was right in that prediction. When August got to Lyckan, the son had disappeared. Both farmers calmed themselves with strong drink and decided that the boy should be forced into marriage as soon as Hanna was of marriageable age, and until then she was to be respected as a daughter in the house.

But nothing much came of the agreement. Hanna said she'd rather jump in the river than marry Rickard. Powerless, Maja-Lisa said nothing. Lovisa got secret messages to her son saying that for the sake of Jesus Christ, he must keep away from the farm; old Anna was talking about the police, saying that when she was small there'd been talk of a man condemned to death for despoiling a servant girl.

But neither August nor Maja-Lisa wanted to cause such vexation to the relatives at Lyckan.

Tongues wagged in the cottages. People began avoiding Lovisa and Lyckan. Until it was clear one day that Hanna was with child, and more and more came to the conclusion that she hadn't been all that unwilling. All the talk about her being so badly hurt was lies. Old Anna's tongue had run away with her, as usual.

*W*hen Hanna's bleeding didn't come twice in a row, Maja-Lisa must have said to herself a hundred times a day that it was because the girl was so torn down below. But then one morning the child began to throw up.

Maja-Lisa took the girl to Anna. The midwife felt her abdomen, rolled her eyes, and said she could make nothing of God's ways. Then she went up to a clearing in the forest where the wild parsley grew, and made a concoction of it. But it had no effect on the babe in Hanna's belly.

" 'Tis gone too far," she said.

Scarcely thirteen years old, on July fifth Hanna gave birth to her bastard, a strong healthy boy with black eyes. He found it difficult to let go, so the birth was long drawn out and difficult. When he at last arrived, Hanna was seized with a strange tenderness for the boy.

Even though he looked like his father.

The feeling was so surprising that it made her bow to the decisions that had to be made. She knew that her parents' land couldn't feed two extra mouths. She had to go back to Lyckan. The master there solemnly promised she would be treated as a daughter and, as far as he was able, kept his promise. He was fond of the boy, who grew quickly and laughed at the world. Strangely enough, he was a happy and energetic child.

Hanna worked just as hard as before, and Lovisa was no friendlier, despite the fact that she talked a great deal about compassion ever since she had been saved by the Mission Society preacher, who came once a month and assembled his flock in the neighboring barn.

All three of them were waiting for Rickard, but not a word was said about the vanished youth. Then a rumor went around the village that he had been seen in the district.

That was when Hanna decided to go to the rune master in the forest upriver behind the Devil's Ravine. She'd thought about it for a long time, but had been frightened by evil whispers about the old man and his troll wife.

She asked her master to look after the child. It was Sunday, and she had to go to church, she said. He nodded encouragingly and said it was good someone from the farm sought out God where He was, giving his wife a malicious look. Lovisa yelled after her to remember to cover her head with the whore-cloth if she was going to God's house.

It was fully six miles to the church by the riverbank, then up the steep hill past the waterfall. There in the calm water, she found the ford, and then it was only half an hour's walk through the forest to the cottage on the ridge at the end of the path. She found her way, for she had been there as a child with her mother and had been made to swear never to tell anyone. Her heart thumped with fear, but the two old people received her with no surprise. So, she wanted a rune staff, did she? The girl didn't dare speak, but nodded, looking in terror toward the corner of the cottage where, according to rumor, the rune folk kept the amputated member of a murderer hanged on the gallows many years ago.

She saw at once it was no man's member. No, it was from a stallion and couldn't frighten her. She'd seen things like that before, in secret corners of cottages where the wife was childless.

The old woman laid her hands on Hanna, on her forehead first and then her heart, meanwhile speaking to her husband in a wild and alien language. He nodded, whittling away, the one rune added to the other on the little staff. When he'd finished, he looked pleased and smiled as he told her she must take care of it, so that her shame would leave her.

She paid with the meager few coins she'd saved, curtseyed low, and ran the whole long way home with the secret rune staff hidden between her breasts. She had her ears boxed for being away so long, but accepted that without complaint, even swallowing Lovisa's comment that maybe she were in heat again, for she were a whore, she were, said Lovisa, who'd seen a strange gleam in her eyes.

Two days later, Rickard came home, brilliant as a rooster in high boots and a uniform with shiny buttons. He swaggered around, laughing at his parents' surprise, bragging the way soldiers do. He talked loudly, particularly loudly when he announced that he'd never be a farmer, wearing himself out on this miserable farm. Hanna could forget him. He wasn't going to marry no whore.

Only once did he waver and that was when the four-year-old appeared at the kitchen door and laughed straight in his face. But then the soldier turned on his heel and left.

Lovisa's weeping turned into loud wails. But the farmer looked at the child and then at Hanna. Both found it hard to conceal their relief, and neither said a word of consolation to Lovisa.

Hanna hugged her rune staff to her under her blouse. From that day on, she woke every morning with a feeling that something singular was going to happen to her.

*A*t midsummer, a man came to the village, a man from Värmland. A miller, said people who'd talked to him, a miller with plans to put the old mill by Norskvattnet in order. Already old, the young ones said. A man in his best years, the older ones said. They all agreed he was a taciturn man, silent about his own life. Only to old Anna had he said that his wife and child had died on him, way up there in Värmland. After that he couldn't stay at the mill in all that loneliness.

He also said he drank to escape remembering.

He went around the farms to find out their needs. He was received everywhere by farmers who assured him they would grind their corn at Norskvattnet as they'd done before, and as their fathers and grandfathers had also done. In the end he realized that if he restored the mill, it would give them all new courage.

Yet he hesitated. These people were more burdened and taciturn than he was used to. There was little joy in the cottages, and the coffee they offered him was like dirty meltwater and tasted of burned rye.

He came from a richer place, more social and talkative. One of the ghosts that frightened him at home was envy, being observed, measured, and compared. Here, where the countryside was meaner and poverty more severe, the same awful disease had struck harder, nourished by the famine years and poisoning every encounter.

Then there was the mill. A great deal of work was needed to put it in order. The railings along the channel were ruined, the landing stage rotten, and the stairway inside the mill in an appalling state. At least the oak drum had held, as had the wheel and the floodgate up by the lake. The two pairs of millstones were new, of natural

stone from Lugnås, and looked as if they had a good edge. He calculated the height of the falls to be about thirty ells, which promised sure running.

A storehouse and barn existed. The dwelling house was in fair
shape, a sturdy house with the living room facing the lake, a small
bedroom and large kitchen.

He had seen many fine landscapes in the forests of Finnmark
and along the banks of the Klar River, but never before an area of
such wild beauty. He gazed at the perpendicular mountains rising
against the sky, saw the peregrine falcon's nests in the cliff walls
and the eagle's flight over the precipices. He listened to the thunder
of the falls and the quiet rippling in the dark Norwegian lakes. He
looked thoughtfully at the soft hills where the sheep grazed, and
did not close his eyes to the poor fields and the neglected forest, im-
penetrable in large parts. As if it had not been touched since
primeval days, he thought.

And yet it was magnificent.

He was a man with a keen ear, and he could hear the mountains
and the lake, the rapids and the tall maples on the mill site speaking
to him with secretive voices.

A close neighbor was the blacksmith, who seemed a good man.
And access to a smithy was necessary for the mill cutters.

Nonetheless, money was the greatest consideration. He had
sold his own mill in Värmland and he would have to rent this one.
Erik Eriksson at Framgården was miserly, like all peasants, but had
reluctantly agreed to contribute to the necessary repairs.

The only person who became his confidant was old Anna, the midwife. She made good coffee, too, so he was seen more and more
often in her kitchen. She was the one to put into words what he had
long thought but had rejected.

"Man, get yourself a woman, a hardworking and tolerant one.
You can't manage with no woman there in the forest."

There was a long silence after she'd spoken. He sat there

suddenly feeling how exhausted he was. And old, far too old to start again.

"Ain't got the right urge no longer," he said in the end.

"You're a young man."

"Over forty."

"A man in his best years."

"I has bad luck with womenfolk."

When he came back the next evening, Anna had done some thinking. She was cunning, so, as if in passing, she began to talk about Hanna, the poor girl who'd had such a bad time in life. Shame, it was, she said. The girl was the grandchild of Eriksson of the big place at Framgården. The miller was taken by the story of the dreadful rape, she could see that on his face, and understood when he interrupted.

"I suppose you ain't got a drop?"

He was given his drink and was slightly unsteady on his feet as he gradually made his way home in the dark. What he was thinking, he said nothing about, but Anna had a shameful feeling of having been seen through.

When John Broman got back to the abandoned mill house, he saw for the first time how filthy it was in the rooms and the kitchen. The discovery gave birth to practical thoughts. He indeed needed a woman. When he went to bed, his need grew into desire, the blood throbbing in his veins, and his member stiffening. Dear Lord, how long ago, how long ago it was since he'd had a woman.

He thought about Ingrid, and his desire deserted him, his member slackening. Things had not been good either in bed or the kitchen. What had she looked like? He couldn't remember, only her eternal nagging about money and how she couldn't make it go around. And about the drink he allowed himself on Saturdays.

If the picture of his wife was misty, the memory of Johanna was as clear as if she was standing in front of him. The consumption had taken his daughter when she was eight.

He still missed the child.

* * *

When he woke the next morning, he had practical thoughts in his mind. The girl would be grateful. He could reckon on keeping her in order. That she had a child was good. He liked children but wanted no more of his own. And it was not bad that the girl was related to the big farm.

Later that morning he turned his steps toward Lyckan.

*H*anna woke as usual with that strange expectation, clasping her hands around the rune staff, as if in prayer. Then she woke the boy on his straw mattress beside her in the box-bed in the kitchen.

"Ragnar."

She was pleased with the name and that she'd had the strength to insist on it. On both farms there'd been objections, for no one in the family had ever been called that. Then they'd said nothing, thinking it was as it should be; the bastard would not bear the family name.

But Hanna remembered a boy at school with her.

She knew now she'd succeeded with her intention. For her son resembled her school friend, sunny and good-tempered. Even now at dawn and just awakened, he was laughing.

She tidied the kitchen and made breakfast. Her master came in as soon as the porridge was ready, sat down heavily, and ate. She stood behind him by the stove, eating as she usually did, the boy on her arm. One spoon for Ragnar and one for Mother.

Both she and Joel Eriksson enjoyed this morning moment. Lovisa did not take part in it, for she had so many prayers to recite.

An hour or so later, the stranger came. The girl observed him, thinking him handsome with his broad shoulders and short squared-off beard. A gentleman. He was looking at her. It was awful the way he stared.

That was just what he was doing, and he found her good to look at and that her eyes were awake. An observant girl—she sees—he thought. Strong, too, amazingly undamaged through that shameful darkness.

So young, he thought, seventeen, not much older than Johanna would've been, if she'd lived.

He was suddenly ashamed of his dreams of the previous night and the practical thoughts of the morning. But he emerged from his embarrassment as the child rushed into the kitchen—a small boy, eyes wide, inquisitive and unafraid. He looked at his mother and laughed. A big laugh, so unusual that it seemed challenging here in this poor district.

The miller squatted down and held out his hand.

"Good day to you. My name's John Broman."

"Good day, good day, good day," said the boy, putting both hands in his.

It was the very first time anyone had been polite to the boy, and Hanna's eyes glowed. Then Joel Eriksson came stomping into the kitchen.

"Hurry up with them turnips, now. Take the boy with you."

The next moment Lovisa was there shouting for the coffee Hanna had forgotten to put on. The girl vanished through the door, and John Broman watched her go, noticing how upright she was as she walked across the field, holding the child by the hand. At that moment, he decided; both she and the boy should be away from this farm.

Then he drank the dishwater coffee and was assured that Lyckan would also grind its flour at the mill at Norskvattnet.

He went home by way of Anna's and told her briefly, "No doubt you'll get your way, old woman. But you has to make sure I can talk to the girl."

That was not easy to arrange, as Hanna had become a daughter at Lyckan and was never free. But Anna went to Maja-Lisa, and she sent one of the boys with a message to Hanna that she should come home on the weekend to see her parents.

On Saturday morning, Broman got up early and cleaned up the house. He didn't have much furniture, a table and a bench-bed was all, so that was soon done, and clean it was, even if it did look rather bare.

There was an old clay pot by the stove. He picked it up and scrubbed it, then went out to pick some flowers. It was already the end of September, but he found some clumps of white and pink yarrow, cut a branch off the birch by the porch, and went up to the Norwegian lakes where he'd seen clumps of blue and white campanulas. They were rather far gone but he removed all the dead leaves and flowerheads.

He was really pleased with his flowers by the time he finished.

At midday on Saturday, old Anna took the girl to Bråten. She said to Maja-Lisa that the two of them, Anna and Hanna, were going to go into the forest, as Anna needed plants for her medicines. Maja-Lisa looked surprised, but Hanna was pleased. She liked roaming around the countryside.

So they came to the mill house where John Broman was waiting. Anna was going to look for belladonna in clumps by the north stream, she said, and disappeared.

He showed Hanna around. To her the house was magnificent, the kitchen, the bedroom, and a living room with two windows facing the lovely view over the lake. There was an upper floor, too, for overnight visitors and storage.

John spoke. Maybe she wasn't listening all that attentively to his words, but his intention was clear. He needed a woman in the house, and she secretly clasped the rune staff under her blouse.

When he started talking about marriage, she turned rigid with surprise.

"But the boy . . . ," she said in the end.

He nodded. He'd thought of that. The boy's to come, too. He liked children. As soon as they decided, he'd arrange to take over responsibility for the boy.

She didn't understand, and he patiently explained that he would speak to Hanna's father and the priest to have it in writing that John Broman would be the boy's guardian.

"We don't know each other," he said.

Then she smiled for the first time and said there was time enough.

"It'll be a hard life," he said. "A lot of work."

"I'm used to that, and I don't eat much."

She seemed to be afraid he would change his mind, he could hear that, and he said rather curtly, "You and the boy'll no doubt have enough to eat."

Then Hanna smiled for the second time and thought about the talk she'd heard as a child. They said they were never short of bread in the miller's house. But then she looked at the rotten bridge and remembered how the old miller had died. He'd gone through it one night and drowned.

Then Anna was back, telling them how secret it all had to be. Not a word to anyone until the banns were read in church. By that time, the papers would be ready and Eriksson of Lyckan would have no chance of finding Rickard and getting him to claim paternity.

"You has to hurry and talk to my father, August," she said. "He ain't no talkative man."

Hanna walked home through the forest with a dizzy sense of it all being too much. She'd be mistress in her own house, a house as big and fine as at Lyckan. The boy would be like a son, Broman had said. It's the end of the shame, she thought. No one could call us bastard and whore any longer.

Too much, she told herself. For she knew good fortune was measured out and was costly if you were given too much. But then she straightened up, tossed back her head, and thought she'd already paid.

"Justice," she said aloud. "I wouldn't never have believed God could be just."

She was troubled by the lack of furniture in the house and the rugs and towels and all the other things she didn't possess. She gave not a thought to the man with whom she was to share her bed and life.

When she got back to her parents' home to fetch the boy, she felt like blurting out her amazing secret. She had to get away, quickly, back to the hell of Lyckan.

There it was easier to keep her joy to herself, and when she had made up the bed on the straw mattress in the box-bed in the kitchen and got the boy to sleep, she took out an advance on her triumph. She even swore. Christ, she whispered. Christ, how I'll laugh the day I can say what I think to those high and mighty beasts.

Then she was frightened and prayed earnestly to God to forgive her for such sinful thoughts.

Before she fell asleep, she wondered about those flowers. She'd never before seen or heard of a man picking flowers and putting them into a vase. Strange, it was, but important, she could see that. She'd have to see to it that there were flowers on John Broman's table. At least in the summer.

That night she dreamed about geraniums, flowers in a pot she'd once seen in the parsonage window.

A few days later it was rumored that the miller had gone back to Värmland and nothing would come of the mill at Norskvattnet.

They're lying, thought Hanna.

But when the week had gone by with no message from John Broman, she gave up, and for the first time in her life, she despaired. This was harder than the shame, and she saw that hope made people vulnerable. You shouldn't hope—or believe that God is just.

"Get a move on!" shouted Lovisa. "You're as white as a ghost. If you're going to be ill, you can go back to your mother."

But Hanna didn't have the energy to walk through the forest with the child.

Autumn came early, storms whipping the leaves off the ash trees. On Sunday morning, the leaves rustled underfoot as she went to the barn to do the milking. August was waiting for her there in the dark.

"Father," she said. "What're you doing here so early in the morning?"

He pointed at the house.

"They're asleep," she whispered.

Then she was told that John Broman had already been to see her father on Monday, told him about the marriage, and asked August to take the message to Hanna. Then he'd gone to the priest to arrange for church papers for the boy.

"I signed, so when the banns is read, Broman is guardian," said August, the sweetness of revenge in his voice.

Broman had gone back to Värmland to fetch furniture and other household goods for the mill house. He would be back in a few weeks, then he and Hanna would have the banns read.

"Why'd you wait so long to tell me?"

"We ain't had time, Mother and I. Autumn's come so early, we couldn't leave the potatoes in the ground."

She nodded, unable to reproach him. She sat down heavily on the milking stool and nodded again as he stopped by the barn door and told her to hurry with the milking. But she wept, the tears rolling down her cheeks and mixing with the warm milk.

One thing that week taught her was that she'd never again live in hope.

On his way home in the faint dawn light, August remembered he'd forgotten to tell her that both he and the boys would have work that winter. Broman had asked him to help with the repairs to the mill.

"Suppose you can work with lumber?"

"Mm."

August also had lumber, mature lumber felled before the famine years, when he'd still thought he'd be able to afford to build a proper barn.

Hanna did her work as usual. When breakfast was over, she said calmly to Joel Eriksson that she was going home to her parents and taking the boy with her. He nodded sullenly and told her to hurry so that she got away before Lovisa woke.

"Make sure you're back for evening milking," he said.

It was bitter cold as she walked along the path through the forest, but she was so warm with gratitude, she didn't even feel the biting wind.

For the very first time, she thought about Broman and how she could serve him. She was orderly and strong, had learned what was required of a mistress on a farm. She'd never handled money, but the teacher had said she was good at sums. She'd see to everything, so he could be proud of his home as well as her.

Furniture, she thought. What kind of furniture would he be fetching from Värmland? Fine, much grander than what they had at Lyckan? Then she remembered she'd promised herself never to hope.

The boy whined. He was cold, so she lifted him up and

wrapped her shawl around him as the path rose the last bit before the forest gave way to August's fields. They were already working in the potato patch, but her mother stopped and came over to her.

"So they gave you time off," said Maja-Lisa, her tone of voice warmer than her words, and when Hanna looked at her tired face, there was joy there. And pride. This was so unusual that after the first greeting, the girl was lost for words.

They brewed coffee, sat down at the kitchen table, and sucked the hot drink through lumps of sugar that dissolved in their mouths.

Then her mother said something terrible.

"Hope you gets away with three or four children."

Hanna straightened up, drew in her breath, and remembered she was a girl. John Broman would do to her what Rickard Joelsson had done. Every night there in the bed in the other room.

He had almost said so, said that here we'll have the bed, my girl.

She remembered flushing slightly, for a moment something frightening in the air. But she hadn't understood, or thought. Though she'd known.

Her mother saw her terror and said calmly, "Don't look so feared. Women just has to put up with it and you gets used to it after a while. Think about being mistress in your own place, and that man of yours seems better'n most."

"Why does he want me?"

"You're young and pretty. And hardworking."

Amidst all her fears, Hanna looked at her mother with surprise. Never before had she had a good word for Hanna. Praise was dangerous, challenging fate. But Maja-Lisa went on.

"We has to make sure you has decent clothes, new for everyday. For the wedding . . . I thought we might remake my old wedding dress."

She looked uncertain. Hanna said nothing, and finally Maja-Lisa said, "Don't know what he thinks. He looks a bit of a gentleman."

She was appealing to Hanna.

I'm being respected, even by Mother. . . .

But it was only a fleeting thought, then the girl was back again to what was fearful in the mill bedroom.

"Mother," she said. "I can't do it."

"Nonsense," said Maja-Lisa, and that was the end of any respect. "Why shouldn't you do what any decent woman can? You gets used to it, as I said. Ain't the bedding that's awful, Hanna, 'tis giving birth."

Hanna remembered when she had given birth. That hadn't been easy, but nothing like as terrible as death in the hay with black Rickard.

"You has to close your eyes and make yourself soft," her mother said, flushing. "Ain't nothing shameful once the priest's read over you. Now let's go try on my old wedding dress."

But they soon had to abandon the idea. Her mother's wedding dress, folded away in tissue paper, was too small. They could see that with the naked eye. Hanna was taller and stronger than Maja-Lisa had ever been.

"I'll have to hang my head in shame and tell John Broman how things is." Maja-Lisa was bitter. "We never have no money."

Hanna wasn't listening. She was still rigid with cold, despite the warmth in the kitchen. When she got back to Lyckan that evening, for the first time she considered running away, leaving with the child and joining one of the bands of beggars that had roamed the roads since the famine. Then she looked at the boy, remembering those emaciated ragged children, and knew she couldn't.

Maybe you got used to it, as her mother had said. Close your eyes and make yourself soft.

Just before she fell asleep in her corner of the kitchen, she again tried to think about the fine furniture John Broman was fetching from Värmland. But it was too difficult and she finally had to give up and sleep.

Her worst fears were gone the next morning. When she got up to light the stove and drag the heavy pans over to the barn, she tried to think about how different everything would be the day when she was lighting her own stove and going to her own cows.

She started milking. With her forehead against the sides of the big animals, she made her decision. John Broman would never know how frightened she was, never. She'd be submissive and soft, just as Mother'd said.

It was snowing when she came out of the barn, great wet snowflakes. She stopped in the wet snow. It was only the beginning of October. A long winter had begun early and primeval terror moved inside the girl.

Long winter, iron winter, starvation. Yes, she'd be good to John Broman.

By midday, however, the snow had turned to rain, and a few days later the sun came out. Winter retreated, autumn glowed in the maples as it should, it turned warm, and the old people talked with relief about Indian summers. As usual in the autumn, the women went out into the forest to pick the lingonberries. Hanna went, too, saying boldly to Lovisa that she'd promised Mother she'd help. Then with the furious Lovisa at her heels shouting abuse at her, she left.

Hanna turned around once, and laughed straight into Lovisa's face.

*T*o everyone's surprise, at the end of October, John Broman came back with a horse and heavily laden cart, and brought a man with him, too, a cousin from Värmland. The gossips were soon able to relate that the two of them were repainting the mill house both inside and out. White inside, red outside. That was altogether too much for them all. Not even the parsonage was painted red, and there was much talk of pride always going before a fall.

Two days later, Broman suddenly put in an appearance in the kitchen at Lyckan and told the Erikssons they now had to say good-bye to Hanna and the boy. On Sunday, banns for him and Hanna were to be read. Lovisa was so astonished, for the first time in her life she could find no words. But Joel Eriksson went into battle.

"The boy stays here. He's the grandson in the house."

"The boy's mine," said John Broman calmly. "I has papers to say so."

As they left the farm, Hanna wept. John was carrying the boy and didn't notice, and her tears were soon over. But Hanna herself was amazed, for tears of joy were new to her.

They went straight to the priest, who received them without surprise, wished them luck, and even shook hands.

As they went on, Hanna said, "He didn't seem surprised."

"He knew," said John. "I had to have church papers for the boy. Can you walk all the way to Norskvattnet?"

Hanna had to laugh. They walked slowly, almost strolling through the forest as if both of them were thinking how much had been left unsaid between them. But it was hard to find words. Again and again, Hanna was about to ask, "Why did you choose me?" but the words wouldn't come.

They stopped for a rest by the stream below Wolf Mountain

and quenched their thirst. The cliff rose straight out of the ground, solid and ancient, still in its deep dark blue shadow. Golden strips of birch swirled below the precipices, and peregrine falcons glided in the upward currents.

" 'Tis beautiful here," said Broman, and Hanna smiled as always when she didn't understand. She moved aside for a moment to wash her face and arms, came back, and sat silently opposite him.

He started talking, a tentative story of the life he'd left, of his wife quarreling over his drinking.

"I has to tell you I gets drunk on Saturdays," he said.

She looked neither frightened nor surprised.

"So does my dad. And Joel Eriksson."

He smiled at her, and went on to tell her about his little girl, who'd died on him and whom he'd dearly loved.

"A man can't put all his joy in a child like I did."

"Consumption?"

"Yes."

He couldn't bring himself to talk about the dark memories of his wife, stingy as she'd been with food. But as if reading his mind, Hanna said she'd learned that consumption took the young who didn't get enough food. And you had to be fussy about keeping clean, for infection was in filth and bad air.

He nodded, thinking about his wife being so plain. Then he flushed, and said that Hanna should know it would be difficult to start again.

"Sometimes I think I can't," he said.

Hanna was downcast, but swallowed and said, "We has to help each other."

Then he said he was pleased to have a new place for a wife who was so young and pretty.

Hanna was frightened for the first time.

At the same time, it was one of the happiest days of her life. The newly painted house was as handsome as the farm on the wall chart at school. Hanna clapped her hands with delight when she saw it.

The cousin from Värmland had left with the horse and cart, but the furniture was all in the barn. They could take it outside so that she could examine it all. Then they'd put everything in order in the house, just as she wanted it. What she didn't want, they could take up to the attic.

Her eyes widened in surprise.

He went into the kitchen and found the toys he had put aside for the boy, a small wooden horse and cart and a pile of building blocks.

"For you," he said to him. "Now you sits quietly while your mother and me gets to work."

But Ragnar went wild with delight and ran after Hanna.

"Look, Mother, look't I got."

Hanna wept tears of joy for the second time that day, then pulled herself together and told him to stay in the kitchen. When John and Hanna went outside again, he looked around with a troubled air.

"There's lots of dangerous places for a young'un here," he said.

His concern for the boy made Hanna cry again.

The furniture was grander than Hanna could possibly have dreamed. Some was polished with brass fittings. There was a sofa with a rounded birchwood back and striped blue upholstery . . . it just couldn't be true!

"Silk," she said, stroking the material cautiously as if afraid it would split on touch.

But his face had clouded.

"Darned great monster," he said. "Can't sit or lie on it. Let's throw it out."

"Are you mad!?" cried Hanna, then slapped her hand over her mouth to stop her wicked words. "I mean," she went on, "I ain't never seen finer, not even at the parsonage. We can have it in the best room."

He laughed.

"You're the one to decide."

He laughed again as they carried the furniture into the living room, the desk, his wall shelves, the chest of drawers, and the chairs with the same round backs as the sofa.

"Ain't no room for people in here now," he said. And to her disappointment, Hanna saw he was right. Some of the fine things would have to go into the attic.

The chest of drawers found a space in the bedroom, and John said, "Didn't bring the bed with me. Thought I'd make a new one. But rugs and towels and them things is all in the chest."

In the end the long benches, the drop-leaf table, and the pullout sofa all found a place in the kitchen. Hanna went through all the linen in the chest. There was a lot and it was good quality, but it had been packed damp and had ugly patches of mold on it. Dismayed, she decided to take it all home to Mother's to wash.

Then last of all she found the crate of porcelain, of a kind that yet again brought tears to her eyes.

He had bread and cheese in the kitchen, so they got something inside them before, heavily laden, they went back to Hanna's parents, John carrying the linen chest, Hanna the boy, and the boy his toys.

Over the next week, Hanna's brothers hauled the dried lumber through the forest to Norskvattnet, while Hanna and her mother washed and rinsed rugs, covers, and towels. The neighboring women scuttled like dizzy hens in and out of the washhouse, inquisitive and envious. On Thursday, old Anna came and said that people hadn't had so much to talk about for years. She'd met Broman, who'd complained about the women making excuses to come to the mill. Maja-Lisa allowed herself a big toothless laugh, and Hanna silently remembered the old saying about tempting fate. Your good fortune is another's misfortune, and don't you go thinking you're someone.

But then Anna said, "The old people is beginning to whisper that Hanna used sorcery to bewitch the Värmlander."

Both old Anna and Maja-Lisa had a good laugh at that, as well, not noticing that Hanna had left the washhouse and was standing outside, her hand clasped around her rune staff under her shift. Fearful thoughts raced through her head. It couldn't be possible, could it? Could the rune master and his troll wife have such power?

Tomorrow she was supposed to go to the mill with food to celebrate their banns. Would she dare tell Broman about the rune staff?

*O*n Friday afternoon, Hanna made her way through the forest toward Norskvattnet. The sun still persisted even at the end of October, the air crystal clear and easy to breathe. But Hanna took no pleasure in the lovely weather, because of the rune staff, and then there was what Mother had whispered as she left home.

"You staying overnight?"

Then she'd laughed. Hanna hadn't wanted to believe it, but her mother's laugh had been strange and lewd.

She was walking past Wolf Mountain when she suddenly decided this was where she would get rid of the rune staff. She climbed up the steep cliff face, bundled the staff into oak leaves, bound it, and then threw it into one of the great hollows.

"You've done what you was going to," she said, adding just to make sure, "for this time. If I ever needs you again, I knows where you is."

Then she went on, crossed the stream, and came to the rise. It was steep but not heavy going, as from here onward there were negotiable roads to the mill. She could soon hear the roar from the falls.

It was quite a while before she noticed other sounds apart from the falls, sounds almost drowned by the rushing water, yet audible. Someone was playing a fiddle! Hanna stopped as if paralyzed by fear, quite still for a long time. The Water Spirit. The wicked spirit was out to lure John Broman to his death in the falls.

The thought made her quicken her steps. She ran until she was out of breath and had a stitch, so she reached the mill with her hand pressed to her side. There she found Broman sitting above the waterfall, scraping away on his fiddle.

"You here?" he said, looking in surprise at the girl running toward him, her skirts flapping. She stopped and looked at him, trying to get her breath back.

"Something frighten you?"

"I thought it was the Water Spirit."

He laughed loudly and put his arm around her.

"Oh, girl, I didn't think you believed them sort of things. You what's so sensible."

She flushed, but heard the amusement in his words.

"I'm playing for the mountains and the falls," he said. "And for the trees and the lake. They plays for me, y'see, and I think I owes them an answer. But I can't find the notes."

He was silent for a moment, then he said, musing, "Finding the right tune is as hard as trying to remember dreams."

He really is mad, Hanna thought. He's escaped from the asylum up there in Värmland. Help me, Jesus, what should I do!

Then she saw the tankard of aquavit propped against the stone where he was sitting and realized with relief that he was drunk. Drunken men have to be humored, her mother had taught her. Never contradict them.

He followed her gaze, picked the tankard up defiantly, and said, "Here, have some to calm yourself."

He poured some into a cup and handed it to her, then raised the tankard to his lips.

"Here's to us, Hanna."

She'd never tasted strong spirits before, and she choked on the first gulp. But he urged her on, and she took another gulp, then felt a strange warmth spreading through her body, in it an unfamiliar lightness. She giggled, then started laughing, right up into the sky, unable to stop. Nor did she want to. For the first time in her life, Hanna was free, with no worries. It's like in heaven when you don't have to worry, she thought. Just as the priest used to say.

Then she noticed the tall trees swaying, and said, "Why don't the trees stand still?"

"They're doing a wedding dance for you," he said.

She no longer thought he was mad now. When he carried her into the bedroom and undressed her, the lightness was still there in her body and nothing was either dangerous or shameful. She liked him caressing her breasts and her loins. Nor did it hurt when he came into her. In fact she thought it was all over far too quickly.

Then she must have fallen asleep and slept a long time, for when he woke her, the autumn outside was quite dark.

"Got a headache?"

Hanna found out that when her eyes hurt when she moved them, that was a headache. She'd never had one before. She nodded, and that hurt even more.

"I'll make some coffee," he said consolingly, but then she felt worse and had to go outside to throw up. Not until she'd turned her stomach inside out did she realize she was naked. The shame of it overwhelmed her as she tried her best to hide behind her long hair as she slipped through the kitchen, where he'd lit the two pinewood logs.

"You're as lovely as a siren of the woods," he called after her. She slipped into the bedroom, where her long skirt and new blouse lay in a heap on the floor. As she pulled them on, she felt great relief. It hadn't been all that bad.

"I was right then, about the evil Water Spirit," she called out through the door. "You must be related to him."

"A distant third cousin, if so," John said jokingly, noting to his surprise that she had a sense of humor and wasn't as shy as he'd thought. He didn't know that was the only time he was ever to see her naked.

Then he taught her how to make coffee as he liked it, clean kettle, fresh water that was to boil until it simmered before taking the kettle off the fire and throwing the coffee in, which had to sink slowly through the water.

"Heavens, what a waste of an expensive gift of God," said Hanna. But when she tasted it, she had to agree it was better to drink strong coffee seldom than dishwater often.

"What did you come for?"

"Lordie me," cried Hanna. "Where's my bag? I was going to do some baking. In case people comes for coffee after the banns."

Then she heard the rain outside where she'd left her bag. At her cry of dismay, John went out to fetch it, and since it was leather, most of the flour was still dry.

She sifted and mixed the flour and yeast, raisins and sugar for the big loaf, then she quickly braided it into a wreath, put a cloth over it, and left it to rise. He watched her, enjoying her quick clever hands and the way she confidently moved around the kitchen.

"Luck's been with me," he said, but Hanna didn't understand what he meant.

She lit the stove so that it would be warm for baking in the morning. She had cream with her, too, and sugar and coffee were in the larder, where the crispbread and a bit of cheese reigned alone. They were hungry.

"If you've got milk, I can make some gruel," she said.

Afterward, they fell asleep side by side in the big bed. He didn't touch her, and she thought maybe he didn't want it all that much and maybe it wouldn't be all that often.

He was still asleep the next morning as Hanna put more wood in the stove to heat the oven. She couldn't resist the temptation to lay the table with the fine china, and was pleased to think how surprised they would be, all those wretched old gossips. When Broman woke, he was heavy-eyed and surly, so, familiar with hangovers, Hanna made coffee in the way he'd taught her. She'd also put aside some dough last night for flat bread.

When he'd eaten and drunk, he said, "Went to market last week and bought a cow."

She clapped her hands, and he went on, "A betrothal gift, too."

A silk scarf, green with red roses.

"I thought it'd go fine with your hair," he said. Now she knew she could go to church like everyone else—with this fine kerchief, in a housewife's knot. No more talk of a whore-cloth.

Those annoying tears dimmed her eyes again, and John looked

at her in surprise. It would be some time before he knew for sure that Hanna cried only from happiness, never from want or misery.

All that Saturday, they scrubbed out the barn, the privy, the storehouse, and the earth cellar. She noticed he soon tired. Toward the afternoon, the heat of the oven was just right, and she put in the huge wheat loaf in the shape of a wreath.

Hanna and John sat up very straight in the pew as the priest read out the banns, and never, neither before nor after, had Hanna felt such pride. Afterward the mill had a great many guests, just as she'd thought. Their eyes took in all the grandeur in the house, and Hanna glowed. As was the custom, they brought gifts with them, her parents bringing four sacks of potatoes, and old Anna three laying hens and a rooster.

Joel Eriksson appeared, too, his horse and cart laden with hay, and he told Hanna that old man Erik had said there was more at Framgården. She drew a sigh of relief, for she had had many an uneasy thought about how she was going to get feed for the cow John had paid for.

Then came copper pans, a coffeepot, and a wall clock from Aunt Ingegerd. They all competed at being generous, for Hanna's marriage had given the family back its honor.

Hanna offered them all strong coffee, and John produced drinks. It was a cheerful afternoon with a great many coarse jokes. Hanna had heard them all before without understanding them, but now she laughed with all the others.

Three weeks later, they were married at the parsonage. Hanna's sister was in labor in Fredrikshald, so she couldn't come, but she had sent a fine store-bought dress for the bride, and Maja-Lisa was delighted. Now she needn't be ashamed of her daughter going to her wedding in clothes that were not new.

John's sister from Värmland came to the wedding with her husband and daughter. Hanna was apprehensive when John got the message.

"What've you written about the boy, about Ragnar?"

"I told her what happened to you."

That was not much consolation, but when Alma came, Hanna calmed down, for she was a good person, and kind.

"He's given to melancholy, my brother," she said. "He's always been so."

Hanna was surprised. Never before had she heard anyone talking like that about people who were present. But John just nodded and said maybe it was good that Hanna knew.

"So you don't go blaming yourself when I get down," he said.

She didn't understand why she would blame herself, but nodded anyhow.

*H*anna left the beautiful wedding dress hanging up long after the wedding.

"For the joy of it," she said.

But there weren't many other joys for her. She had plenty of troubles, the worst the potato field that had to be turned before the frost came. She could pull the plow, but Broman didn't have time to steer the plow now that he was working on the mill full-time. I could borrow Father's ox, she thought. But it'd take several days to trudge the critter here and back through the forest. I ain't got time. The earth cellar has to be filled, and we has to have more hay before winter comes.

One evening, John looked at her and said, "What's troubling you?"

She grew quite talkative as she described the field and all its weeds, and the time it would take to get the old ox through the forest. As so often recently, he thought what a child she was.

"I'll talk to your father tomorrow," he said. "He'll bring the critter over."

She slapped herself across the mouth, and said, "Stupid I am, not to have thought of that before."

"Ain't so easy with the cow," he went on. "That has to be fetched from the market in Bøttlen on Tuesday. But I can't get away. Could you go on your own?"

"I think so," she said. "I'll have to leave the boy with Mother."

That's what she did. Hanna left in the darkness before dawn with the receipt for the cow and a pouch of money hidden in the lining of her blouse.

"The money's in case the cow don't please you," said Broman. "Then you'll have to add to it to get a better'n."

The responsibility for such a major decision was great. When the morning light came, walking the long way seemed easier. She'd manage.

She'd never seen so many people as there were at the market. But she found Anders Björum and learned the cow Broman had bought was young and had just calved. That meant milk for the whole winter.

"Expect you wants a heifer calf, too," the cattle dealer said.

Hanna was sorely tempted, but Broman had said nothing about a calf. And yet it was a fine creature. Hanna looked longingly at the calf, thinking she already had plenty for the winter, but it'd be even better if she could take the heifer to the bull next spring, and then have a calf for meat as well as fresh milk.

With two cows she'd always have milk for the boy and Broman. Before she had time to think it over, the question came blurting out.

"What do you wants for it?"

He told her the price, and she had enough money. Nevertheless she haggled, beating him down by a third. The dealer laughed and said she wasn't as foolish as she was young.

They met halfway, and Hanna started off home with two creatures and worries over what her husband would say. It took a long time, too, for the calf was difficult to manage and couldn't walk for long stretches at a time. They didn't get back until midnight, and there was no mistaking John Broman's relief.

"I bought a calf, as well," she said, to be rid of her fears as soon as possible.

"Probably right in that," he said. "You knows more about them things than I does."

That made her plump to the ground with relief, and she stayed sitting there in the yard while John took the creatures into the barn and gave them hay and water.

Hanna fell asleep almost the moment her head hit the pillow, and she slept soundly all night.

"You must've been tired," said Broman in the morning, and she nodded.

"Wasn't the tiredness that were difficult," she said. " 'Twas the calf I bought with your money without permission."

"Don't suppose you wastes much unnecessarily."

She smiled, her eyes as usual on a point somewhere behind him.

"Hanna," he said. "Look at me."

For a moment, their eyes met. Hanna flushed and rose.

"Time for milking."

John Broman had noticed even at the wedding party she found it difficult to look people in the eye. She was just as he had thought at their first meeting, a wakeful observer, but only in secret. She averted her eyes the moment anyone looked at her.

By the time Hanna came back from the barn, August and his sons had arrived, so there was no opportunity to continue the conversation. But Broman did not give in, and asked again at their evening meal.

"Why don't you looks people in the eye?"

Her face and neck flared again as she thought, but she was unable to find an answer.

"Don't know," she said finally. "Never thought about it. Maybe because I ain't got no looks."

"But you're pretty."

Her flush deepened to scarlet. Silence fell while Hanna sought for words.

"You're the only one what thinks so," she said in the end. "And you sees things in a peculiar way. Like them horrid mountains you thinks is beautiful."

Now it was his turn to be at a loss for words.

Hanna cared for her cows as if they were infants, and everyone said her barn was so clean you could eat off the floor. The cow answered to the name of Lyre, but the calf was nameless until one day John Broman said they'd call her Star. That's good, Hanna thought, looking lovingly at the brown calf with a spiky white patch on its forehead.

As soon as the work on the mill was almost finished, Broman had a letter from his sister saying that their mother was ill and wanted him to come and see her. He thought of taking Hanna with him but she begged so miserably not to have to go, he gave in.

He was in a black mood as he left.

"Are you worried about your mother?" Hanna said in farewell.

"Not much. She's been dying so many times before," he said curtly.

As soon as he reached the main road, he got a lift with a man taking his sheep to slaughter in Fredrikshald. Once at the border, though, Broman was glad to be alone. He wanted time to think.

He had heard old men saying that the worst part of a difficult wife was that you never got her off your mind. And it was the same for him as he pondered his young wife. But Hanna wasn't difficult. As he took a shortcut through the forests up by the Värmland border, he found himself making a long list of her virtues. She was obedient and quiet, didn't run around gossiping, was a good cook, and kept the critters' place clean. Best of all, she never complained or reproached him. And she was orderly, clever at keeping house and with money. Plus she was good to look at and not unwilling in bed.

That far in his thoughts, he then remembered the night the boy had cried and she had opened her eyes in the middle of their lovemaking. Her eyes were so full of terror, he had to stop.

"What are you afraid of?"

"Maybe that the boy's so uneasy."

She was lying, and that was unusual for her.

It had taken him a long time to shake off the memory of her eyes that night. He had lost his desire and hadn't touched her for a week.

She was so full of mysteries, and he was the kind of man who had to understand. Like all this God business. Every Sunday she walked the long way to church. He occasionally went with her, for he, too, might need the word of God. But the service simply increased the emptiness inside him, although the organist was good. Hanna sat bolt upright in the pew, apparently listening devoutedly, not looking around. Yet he was almost certain she was as bored as he was.

On the way home he tried to talk to her.

"You believes in God then, do you?"

"Believe?" she said in surprise. "But He is."

She said it as if talking about the ground she was walking on, but he persisted.

"What's He like then, do you think?"

"The worst thing about Him is you never knows where you is with Him. You has to submit, whatever happens."

"You mean . . . that God's cruel," John had said, tentatively, as that seemed blasphemous.

"Just that," she said. "Blind and unjust. He don't care about us. That sort of talk's all nonsense."

"Sounds as if you're talking about destiny," he said.

She frowned, thought for a moment, then said, "Yes, He's probably like fate because you can't escape Him."

Surprised, John Broman asked what she thought the priest would say if he knew what she thought. She laughed.

"The priest's daft."

John Broman laughed now, too, as he walked through the wet autumn forest remembering their talk. But it was no happy laugh, for there was something frightening in his wife's faith, something heathen and witchlike. Then he abandoned the thought. Hanna was no witch. She was just more honest than most.

Before reaching his native parish, he took a rest and ate his packed food. He found that Hanna had treated him to butter on the bread and a slice of pork. It was good, and he would have preferred to stay there by the stream in the forest. But then he sighed heavily before turning onto the road to his home farm. When he saw the farmhouse, it struck him that perhaps he'd been thinking so much about Hanna in order to avoid thinking about his mother. He stood for a while on the edge of the forest trying to see Brogården as a stranger would see it, thinking it looked grander than it was. In the end, he pulled himself together and walked up the gravel path to the door.

He was afraid of his brother-in-law who ran the farm, almost as afraid as he had been of his father. The old man had been dead fifteen years, but his mother ruled the family from her sickbed. Both parents were the kind you were indebted to no matter what you did.

His brother-in-law was not at home, but Agnes received him with her usual resignation, like greeting a dog you know is going to cause trouble.

"Alma wrote . . . ," he said.

"I know," she said. "But Mother's no worse. She's asleep now, so you got time to wash and have a cup of coffee."

He rinsed his face and hands in the tub out in the yard and drank coffee as weak as Agnes herself.

As he went toward his mother's room, his sister whispered, "Don't wake her. It's best for us all if she sleeps at night."

"How is things with Aunt Greta?" he said quietly.

"She's living with Alma now but still has her wits," whispered Agnes.

He sat there looking at his mother. She was panting, her breathing light and thin, as if a hairsbreadth from death. She looked peaceful, and for a moment he wished he could feel tenderness for her. But then his bitterness took over, and he thought that if God were merciful, she would die. I'd be free, he thought. I'd get my inheritance. God knows, I need the money.

They were only thoughts, but his mother woke and looked at her only son with eyes so full of reproach that he had to look away.

"So, you've come, has you," she cried, suddenly with air in her lungs. "But not brung that new wife with you, the whore from the gyspy village down in Dals. I suppose she don't dare come and see her mother-in-law."

He didn't reply, knowing from experience that sensible talk simply made things worse. But this time his silence provoked her into raging and shrieking insanely. Agnes came rushing in.

"I told you not to wake her."

He got up and left, but turned in the doorway and said meekly, "Good-bye then, Mother."

She shrieked at him again, the same old words about him bringing shame upon family and farm, just as his father had predicted.

John Broman hurried through the kitchen and across the yard to the path leading to Alma's farm. Alma had no share, and until their mother died lived with her husband and children as tenants of the outlying farm up toward the forest.

"You looks terrible," she said when he arrived. "I can see it went all wrong."

They fell silent as people do when faced with the inevitable. In the end, Alma spoke first.

"And yet she kept urging me to write. I thought she wanted to be reconciled."

He could find no answer to that, and felt the melancholy descending on him.

But Alma started asking about Hanna, the boy, and the mill, so for a moment he could keep the darkness at bay by telling her how well things were going at the mill house, how clever Hanna was, and how fond he'd become of the boy.

He asked about Greta, their father's sister, to whom they had turned during their childhood years, the aunt with all the stories and delights.

"She's went to sleep for the night," said Alma, but when she saw the darkness in her brother, she hurried to say, "Go in to her. She'll be glad to see you. But wake her slowly. She's in the bedroom by the baking oven wall, where it's warmest."

They crept in, but that proved unnecessary, for Greta was awake. She sat up in bed saying she'd dreamed John had come home to see her.

"That were no dream," said John, taking both her hands in his and looking at the toothless smile and her thousand wrinkles. She was just the same, strength pouring from her hands and into his body. They talked about old times, and she didn't ask about his visit to Brogården, as if she'd known beforehand what would happen. Then she wanted some coffee, but Alma laughed and said there'd been enough madness for one evening. They would have their evening meal now and then the house would sleep.

To his surprise, John felt sleep coming the moment his head touched the pillow in the attic room. He slept all night and woke no longer brooding over his mother. As he walked home through the forest, he was laden with a new oil lamp and an old gilt-framed mirror Alma had cleaned up for him.

"A few more wedding presents for Hanna," she'd said, and as he walked on he reckoned they would please his wife. But most of all, he thought about the agreement with Alma's husband. By threatening his mother with the law, he was going to try to get some of his inheritance in advance. The next time John came home, the horse and cart would be his.

He took a rest where the road came to the long lake and the high mountains soared into the sky. A goat track ran up the mountainside, and he climbed a short way up it to look out over the land in which he now belonged. A valley ran down from the hills on each side of the long lake, with poor strips of soil along the shores. From his perch he could see about ten of the hundred or so lakes in the parish, all winking like mirrors flung out into the wilderness.

This was not farmland, but intended for wildlife and bold hunters. Yet the stubborn earthbound peasants had stuck firmly to the poor fields, built a church and school, married and had children. Too many children.

It's always been a hard life here, August had said, but real hardship came when people began to breed like rabbits.

On his long walk, John had seen the clouds roaming across the sky in the south, and now they were gathering on the horizon over where his house was and his wife was waiting.

He got up, pulled on his pack, and set off into the rain. He was soon soaked through before the clouds gave way and the sun used the last hours of the day to dry off forest and paths, people and creatures. John Broman was not surprised. He had gotten used to the weather here being as changeable as the landscape.

By the time he got home it was long into the night. But the resinous pine log was still burning in the kitchen, and Hanna was ironing. Probably afraid of being on her own, he thought, and he called out before thumping on the door, "Hanna, it's me."

She flew toward him, and in the dim light he could see her wiping away those annoying tears with the back of her hand.

"Oh, dear Lord, am I glad to see you."

"Was you afraid?"

"No. My brother's asleep in the attic."

Then he remembered he and August had agreed that Rudolf would sleep at the mill house while Hanna was alone. At that moment, his melancholy left him, for this time.

"You ironing here in the dark?"

"Hours of the day is never long enough for me."

They didn't touch each other, but their joy lit up the kitchen. That made Broman remember the oil lamp.

"Put them clothes away and sit down here, Hanna."

He didn't look at her as he put the lamp together and filled it with paraffin. But when he lit it, his eyes never left her face, and as he stood there in the clear light, he reveled in the sight of her surprise and almost unfathomable delight.

Finally, she whispered, "It's as light as a summer's day."

It was so light, it woke Ragnar, who sat up and said, "Is it morning already?"

Then he saw John and ran straight into the arms of his stepfather, who hugged the boy as he had wished to hug his wife, but hadn't dared to.

Not until the next morning did John Broman remember the mirror.

"I has a present from Alma."

He hung the handsome mirror on the wall in the front room. Hanna stood beside him, gasping with delight, running her hand over the gilt frame, but not meeting her reflection in the glass.

"Look at yourself in it. See how pretty you is," he said.

She started to obey, her face flushing, but then covered her eyes with her hands and fled.

When she gave him his morning coffee, she said, "How was your mother?"

"As usual," he said, and that was all that was said about his visit to Värmland.

*T*he next week, the mill started up, the roar from the millstream grew more subdued, and the wooden drum held the floodgate. Broman was satisfied, pleased he also had money left over to pay August and his sons for the work they'd done.

But he told Hanna what the situation was, that the last coin was now gone from the money pouch.

And she replied as he'd hoped, "We'll manage."

She was sure. She considered herself rich. She had the cows. The earth cellar was full of potatoes and turnips, lingonberry and cloudberry preserves. The hens were laying, and a cousin had given her a pig. The beer was brewing in the brewhouse, and Broman's aquavit was bubbling away in its keg. They would have more than enough flour, so there would be no shortage of bread in the miller's house.

Then there was the fishing. John Broman knew many arts that surprised the peasants of Dals, but the one most talked about was his ability to take fish from the lake. The villagers seldom owned boats and not even during the famine years had they reckoned on fish as everyday food. Broman had acquired a flat-bottomed boat as soon as he'd decided on Norskvattnet, and he put out his fish trap every evening.

The only fish Hanna had ever eaten was salt herring, so at first she had difficulty with pike, perch, and whitefish. But she believed him when John said fish was wholesome food, and she soon learned both to cook and eat it.

The days were all work. Hanna hadn't known that the men would want coffee while waiting for their flour to be ground. And preferably a bit of bread or a bun with it.

"It's like an inn," she said to her mother. But she liked having people around her with all their chat, joking and laughing.

With the snow came other visitors. As always in winter, beggars appeared at the cottages, standing at the kitchen door, their eyes sunken so far back in their heads they looked black. Worst of all were the children. Hanna couldn't bear it. She baked bread and gave it away, then set about baking again.

"I can't turn them away," she said to John, who nodded with understanding. But the more baking Hanna did, the further the rumor spread, and the stream of beggars increased day by day.

"It's hard work for you," he said, watching her scrub the kitchen at night, the floor, table, and benches. She wasn't afraid only of fleas, but truly believed that disease lived in the dirt left by beggars. Broman laughed at her, but said nothing. He knew he would never overcome her superstitions.

What was most difficult that first winter when Hanna was learning to be a miller's wife was seeing Broman wear himself out. He developed a cough from exhaustion and from the flour dust, a bad cough that kept him awake at night.

"You'll work yourself to death," Hanna said.

When things were at their worst, she helped him carry the sacks into the mill, but that embarrassed Broman, who said, "You see to yours and I'll see to mine."

Hanna spoke to her mother and together they drew up a plan. Hanna's youngest brother was no longer needed at home, so he could come and work at the mill. He was fourteen and strong, and they could pay him in flour.

For their plan to come about, though, Hanna had to learn women's cunning. In passing, she said to Broman that her parents were worried about Adolf, who just idled around at home. At the same time, Maja-Lisa told August that she was worried over the flour maybe not lasting through the winter.

So in this way August got such a good idea and went to Broman to ask if Adolf could go into service as the miller's laborer at Norsk-vattnet. Adolf was paid in flour as agreed, but he didn't have to sleep in the laborer's box-bed in the kitchen, for Hanna had plenty of firewood and put the attic room in order for him.

Broman was less exhausted, but his coughing continued at night and worried Hanna.

Hanna also worried about the flour. The peasants of Dals paid the miller in the old way, two bushels of flour taken out of each barrel of the grain he milled for them. And the flour had to be carted the miles to the village on the border, where it was bartered for coffee, salt, sugar, and money. When the ice froze on the long lake, Hanna undertook the task, hauling the heavy sled to Alvar Alvarsson's store and returning home with the necessary goods and ready cash.

But Broman was ashamed. It was hard work for a woman even if she was young and strong. He was pleased, however, when he was at last able to pay her brother one riksdaler a month in addition to the agreed flour. Every day he waited for news of the horse from Värmland, but it didn't come. Hanna said it was all right. They didn't have enough feed for a horse in winter.

After the early service at Christmas that year, they took breakfast with August and Maja-Lisa at Bråten. The table was laid with the Christmas pork and porridge. Hanna made the coffee, because Maja-Lisa stayed behind for a while at the churchyard, where she laid spruce wreaths on her children's graves. John Broman went with her, and perhaps it was his friendliness that made her speak about her dead for the first time.

On the long way home, she said, " 'Tis a heavy burden, for I was that fond of them. Much more than the children who came later that I was allowed to keep. They was Anders and Johan, they was almost like twins. So happy and lively. Then there were Elin, she were so weak I never got to know her. No point in that, either, for Death already stood right there by the cradle."

She wept then and wiped her eyes on her best apron. He said nothing, but ran his hand down her back.

"Worst was Maria, losing her. She was such a bright one, fine both inside and out.

"I ain't never said this to no one, but now it's got to come out of me. When Astrid was born, only a year after Hanna, she was like . . . it was as if Maria'd come back. Things like that is called foolishness. But I thinks it's true, for she's like the dead one in both her ways and looks."

They were nearing Bråten. Maja-Lisa went around the corner of the house to wash her face, while John slipped into the warmth and sat down at the Christmas table. He needed a big drink. Hanna could see that and handed him a full tankard.

*O*ne Saturday toward spring when the snow was melting but the nights were still cold, Broman came back with the news that Rickard Joelsson had been accidentally shot on a bear hunt in Trysil.

"So he's dead now, Ragnar's father," said John.

Hanna turned as white as a sheet and as rigid as a hayrack.

"Is it true, or just talk?" she whispered.

"It's true all right. The policeman's been to Lyckan and told the old folks. Things is bad for them."

Hanna's face flushed scarlet, and she began to shake. Then she suddenly cried out, "Serve 'em right, them devil's asses."

Broman looked at his wife in surprise, seeing all her shame running out of her, and with it, all her sense and dignity. She rushed out the door and ran around the yard, shrieking and laughing alternately, like a mad thing, oaths pouring out of her mouth, words he would never have believed of her.

"Hell and damnation, the devil take 'em, that damned Lovisa's got her desserts—Christ, how she deserves it. You got it coming, got it coming, dear aunt!"

Then she laughed again, so loudly the birds rose from the trees.

"Ragnar, Ragnar, where are you, boy? You're free, at last you're free from that evil."

Alarmed, John went after her as she rushed off down toward the lake, crying out, "I'm free, Ragnar, we're free of all that horror. For now your father's sizzling in hell."

Then she ran back toward the house and threw herself onto her back on the ground, her skirts flying over her head, exposing her legs, but she didn't care. She just pulled her skirt off her head and clenched her fists. Shaking them up at the sky, she shrieked, "I'll never forgive you if you forgives him, you damned God. Do you hear me, do you hear me!"

Then she suddenly quieted down, gathered her clothes together, turned over on her side, curled up like a baby, and started crying. John went over to her and stroked her head. She stopped sniffing for a moment and whispered that he knew she cried only when she was happy.

"I knows that, all right," said Broman. Then he said nothing for a long time before going on. "I didn't know things was that bad for you."

Her wild weeping had stopped and her voice was steady when she said, "You, John Broman, is much too kind a man ever to understand."

He was silent for even longer, then said, "That ain't true. I were pleased when my father died."

Her weeping stopped altogether. She sat up, wiped her eyes on her apron, and said in wonder, "Then we're alike, you and me. A little, anyhow."

For the very first time, she looked him straight in the eye. His eyes met hers, and she did not turn away when he replied that it was true all right.

He saw that she was cold and told her to go with him into the warmth before she caught a chill. She obeyed, and as soon as she was in the kitchen, she washed her hands and face. Then she went over to the mirror in the front room and for the very first time stopped in front of it and looked at herself in it for a long time.

"I looks like anyone else," she said at last.

Then her shame caught up with her.

"Where's the boy?"

"Playing at the smithy."

"That's good, then."

"Yes, that's good."

"I behaved like a loony," she said, her voice uncertain.

" 'Twere good you got it out of you."

To his surprise, she understood what he meant and agreed.

"Yes, probably were. You won't tell . . ."

"Don't be silly."

The next moment the boy came rushing into the house shouting that the smith had said Rickard of Lyckan had been murdered in the forest.

"No," said John Broman in a firm voice. "He had an accident. The man what shot him thought Rickard were a bear."

"Was he wrong?"

"Yes, things like that happen. It's called accidental."

"I knows," the boy said quietly.

But when John said now he was going out on the lake with the trap, the boy brightened.

"Can I go in the boat, too, Mother?"

"Yes, you can," said John Broman for her. "Mother ain't got no time to row for me, so you can do that while she gets our evening meal."

In the boat, the boy grew serious again, and finally found the courage to ask the question.

"He were my father, weren't he?"

"Yes," said John Broman. "That he were."

That night, for the first time, Hanna turned to her husband in bed. She abruptly fell asleep afterward, but John lay awake a long time worrying about his wife. He had been more afraid than he cared to admit, and thought she was perhaps a bit mad, and that anything could've happened. But he also thought about his own wild joy when the message came that old Broman had gone through the ice. John had caused some wonder because he had wept so loudly at the funeral.

Was he like Hanna, who wept for joy?

In the morning as Hanna lit the stove, she felt a sense of destiny. Now I'm with child, she thought.

After that day, the air cleared somewhat at the mill house. And on Thursday, when her parents arrived unexpectedly with the terrible news that Joel of Lyckan had strangled his wife, then gone into the barn and shot himself, Hanna managed to look decently horrified. But her eyes did not leave Broman's, and sought deep down into them.

He did not turn away, but in some strange way felt guilty.

On Friday, they cleared the potato patch. Hanna pulled the plow, and John Broman, ashamed, walked behind his wife in the furrows. He had to get a horse somehow.

He had finally gotten a letter from Alma shortly after Christmas. Their attempt to acquire an advance on their inheritance with the aid of the law had failed, and their mother refused to talk about it.

"She'll survive us all," Alma wrote. He thought that was probably true. His cough would be the death of him long before the old woman gave up.

There was no reproach in his sister's letter, but John could read between the lines. The fact was, he was the only son, and if he'd stayed at home and taken over the farm, their inheritance would have been distributed, and Alma and her family would have been better off. But he had left the farm when young, apprenticed himself to a miller in the neighboring village, then married unhappily.

Although suicide was much disapproved of, a great many people came to Joel Eriksson's funeral. And as if everything was as it should be, husband and wife were buried alongside each other, beside them their son, whose shattered body had been brought from Trysil. Erik Eriksson stood as upright as a pine tree by the grave, and after funeral coffee had been taken and the guests had left, he told them his plans. August was to take over Lyckan, and August's eldest son was to have Bråten. But for the first time in his life, the old farmer met with opposition. August said he didn't want Lyckan, but the deeds of Bråten. And his son said he'd decided to go to America.

Then they all said with one voice that no one wished to live at

Lyckan, haunted as it was by both Joel and Lovisa, not to mention the unfortunate Rickard. This talk frightened Hanna so much she took a firm grip on John Broman's arm.

Erik Eriksson, never before opposed, crumpled as he sat at the table at Bråten, his back bowed, and suddenly they could all see he was old and that their misfortune had badly affected him. As usual, Ingegerd was the one to find a solution. She suggested the farms should be combined and transferred to August, who in his turn would have to decide on their inheritance.

"It'll be long roads for you to go if you insists on staying on at Bråten," she said to her brother-in-law. "But that's up to you."

August made a special effort not to show how pleased he was. This was the solution he'd hoped for. Hanna looked wide-eyed at Aunt Ingegerd and, as so many times before, thought how upright and handsome she was, Erik Eriksson's elder daughter. She was fifty now, and seven years older than Maja-Lisa, but she looked much younger.

People spoke contemptuously of daughters who stayed at home, but as far as Ingegerd of Framgården was concerned, people had little to say. It had long been said that Erik Eriksson never made a decision without first consulting his daughter.

A woman can be like that if she escapes husband and children, Hanna thought. Then she was ashamed, for she knew women had to bow to established custom and children had to be born.

After Erik Eriksson and his daughter had left in their cart, August, his sons, and John Broman celebrated their victory. They drank so deeply, there was no question of John and Hanna returning home. Together with her mother, Hanna dragged the menfolk up to the attic, laid them out on the floor, and covered them with quilts. Then the two women went down to the kitchen to clean up after the funeral and the celebrations. They talked about Ingegerd, who had been beautiful and clever when young.

"She never lacked for suitors," said Maja-Lisa. "They came in droves, but she just laughed at them. And Father were pleased, as he didn't want to lose her. Poor Joel had to keep hearing that he'd been born an old woman, that Ingegerd were the heir Eriksson and the farm needed, and it were the misfortune of his life that she were a girl."

Grumbling, Maja-Lisa told the story, and Hanna thought she was lamenting Joel and his unhappy life. But suddenly Maja-Lisa cried out that she would never forgive her brother, who'd taken the honor from the family, murderer and suicide that he was.

Five great Norway maples grew in a clearing above the house, on the very edge of the shores of the Norwegian lakes. When they flowered that spring, there was a smell of honey all around the mill house, and Hanna said it was a great pity they couldn't take the sweet juice straight out of the trees. Broman laughed at her as he gazed at the pale green pointed flowers swooping down toward the dark water, and he saw she didn't mind.

"You has to help me carry the best sofa up to the attic," she said. "I needs the space for a loom in the living room."

He was pleased and said she knew what he thought of that sofa.

She snapped back that it was only temporary, this loom business, and she'd soon have her fine sofa back down again.

"Nothing but a showpiece a man can't even sit on," he said.

At that she grew ragingly angry, saying there were better things in life than sitting. He looked at her in surprise.

"You're very short-tempered these days," he said.

"I'm to have a child," she shouted at him, then clapped her hand to her mouth, thinking this was just like her. Here she'd been pondering for weeks about when to tell him and how she would choose her words!

She could see he wasn't pleased, but he put his arm around her shoulders as he finally said, "Yes, well, it's to be expected, ain't it."

She managed to lift the potatoes in time and stock the earth cellar before the boy arrived in November. The birth almost frightened the life out of Broman, and it was made no easier when old Anna slipped out into the kitchen for a cup of coffee and said Hanna was so torn down below, this was only to be expected.

"You get on out, Broman," said the midwife.

He obeyed, thinking it was lucky Rickard Joelsson was dead, for today he could've gladly killed the man himself. Then he went across to the mill, pulled some sacks over himself, and fell asleep on the floor.

At dawn, old Anna woke him and said solemnly that he had a son.

"How's Hanna?"

"She's sleeping and healing. She's strong, your wife."

Relief washed over him, and Hanna's stoicism moved him. He washed thoroughly in the kitchen and put on a clean shirt before creeping into their bedroom. She was pale, his girl, but sleeping soundly, her breathing deep and even.

The boy was already in the cradle at the foot of the bed, an ugly little creature with a bright red tuft of hair. Broman gazed at the infant, recognizing those features and thinking he would have trouble with this boy. Then he heard the first cart coming up to the mill and went off to the day's work.

Toward evening, Maja-Lisa and August arrived with Ragnar, whom Broman had taken over to Bråten when the birth pains had started. He'd not wanted the boy to be frightened, he'd said. Maja-Lisa had taken the boy, but thought it a strange idea. Children had to learn what life was like. When she told August, he'd agreed. He had long thought the miller was soft on the boy and was embarrassed when Broman stroked Hanna's cheek.

Now they'd come to see their new grandchild. They soon found he was nothing like anyone in the family, for none had a round face like that, a turned-up nose like that, or red hair like that. So Broman had to say that the child was like his own father, but Hanna was the only one to notice that he looked miserable as he said it.

"Looks like a frog," said Ragnar, and both Hanna and Maja-Lisa scolded him. But Broman sat the boy on his knee and said comfortingly that newborn babes often looked peculiar.

"He'll soon be as handsome as you," he said, knowing it was a lie. This new child would never be as handsome as his brother.

It was decided that the boy would be called John after his father. Hanna was given a long list of things she must do. No uninvited guests at home for the next week. And Hanna must watch out for Lame-Malin, the blacksmith's wife, as she was suspected of having the evil eye.

When his in-laws had gone, John made a bed up for the boy and himself in the box-bed in the kitchen. They fell asleep immediately, exhausted by all the excitement. But Hanna lay awake for a long time in the bedroom, looking at the new child and thinking to herself, ugly little thing.

Still, she felt the same strange tenderness as she had for Ragnar. Then she gave thanks to God that it was over and it was a boy. For a moment she thought with anxiety about what Broman had said, that he was almost insane with joy when his father died. Must have been an evil man, she thought, looking again at her newborn son.

"He won't be like him in his ways," she said aloud as if pronouncing an invocation. Maybe that helped, for the ugly infant grew into a good and compliant child.

The snow came at the end of the month, but, thank heavens, gave way to rain from Norway. John Broman swallowed his pride and went to Erik Eriksson to borrow a horse and cart. The old man was in bed with a high fever and pains in his chest, Ingegerd said, and John was ashamed of his relief.

He liked Ingegerd, one of the few in the valley he could talk to. She offered him coffee, and they sat in the kitchen discussing all manner of things. About Rickard, she said that the wretched boy went mad when his father beat Lovisa.

"I tried to do something to help Hanna," she said. "But Father were against it. You know how the old thinks, that a whore is a whore whatever she's done. And there's something strange about Maja-Lisa's children."

"Something strange?"

Ingegerd regretted saying it, he could see that. But he pressed her, and she told him about Astrid, Hanna's sister, who had married well in Fredrikshald.

"She had fits," Ingegerd said. "Went clean off her head one day. Then she ran all the way to the churchyard and tore the flowers and crosses off the graves of her dead brothers and sisters. To the priest, she said they wasn't dead. They was alive and it were wrong to have them in the earth."

Ingegerd shuddered as she sat there, then took a sip of her coffee.

"You can imagine what was said in the cottages. But I made sure Father didn't hear none of it, and took the girl in here. She was a good girl, and clever. Pretty she was, and she was never once mad here. I was fond of her and wanted to keep her. But the village tongues wagged and I was pleased when a job in service was arranged for her in Norway. I went to Fredrikshald myself, so I knows it was a good family she was going to, not a farm but a merchant's household. Then the fish merchant fell in love with her, and there was a wedding in Fredrikshald. Her man is the kind with his feet firmly on the ground. He knows nothing of madness."

"So it turned out well in the end?"

"That's right. Letters I get from her is happy. I think them peculiar thoughts of hers went away when she got away from Maja-Lisa."

"Maja-Lisa says she's like one of the dead children."

"That she is. But it's not all that strange, siblings is often as alike as peas in a pod."

John was comforted by her calm voice and sensible explanation. He'd had some strange thoughts ever since last Christmas, when Maja-Lisa had told him about Astrid and the dead sister.

In the end, he told her what he'd come for. To his own surprise, he told her all about his mother refusing to die, the inheritance that couldn't be divided, and how long he'd waited in vain to get a horse from the farm.

"We can't manage without it," he said. "No man pays money, and once a month I has to go off and sell my flour. Alvarsson pays poorly. He knows how to make the most of the trap I'm in."

"You could borrow our horse and cart and go to Fredrikshald," said Ingegerd. "Father don't need to know. He won't be on his feet for the next few weeks. Meanwhile I'll think up something."

He was surprised at her benevolence as he harnessed the horse, young and strong and not all that easily managed, to the cart. But when he said good-bye, he understood better.

" 'Tis the same for us both, Broman, you and me," said Ingegerd. "It must be hard to wish the life out of the old."

Hanna was hugely surprised when he came back with the horse. But unease took over from her joy when he said he intended to go all the way to Fredrikshald with the flour.

"Then you'll be away for many a day."

"You've got your brother here."

"But that ain't the same. He mostly says nothing."

Broman thought all the children from Bråten mostly said nothing, not least Hanna herself. But aloud he said, "I thought you didn't like me telling my stories."

"But that's only because I shouldn't like them," she said.

He laughed at her, then saw too late that she was saddened.

"Hanna, tell me why you pretends not to like what you like."

"They ain't necessary."

"To tell stories to your boy?"

"Yes," she said, and she was angry now. "That don't bring no bread to the table."

"I didn't think you lacked for bread," he said, and he went out, slamming the door behind him with such force it shook the house.

Then she was afraid.

But Ragnar, on the floor with his building blocks, looked thoughtfully up at her and said how stupid his mother had been.

She tried, but as usual couldn't be angry with her son, so she just snapped at him that children should keep quiet about things they didn't understand.

"It's you what doesn't understand," said Ragnar, and for a moment the thought that he might be right raced through her mind.

Meanwhile the boy slipped out to John, now grooming the horse and making a place ready for it in the barn. Little John was yelling in his cradle, and Hanna calmed him by putting him to her breast. When her husband and son came back, she heard them laughing outside, and she thought they were laughing at her. That hurt. But she would get used to it. All through her life, her sons would make a great deal of fun of her.

*E*ighteen months after Little John was born, the next boy arrived, and, as expected, was like the Eriksson family, large brown eyes, straight nose, and dark brown hair. Maja-Lisa was as proud as if she had given birth to him herself and decided that the boy was to be called Erik after her father.

The birth had again been a difficult one, and when Broman saw Hanna's suffering, he solemnly promised himself he would never again touch his wife. But it was a promise he couldn't keep, for when Erik was two, their third boy was born and named August after Hanna's father.

The last boy was frailer than the other two. Hanna could see that at once after the birth, even before the midwife had washed the child. When she put him to her breast for the first time, she sensed little will in him to live.

Takes after his father, she thought.

She lived in constant anxiety over her husband as his cough grew worse each year, often so bad he found it difficult to breathe and had to go outside and gasp for air. When it was at its worst, old Anna came to put hot compresses on his chest and to speak soothingly to him.

"You should go to the doctor," she said, and in the spring when there was the least to do at the mill, Broman and Aunt Ingegerd traveled the long way to Vänersborg, where an ill-tempered doctor told him he had asthma and must stop working in the mill.

"Nothing about how I'm supposed to support my family if I close the mill," said John to his wife, when he got back. The medicine he had been given soon ran out, though that didn't matter much as it had been of little help.

But shortly thereafter, Erik Eriksson made a decision about his horse. August received two-thirds of the creature and John Broman one-third. Broman was bitter, but Hanna considered it a good agreement. They didn't have enough grazing for the great beast up there, and they needed the horse for only one week a month, when the flour had to be taken to Norway to be sold.

As Ingegerd had predicted, living up at Bråten and looking after the Lyckan farm became too much for August. Cautiously, he took the matter up with Maja-Lisa, who immediately said she would never go and live at that place of misfortune. When John was brought into the dispute, he pondered for a long time and eventually came up with a suggestion.

"Let's pull down the old house and build another on the hill," he said. "It'd be better, a fine new house, with a view across the river and lake."

But August had neither the money nor the energy to build anew. That meant a move to old Lyckan, where August, his sons, and John Broman painted the ceilings and walls and whitewashed around the stove.

At midsummer, all their belongings were taken to Lyckan. Maja-Lisa stopped complaining, but she never really liked their new home, and some time went by before they noticed what was wrong with her. One day John said to his wife that her mother was fading away up there at Lyckan. Hanna was shaken and frightened, whispering that there they were again, the evil spirits. Broman snorted and told her that what was troubling Maja-Lisa was a sickness of the kind that set in the body.

Hanna went with the children to see her as often as she could and each time saw that she was thinner and paler.

"Are you in any pain, Mother?"

"No. Just so wretchedly tired."

Maja-Lisa's housework went by the board. Hanna cleaned and did the baking, but soon had to tell August that he must get hold of a servant girl.

"You can see she can't manage."

But it was no longer possible to get hold of servant girls. Young girls left in a steady stream for Norway where they got work in households and at guest houses in Moss and factories in Fredrikshald. Some went on to America; some stayed and married Norwegians. Others sometimes came back on weekend visits in fine store-bought clothes and big hats with roses on them. That annoyed all decent housewives, who said what hussies they were, if not worse. For you could well imagine how much such fripperies cost.

Hanna did what she could for her mother, leaving the children almost every day at old Anna's and taking the infant August to Lyckan to make sure her parents and brothers at least had some food. One day a question slipped out of her, a question she had never considered asking.

"Is it true the dead walks again here, Mother?"

"Yes," said Maja-Lisa, smiling. "But it ain't not Joel and Lovisa who're here. It's the children, Anders and Johan. And sometimes little Elin."

"But they never lived here."

"They does now, anyhow."

When Hanna got back home and told John Broman what her mother had said, he told her folk never got over grief. It's there to make inroads into life, taking a bit at a time away from you.

"People with a lot of dead begin to lose the desire to live."

August couldn't endure his wife's illness and wrote a letter to Johannes. August was related to this well-known healer, and wrote, "Now, Cousin, you must come, for I cannot manage without the wife."

When Hanna told John about the letter, he was surprised and said he thought Johannes cured animals.

"People, too. You must've heard about the soldier at Piletorpet who was dying of cancer. Johannes went into his cottage and made him a drink. Then he told him to get up. Johannes said he was going to live to ninety. And he did."

John hadn't heard that tale, but he had heard many others, each one more amazing than the one before. For Johannes's reputation was great even in Värmland. John had never believed all those tales, but he said to Hanna that perhaps a visit might comfort August and Maja-Lisa.

But John was wrong. On Sunday afternoon, the family was all assembled at Lyckan. Johannes came, shook them all by the hand, and went into the room where Maja-Lisa lay. He took one look at her and said, "So you're on your way now, are you?"

Then she could admit it to herself and to the others.

"I'm so weary," she said. "When will it be?"

"Probably already this week. You don't need to fear for torments. You'll go in your sleep."

"Will I see my children then?"

"Expect so. All except Maria, but you knows that."

John Broman, in the kitchen and hearing every word, couldn't believe he'd heard right. Then Hanna came out as white as a ghost, closely followed by her father, who looked as if he were the one sentenced to death. They couldn't bring themselves to speak, but finally Ingegerd said, "Must send a message to Astrid."

Although she whispered it and Johannes was still in with Maja-Lisa, he heard and said loudly, "No, Astrid's not to come."

"That's right," said Maja-Lisa. "Astrid's not to come. But I wants the priest, if the boozer can stay sober for a whole day."

Hanna stayed at Lyckan to cook food for them all. But John went back to the mill where Ragnar, now ten, was alone with his younger brothers. John got a ride with Ingegerd, now hurrying back to Old Erik, who'd been in extremis for over a year now.

In the cart, John said, "What should we believe?"

"Johannes has great experience of sickness. It ain't too hard to see that Maja-Lisa is on her way out."

"But what Johannes said about Maria and Astrid?"

"Don't take it so seriously, Broman. Johannes has been in America for a long time and got himself a new religion. A strange teaching that says the soul leaves the dead and goes into the new-born. 'Tis all nonsense."

She glanced at John but saw he wasn't convinced.

"Listen now. Johannes stayed at Bråten all one winter when Astrid was small. That was when he put those strange ideas into Maja-Lisa's head, what sent the poor girl crazy later."

John heaved a deep sigh of relief and agreed with her from the depths of his heart when she said, "The dead is dead, and you knows that, Broman."

The priest was only half-drunk when he arrived on Monday to give Maja-Lisa communion. She was calm, almost expectant. But August was rigid, dumb with terror, as if exiled to another country.

On Tuesday, Maja-Lisa had a pain in her chest and found it difficult to breathe. The family sat by her bed all night, and things went just as predicted. She drew a deep sigh and stopped breathing.

John was not at the deathbed. Someone had to be at home with the children, and he had just gotten them to sleep when there was a knock on the door and Johannes came in.

John made coffee and put out a bite to eat, moving about awkwardly, for he did not like his guest. They said nothing until they'd finished their coffee, then John spoke.

"Do you always condemns people to death straight out like that?"

"Only those who wants to hear," said Johannes, smiling. "August ain't got long to go, either. But he wouldn't benefit from knowing."

John thought about his asthma and his wretched tiredness, but he didn't dare ask. Nor was that necessary.

"Broman, you've got several more years to go than you really wants. And that's for a definite reason. Can I sleep up in the attic room?"

John was astonished. But as he was lighting the stove in the attic and preparing the bed, he felt happier than he had for a long time.

* * *

Hanna was pale when she returned, and tense as she fed the hungry infant. As she sat there with the boy at her breast, she looked long and hard at John, and said, "Dear Lord, how I wishes I could've cried."

She slept for only an hour or so, but despite the sleepless night, still had the milking to do. As she'd expected, Johannes came to the barn, praised the creatures, and told her she needn't worry about her husband.

"He'll live on a good bit into the 1900s. He'll be here all right when we has to write 1910."

Hanna was greatly relieved. It was still the summer of 1894, a long time until the turn of the century. She didn't have time to work it out until Johannes had left, and she found to her surprise that he'd promised no more than sixteen years. But that was enough, for by then Ragnar would be twenty-six, John nineteen, and Erik eighteen. There'd be three hale and hearty men at the mill.

"Even you, poor wee thing, you'll be sixteen and grown," she whispered to August as she put him to her breast.

"You looks a mite more cheerful," said Broman as he came in for his midday meal. She nodded, but pursed her mouth, Johannes's final words still ringing in her ears. One word to Broman, and he'd die just out of sheer cussedness.

After they'd gone to bed, despite her exhaustion, Hanna again found it hard to sleep, memories of her mother coming and going in her mind, and some of them hurt.

"You looks worn out," said John at breakfast.

"Been having bad thoughts." She flushed but couldn't stop herself. "Like that winter I was carrying Ragnar. Mother made me help with the slaughter, and she actually had me hold the blood pail. Then an old woman in a cottage by the river died, and what do you think, Mother told me to go and wash the body! All that so the boy inside me would be unhealthy and die."

Hanna smiled wryly and pointed at Ragnar asleep in the box-bed.

"Then he was healthier and finer than any of her own children."

John could only shake his head. But as he reached the door on his way to work, he turned around and said, "One thing we can learn from this. Them old superstitions don't got no effect."

In the middle of the busy harvest, August Olsson had a pain in his chest and lay down under a tree to rest. When his sons went to wake him an hour or so later, he was dead. They stood around him in silence, neither really surprised nor frightened. Old August had not really lived since Maja-Lisa had gone into the ground.

There was no will, so the farms went to the sons. Robert had not given up his America plans and Rudolf was as hardworking as Hanna, so Rudolf established himself at Lyckan. But Adolf stayed at the mill at Norskvattnet for a few more years. When the miller's sons were old enough to take over the work, Adolf took out his share of the inheritance and went to America.

None of Hanna's brothers ever married.

*A*strid came to her father's funeral with her husband and children. John Broman often looked at his sister-in-law with appreciation, grand as she was in her store-bought floral dress. She was a sight to see and friendly to them all, loved a good talk, sang lullabies to the children and critter songs to the cows.

In temperament, she was nothing like her other siblings, yet had the same stature as Hanna, and if you looked closely, you could see the likeness in her features.

But her sister made Hanna seem heavy and countrified. While Astrid flew across the ground, Hanna plodded. Astrid's face reflected every emotion and was as changeable as spring weather, while Hanna's expression was closed. Astrid chatted and sang, while Hanna said nothing, giggling occasionally, but at once putting her hand to her mouth, always embarrassed when it happened. John felt sorry for his wife, but sometimes angry; she could well have taken off her kerchief to show her lovely hair, and wear something else besides black and brown striped wool.

Astrid said so.

"Why do you has to look like some old country bumpkin? Come on. Try on my green skirt with this flowery blouse."

"I'd never dare," said Hanna, tittering, and Astrid realized that things were just as her sister said; she didn't dare.

One thing was unmistakable: the two sisters were fond of each other, not a scrap of either envy or distancing in Hanna, though now and again she did speak of conceit and vanity. Astrid could smile at those words, tenderly and compassionately.

"You're too hard on yourself," she said.

"Things went for me as they went."

They never got any further than that.

John was attracted to his sister-in-law, entranced by her sunny nature. But she disturbed him, too, so they never became truly intimate. Once he said, "You're not really of this world."

She laughed at him, but he saw Hanna was frightened.

His brother-in-law agreed.

"The wife's an angel," he said. "When she ain't being a troll. It ain't easy, as you can imagine."

They could all laugh then, all except Hanna, who flushed and bit her lip. She's remembering the madness, John thought.

He grew to like the fish merchant, a trustworthy man with a big heart and a good head. They became friends when out fishing on the lake in the early mornings. In the boat, Broman began to realize a crisis was blowing up, maybe something worse, between Norway and Sweden.

Arne Henriksen's voice rang across the lake with such force, he frightened the fish away.

"There's got to be an end to this Swedish lording over us," he said. "Otherwise it'll all blow up. You can be certain of that. We've got both arms and men."

John thought about his trips to Fredrikshald, where the poor peasants from Dals stood humbly in the market square to be rid of their sheep, their hay, and tubs of butter.

"I means them gentlemen in Stockholm," Arne went on. "Not you."

"But we'd be the ones slaughtered if you comes with arms."

"You has to join the cause and get rid of the king, the damned old fox."

John Broman was surprised at his own feelings. Never before had he felt how Swedish he was. For a moment, he felt like flinging the loudmouthed Norwegian overboard. But Arne noticed nothing of his anger and launched into a long explanation, talking of the law in Eidsvoll that gave ordinary people greater rights than anywhere else in the world. Then he came to the consulate dispute.

Broman had heard about it but, like most Swedes, hadn't taken the matter seriously. Now he was told about the Left party and its demands for a foreign minister of its own with power in the Riksdag, the Swedish parliament, and about Norwegians who were already taking the Union badge off the flags of Norwegian ships sailing around the world.

The miller listened without really understanding. But when Henriksen told him the Riksdag had bought new warships for eight million riksdaler, and the new Norwegian defense minister, a man called Stang, a lieutenant-commander, was building forts along the long border with Sweden, John Broman was frightened.

"Stang's a damned good man," said Henriksen, then went on to say the defense minister had bought new German arms, and Fredriksten fortress had been given cannons with much greater range.

Henriksen tested John out with a long look before rounding off his speech.

"We don't talk all that much about it, but every single Norwegian knows . . . arms first, then . . ."

They went on talking about it over their evening drink. Henriksen was unusual—voluble and vociferous when sober but calm and factual once he had a drink inside him.

"You has to see it's sheer madness, Norwegian seamen sailing all over the world without their own countrymen looking out for them."

Broman understood that.

"The Norwegian parliament's decided on a consulate of its own," Henriksen went on. "We've allocated money for it. But the king in Stockholm refuses."

John nodded.

"King Oskar's a shit," said Henriksen.

The sisters serving up their evening meal heard him. Hanna looked as if about to faint, but Astrid laughed.

The Norwegian relatives were offended when they heard that John Broman went to Fredrikshald once a month. Why hadn't he let them know? John found that difficult to answer, but in the end said he'd probably been too shy.

"Nonsense," said Arne, and Astrid laughed as usual and said there would have to be a change. Broman could stay over with them next time, and he had to agree to that. In a few months' time, little August would be weaned and then John was to bring Hanna with him.

"Mother'd never let me," said Hanna, then flushed when she remembered that Maja-Lisa was dead. "I means," she went on, "that if children is to be healthy, you has to breast-feed them for two years."

For once, Astrid was angry.

"It's time you got free of Mother and her awful superstitions," she said. "Times has changed, Hanna."

Then Hanna said something that truly surprised John.

"Mm. I think I knows that. But it worries me. What am I supposed to believe in if all the old things is wrong?"

"You has to believe in yourself," said Astrid, as if that were the simplest thing in the world.

The two sisters gossiped their way through the local news. Astrid was horrified at all the changes, the Kasa people in America, only the old people left at Bönan, the forest growing over the big Kleva farm, Jonas dead, Klara dead, Lars dead.

"But they wasn't old!"

"No. Neither was Mother and Father."

"What did they die of, Hanna?"

"They was worn out."

"I reckon they died of grief after the famine."

They went through all their school friends. Where was Ragnar and where was Vitalia, Sten, Jöran, and Olena?

Hanna replied: In Norway, in Göteborg, in America, at sea.

Hanna hadn't thought about it before, how deserted it had become in the valley. Now it was put into words.

"Soon a wasteland," said Astrid.

Astrid fell in love with Ragnar, the dark-eyed eleven-year-old with his quick smile and lighthearted nature.

"A Sunday's child," she said. "Life's incomprehensible, ain't it, Hanna?"

"He's like his father," said Hanna, adding hastily, "only on the outside. Ragnar's kind and good by nature."

"Must be hard not to spoil him."

Yes, Hanna had to admit Broman had a weakness for the boy and was much fonder of him than of his own sons.

But Henriksen told John he would have to look out for the boy.

"They finds it difficult to grow up, them what can sweeten themselves to get what they wants."

John nodded. He'd thought about that.

When the Norwegians left to return home, it had been decided that John would stay with them whenever he took his flour to Fredrikshald, and that once every summer he would take Hanna with him.

"We'll buy you some fine new clothes and take you to the photographer," said Astrid, but Hanna cringed with dismay. And delight, John noticed.

It was early morning, the sun low as the Norwegian wagon with their children asleep in it set off downhill toward the border. Hanna stood waving in the yard outside while Broman went with them to the gate. After their guests disappeared around the bend, he turned around and stood still for a moment, looking at his wife, her shadow long in the slanting light, dark and sharply outlined.

Hanna's first trip to the busy town became a great event. She liked everything she saw, the crowded street life, the many shops, and best of all being surrounded by strangers.

"Just think," she said to John. "Just think, being able to walk the streets and into all the shops without having to speak to a single person."

Pressed by her sister, she tried on clothes in the shops. It was painful to watch her, deeply embarrassed as she was, sweat pouring off her.

"I feels so awfully ashamed," she whispered. But Astrid refused to give up. She got Hanna to try another dress and told her to look at herself in the big mirror, though she didn't dare for more than a brief moment, then clapped her hands over her eyes.

In the end she relented and bought a dress with flounces and green flowers on a white background. But when she was made to go to the photographer's, she put on her best dress from home, the brown checked one, and once there, did nothing but gaze solemnly straight into the camera.

She was profoundly taken by the photograph. She had it framed and hung up back at home, and she often stopped to look at it, as if she couldn't have enough of those eyes meeting hers.

On their way home, she told Broman she had never imagined Norway like that . . . so bold. She'd been there when she was small, but couldn't remember they were all so cheerful there.

John agreed. He'd also been across from Värmland quite often as a child and hadn't noticed much difference. But now there was a kind of rousing force in Norway, a liveliness and joyousness you could feel the moment you crossed the border. He understood it better now, since he had gotten to know Henriksen. The Norwegians had a common purpose and a great dream. But he didn't want to worry Hanna, so he said nothing about the Union crisis. They talked about Astrid, instead, and Hanna said she was like a whole lot of people in one.

"She's got lots of aprons," Broman agreed, but Hanna misunderstood.

"She don't dress up too much, my sister."

"No, she don't," he said. She was all of them at once, angel and troll, mother and child, grand wife and cheerful country girl.

He wondered what held her together, thinking perhaps it was a secret, that the great secret was the core of her nature.

* * *

As soon as Hanna was home, she started making curtains with the thin white cotton material she'd bought in Norway. The little windows in the house looked softer.

"How fine, how fine," she said, as if beside herself with delight.

The people in the district looked askance upon her newfangled curtains as vanity, but Hanna persisted and the curtains stayed.

But she never dared put on the flowery shop dress.

*H*anna had a hand with the butter. No churning failed for her, not even if a beggar woman came into the kitchen and put the evil eye on the churn. But then one day the blacksmith's wife, Lame-Malin, said it'd always been said whores had luck with butter.

Hanna had lost her temper, and shouted back, "Get out, you lame bitch. And never show your face in the mill house again."

From that day on, there was hostility between the two houses by the lakes. Broman was never told what had happened, but it was difficult for him, as he was dependent on the blacksmith in many ways, not just because they drank together on Saturday nights. Every other month, the grindstones had to be lifted for chaff-cutting. That was heavy work, and for cleaning the millstone ridges he needed sharpened cutters.

He reproached Hanna.

"We has to keep in with the neighbors we has."

But she was unmoved. Malin was never to cross her threshold again.

"Ask her," she said. "Ask her why I has a hand with the butter."

So Broman went to the smith's house with his question, and Malin said it was probably just as Hanna said, that she had luck with the butter because she kept both kitchen and barn clean.

That evening when he got home with Malin's reply, he was told what she'd actually said to Hanna. He was so angry, he went straight back to the smithy and scolded the smith's wife. So the men had to take their drink down to the big cave by the long lake.

Then Hanna regretted what she'd said, thinking she'd gone too far. Especially as she couldn't keep her sons away from the smithy and the blacksmith's boys, who were mostly the same age as hers.

In the old days I didn't even blink when they called me a whore, she thought. Now that I'm respectable I gets so horribly angry.

She was disappointed with respectability. It hadn't lived up to her expectations. At first she'd gone to church to sit among the other wives, even on an aisle bench so the young had to squeeze by. But it was no pleasure and when Broman asked her what consolation she sought in church, she was ashamed. It was now many years since she'd been to divine service.

Then one late winter's day, Ragnar came home from school covered with blood and bruises. Yes, he'd been in a fight. The others had come off worse than he had, he said, wiping the blood from his nose off his upper lip with the back of his hand.

Hanna sent for Broman.

He came, demanded hot water to wash the injuries, scraped the worst of the blood from the boy's face, and asked what had happened.

"They says I'm a bastard," said the boy.

"Heaven's above!" cried Hanna. "That ain't nothing to fight over, is it? It's only the truth!"

Broman at once turned abruptly around and struck Hanna across the face with the flat of his hand, sending her flying across the kitchen floor until her back hit the long bench under the window.

"Are you mad!" she cried.

"Nay, I ain't," shouted Broman. "But you'll drive me mad." Then he went out and slammed the door behind him.

Ragnar was crying, but she could see his eyes were ice-cold behind the tears.

"It's you, Mother, what's crazy."

Then he, too, disappeared.

Hanna was shaking all over, but managed to pull herself together. She looked hard at her face in the mirror. It was swollen and bruised, but not bleeding. Her back was worse, aching from the blow against the bench.

Thank goodness the children's out, she thought, but then remembered where they were, at the smithy, where Malin gave them bread and juice.

She made their evening meal, and her sons came home. She sent Erik to fetch their father and Ragnar. Broman appeared looking miserable, but said not a word.

"You hurt yourself, Mother?" said Erik.

"Where's Ragnar?"

"Gone into the forest," said Broman.

"Dear Lord," whispered Hanna. "We has to go and look for him."

She looked terrible, white as sheet beneath the bruises and swellings. He was ashamed but said in a steady voice, "He'll be back. He told me he had to be alone to think. I can understand that."

Hanna moved with difficulty as she set about the dishes and served the food. When Broman noticed, she said apologetically that she'd hit her back on the bench. That made him even more ashamed.

Ragnar came in as they were getting the beds ready for the night. He did the same as Broman, said nothing.

Dear Lord, how can I explain?

When they'd gone to bed, all Broman said was, "I wants to know why you can't forgive it when Malin calls you a whore, but it's all right when Ragnar's called a bastard."

She said nothing for a long while, then finally said, "I ain't no whore. I was attacked. But Ragnar . . . he's illegitimate and that can't be denied."

"So you're innocent and he's guilty?"

"I don't mean that."

In the morning, she could scarcely move, but Broman ignored her pains and tried again.

"Hanna. You ain't stupid. You can think. Now you has to explain to the boy and me."

She thought about it all day, but could find nothing that would make her words understandable to others. To her it was obvious. At their evening meal, she said to Ragnar that her tongue had run away with her.

"I were that frightened, I didn't know what I were saying," she said.

That was as near to asking for forgiveness as she could get, but not enough for the boy. His eyes were still icy cold, and it was a ghostly silent week in the house. They were all good at saying nothing, Ragnar, Hanna, and Broman. The days went by. Her back got better, and the bruises and swellings disappeared. But her eyes were dark with shame and grief.

Then one morning before Ragnar and his brothers went to school, the boy said, "You're a bit thick in the head, you is, Mom."

That was the first time he had ever called her Mom. She sat quite still at the kitchen table, thinking she'd lost him now and he was the most beloved she had.

Again she wished she could cry, but as usual, she was dry to her very soul.

*B*roman took his flour to Fredrikshald, and Hanna worried whether he would tell her sister what had happened. She tried to calm herself with the thought that he didn't make a habit of going around gossiping and telling tales.

But when he came home late that night, she realized she'd been wrong. He said curtly that he and his brother-in-law had agreed that Ragnar could go to work in the fish trade in Fredrikshald as soon as he was thirteen.

When John saw her despair, he told her she must realize the boy was growing up and had to make a life of his own. At that moment, Hanna made a decision.

"I suppose he has to choose for himself," she said.

"Yes, he'll decide for himself."

"He's needed at the mill."

"No, 'tis enough with Adolf and the boys."

"We'll ask him at midday tomorrow," said Hanna, and Broman nodded.

As soon as the men had left the next morning, Hanna started making a sponge cake, generous with both butter and sugar, and tasting until the mixture was smooth and sweet. Then she took the cake to the smithy where Lame-Malin almost swooned with surprise.

"I thought," said Hanna, "we neighbors should stay friends."

Malin was so astonished, she never even got around to putting on the coffee. Hanna was grateful for that, for she found it difficult to bear the filth and bad air in the smith's house. She talked for a while about Malin's boys, who were shaping up well, she said. And about the winter that refused to let go.

Then she went home and said to Him up there in the heavens

that now she'd done what she could. Now it was His turn to do something for her.

But at dinner when Broman told the boy what had been agreed in Fredrikshald, Ragnar went wild with delight.

"If I'd like . . . ," he cried. "You mad, Father? If I'd like . . ."

Broman went on to explain that Henriksen had customers all over the town and needed an errand boy to cycle around with the orders. Some wanted fresh herring on Wednesday when they were brought in, others mackerel on Thursday. And then there was the cod that nearly everyone wanted on Saturday.

John was quite voluble as he described this trade, but Ragnar had heard one word only.

"Cycle?" he said. "Father, do you means I'd have a bicycle?"

At that moment Hanna knew that, yet again, God hadn't listened to her.

The house seemed empty after Ragnar had gone, and Broman was made to think about how much the boy had filled the place with his laughter. He was troubled about Hanna, too. She was so tired and upset, not at all herself. He tried talking to her.

"It was good you settled with the smith's wife."

" 'Twere useless."

As usual, he didn't understand her.

By the time spring came with the snow melting and the starlings, they'd gotten used to it. Even Hanna began to regain her old briskness and took a greater interest in her other sons. Broman looked at Little John, their small red-haired eldest son, and to his surprise found the boy was himself filling the space left by Ragnar. He was full of ideas, had the same laugh as his half brother and the same liking for what was lighthearted and amusing.

He was tender, too, noticing his mother's grief and doing what he could to console her. He'd never been on good terms with his father, but now Broman had to admit what was obvious, that Little John was the son who worked hardest at the mill.

"You sticks to things more than your brother does," he said, almost reluctantly one day. When the boy flushed with pleasure, Broman felt guilty. He had neglected his sons. Not only Little John, but Erik, too, and August, the youngest a constant source of annoyance with sickliness and whining.

Erik was good at school. Hanna had said so long ago, that he had a scholar's head. It wasn't long before the schoolmaster had taught him most of what he himself knew.

Broman started hunting out his old books in the attic, never unpacked since the move from Värmland. He found *Robinson Crusoe* and smiled wistfully as he remembered how the book had fed all his boyhood dreams.

"Not an uncalled-for word," he said warningly to Hanna as he brought down the book. As they sat down for their evening meal, he just said to the boy, "Here you are, a present for you."

Erik flushed just as his brother had and disappeared into the icy upstairs. Then he took to vanishing there at every free moment. Hanna was troubled and took up blankets and sweaters so that he wouldn't die of cold.

In the end, she gave in and lit the stove for him.

A few days later she told him his blood would rot in his veins if he lay there every evening with his nose in a book. But Erik laughed at her. She recognized that laugh—superior, just like Ragnar's.

Erik soon found his own way to the chest of old books.

August caught whooping cough that spring. Hanna walked around with the boy in her arms at night and gave him hot milk and honey. But that didn't help, and he usually brought up all his food. John tried in vain to find some rest in the bedroom, but the boy's terrible cough started his own up again. Father and son competed at coughing together.

"You've been so well for so long now," said Hanna uneasily.

For the first time, Broman realized his cough had not really troubled him since Johannes the healer had promised him a long life.

* * *

Henriksen was given to jealousy. Astrid could always sense bad weather in other people's minds long before they noticed themselves, and she hadn't interfered with the decision to bring Ragnar to Fredrikshald.

She was fond of the boy, but she kept that to herself, greeting him kindly but briefly when he arrived, then she showed him the worker's room up in the attic. He was to have no advantages just because he was a relative, she'd said to Henriksen.

"They've spoiled him at home," he said.

"Yes, they has. We'll get that out of him."

So Henriksen was more friendly to the boy than he'd intended, just to outweigh his wife's prejudice.

The first thing Ragnar had to learn was to rid himself of his Swedish words. He was to speak Norwegian. It wasn't that different, and in a week he had learned it.

"He's got a quick head on him," said Henriksen.

But Ragnar never understood why he had to avoid Swedish words. Fredrikshald was not a big town, and most people he came across knew he was Swedish, nephew of the fish merchant's wife. People had nothing against ordinary folk from Dalsland and Värmland.

Much more important to Ragnar was that no one knew his origins. Here he was the son of the miller across the border.

He had to wait for the bicycle until he had learned his way around the town, so for the first six months he pulled the cart with the fish orders himself. At each door he smiled his warmest smile and the housewives melted. He was soon telling Henriksen that he could do more than just make deliveries, and after a while the little cart had also become a stall.

"He's a clever businessman," said Henriksen. When his wife didn't reply, he was angry and added, "He's honest and hardworking. He never complains about long workdays, and he accounts for every øre."

* * *

One day, in one of the narrow alleys below the fort, Ragnar was confronted with something that would color the rest of his life. A gentleman from Kristiania arrived . . . in a car with a chauffeur! The incredible vehicle had to stop for the boy to pull his cart into a porchway. Ragnar stood there for a long time, his eyes gleaming as he watched the amazing vehicle disappear down toward the market square. Father had talked about cars and had once read aloud a newspaper article about these newfangled vehicles that went by themselves, frightening people to death and making horses bolt with their noise and fearful speed. But words had never made much impression on Ragnar, for he lived by his senses. He was now so astounded and happy that he dawdled that day and was late with his errands.

He asked Henriksen what a machine of that kind cost.

"About five thousand kroner."

An inconceivable sum for the boy. He tried to imagine five thousand kroner lying gleaming in a great heap on the floor. Would it reach right up to the ceiling?

From that day on he saved every øre he earned.

Over the years, John Broman kept his secret promise not to approach Hanna in bed. She was thirty now, and the midwife had told him that another birth might cost Hanna her life.

Old Anna had been widowed, but still lived on at her farm. Her sons were in America, so she had to rent out her patch of land to her neighbor. When the winter was at its worst that turn-of-the-century year, John and Hanna persuaded her to come and live at the mill. Both thought she brought good cheer with her, and they missed her when she insisted on going back to her own farm once winter was over.

When Broman came home after helping Anna move, he was gloomy, his old melancholy on him again. They were alone again now, and silence settled beneath their roof.

He had become more taciturn than ever over the years and had accepted that he would never be truly intimate with his wife. For weeks on end he said nothing, and if he occasionally said anything, it was always unpleasant.

"Your head's all sawdust," or "You looks like a crazy old hag."

They also had worries over their livelihood. Farm after farm in the district had been abandoned, so there was less and less flour, even in the miller's barrel. They grew increasingly dependent on the potatoes, the cows, and fishing.

John was also worried about the crisis with Norway. The newspaper he fetched twice a week from Alvarsson's store on the border was full of antagonistic and increasingly violent speeches. Hostility also began to infect the people. Ragnar came home once a month and told them about insults hurled at every Swede across the border. When Astrid and her husband came to see them, they kept off politics. Henriksen was quieter than usual, and

Broman could see the Norwegian was also afraid about what might happen.

These days Ragnar took the flour from the mill to Fredrikshald. Broman said he was pleased to be relieved of the burden, but he missed the trips.

That spring he was forced to take out a loan to survive. Ragnar contributed, too, with what he earned. Things were going well for the boy in Norway, so well Arne told John that if he'd not been Swedish, he'd have made him a partner.

That summer was cold and wet, keeping them indoors, chafing against each other more and more. Broman's cough grew worse than ever at night when desolation crept over him, and it was on such a night he approached his wife.

She received him with warmth, as if even for her the loneliness had become too much. Their union softened them both. By the time late summer arrived, at last bringing with it the sun and warmth, they had made a habit of being together at night.

In November, old Anna moved back and was welcomed with coffee and newly baked bread. She brought with her great news. Anders Olsson, August's younger brother and Hanna's uncle, had been to see her with an offer to buy her farm. He'd worked at the shipyard in Fredrikshald for many years, had saved his earnings, and now wanted to return home.

"But this ain't never been his home," said Hanna in surprise. "He was born in Norway, like our father."

"I asked him about that," said Anna, "but he thought that as things was now, Sweden was home for anyone Swedish."

Hanna looked at John, her thoughts on Ragnar.

"There'll be another solution for Ragnar," said John. "He'll soon have to come back for his military service."

"Do you think there'll be war?"

"We has new laws for national service."

Was Anna going to sell? Another neighboring farm would be important, bringing more life to them all. Anders Olsson had four

sons and three daughters. The eldest son had already made in-
quiries about buying Svacken, the farm below Troll Ridge. It had
been derelict for several years, but had good grazing land.

Anna sensed what the miller and his wife were thinking and
nodded. She'd thought that, too. But she also knew what she
wanted.

"I wants to have a room and furniture of my own. And I'll pay
well."

"Payment'll have to be as it will," said John.

"Your work is enough," said Hanna.

"I knows how things is for you for money," the old woman went
on. "And I've grown fond of you both. But I don't wants to be a
burden so it'll have to be as I've decided."

John was almost happy as he rowed out onto the lake. He got
two pike on the line. She's already brought me luck, he thought.

Their new joy lasted a few months. They made preserves and juice,
the kitchen full of good aromas and women's chatter. But as autumn came it became clear how things were with Hanna.

"You has another on the way," she said to Broman, her voice
and expression harsh, but when she saw how frightened he was, she
softened.

"We has to pray to God," she said.

John went out into the forest, burdened with fear and guilt.
"Dear Lord," he said, but couldn't go on. He hadn't prayed since
he was a child, and then it'd been no help.

On his way home, he thought perhaps they could go to the doctor and have the child taken away.

"Should be possible," said Anna after thinking for a while.
"They does things like that, the doctors, if it's necessary. And that
it is for Hanna."

They both looked at Hanna standing stiffly by the stove, a
clenched hand over her mouth. Time and time again, she took her
hand away and gasped for breath, but found it difficult to get a word

out. In the end she cried, "Never! Don't you see it's a sin what takes you straight to hell?"

"But, Hanna, if you don't get through it, the children will be motherless."

"Then it's God's will."

"You usually say no one knows that."

"No. Then there ain't nothing to do but bow to it."

Nothing more was said, for at that moment their sons came in, tired and hungry. They ate as usual, but when Hanna went to bed, she said to Broman in a quiet but steady voice, "Don't worry. Maybe I'll manage."

For a moment he dared believe her, and he brightened.

"How strong you are," he whispered.

She was back to normal the next morning, brisk and active. As on every morning since old Anna had come, he heard her saying to herself that she missed her sofa that had ended up in the attic now that Anna had the bedroom, and John and Hanna had moved their bed into the parlor.

Can she have forgotten? he thought. Or ain't she afraid of death?

She hadn't forgotten, that was quite clear when one day he happened to hear her talking to their sons, whispering advice to them, about keeping clean their clothes, bodies, and way of life. And they must promise her to look after their father should anything happen to her.

He was moved, but the boys laughed at her.

"You'll live to a hundred," said Erik.

"Maybe," said Hanna. "But if I don't, you has to remember what I've told you."

Anna had worked out the child would arrive in March. By the middle of February she was making Hanna stay in bed, to rest and gather strength. Anna mostly sat with her, talking away to make

Hanna forget the shame of her, a healthy person, lying about in the middle of a weekday. They talked about many things, about death, as well.

"I wants to go decently to the grave," said Hanna. "I've saved my butter money, what I've put aside, in the cupboard over there. You can take it and make sure the boys has black mourning clothes."

"I promise."

Hanna had to get up sometimes to go to the privy. On February the fifteenth, she came back from it and told Anna she was bleeding. The midwife looked pleased and made an astringent herbal drink for her.

"Drink this down now, so we can get it started. It's good it's come too early, then it won't be too big."

"You has to send Broman away," said Hanna.

But Broman refused to go, and he would never forget the three days that followed. Hanna pushed and screamed, but the child seemed to have grown into the womb. Anna tried all her old arts, and in the end even had Hanna suspended from a beam in the ceiling, the pains coming at shorter and shorter intervals, but the child would not budge.

"I has to cut you now."

"Do that."

"Go on out," the old woman said to Broman.

Anna had the sense to dip her sharp scissors into boiling water on the stove before she cut the mouth of the womb. The child shot out like a cork from a bottle and Hanna fainted, though she didn't bleed as much as Anna had feared. She couldn't stitch, but clamped the cut together as best she could and smeared it with mistletoe ointment.

Hanna slowly came back to life.

"You've managed, Hanna," whispered Anna. "It's over. Sleep now."

The child was blue and bloody, but with a slap, Anna got it breathing, cut the cord, and washed the babe.

"It's a girl," she said.

"God have mercy on her, the poor wee wretch," whispered Hanna.

Broman had gone to sleep at the mill, curled up and as cold as ice. When Erik came with the message that it was all over and Hanna was asleep, at first he didn't dare believe it. When Anna brought him a stiff drink, the message at last sank in.

"You has a daughter," said the old woman.

Her words touched on an old memory. But he drank back his drink, and the fiery spirits made him forget. Once he had washed, put on a clean shirt, and was holding the babe in his arms, the memory came sharply back to him.

"She's to be called Johanna," he said.

But the midwife objected.

"It don't never bode well to give babies names of dead siblings," she whispered.

The look he gave her said more clearly than words that she hadn't understood.

Hanna wept and whimpered alternately when she woke the next morning.

"She's in pain," said Anna, but she knew Hanna was grieving over having a girl, for the terrible fate that awaited all women.

Hanna had nothing against the name, and both John and Anna took it for granted that she'd long forgotten the name of John Broman's dead daughter. They were wrong there. Hanna remembered and felt great satisfaction at having borne him a daughter in place of the one he'd grieved over so long. With her own eyes, she could see the newborn was like her father.

She also saw that she was an unusually beautiful child.

"Poor wee thing," she said as she put the baby to her breast.

*T*hey never found out what old Anna put into the water she washed Hanna's torn body with, but the strong odor of her secret brews filled the kitchen over the next few weeks. She made Hanna lie still in bed and drink her vile herbal concoctions.

Her labors all had a good effect. Hanna healed, and a fortnight later, she was out of bed. And though it took a while, since her legs were still weak, she then returned to running the household.

"I'll see to the house," said Anna. "You sees to the babe."

But that didn't happen. Broman looked after the child more or less on his own, changed her, rubbed in ointment, prattled to her, and rocked her.

"Just like an old woman," said Hanna, embarrassed.

"He's old and tired. Why should we grudge him the child when he has such joy from her?"

"It ain't natural," said Hanna, glad they lived so far away from others. Lame-Malin no longer came to see her, so there were no prying female eyes here, nor tongues to wag bad talk all around. When their new neighbors came to see them, she made sure she had the child at her breast.

They were pleasant people, her aunt and uncle from Norway. Hanna was pleased to have relatives back again after the long lonely years. Ragnar came home and was almost as attached to his little sister as Broman was. He brought gifts from Astrid with him, dresses for the little one and the finest bed linen for her cradle.

He brought presents for Hanna, too, a jet necklace so long she could wind it three times around her neck. He had bought it when Astrid happened to say once that Hanna had always gazed longingly at the strings of jet beads when she was last in Fredrikshald.

As always when she was pleased, Hanna wept, and the tall youth flushed. Never, he thought, never is she to know what Astrid and I gets up to in the bedstraw when Henriksen is away on business in Kristiania.

Spring came early and was warm. Broman wove a birch-bark knapsack, lined it with sheepskin, and then went walking along the banks of the lake with his daughter on his back. He taught her to look, to see the blue anemones cautiously appearing in last year's grass, the fish slapping the surface of the water, the first butterfly, and the clouds wandering across the sky.

Old Anna laughed at him. "The babe's far too young to understand that sort of talk," she said. But Broman could see from the glint in the child's honey-brown eyes that she understood.

He taught her to listen, too.

"Listen to the diver calling."

At midsummer, at last old Eriksson at Framgården died, after having lain like a log in his bed for many years with neither speech nor reason. Ingegerd herself came to the mill with the message, congratulated them on their daughter, and asked Broman to assemble the family at the mill the following Saturday, when everything was to be settled.

"I suppose there was a will?"

Hanna was the one to ask, but Ingegerd shook her head and said the old man had never gotten around to writing one before his illness took his mind away.

On Saturday, Ingegerd clearly and sensibly described her plans. She was going to sell Framgården and share the money equally with them and Hanna's brothers. Hanna would have the rights to the mill and the mill house, and any articles she wanted from the old family farm. She was also to have whatever creatures she wanted from the barn, the stable, and the pigsty. Astrid was to have all the old family heirlooms, jewelry from both their maternal and paternal grandmothers.

"I've had them valued, so I knows Astrid's inheritance ain't no worse than yours."

They all found the settlement reasonable. Broman was pleased. It was good to have your own mill. And they could sell many of the creatures. Only one thing surprised them, and that was that the illegitimate boy, Ragnar, was to have a thousand riksdaler.

"He's family, on both his mother's and his father's side," Ingegerd said.

"But what about you? What're you going to do?"

Then they were told that Ingegerd had gotten work as housekeeper at a merchant's house in Stockholm.

Stockholm! That was a great surprise. Those who left Dalsland didn't go there, so far away as it was, almost at the end of the world. Ingegerd laughed and said it was a good deal closer than America, then added that she'd long wanted to go to the capital.

"I wants to see the king," she said. "Seems right in these bad times."

She had papers, all of it, every detail, clearly written down.

"Read it carefully now," she said. " 'Tis important you understands, because I wants no family squabbles behind me."

They read it and signed their names to the settlement.

Ingegerd was hardly out the door before Hanna started wringing her hands. How ever were they going to find grazing for all those cows and the handsome horses? Broman said they would probably have to reckon on selling some in Fredrikshald. Ragnar could see to that, for he was a good businessman. Hanna looked miserable, but had to agree when Broman said they needed some ready money.

He reckoned he was going to miss Ingegerd.

That autumn they experienced a miracle at the mill house. The diver called one evening as usual, and suddenly Johanna, sitting on her father's knee, said, "Lissen, lissen. The diver."

Her father and brothers rejoiced, but Hanna exchanged an uneasy look with Anna. She'd never heard of an eight-month-old child who could talk.

"I'm terrified," said Hanna, when the women were alone in the kitchen. "Don't it mean her life's going to be short?"

"No, that ain't naught but superstition," said Anna. But during the autumn she recalled that old saying that those whom God loves often die young. The little girl was an unusually beautiful and clever child.

A few months later, when Johanna took her first steps across the kitchen floor, the two women had to agree in their delight.

"Ain't never seen such a forward child," said Hanna, torn between fear and pride.

Broman was tired and spent a lot of time in the warmth of the house that winter. But his cough didn't afflict him too badly, and he was cheerful of mind.

"I ain't never seen him so happy," said Hanna.

"And I ain't never imagined he had so many tales in him and such a good singing voice," said Anna.

Johanna laughed as much and as often as Ragnar had, and Hanna thought it strange that the children she'd borne with the greatest pain were the sunniest of the lot.

"*O*nce upon a time there was a poor peasant couple who had a child. But no one would take the child to the priest, because, you see, they was so poor, people thought it were shameful to have anything to do with them. So the peasant himself had to take the child to the priest."

John was telling Johanna the tale of the peasant and Death in his broadest country accent. She kept asking him to tell it over and over again, so that in the end she knew it so well, if he changed a word or skipped a bit, she at once corrected him.

"She can't understand that peculiar story," said Hanna.

"She must. She's always asking for it," said Broman. He laughed when he remembered the first time he'd told Hanna the story about Death. She had been so taken by it, she'd dropped the kettle at the moment when the peasant was walking along the road and met God himself, and God asked to go with him to the priest. But the peasant had said, "I don't think I wants to have anything to do with you, for you're such an unjust Father. Some people you gives a lot to, others so little, and to me you ain't given nothing. Nay, be off with you."

It had caused a great stir when Hanna dropped the kettle, then had to get down on her hands and knees to mop up the water. All the time she was wiping and wringing out the cloth, she kept laughing.

John was laughing, too.

"And then," said Johanna, her eyes shining, "then he met the Devil."

"Yes, Satan himself, and he, too, asked if he could go with the peasant to the priest.

" 'Nay, nay,' said the peasant. 'I'll not get myself caught in your claws. Nay, be off with you.' "

"And then," said Johanna, "and then he met Death himself!"

"Yes, and Death asked if he could go along with the peasant to the priest. And, you know, he was allowed to, because the peasant considered Death a good man.

" 'At least you're the same to everyone, whether rich or poor,' said the peasant."

John expanded on the story, making a detour through the forest until the peasant and Death were brought before the priest and they had the child baptized.

"Now comes the wonderful bit," said Johanna. And it did, for Death invited the peasant back to his home.

" 'Come back home with me and you'll see how fine it is.'

"When they got to Death's house, the peasant was dazzled, for so many candles was burning there, one for every living person on earth. And one for the peasant's new child, as well."

"Wait, Father, wait," whispered Johanna, for she wanted to stay on at Death's house to look for her own candle to make sure it was tall and burning steadily. Her mother's candle was fine, too. But she couldn't find her father's.

The fairy tale ended with Death taking the peasant into his service and teaching him first how to cure people and then when to tell people that it wasn't worth extending life further. The peasant became famous and rich and lived well right up until his own candle burned down and went out.

"In Death's house," said Johanna, shuddering with delight.

"*I* thinks you should go," John said to Hanna. "No one knows when you'll see the other again, you and Astrid."

"Is it that bad?"

"Yes. Take the girl with you, for she's something to show."

Hanna nodded. What he'd said was so true.

Ragnar was home on a short visit before going back to Fredrikshald for the last time to say good-bye and pack his things. From Fredrikshald he was going to Vänersborg, where he would be recruited into the Västergöt-Dals regiment for his twelve months of military service.

He was glad to be leaving Norway. It was now May 1905 and the Norwegian government had resigned. As the king in Stockholm had refused to approve it, the Norwegian parliament had stated that as far as Norway was concerned, royal power no longer applied to them and the Union was dissolved. In Sweden that was called revolution. The Norwegians reinforced their border defenses.

John Broman read in the papers that the Swedish people were full of righteous anger. But here in the border areas, they were terrified of what might happen, although there were some malicious comments about those loudmouthed Norwegians.

Hanna hadn't taken the talk about the Union crisis seriously. As usual she had enough to do with her everyday troubles, but now when she saw soldiers all over the place at the border and in Fredrikshald, she was frightened. Even more frightening was finding Astrid flapping around like a captive bird, far too nervous to sit still and talk. Relations between her and her husband were also bad. He had come to hate everything about Swedes.

"Maybe I'll go back with you," Astrid said to Hanna.

"Nonsense," said Henriksen. "You're Norwegian now and your

home is Norway. If you're afraid of war, then you're safer on this side." He was curt and unfriendly to Ragnar, but he took his sister-in-law and her little girl to Fredriksten fortress to show them how impregnable it was.

"That's where we shot him, the damned Swede," he said.

Their visit lasted only two days. As they crossed the border, Hanna heaved a sigh of relief, and said to Ragnar, "Can't make out how you stood it."

"It ain't been easy."

To her surprise, Hanna noticed he was blushing.

Ragnar had a brief talk with John Broman before going on south to Vänersborg.

"Father, you has to get the cave in order."

But John shook his head.

In August, Ragnar came home on his first leave. Negotiations were going on in Karlstad, and the Swedes were demanding that the Norwegians demolish not only the defenses along the border, but also the old forts of Kongsvinger and Fredriksten.

"They're insane," said Ragnar. He was able to tell them that other countries agreed with Norway, that England had said that the country should be recognized, and that Russia and France had stated that they "highly disapproved of " the demands made by Sweden regarding the two forts.

That was when he got his family away to the cave.

Only a few weeks later, agreement was reached in Karlstad. The border forts disappeared, people on both sides sighed with relief, and Broman's conservative newspaper quoted what Hjalmar Branting had already said in the *Social-Democrat* in the spring:

"On May 27, 1905, the Royal Union between Norway and Sweden died at the age of ninety years six months. All that remains is the funeral and the inventory. We must part in peace like brothers."

"We should've suscribed to the *Social-Democrat*, then we'd've had a more peaceful summer," John said to Hanna.

"You're mad! People'd think we was socialists."

"Well, for me, that ain't far wrong."

Hanna stared at her husband before she could bring herself to speak.

"So you'd both renounce God and kill the king!"

"Where'd you get all that nonsense from!" laughed John.

Johanna was sitting on the floor with her doll. She would always remember that exchange of words.

*J*ohn Broman was not the only one to spend all his free time on the girl. Old Anna also took care of her, taught her women's things, and told her all the strange local tales.

So as a result there was little room for Hanna in her daughter's life. All that was left for Hanna was to teach the girl to behave and obey. Johanna did both willingly, but there was no intimacy between them.

Johanna was five when she learned to read and write. When Hanna found out, she was very angry. What would people say? She knew how tongues wagged when it came to anything different and precocious. And what would the teacher do with Johanna when she went to school?

Broman told her to be quiet. But he realized there was something in what his wife had said. As he was on a friendly footing with the new teacher, he went to see her and explained about Johanna.

The teacher was still young enough to believe in her work. She just laughed and said having a girl who could read would be a pleasing problem. She was a good enough teacher to be able to keep the child occupied while she hammered the alphabet into the other beginners.

"She can draw and paint," she said. "And I'll find some books she can read for herself during school hours."

John was pleased. But neither he nor the teacher had reckoned with the other children. Johanna had a bad time, was ignored and disliked, and exposed to a lot of aggravation. The talk also got around, just as Hanna had predicted.

But the girl said nothing about the torments of school. Mother would be angry and she could bear that, but Father mustn't be sad.

* * *

When Johanna was just seven, old Anna had a pain in her chest, and one Saturday evening Hanna saw her concocting some medicine to relieve it. Hanna watched with some surprise as Anna mixed large quantities of belladonna and henbane in the drink.

"Don't you go taking too much, will you?"

"I knows what I'm doing," the old woman said.

In the morning, they found her dead. White and rigid, Hanna stood by the bed, the boys sobbing and sniffling. John Broman's eyes were glistening and grave as he stood with Johanna in his arms.

"She's gone to God, now," the child whispered, and John nodded, glancing sternly at Hanna, afraid she might take the consolation away from the girl. Hanna never even noticed, as her mind was full of strange thoughts, but she said not a word to anyone about the drink the old woman had made the night before.

One day in the thaw, the mill-house family was to experience an event not one of them would ever forget. They were at their midday meal when Broman suddenly crashed his fist down on the table, and roared, "Quiet!" In the silence that followed, they could hear a rumbling, growling, screeching sound. John and the boys rushed out, fearful of what might have happened at the mill.

The floodgate!

But nothing was wrong with the dam. They just stood there, but then realized all that noise was coming from far away down the road.

It was coming closer.

Hanna took the terrified Johanna into her arms and thought about the Devil himself, the one who came on the Day of Judgment in his chariot of fire to take the wicked to Hell.

It *was* a kind of fiery chariot. They could see that as the monstrosity came roaring over the crest of the hill as fast as if shot from a cannon. But it wasn't the Devil at the wheel, but Ragnar. He drove straight in, braked with a screeching, and tooted like a madman.

Then it fell silent and they all stood there, eyes wide and

mouths open. Never had it been so quiet at Norskvattnet as at that moment.

"An automobile!" said Broman. "The little devil has got himself an automobile!"

Then he started laughing, and when Ragnar climbed down from the monstrosity, both father and son laughed and laughed until tears rolled down their cheeks.

In the end, Ragnar collected himself sufficiently to be able to speak.

"Now, Mom, I want something inside me. I'm as hungry as a lion."

Hanna took her trembling legs back inside to heat up the cooling food while the brothers buzzed like bees around the vehicle.

"Did you buy it with your own money?" said Broman.

"Yes. I saved every riksdaler ever since I started working for the fish merchant. And everything I've earned building in Göteborg. Then I got my inheritance. That automobile is going to earn my living now."

John didn't dare ask what it cost. A thousand? Several thousand?

Ragnar ate and explained, his mouth full, but Hanna didn't dare say anything about table manners. He told them Göteborg, the town at the mouth of the Göta River, was growing. Fredrikshald was nothing but a country village in comparison with the city by the sea. Lots of people were building houses and factories there, but there was a shortage of lumber and tiles and bricks.

"Transport didn't keep up with development," he said. "Horses and carts blocked the roads." The motor vehicle was the solution. He could get as much work as he liked.

Hanna understood most of what he was saying, but one question wouldn't leave her. What on earth kind of language was he speaking?

In the end, she asked, and Ragnar laughed again.

"Swedish, Mother. I've at last learned to speak proper Swedish."

"You sounds like it is in books," said Johanna, profoundly impressed.

Ragnar decided they should go on an outing that afternoon. They had to take some old straw mattresses and make themselves comfortable on the open back of his vehicle.

"Mother can sit in the cabin with Johanna on her lap."

But by this time Hanna had become herself again.

"Never, never will you get me into that monster. Not my girl, neither."

So it was John who got up into the cabin, while the brothers clambered up onto the back. Johanna forced back her tears, but Ragnar noticed, and whispered in her ear, "Another day, girl. I won't leave until you've had your ride."

When they were back after a hour or so, they talked nonstop, all at once, about how people's jaws had dropped in amazement, and how the old women had screamed in terror, the children with delight. Alvar Alvarsson had raised his cap when Broman got out to fetch his newspaper, and the priest himself had come up to inspect the vehicle.

"I knew it'd come, even to these remote places," he'd said. "But I'd no idea it'd come so soon."

It was clear all this pleased Hanna. And when Ragnar said that she and Johanna must go out in it with him tomorrow, she said, "I ain't no worse a person than I can change my mind."

*T*he spring of 1910 came kindly and early to Dalsland, not the usual kind of spring with its great strides and changes of mind. No, it crept in so cautiously not even the blue anemones felt the cold.

The starlings came early and found their home in the north friendlier than usual. It rained, the sun shone, and white wood anemones replaced the blue ones. One May morning, the maples flowered, and Norskvattnet was enveloped in the scent of honey.

John Broman was wearier than usual as he roamed the forest with his daughter. But it was his body that was weary, not his mind, which had never before been so clear.

Together, he and Johanna watched the migrant birds arriving and occupying their old places. By the time the swallows had built their clay nests on the ridges of Wolf Mountain, the diver already had a clutch of eggs and the peregrine falcon chicks had hatched.

He was happy, and the girl lodged that in her memory.

That was the spring when Johanna became religious. She would remain so, even when she became a socialist and an atheist.

Not until the summer did John draw any conclusion from the strange state of exhilaration he found himself in: life and death were confronting each other within him. He imagined them drinking together like good friends, for the feeling spreading through him was like the slight intoxication felt from that first drink.

He wasn't afraid once he understood what was happening, as he sat by the stream watching Johanna slaking her thirst in the rippling water. He was relieved. And sorrowful. But it wasn't the weighty kind of sorrow. It was blue like melancholy, just what gave the world depth.

In the following weeks, he often tried to summarize it all. Occasionally he got as far as that life had been good to him and that he had largely done as he should have done. On other days, the final reckoning frightened him. Full of remorse, he thought about the mother he hadn't seen for twenty years, and about the sons he had neglected and pressed into work far too hard for their growing bodies.

Then there was Johanna, the girl scampering around him on the forest tracks and along the lakes. Perhaps his love had been selfish and the child was badly equipped for a hard life.

Johanna was now eight, exactly the same age his first daughter had been when she died. This little girl would live, well fed and healthy as she was.

Thanks to Hanna.

He thought about Hanna. Surprised, he realized his wife was the only one he did not stand in debt to. Not that he had been a thoroughly good husband, no, things had happened that he regretted, but he was exonerated from any blame, for there was no reproach in her being.

He pondered on that for a long time and came to the conclusion that anyone expecting injustice does not keep a collection of injustices.

He thought also, of course, of all the worldly things that had to be arranged, but for that he could rely on Ragnar. The mill was worth quite a lot, although it was mostly silent now that the farms were being abandoned all around them, but John had had a surprising offer.

There was also his eventual inheritance from Värmland.

He was suddenly struck by the certainty that his mother would die as soon as she heard he had passed away.

He must write to Ragnar. They needed to have a long and clarifying talk before it was too late.

How long did he have?

Ragnar came at the end of July, and he had a woman, city-pale and shy, with him in the van.

"A shilly-shallier," Hanna said.

But Johanna said Lisa was nice.

"She's got a haberdashery shop in Göteborg, so whatever she looks like, she can't be," John said to Hanna. And John had seen from the start that Lisa's submissiveness was for Ragnar alone, that she was one of those poor wretches who loved too much.

"Take care, Hanna," he said. "That you don't become a shrewish mother-in-law."

John had put the upstairs room in order, pulled out the dropleaf table, and assembled all his papers. He told his wife he'd asked Ragnar to come and help him draw up a will, and that he wanted her to be there to go through everything. When he saw her eyes darken, he tried to calm her.

"Every husband gone sixty-five has to do this."

She didn't answer, her hand stubbornly covering her mouth, then she turned and went stiffly down the stairs.

She knows, he thought.

Hanna said little as Broman, Ragnar, and she sat around the table for the whole afternoon, not even when Ragnar said that if the worst should happen, Mother and the children would have to move to Göteborg.

"What do you think, Mother?"

"I has to think about it."

"There ain't no future for the boys here," Broman said. "They can't make a living out of the mill, you knows that. And I don't want you to stay here alone in the wilderness."

"Can't you try to live a bit longer?" she said, but at once regretted saying it.

Ragnar stared at his stepfather. At that moment, it was clear to him that Broman would be gone before winter.

That stuck in Ragnar's throat.

But Broman went on as if nothing had been said. This was the moment to mention the offer.

The previous autumn, when Hanna had been in the forest picking lingonberries, an engineer from the electric company in Ed had come to see him in Norskvattnet. He stood for a long time by the falls, and even asked John to open the floodgate. Then he said he might buy the place. They would pay five thousand riks-daler. Cash.

"Why haven't you said nothing?"

"Didn't want to worry you."

Hanna was silent. Ragnar said he would contact the company in Ed, his tone of voice revealing that he was relieved.

Then there was the Värmland business. John didn't know how much the farm up there might be worth.

"It's beginning to be a wasteland up there, like here," he said. "But Mother can't live much longer. She's ninety-eight. Ragnar, you has to keep in contact with my sister Alma. She and her hus-band is honest folk, and they won't cheat you of your inheritance."

He said nothing about knowing his mother would give up the ghost as soon as she got the message saying her son was dead.

The next morning, Ragnar wrote out the will with an unaccus-tomed hand and poor spelling, for it was only the spoken word he found easy.

"We'll have to ask Lisa to write it out properly," he said, and his parents nodded. Broman hesitated, but finally plucked up the courage to ask if a marriage was in the offing. Ragnar blushed and said things were probably heading in that direction.

Even Hanna had to admit the will looked very fine and that Lisa wrote like a priest. The blacksmith was summoned to witness the will together with Lisa.

When Lisa was packing the van that afternoon, she noticed Ragnar standing there holding both his father's hands in his for a long time. John was bright-eyed and Ragnar weeping. Hanna also looked at the two of them, remembering that day many years ago when the strange miller had held out his hand to her bastard child and said, "Good day, my name's John Broman."

Just as the first autumn storms were ripping the leaves off the trees, John Broman coughed his last.

*I*t was the first and only time the child at Norskvattnet ever saw her mother cry from sorrow. Hanna herself was surprised. She'd never imagined there was so much water in her head, she said. She sobbed and wept day and night as she made all the arrangements for the funeral.

No one gave a thought to Johanna, who was going around in a strange way, feeling horribly cold.

"Hurry now, girl," Hanna might say when something was to be done. Only occasionally did she notice the girl was cold and, feeling her hands, said, "Put your thick sweater on."

They never noticed the child said not a word.

The moment Ragnar arrived, however, it was obvious to him.

"Johanna's gone dumb!" he cried. "Haven't you noticed, Mother?"

Hanna was ashamed. Ragnar walked around with the girl in his arms, talking, tempting. She grew warmer but showed no desire to see the Norwegian lakes, the falls, or the long lake, and he could not get her to weep or speak.

Indoors, Hanna baked bread and cakes, while Lisa laid the table for the funeral meal. Ragnar went straight up to Lisa with the girl, and said, "Will you try, Lisa?"

Lisa couldn't carry the child, but the little girl took her hand as they walked across to the stable where Broman was lying in his coffin. Hanna was about to call out to them not to, but Ragnar snapped at her.

"Quiet, Mother!"

Lisa drew back the sheet from the dead man's face.

"Johanna," she said. "This person lying here isn't your father, only his shell. He's waiting for you in heaven."

It was enough. Johanna wept in the stranger's arms and at last could whisper that she'd thought that, too.

They stood there for a long time. Then Lisa said she wanted Johanna to go back with her to Göteborg as soon as the funeral was over. The two of them would have a good time together while they waited for her mother and brothers to come later.

That is what happened. The day after the funeral, Ragnar drove Lisa and Johanna to the train, then he went on to see the engineer in Ed. After that he would return to his mother and brothers.

"To clear up the worst," he said.

At the electric company things went better than expected, and the sale would be completed by the spring. As Ragnar drove his wretched old vehicle northward along the lake, he felt satisfied. But most of all, he thought that now he understood what Broman had said at their farewell. "You has to promise me to take care of Johanna. You sees, she's of a different kind."

On the train, Johanna sat on Lisa's knee thinking that this terrible new life of hers was beginning right there in this carriage rushing through the darkness and hooting like a monster.

The morning after John's death, Hanna had sent Erik with a message to Alma in Värmland. He had returned home wide-eyed as he described how magnificent Brogården was with its many fields and extensive grazing lands.

John'd never said anything about that, Hanna thought. But then neither had she asked.

On the same evening Ragnar left to join Lisa and Johanna in Göteborg, there was a knock on the door and there stood a man she had never seen before, a Värmlander who said he was Alma's son-in-law. He had brought a message that the old lady of Brogården had died on Sunday. Could they come to the funeral?

Hanna fried pork and put out bread while the stranger stabled his horse in the barn. Erik lit the stove in the attic room, and Hanna warmed bedclothes for her guest. The next morning, she told him that she was going to send her two older sons to the funeral. She had no place there, she said.

The man nodded as if he understood, and they parted friends.

After he'd gone, Hanna sat for a long time on the bench in the kitchen, wondering about how amazing it was that the old woman had died exactly one week to the day after her son.

On Saturday, April 22, 1911, Hanna went to the neighboring farm to say good-bye to the relatives who had moved in from Norway during the Union crisis. With her she had the cows, the pig, and five sheep. It was a dismal walk, and it did not help that the Olssons at Kasa paid modestly for the creatures.

From Kasa, she went on to the priest to get the moving certificate to Haga parish in Göteborg for herself and her four children. They exchanged few words, and as she said good-bye, she thought the priest had shrunk since—to everyone's surprise—he had stopped drinking.

Last of all, she went to the smithy. The smith and his wife were old now and received the news about the power station with dismay. Hanna kept the visit as short as possible, but as she was leaving she said there would be a few things left behind, things not going to Göteborg. She would put them in the shed, and they could take anything they could use.

Lame-Malin's eyes brightened, covetously and acquisitively, so as Hanna crossed the yard to the mill house, she decided to make sure there wouldn't be that much left behind for Malin. But then she remembered Ragnar's words.

"None of that old rubbish in the load. Just bring the bare essentials."

That remark stayed with Hanna to such an extent that she didn't grieve over her departure from Norskvattnet or worry about the future. What in heaven's name was all this she'd collected over the years?

She flung out all the rag rugs, Broman's clothes, and the two box-beds in the kitchen, though she was to regret the latter.

She was determined to take the Värmland furniture with her. If he says a word about the best sofa, I'll have something to say, she thought.

But when Ragnar arrived, all he said was, "It'll be difficult to find room for the sofa, Mom. But maybe you could sell it and get a good sum for it."

When everything was loaded and lashed onto the back, and the boys had made themselves as comfortable as possible, Hanna stood for a while in the yard, looking at the house, the falls, and the long lake. Then she sighed heavily and as she took her place beside Ragnar in the cabin, she was sobbing.

"Not crying, are you, Mother?"

"Course not," said Hanna, the tears pouring down.

"We'll come back on a visit in a few years."

"No, boy, I'll never come back here."

After they'd gone quite a way, she asked after Johanna and how she was getting on in the city with Lisa.

"She's not as cheerful as before. But she's pleased to be so fond of Lisa."

"Can imagine that," said Hanna briefly.

They said nothing for the rest of the winding road along the lake to Ed. When the church tower appeared, Hanna said, "When're you getting married, you and Lisa?"

He flushed, and his voice was cold when he answered.

"Mind your own business."

That made Hanna angry.

"Ain't a mother got the right to know when her child is to marry?"

Ragnar already regretted his remark, but persisted.

"It's different in the city, Mom. They don't mind so much about when people who like each other live together without marrying."

"Terrible lot I has to learn," said Hanna in astonishment.

"Mm, you'll probably have to relearn most things, Mother."

*   *   *

They left Ed, and then Hanna was in unknown country. She had never been further than this. At Vänersborg, they stopped for a rest and ate the sandwiches they had brought with them. Hanna stared out across Lake Vänern and could see where the water met the sky, far away.

"Is that the sea?"

"No, Mom. The sea's much bigger than that."

He laughed at her, so she didn't ask any more questions. But she found it difficult to understand how any sea could be bigger than this. She said nothing all the way through the valley and didn't even answer when he said, wasn't this lovely countryside; this, too.

Not until they drove into the stone city of Göteborg did she get her voice back.

"I never even dreamed of nothing like this."

They inched their way between people, horse-drawn carts, and motor vehicles up to Järntorget, the apartment block they would be living in. To impress his mother and brothers, he took a long roundabout route to get to Haga.

"Is it market day? There's so many people."

"No, it's always like this."

"Heaven's a mercy," said Hanna, exhilarated rather than frightened, and when they finally drove in through an entrance gateway to the great building, she was glowing like the sun.

"So . . . so grand," she said. "Where are we going to live?"

"Up there," he said, pointing.

Toward the sky, she thought.

"Three floors up with a view over the street," he said proudly. "Lisa's put up new curtains for you to hide behind."

"That's awfully kind," said Hanna, who'd been worried about curtains. The next moment, Johanna came running out one of the many doors.

Hanna stood gazing at the girl, thinking, my girl, my girl. Then she said, "How fine you looks."

"I've got new clothes, town clothes. Lisa made them."

Hanna did not look pleased, but made an effort to think that she must learn to like her, that kind creature.

Inquisitive eyes stared at them from windows and entrance porches as they carried up the furniture. We look countrified, Hanna thought with shame, wishing herself out of their sight. Yet she had to ask what kind of little houses they were under the chestnut trees on the great courtyard.

"They're privies and sheds. Each family's got its own key."

"Mercy, how grand!"

The door opened straight into the kitchen, and it was a fine kitchen with an iron stove, the kind Hanna had admired at Astrid's in Fredrikshald. Then she noticed the sink unit, with a drain and a faucet. Hanna had heard about that amazing thing, running water, and now she stood there turning the tap on and off.

"Don't it never run out?"

"No, Mom, it never runs out."

"Mercy me!"

There was a tiled stove in the living room and shiny pine floorboards, real gentry stuff, Hanna thought.

What was most amazing of all, and they were to talk and laugh about it for many years to come, was the light. Fortunately it wasn't Hanna who made a fool of herself this time, but John.

"Getting dark, Mother. I'll run down and get the oil lamp."

"No," said Johanna. "Look, all you do is this." She flipped the switch on the wall inside the kitchen door, and the light flooded down on them.

Once Hanna recovered from her surprise, she was pleased Ragnar hadn't been there to see her standing with her mouth open. He'd gone out to buy food and get Lisa. They brought hot soup Lisa had made and bread and butter Ragnar had bought.

"Welcome to town," said Lisa.

"You're kind," said Hanna. "Thank you for the curtains. And for looking after the girl so well."

Lisa said it had been nothing but fun.

"Tomorrow we'll go and get some new clothes for you, too, Mother-in-law."

"I'll be needing all the help I can get," said Hanna to Lisa, who didn't really understand what an incredible remark that was.

But the sons were scared. They'd never heard their mother ever say anything like it.

So they settled into the one-room apartment with a kitchen in the great block. The two older boys were given a pullout sofa in the main room and August a modern folding bed that could be put away in the wardrobe.

A large round table commanded the middle of the room. The table was modern, too, but went well with the old chairs from Värmland, Hanna thought.

Hanna and Johanna slept in the kitchen. That was where the box-bed from Dalsland would have been of use, but Hanna consoled herself that the new kitchen sofa was also modern.

"An awful lot of money's slipping through my fingers," Hanna said to Ragnar.

"You can afford it, Mom," he said comfortingly.

Once all was ready, Hanna invited the neighboring housewives for coffee and a horribly expensive store-bought cream cake. That's what everyone did, Lisa said. Hanna wore a new store-bought dress. Modern. The neighbors were people of all kinds, lamenting when she told them she'd just been widowed, and making no comments on her odd speech.

"You're from Norway?"

"Not quite," said Hanna. "We're Swedish all right, but we lived right on the border. My father was from Norway, and my sister is Norwegian."

Hulda Andersson lived on the same hallway and was similar to Hanna in her ways. The two of them were soon on good terms.

The day after the party, Hulda said, "Are you rich or do you has to work?"

"Of course I has to work."

"They needs people at Asklund's bakery in Risågatan. I works there myself. Can you bake?"

Hanna gave a great laugh, and said, "If there's anything you learns from being a miller's wife, then it's to bake."

*T*hat was how Hanna became a bakery worker, heavy work, every day starting at four o'clock in the morning. But that was good, for she finished work at two, and so had plenty of time to look after the home.

On May Day, she stood in Järntorget watching the red flags fluttering above the marching people singing, "Rise, ye slaves . . ."

Hanna was afraid.

"They're mad," she said to Hulda. Hulda agreed.

Even more frightening was one morning when the two bakery women were crossing the market square and met some dolled-up women with their mouths painted red.

"What kind of people is them?"

"Whores," said Hulda. "Sell themselves to seamen in the harbor. Them's on their way home."

Quite a long time went by before Hanna could bring herself to say anything.

"Do you mean they has a different man every night?"

"Oh nay, they has to have *several*, otherwise they can't make ends meet."

Hanna was speechless, her head quite empty.

But what made the greatest impression during those early days was the man who employed her at the bakery. Not that he was unpleasant, only supercilious, and he had a right to be that, fine gentleman that he was.

"What's your name?"

Hanna hesitated for a while before answering.

"Hanna, Lovisa, Greta . . . Broman."

"Married?"

"Yes, but my husband's dead."

"Widow, then," said the man, noting it down. "Date of birth?"

She was silent. She'd never heard anything so silly. He had to repeat it.

"When and where were you born, woman?"

She stated both year and parish, got the job, and was given a white coat and put to work making braided wreath-shaped wheat loaves. That she did, and the foreman looked satisfied.

She soon came to enjoy the warmth and the women's chatter in the big bakery, where the gossip started the moment the foreman had left. There were many women like her there, farming wives speaking dialects even cruder than hers, and whose situation was much worse than hers because they had small children at home.

But she never forgot the foreman's questions and repeated them to herself every evening for a long time afterward. Name, married, born? To her it was if she'd fallen into a gigantic hollow on Wolf Mountain. Who on earth was she when no one knew she was Hanna Augustdotter from Bråten, granddaughter of the rich Erik of Framgården, and who became the miller's wife at Norskvattnet?

Fortunately she wasn't given to brooding. But many a time over the next few years she had to fend off the feeling of having lost her foothold.

The bakery was as big as a palace and built like a fortress around a large courtyard. All four wings were three floors high, faced with brick and decorated with green soapstone figures. There were departments for the hard crispbread, for the ordinary bread, and for the finer confectionaries. There was the sweet bread bakery for braided ring-shaped wheat loaves and Danish pastries. Finest of all was the big corner shop at street level.

It was an awful lot to take in, and she often felt as if there was no room in her head for it all. One day Hulda asked the foreman if she could show Hanna the mill high up in the fortress where there were millers and a whole series of laborers mixing and sifting flour for the different kinds of bread.

"Where does they get power from," whispered Hanna, and was told about the steam engines growling away day and night and the generator turning the energy into electricity.

Broman would've fainted if he'd seen this, Hanna thought.

But most amazing of all was the third floor, and Hanna was struck dumb. There, one huge dough-kneading machine after another did all the heavy work previously done by women.

They took the elevator down, and that scared her, too.

Her sons roamed around town doing nothing much and filling the emptiness with strong drink, just as their father had. But their fears were not driven out that way.

Ragnar got them jobs in the building trade, where they were scoffed at for their strange accents and soft miller's hands. They quit the jobs and went home for another strengthening drink. When things got so bad that they never even got out of bed all day, Ragnar took them seriously to task. The brothers laughed scornfully at him. That led to a fight, and Hanna's fine Värmland chairs were smashed to matchwood.

"Never!" shouted Ragnar. "I'd never have believed you were so damned spoiled. Have you no shame? Letting Mother keep you, grown men like you?"

Then he threw them out onto the street, locked the apartment door on the outside, and left.

Hanna had never been so frightened as that night when she was locked in and alone in the apartment, trying to clean up after the fight. Ragnar had taken Johanna with him to Lisa's.

"The girl's to live with us until you knock some kind of sense into those damned boys of yours."

When he came back on Sunday morning, he had calmed down.

"What shall we do, Mom?"

"You can start by letting me out so I can set about finding where they is."

"Go to the police. I expect that's where they are. The police pick up all the drunks around town."

"Oh, my good Lord," said Hanna, shaking her head, knowing better than most that the Lord was not good. But she tidied her hair, put on her best dress and new hat, and went to the police station. There they were, behind bars. They had to sign papers and pay fines before she could get them out.

"If it happens again, it'll be prison," said the sergeant as they left.

Ragnar eventually took John, the eldest and strongest, with him in the truck.

"Can't afford to pay much," he said. "But if you drink on the job, I'll kill you."

The other two went to sea.

"They'll teach you how to behave there," said Ragnar.

Hanna didn't dare protest, but she often whimpered in her sleep in her anxiety over her sons, worries that followed her for a whole long year. But they survived and returned home, coarser, heavier, and more serious. They got steady work, married eventually, and drank only on weekends.

Hanna's life had become lonely, for her daughter spent most of her time with Lisa. John was indeed still living at home, but they exchanged few words. She did have Hulda across the hallway and, as she often told her, without her she would've gone mad.

She never became really intimate with Lisa, though she did have one opportunity to pay back her daughter-in-law for her help, this daughter-in-law who wasn't really a daughter-in-law because Ragnar refused to marry.

Lisa was with child and came to see her mother-in-law in her distress. Hanna undertook to speak to Ragnar. What she said during their long talk in the kitchen no one ever knew, but it was assumed to be about bastards and the awfulness of condemning your own child to a life of shame.

Anyhow, Ragnar said to Lisa that they might as well get married. "But you'll have to take me for what I am, and you know I'm not to be relied on when it comes to women."

Lisa was grateful.

*H*anna grieved over her ruined lovely chairs but with Hulda's help managed to install her sofa. Though there really wasn't room for it, both she and Hulda thought it was rather grand.

When her sons came home, they simply flung their filthy clothing on the silk-covered sofa, making Hanna moan and scold Johanna for not picking up after her brothers. Johanna grew more and more silent, but Hanna didn't notice, closing her eyes to the fact that there was little comfort in the home with all these quarrels and drinking every weekend. Her back was aching.

The ache spread from her shoulder blades down her spine. At first she thought it would pass, but then she heard that most of the women at the bakery suffered from the same affliction. And that it only grew worse.

You had to endure it, they told her. Not a word to the foreman, for then they would lose their jobs.

Lisa gave birth to a son, and amazingly Ragnar was so delighted with his boy, he spent all his free time at home, so he had less and less time for his mother and brothers and sister.

The years went slowly by, the first world war broke out, and the shortage of food was acute. In Haga, there were hunger riots, and police and soldiers were brought in. People screamed their hatred at the queen, who was German and was accused of smuggling food out of Sweden to give to the mad Kaiser. Hanna bit back the pain in her back and gave thanks for her work at the bakery. She could take out her wages in bread, so she and her children did not starve. Then the Spanish flu came, and again Hanna was grateful that none of her family caught the terrible disease.

Johanna left school and was able to help with their keep. It was quieter once the boys left home. And more orderly. But Hanna and

Johanna did not get on well together. The girl was insolent and up-
pity, not good and submissive like Hanna's sons. She reprimanded
her mother for being stupid and uneducated, corrected her speech,
and told her to shed her superstitions and begin to think. At first
Hanna tried to defend herself with words. But Johanna had so many
more words than she had, and a much clearer mind.

She's always been cleverer than the others, Hanna thought.

When Johanna joined the Social Democrats' May Day procession, Hanna almost died of shame.

"You gone out of your mind?" she cried.

"You wouldn't know, for you've never had one," the girl
retorted.

Hanna's bad back got worse over the years. She grew bent and
moved heavily, but she stuck it out until pension age when, for the
first time in her life, she was able to rest. She had definite views on
the old-age pension that came every month. It was shameful to get
money not honestly earned, she said to Johanna. But only once, for
the girl got so angry that Hanna was frightened.

Johanna married. Hulda Andersson died.

Hanna had so many grandchildren, she couldn't tell them apart.
The only one she recognized was Johanna's horrible girl, a child
with strong eyes that stared accusingly and looked right through
people. Badly brought up and plain she was, thin in body and hair.

In the 1940s, an apartment block for pensioners was built in
Kungsladugård, and Johanna arranged for Hanna to have a modern
one-room apartment there. Hanna believed she had come to paradise, for she had a bathroom, hot water, and central heating.

"What in heaven's name will I do when I don't even has to light
a fire?"

"Rest, Mother, rest."

Hanna rested, and strangely enough never disliked it. She could
read, but had such difficulty with her letters that she never grasped
what it was all about. Sometimes she listened to the radio, but both
the talk and the music irritated her.

On the other hand, she loved going to the movies. Her sons often took her with them if they had time, her daughter more rarely. Johanna did not approve, and was ashamed of her mother's loud laughter at bad films. And it was really painful when men kissed women on the screen, for Hanna just covered her eyes and cried out loudly, "Shame on you!"

The audience laughed at her. Didn't she notice? No, Johanna decided.

Over the years, Hanna grew very fat. After a long battle, Johanna got her to a doctor, who talked about a stomach ailment that was easy to operate on. His talk frightened Hanna to death, as she was just as afraid of the knife as she was of the hospital. After the visit to the doctor, Johanna had to promise to look after her at home when the time came for her to die.

"I won't be no trouble to you."

"I'm sure it'll be all right, Mother dear."

When August committed suicide, her grief almost did away with her and she aged ten years in a month.

But she was crystal clear in her head up until her death at almost ninety. A week later to the very day, Ragnar died on an elk hunt in Halland.

Accidentally shot, just like his father.

But there was no longer anyone who could remember Rickard Joelsson and his death in the days when the peasants of Trysil hunted bears in the forests of Dalsland.

ANNA

INTERLUDE

*A*nna sat in her study with the fat blue notebook in front of her. On the front she had written JOHANNA, and on the flyleaf, "Try to chart what attitude to take to your mother without denying her worth or sacrificing yourself."

She now thought that rather pretentious.

On the first page were a few scattered disconnected notes. The rest was empty, page after page of unwritten whiteness. I'm not there yet, she thought, haven't arrived.

So she went back to the gray book, a hundred pages, full, stuffed with loose notes, letters, newspaper cuttings. On the cover she had written HANNA.

Grandmother.

She had started in the parish registers in Dalsland, that alone an adventure, seeing the old family branching all over the landscape, into Norway, down to Göteborg, across to America. Then she roamed along the shores of the long lake and seriously attempted to make herself receptive to secrets in the unfathomably beautiful landscape.

Once back home, she had gone searching in libraries and secondhand bookshops. She read cultural anthropology and wept for Grandmother, the woman already labeled a whore as a child. She found the rune master and his troll wife in an old newspaper cutting, astonished by how long heathendom had survived in the distant border communities. She looked at the economic history of the area and tried to grasp what the parish registers told her, that Grandmother's four older siblings had died of starvation during the famine.

She came across a number of local history books from the parishes around the lake. Old people wrote in them about Sundays and weekends, and weekdays that followed the seasons, not the clock. In them she read stories of ordinary people, but more often about unusual people, the kind long remembered in communities. There was a light serenity in the memories of bad times, and great melancholy over what had been forever lost.

She now sat by the big window in her study, ten floors up, and looked out over the modern world spread out below. It was autumn, gray light over a colorless world. Here and there a few pines had been left standing between the buildings, like toy trees carelessly flung there by children tired of playing with their building bricks.

Her view brought with it noise, for the highway ran close to the high-rises.

Hanna first came flesh and blood after Anna had discovered a chest in the attic of her parents' home. There she had found what Grandmother had left, papers, inventories, copies of wills, announcements of births and deaths, and also whole bundles of yellowed letters from relatives in America, Norway, and Göteborg.

Innocent letters, most of them, written in fine handwriting. Not a word about injustices, hunger, or shame. The letter writers kept themselves inside the limits of the world they had grown up in and never left, even if they had lived for decades in Minnesota.

Anna had taken some of the letters and put them between the pages of her notebook. She took one out now, read it again, and for the first time thought that the letters really were true in their way. They reflected a reality in which bitterness and ingratitude were not admitted, so didn't exist.

Only the letters from Astrid in Halden, which was called Fredrikshald back then, and Oslo were different, written in large meandering handwriting, full of ideas, thoughts, and gossip. A gold mine, a personal testimony. Anna well understood that Astrid was not a true witness, but was more of a writer, but then it was a writer's view and truth Anna needed.

Had her mother gone through Hanna's letters when she had inherited the collection? Anna didn't think so. She was like me, troubled by the family.

Anna had always known Uncle Ragnar had another father. The parish registers confirmed that in their crude language. "Ill.," it said. "Father unknown." Her research in cultural anthropology had taught her what it was like to be illegitimate, a bastard, or for that matter a single mother and whore.

Hanna was thirteen when she gave birth. When Anna worked that out, she had wept with compassion and rage.

You must have been strong. As Mother said.

Anna had a great many memories of Uncle Ragnar. She thought of him as a king in a fairy tale, handsome and huge right into old age, exotic and extravagant. She remembered his smile that began as a glint in his dark eyes, continued downward, and creased his brown face on its way to his mouth below the clipped mustache.

"He'd melt hearts of stone," Mother said.

"You mean hearts of women," said Father.

Now and again, and always surprisingly, Anna's amazing uncle would come tearing up in his great truck, which was as overwhelming as he himself. "Now, little sis, on with the coffee." She remembered his great laugh rolling through the house, frightening and delighting. And she remembered what he smelled of, sweat, tobacco, and beer.

And money, warm silver coins. She often sat on his knee, and somehow or other he managed to slip a krona into her hand or pocket, always when Mother wasn't looking. Then he winked with his left eye as a sign that they had a secret together, he and the child.

It was magnificent.

He could also wiggle his ears.

She found out who the unknown father was in a letter from America. "We heard that Rickard Joelsson at Lyckan had been accidentally shot. So he got his punishment in the end, that beast who ruined Hanna's life."

She had drawn a large exclamation mark next to the name. Anna's husband, her children's father, was also called Rickard. He was no rogue like the Joelsson boy, but had the same unfortunate tendency to be a victim of his own power to charm.

Anna sighed.

Then she hunted out the envelope of photographs she'd taken from the album at home. There he was, Ragnar, like his father Rickard, but so improbably unlike the others in that family. Perhaps Lovisa had allowed herself a wild love with a gypsy boy; perhaps lust had cracked her shell one night in a deserted house in the forest.

It suddenly struck her that there was a similarity between her own husband and the rapist in Dalsland. They had both had violated mothers, the kind who tried to make their children share their bitterness. They often succeeded with the daughters, who identified themselves with the resentment of their mothers and carried the female anger on through the generations. But what about the sons? No, the strongest refused and became men constantly fleeing from all things emotional and difficult.

Signe, her husband Rickard's mother, was more sophisticated and much wilier than Lovisa at Lyckan. Signe's husband, unlike Lovisa's, had found no real reason to kill her, but had chosen to die young. Still, it had been no easier for young Rickard Hård in the dollhouse apartment in Johanneberg than it had been for Rickard Joelsson at Lyckan.

*T*he clock struck twelve. Now they're feeding Mother.

Anna took a yogurt out of the refrigerator and crumbled a slice of crispbread into the soft mixture. As she ate, her thoughts about Rickard gnawed at her as if she'd happened to reopen an old wound that refused to heal.

She thought about the time before their divorce, the worst years when she had cried as soon as she was alone. At first, she hadn't taken those daytime tears seriously, regarding them as self-pity. But when she started crying in her sleep, she was frightened and went to a psychiatrist. A fashionable man.

"You're one of these modern women who castrate their husbands," he said.

She got up then and left.

That was stupid. He had had the last word, and so she had to fight with him in her head for years.

She put her plate in the dishwasher and determinedly went back to her notes on Hanna. The differences between her and her grandmother were many, just as she'd expected. Hanna accepted, Anna defied. Hanna was spontaneous, Anna sought expression. Hanna belonged in her hard and unjust world. Anna felt she belonged only for short moments, when she could nod at a tree and say, I know you from somewhere.

They were not even as alike in appearance as Anna had thought. Hanna had been darker and heavier.

Once again she stopped at the description of the rape. Only twelve, it was crazy. How old was I when I was taken by Donald, the American exchange student lured here by rumors of Swedish sinfulness? I must have been over nineteen, my first year at university.

And it wasn't rape, though it was, of course, mutual rape, if there is such a thing.

She hadn't given Donald a thought for many years. And yet they had had a long relationship. It had been hard, for they had excellent opportunities to hurt each other's deepest feelings, despite the fact they neither understood nor knew each other. It was a strange relationship, like kinship.

And, of course, I became pregnant, Grandmother, just like you. I had an abortion, easily arranged in university circles at the time. Nor did I have any second thoughts. My only fear concerned Mother, that she would find out in some way. But I was in Lund and she in Göteborg, so thank heavens, she had no idea.

Naturally I thought it was love driving me into Donald's arms. In my generation, we were obsessed with a longing for grand passion.

Hanna, you would've understood nothing whatsoever about love of that kind. In your day, love hadn't penetrated from the upper classes to the depths of peasantry.

There was romantic influence, tragic stories told in country communities. But they had nothing to do with the basic conditions of life. They were like penny dreadfuls. If Hanna ever listened to the songs at all, she surely thought the men in them were conceited fools and the women silly girls. The Älvsborg song would have upset her: "I have killed a child for you . . ."

Heavens, such rubbish! Why didn't you just slit the man's throat? she would have said.

By the 1920s, great love held sway over ordinary people. Johanna and her friends called their search for love "finding Mr. Right." That Mr. Right in her case was a copy of her dead father, whom she had never known, reinforced the myth but didn't make her life any the less complicated.

And yet Johanna wasn't romantic and consequently not so demanding as the next generation of women were to be.

For Anna and her contemporaries, love was a fact that couldn't be disputed. Woe betide the poor creature not afflicted. Added to that was yet another demand: perfect sexuality. Being in love for life, and constant orgasms.

Then the dreams burst like bubbles in the wind. But change takes time. When people fail at love despite the overwhelming desire for it to last a lifetime, they think they have something wrong with them. Only now when every other marriage ends in divorce have people begun to understand that infatuation seldom grows into love, and that not even love can free a person from loneliness. And that sexual enjoyment does not make life meaningful.

Jesus, how stupid, thought Anna. And then a moment later, And yet?

She almost swore when she saw the way her thoughts were heading. To Fjärås Bräcka, the ridge they escaped to every free day of that hot summer in the late 1950s. They nuzzled each other, snuggled, bit, licked, and laughed. In front of them was the sea with its gulls and long salty breakers, behind them the enchanted landscape of lakes with its birdsong in the forest that ran steeply down toward the deep lake. The way he smelled, tasted, laughed. The joy, his joy in her body. And his devotion and her gratitude, his gratitude.

He came from the sea, he said, and she believed him, could envision him as he stepped out of the waves one bright morning with a wreath of sea grass in his hair, his trident carelessly on his shoulder. She came from the forest, he said, finely shaped by wind and rain, as light as the mist rising from the lake. An elf, hidden away in the forests for millions of years, forgetting the language of elves and now with great solemnity trying to learn the language of humans, he said. It was his task to give her substance, turn her into an earthly woman.

"And mine to hold on to the sea god so that he isn't dragged back by the next wave."

She had laughed, but his eyes had darkened before he closed them, then clasped his hands.

"What are you doing?"

"Praying for the strength to not hurt you."

Strangely enough she hadn't asked him whether he was a believer. The moment had seemed too great for that.

Nor had she had the sense to feel uneasy, either.

Hanna's relationship with the mirror had made a profound impression on Anna, who herself had always had a complicated attitude about her own appearance. She wondered when that had begun. And how. Whose looks, whose words had given her a lifelong feeling she was plain, clumsy, almost deformed?

Johanna was beautiful but had the same handicap. Anna had filmed her children when they were small and had plenty of sequences in which her mother had slunk away or covered her face with her hands whenever a camera had been directed at her.

To a thin uncertain teenage daughter, Johanna had said, "You're really pretty, my dear. Anyhow, what you look like doesn't matter at all."

Divided attitude, double message.

When Anna was small, there had been much talk about who in the family a child resembled, though never any discussion about Anna. She was like her father's mother. The child detested the old woman, a wrinkled old witch with sharp features and watery blue eyes, with something gloomy and grandiose about her.

Johanna was afraid of her mother-in-law.

Everyone said her grandmother had been a beauty. Anna couldn't understand that until the old lady died and photographs from her youth were brought out. Then even Anna could see they were right, she had been beautiful and there was a likeness.

But it was too late. The self-image of the plain girl was fixed forever in her mind.

Of course, by falling in love in that tempestuous way, Rickard Hård made her, yes, actually made her believe she was elflike. He did that from the very first moment, miraculously, as if he'd touched her with a magic wand.

Though he had used a wolf whistle.

*   *   *

In the summers, Anna went back home from the university in Lund, where she had worked hard but had never really liked it. She got a temporary job proofreading at one of the newspapers in her hometown.

She closed her eyes now and could see the pleasant shabby premises, hear the clatter of printers, and smell paper, dust, printer's ink, and tobacco smoke. On the very first day, he was there in the doorway of her room, one of the young reporters, the most lively and the best looking. He whistled like a street boy with delight, pulled himself together, and said, "Are you a woman or a dream?"

"Probably the latter," she said, and laughed.

What had he looked like? Tall, craggy, dark, a sensitive face full of life, playful gray eyes. Anna again hunted out the photograph of Uncle Ragnar; perhaps there was a resemblance. In their smiles, their kind eyes. She thought about Astrid, who used to call Ragnar a Sunday's child. Maybe gods are still born on earth, full of life and warmth, lightheartedness and charm. Faithless and sensual as Pan himself.

Anyhow, he at once fell in love, this young god in the grubby newspaper office. Naturally she was so flattered, she soon gave in and was then grateful to the American for what she had learned from him in bed. Everything went very quickly, too quickly. Suddenly Rickard was in their kitchen with Johanna, dispensing warmth, laughter, and crazy stories.

When he said good-bye that first evening, Father said, "Now, there's a man for you."

Over at the sink, Mother had nodded silently, over and over again. Anna soon saw she had found Mr. Right.

Johanna never changed her mind. It took Anna only a month before she began to waver.

"Mother, everyone says he's a womanizer."

There was a long silence on the phone before Johanna answered.

"That's a pity, Anna. But I don't think you'll escape."

*   *   *

As she sat there now in her study in Stockholm, remembering and taking notes, she grew annoyed. You should have told me to run away, quick as quick, away from that man. Then she had to laugh, and her mind went quite blank—in surprise.

For she had been thinking just as Hanna would have done.

It was fate.

For a long time she thought about Aunt Lisa, Ragnar's wife, who had found herself married to a womanizer. Yet she was also one of the first independent women, owner of a business and with an income of her own.

But so tired, always tired.

The memory of her own grandmother led her to think of her husband, Rickard's, a frail, unreal old woman, transparent and clear. Anna had met her only once and that was in a nursing home where she was awaiting death.

To Anna, she'd said, "I hope you're gentle and pliant. A hard woman could turn the boy into a monster."

"Why is that?"

"I don't know. Perhaps it runs in the family. That's what . . . his mother's like. Sometimes boys have to be as hard as flint to survive. And, you know, flint's hard but breaks easily."

Then she had fallen asleep in that abrupt way old people do, and she died only two weeks later.

How strange I'd forgotten her and what she'd said. How quickly I forgot. For I grew hard in the end.

"You're made of stone, so you'll always manage," he had said during a quarrel.

She hadn't been able to bring herself to answer, not then. She'd just screamed, "You're a quitter."

It's four o'clock now. They'll be tucking Mother in for the night.

*O*h, Mother, what a lot of guilt.

Like when an old sheet with my finely embroidered monogram on it turned up, Anna remembered, A. H. in curly letters. Or those towels you made. You'd found such wonderful toweling, you said. It was true. I've still got them, and no other towel dries so well or feels so pleasant.

You sewed all my "bottom drawer," and I laughed at you, saying I could buy things like that whenever I needed them. I hope you didn't think I was defying or condemning you. No doubt you just felt a vague sadness.

Your mirror. You brought it, proud and happy—a mirror for my hall. I was modern, had "good taste," and liked the simplicity of the day. God, I hope you didn't notice my dismay as we stood there in the hall with that mirror and all its elaborate gilding. My children have it now; their generation loves curly-whirlies.

I must phone Father soon.

All her life, Hanna kept her faith in what had once been laid down, and she had a deep distrust of anything different, unknown, or new. She despised those who sought out secret detours in a world in which everything was measured. An unusual thought, a new idea, or an incomprehensible longing threatened her very foundations.

As this obstinate creature grew out of all those notes, Anna was annoyed. How impoverished she had been, how limited.

Then Anna thought she was like most people, today as well. When our patterns are threatened by new facts, reason is seldom the victor: "I know what I think, so don't go confusing me with new opinions." She did that herself, automatically discarding knowledge that didn't match up with her own values. And finding with blind but unerring certainty the information that suited her and justified her actions.

Just as Hanna had done.

But the truths were different today, more substantial, equipped with evidence and supported by science.

Anna's consciousness had been raised, as it was called, about injustices toward women, for instance—what so much of her research was about. Those injustices led to bitterness, that feeling visible in so many women's faces and heard in their laughter.

"I want to believe in a just world," she said aloud to the framed photograph of Hanna on her desk. "I need to, don't you see? The world must be the kind in which the good are rewarded and the wicked punished. So that everything has some meaning."

God, how stupid!

Much stupider than Hanna's belief in a justice that makes the victims participants in the guilt. In a just world, little girls wouldn't be raped.

And yet, Grandmother, listen to me. It was the dream of the good being possible that built our new society. You were also given a share of it, a pension, hot water, bathroom.

Human values?

I am always surprised by women's compassion, Anna thought. What use is it? There is a better word: empathy. If the psychologists are to be believed, the individual's ability to empathize depends on how much love one received as a child, the way in which the child was regarded and loved. Yet boys were often loved more than girls, but all the same grew up into adults who never had to feel other people's torment all the time. So?

Mother had had endless compassion for the weak, the sick, and the wronged. So there it fitted, for Johanna had been exceptionally loved and regarded for a child born around the turn of the century.

Suddenly a new thought, new notes. Was it her father's love that made Johanna think she had some rights of her own? She was politically active all her life. She and her generation based the welfare state on the conviction that justice was possible. And they brought up a generation of disappointed men and women, badly equipped for sorrow and pain, and quite unprepared for death.

*A*nna looked again at the photograph of Hanna.

You were jubilant when Rickard Joelsson died. I wept when I divorced Rickard Hård. You welcomed joy and became pregnant. I had just had a child when I found that my husband had had a six-month relationship with a colleague. I wept floods of tears over the baby's crib. My friends said it was good for me. It wasn't, either for me or the child.

You never cried from sorrow, not until Grandfather died.

Anna turned back to the account of Hanna and her whore-cloth, something she hadn't been able to make much of. She knew why. She could feel Hanna's shame on her own skin.

She remembered every single second.

They were at a party in Lidingö given by some newspaper people. She was eight months pregnant and enveloped in a silver lamé tent. White, stiff, wrong. As soon as they all rose from the table, Rickard vanished upstairs with his gypsylike table partner. Remained absent. The others avoided looking at Anna. She didn't exist, only the shame. She couldn't remember how she managed to get out of the house, only that she had walked along slippery streets until a taxi appeared and took her home.

He wanted to talk about it the next day.

She didn't listen.

He always wanted to talk about it, his "sidestepping," as he called it. She needed to understand.

But she never listened. She couldn't understand. He wanted forgiveness, and she was unable to forgive.

They weren't able to talk to each other for several years after the divorce, and even then it was on the wrong day at the wrong time—

when he was just about to leave in an hour's time, for Rome, where he was to cover an environmental conference. They must try again. For the sake of the children, he said.

"But you live in the same building as we do," she said. "Our children are much better off than children growing up in homes where their parents quarrel."

"You're always right," he said. "That's what's so awful. I hate you for it. You're so damned practical. But I can't cope without you. Do you want me to go down on my knees?"

He never noticed she was crying.

"What you've never grasped is that my silly affairs were only a way of reaching you. But that didn't work, either. You didn't care about my infidelities."

This raging man, her husband, went on.

"Women like you always make me think that you see through me. That's why I'm intimidated when I come near you. Not because of your intelligence, no, something much worse."

The kind of woman who castrates her husband.

That broke her paralysis.

"But why is it so bad to be seen through and so important to come out on top?"

"I don't know."

That was when she saw he was a victim of the male legacy and he was not sufficiently stupid to not understand it. Not like Father.

"Anna. There'll be no more of these silly affairs. I promise."

Then she was able to cry, "You're an idiot. Your faithlessness killed me, everything that was me, my confidence, my innocence. I died, don't you see? What's left of me is nothing but the witch, the one you're so afraid of."

She could see that he understood, that at last he had understood. "Oh God, Oh God," he said.

Then finally, almost inaudibly, "Why did you never say so?"

She wept, incapable of answering. Suddenly he was raging again.

"You made me treat you badly. It made me hate myself. You just looked on when I failed at what I wanted most of all, and I thought it meant nothing to you."

"That's not true," she cried, and now he couldn't help seeing she was crying.

"Are you crying? You've never done that before!"

She laughed so hysterically she frightened even herself.

"My dear," he said.

But the terrible laughter went on. She was unable to stop herself. When she at last fell silent, he said, "I probably didn't want to see things go wrong for you. I'd have gone mad if I'd understood. You were so intelligent and clearheaded, I was proud of you. Maybe I wanted you to be like that. Then got furious because you were. So damned strong."

"I wasn't. I was going mad."

Then the taxi horn sounded, and he had to go.

Naturally she knew she would take him back. Her loneliness had already made that decision. And the hunger for his body in hers.

Anna looked at her watch, past five, must phone Father! That was just as difficult every day. Reproaches.

"Oh, so you've suddenly remembered your poor old dad, have you?"

"I phoned yesterday. How was Mother today?"

"All right. I got her to eat all right. I took one spoonful of the hamburger and one of the fruit custard. You know, she's just like a child, wanting dessert first."

"Clever of you."

"When are you coming to see me?"

"I was with you last week. Have you forgotten?"

"I forget so easily."

"I'll phone tomorrow as usual."

It was over. It had gone unusually easily but the receiver was wet with sweat. Why the hell was it so difficult, this phone call she had to force herself to make every day?

I wish you were dead, both of you.

* * *

A few days after the quarrel with Rickard, she found a sentence in a book that made a great impression on her. "A free man's love is never secure."

That's true, she thought.

She was so taken with it, she bought a postcard, wrote the sentence down on it, and sent it to the hotel in Rome.

Then the reply came. She had to find it now, rummaged in drawers for the key of her secret case, opened it, found the letter with the Rome postmark, and read it.

You've never wanted to listen to me. But you find it hard to resist the written word, so now I'm trying a letter.

You're naive. A free man—that must be a man no one has any power over. He doesn't need revenge. My women are like me, they want revenge. At least it started out that way. The first, Sonja, at the party, I'm sure of because her lover was at the dinner. He was a shit I'd known for a long time.

The one I wanted to humiliate, take my revenge on, there's no doubt about that. It was you. We, she and I, were suffering from the same kind of madness. We wanted to demonstrate what love is—not power, but desire in the encounter between an arbitrary male/female. It's perverse. But perversion doesn't reduce the desire. I think even you can understand that. On the other hand, what you probably can't understand is the excitement when two people deliberately behave badly, intending to hurt.

It was the same with all my women. Though I did make a mistake with Lilian. She fell in love with me, and I was furious with her. As I saw it, that wasn't included in the agreement.

That was why it took so long to get rid of her. You were pregnant with Malin, more goddesslike than ever. Christ, what a shit I was.

That brings us to the main question. Why do I have to take revenge on you? You're honest and lovely—everything I've ever dreamed of.

I knew nothing about love until I met you. If I had, I would have run away. I didn't really want it, this consuming submission that makes a man a slave. So this "free man's" answer is that you had unlimited power over me. If you were sulky at breakfast, my day was sheer hell. When you were happy, I was drunk with my victory. If you were ever angry and scolded me, I deserved it. It's still your power over me I'm afraid of. But I can't live without you. My position has no underlying base. I'm the one who's been whoring, lying, betraying you. And yet I like to believe it could have been different if you'd just for once tried to listen. You're a very proud person. You were brought up like that, so I'm not blaming you. It was beneath your dignity even to try to understand. Or what?

The letter wasn't signed. She had wondered why.

She smiled as she remembered how she had spelled her way through her telegram to Rome.

"Meet you Pentecost Sunday at Fjärås Bräcka."

She thought, just as she had when she had received the letter, that Rickard required attention in abundance. To maintain his hold on life, he needed to be able to choose and wreck, take and throw away. That was his weakness, his fundamental flaw.

Just as he had written, it was incompatible with love, with the dependence that lifelong fellowship entails.

Anna remembered Maria's teens, her rebellion, particularly a quarrel about Sandra, a school friend, with whom Rickard had flirted. Maria was scarlet with shame, and cruelly shouted at her father.

"You're a silly fool, a damned tomcat, thinking you're irresistible. Some boys at school are like you, but the girls who know anything simply laugh at them. I've never understood how Mom could stand you."

Maria hadn't married, nor had Malin. They lived like men had always done, in love sometimes, brief relationships. But they each had a child, free children who had escaped the game in that hellish triangle, father, mother, child.

Right from the beginning Anna had had an inkling that Rickard had little self-confidence. An autocratic mother? A weak father? But when she was young she hadn't wanted to understand. Constantly understanding was a danger to yourself. Her mother's life had taught her that. Johanna always understood, and so had to endure a great deal.

Suddenly Anna remembered another quarrel, much later. The memory was knife-sharp. She could see the evening sun falling in through the big picture window in the living room back in Minkgatan, dust whirling in the rays. Rickard had fallen into the habit of calling her Mother, even when they were alone.

"I'm not your mother," she shrieked at him. "Never have been and never will be."

She saw he'd taken it badly, had stiffened.

"Of course not," he said. "It's only a manner of speech, a silly habit."

At that moment, Anna knew it was neither a manner of speech nor a habit. But she couldn't bring herself to say so.

"Sorry I lost my temper," she said, and the moment went by.

But Anna had seen her mother-in-law's face, lovely and self-absorbed, and had wondered how often and intensely the little boy had longed for her in vain. And she thought, that's why he's so furious with me. He's having his revenge on her.

She jotted down notes now, thinking she might find some

answer, but then hesitated, put a question mark in the margin, thought for a while, then wrote:

Rickard is always considerate toward his mother and defends her against the slightest criticism. But of his dead father he speaks only with contempt: "He was a fool."

She heard the key in the door.

"Got some plaice," he called. "Fresh."

"Lovely. Coming."

"I'll get us a drink."

They raised their glasses, and slightly formally he said as usual that it was great to be alive. Then he picked up the thick gray notebook, the Hanna book, and leafed through it.

"Read it while I peel the potatoes," she said.

When he came out into the kitchen, he said, "This'll be a book, Anna. It's damned powerful."

She was pleased.

"Rather too much nostalgia, don't you think?" she said.

"No. Anyhow, there's nothing wrong with nostalgia."

He'd always helped her with her work. Right from the start.

He was the one to come up with the idea of writing a popular version of her thesis.

"It's worth a better fate than just collecting dust in a faculty."

She wanted to reach a lot of people.

"Do you think I can?"

"We'll manage it," he said. So she went to journalism school and learned to express complicated matters in a simple way, universalizing and using examples. She was expecting a child, and wrote at home in the daytime. He corrected the manuscript every evening.

It was fun. They were newly married, in their first two-room apartment in one of the new suburbs of Stockholm.

He was strict at first.

"For Christ's sake, that isn't correct Swedish. Listen to it yourself."

She listened and took it in. A language entirely of its own soon began to emerge, hers. It was like a miracle, almost as wonderful as the child growing inside her.

"I've met my match," he said.

The book came out a few months before their daughter was born. Both were surprised by the attention it received.

Success. Happiness. Until that evening at the house in Lidingö.

He cleaned the fish and fried it. She sat at the kitchen table with her drink, watching how deftly he handled the knife and spatula, precisely and elegantly.

I know no one as sensuous as he is.

"Hello there, öre for your thoughts."

She blushed, then told him, and listened to that dark laugh that came from deep inside him.

"I'm hungry," she said. "We must eat first."

"I haven't made the slightest approach."

"Just you dare."

He wanted to have a house.

"Live on the ground, Anna. Before it's too late."

The first time he'd said that, she'd thought it was already too late.

"Who plants apple trees after they're fifty?"

"Me," he said calmly.

Then the idea had grown. Suddenly she dared feel how tired she was of high-rise apartment blocks, the anonymity, and the highway thundering through her days and nights. Not to mention those poor pine trees.

A garden!

"There were always arguments about the garden at home," she'd said. "Mother had to do it all while Father went out sailing."

Rickard had been angry.

"For Christ's sake, we can't have the whole of our life steered by what your parents did."

"You're right."

She knew what he meant by "the whole of our life." He was upset by her ties to her mother and furious about his relationship with his father. She thought he was right in principle, although his motives were dubious.

That day he had been to look at two places. One was too big and expensive. The other was two smaller houses on one large rural site. Lovely situation, he said. Solid buildings. One house for work, hers and his as soon as he retired. And one to live in.

"There's an old farmhouse there, too, derelict."

"There must be a snag. Is it too expensive?"

"No, but it's a long way from town. Over twenty miles."

"I've no objections. Better proper countryside than another suburb."

"You're not afraid of being isolated?"

She suddenly felt that old unease.

"How would you get in and out of town?"

"There's a train," he said. "You'll have to be one of those wives who drive their husbands to the station. And pick them up in the evenings."

Before she fell asleep, she lay there a long time thinking about those two little houses, about giving them apple trees and roses. He was going to talk to the seller the next day and set a meeting out there.

On Saturday, she thought. She'd already decided.

As she tackled the notebooks the next morning, it all seemed more serious, weightier, all because of Rickard saying, "It'll be a book."

How strange of me, she thought. I've actually known that all the time. But it was easier as long as I pretended it was just a journey, an outing into my own background. A little psychology, a little sociology, a little increased self-knowledge.

It had worked out like that, too. She had grown calmer in the course of the journey, made some discoveries and acquired new insights. She had stopped searching so desperately for childhood memories, out of "reality," as she used to say. She had realized there are only fragments, that "memories" always consist of fragments the mind puts together into a pattern, adapts to a picture staked out early without the need for a connection with anything that really happened. A great deal is misunderstood by small children, then stored as images that attract similar images, confirming and reinforcing.

Then she thought what hadn't happened might be more truthful than what had happened, would have more to say.

She left her fragments lying there, scattered about, and found that was the only way she could acquire information on the past, only briefly, of course, just moments.

She avoided the worst, that which hurt. But that wouldn't do, if she was serious about it all. She would have to search more deeply. Into Hanna, especially, rather than sliding over her grandmother's grief when August drove through the bridge railing straight into the sea one dark night somewhere in Bohuslän.

Anna was in her teens when it happened and couldn't understand the old lady's despair. August was a grown man and made decisions about his own life for himself. He was divorced and had no children.

She asked Johanna, who looked at her with distance in her eyes.

"He was her child, Anna."

I must understand why she mourned so terribly. And aged so cruelly in only a few weeks.

August had always had a weak will to live, it was said. He had had all kinds of illnesses. For years, Hanna had walked the cottage floor at night with the boy in her arms.

"He was her child, Anna."

Peter, she thought. Peter.

Like her grandmother and her mother, Anna had had difficult deliveries. Inherited, that too? Genetic? Psychological? Peter was born after their divorce and reconciliation, six years after Malin. He arrived two months too early, the wrong way around, and as thin as a baby bird. The first time he was put to her breast, Anna knew something was wrong with him, something ill-fated. He had no vitality.

The doctors laughed at her anxiety. The boy was healthy. She should be grateful he didn't have to go into an incubator.

Rickard was in some eastern state where a crisis was going on. He was supposed to be back in good time for the birth. If she had gone to full term . . .

Johanna came up and sat beside her at the maternity hospital, her eyes as uneasy as Anna's.

"The best help to me would be if you took the children back with you to Göteborg. Then I can devote all my time to the boy when I get home."

Johanna hesitated, but talked to the doctor and grew calmer. They agreed not to tell Rickard, not to worry him.

Johanna took the two girls home with her, but telephoned twice a day.

"Haven't you got a friend, Anna? Where's Kristina?"

"In Åland. They're all away."

It was high summer when Anna, alone with the boy, went into the darkened apartment. The child whimpered for light. He couldn't cry, but he whimpered the moment he was out of Anna's arms.

Oh, that lament, humble, hopeless.

A week, two, four, then six. Forty days later, all carefully counted, he died one Wednesday afternoon. She looked at the clock. Three. A banality from the world of death announcements was turned into a profound truth: "Little angel came today, smiled at us, and turned away."

But Peter had never given her a smile.

Anna did not put the child down as she drew back the curtains, the light slicing like lightning in her eyes. She looked out at the world with surprise, that it hadn't changed, people coming and going, children on swings down in the playground and squabbling in the sandpit. The telephone rang and she didn't answer it. She would never again respond to calls, she thought.

Then she fell asleep with the baby in her arms, going with him into the cold and death. Ten hours later she was woken by Rickard, who'd had a telephone message from Johanna and had flown home via Berlin.

He dealt with all the practical matters, doctors, undertakers, telephoning parents and friends. He also looked after her, bathed her in warm water, made her drink, remade the bed, wrapped her in warm blankets.

She heard him crying at night.

She herself didn't cry for weeks. Weeks of unreality, as she was to call them later, weeks filled with peculiar experiences.

Like the day Rickard had to go in to the paper. "Only two hours, Anna. Promise me to stay in bed."

She promised.

When he got home, she had gone. He ran all around the neighborhood and was just about to give up and phone the police when she came walking along the street, straight at him, smiling.

"What luck I found you. You must help me."

"But where've you been?"

"At the children's clinic, Rickard. That's where you take babies."

"Which clinic?"

"The usual one, behind the market square."

"But, Anna, that was pulled down years ago."

"How peculiar," she said. "So that's why I couldn't find my way back. You see, I've left Peter there. With the nurse."

When she saw the look in his eyes, she misunderstood.

"Don't be angry with me, Rickard. He won't come to any harm. I mean, they're trained and all that . . ."

"Let's go," he said, and taking her arm, he steered her across the square with the pool and its idiotic sculpture, around the corner and down to the site where the children's clinic had been, now a parking lot.

"But I don't understand. I was here only an hour or two ago. Where's Peter?"

"He's dead and you know it."

Their eyes met and he did not turn away. In the end, she nodded.

"I know."

That evening her head cleared, but she was frightened.

"I was there, I remember, it's all so clear, the door they painted pale blue, Sister Solveig who was tired but just as patient as usual. I was there, Rickard. And yet I can't have been there."

"Sister Solveig died when Maria was quite small. Of cancer, don't you remember? We went to her funeral."

"Dead? Like Peter, then?"

"Yes."

She closed her eyes, her face smoothing out as if she had understood. And when she at last opened them again she was sensible.

"Rickard. I promise you I won't go mad."

"You almost frightened the life out of me."

Then she noticed how tired and pale he was and realized she must pull herself together. More experiences in unreality came, but never again did she involve him in them.

* * *

What helped her through the wall was her mother-in-law, who came to see her and said, "But you mustn't grieve. It was practically only a fetus."

"He was my child," said Anna.

Then at last she was able to cry. She wept almost without stopping for two days.

Afterward she cleaned her home, put away the sleeping tablets, and went with Rickard to the west coast, to her mother and the other children.

*B*y the time Rickard came home, she had put the memory of Peter into the computer. He looked at her uneasily.

"Anna, how pale you are."

"You read it while I get dinner."

She had already bought and cooked a piece of salted beef brisket that afternoon. She peeled rutabagas, potatoes, and carrots, cut them up into small pieces, boiled them, and mashed in the stock.

He liked mashed rutabagas.

He was dark-eyed and pale when he came out into the kitchen. They didn't have the strength to talk as they ate, but afterward, in the living room, he said, "I often think about Peter, that it was as if he had a mission. For that was when things went . . . as they did. Between us, I mean."

She couldn't bring herself to reply.

*D*id Mother ever tell Grandmother I was divorced?

Anna wrote down the question, then looked at it.

Then she wrote:

I don't think so. She probably didn't want to worry her. Hanna was very fond of Rickard, too, and said he reminded her of Ragnar.

That was more true than Anna had realized.

After a while, she found yet another explanation. Mother had kept silent about the divorce because she had never really believed it, and had said so occasionally over the lonely years.

"I don't think you two will ever get away from each other."

Anna made the decision when she got back home from the maternity hospital with Malin. For months Rickard had been sleeping with someone else, the smell of her on his clothes, in their living room, and in bed.

When she told him she wanted to separate, he was desperate and refused to believe her.

"Anna, it was just stupid of me . . . and then I couldn't get rid of her."

"I haven't asked for an explanation."

"But listen to me."

"No, Rickard, I don't want to hear. It'll have to be as I said. You've got the spring to find somewhere else to live. Then we'll talk to Maria together."

"You've thought everything out."

"I've talked to a lawyer."

"Maria will be very upset."

"I know."

Maria was the center of the course of events running relentlessly on its own volition. All anxiety and guilt was drawn toward her. She filled Anna's days with torment and nights with nightmares. She appeared in a thousand guises, the abandoned child, the knifed child, a child lost in the forest, looking for her father.

Maria loved Rickard.

Rickard was a good father, amusing, enterprising, and as inquisitive as the child. Safe.

Maria was a sensitive child, full of tenderness toward everything and everyone, quick-thinking and with an inquiring mind. Beautiful. Like you, Rickard used to say. But it wasn't true. Maria was a fair-haired copy of Johanna.

Malin was different. So far, she had been entirely Anna's baby.

He said what she had most feared, that he would contest custody.

That was Friday evening, and he left. Didn't come back until Sunday, hungover, scornful, almost crazy with despair. Anna took the children down one floor to Kristina. "Please look after them."

When she got back, he was in the shower.

"We must talk like grown people," she said as calmly as she could.

"What about?"

"About how this can be arranged so that it causes the least harm to the children and you. And me."

"As you're made of stone, things are sure to be all right for you. I'm going to drink myself to death."

"Rickard!"

But he went to bed.

The next morning he was calmer and she could talk to him. He took Maria to kindergarten as usual, came back, and phoned the office to say he was sick.

She was feeding Malin as she told him. He was to have the children every other weekend and for a month every summer.

"Magnificent."

She needed maintenance for the children, a thousand kronor a month.

"To manage," she said. She had already decided to move to a smaller apartment and take a lecturing job at the school of sociology. She also made quite decent income from freelance work.

"But you didn't want that job. And what about your book?"

"That was then," she said.

He wept and found it difficult to get out the words when appealing to her.

"Is there nothing, nothing on earth I can do to get you to change your mind?"

"No."

That was all she could find to say.

It didn't work out as Anna had thought. Rickard got a job as a foreign correspondent in Hong Kong.

"Covering the whole of the Far East."

To blazes, thought Anna, and congratulated him.

Together they talked to Maria. He said he had to go. Anna said they were having a difficult time. They needed . . . to be apart.

Maria said that was good.

"Then maybe you'll stop crying so much, Mommy."

Anna and Maria drove him to Arlanda airport. The five-year-old held out her hand.

"Good-bye, Daddy."

That was all.

He looked weighed down and old as he headed for the gate, and Anna almost cracked with pity. And doubts.

Those first lonely months . . . heavens, how she missed him. She fumbled for him in her sleep, flung her arms around his pillow, but couldn't sleep. Dry, parched, she looked for him on every street corner, in the square, and in the shops.

That was when her desert dreams began. Night after night, Anna wandered in an endless desert, seeing his back disappearing among the dunes. It was heavy going, her feet sinking into the sand. She was exhausted and parched with thirst, searching for water, finding none, trying to rest, but then she caught a glimpse of his back again and had to go on.

She borrowed some sleeping pills from Kristina and managed a few nights' rest.

Her last desert dream was the worst. The man walking ahead of her across the parched ground turned around, and it wasn't Rickard, but the doctor, the one who had said, "You castrate your husband."

She found a two-room apartment right above the kindergarten. A man appeared and helped her move, an old friend, practical and handy. From gratitude or loneliness or desire?—she went to bed with him and found sex much like her desert wanderings, sterile and meaningless. She woke with sand in her mouth, whispered that he had to go, that Maria might find him there. He obeyed, and she realized that the sex had been a disappointment to him, as well.

She told Kristina.

"I'm a one-man woman."

"Sounds fine," said her friend. "Pity Rickard's a many-woman man."

They agreed that he was having a good time in the Far East, free to devote himself to geishas, diplomats' wives, and sophisticated women reporters, the kind they saw on television.

But Anna knew it wasn't true, that Rickard was lonely and desperate. For the first time she asked herself whether that was so, whether it could possibly be true that what lay behind his womanizing was an attempt to reach her.

Then she told herself she was foolish. And the next moment she thought that if that were true, then it was even worse.

* * *

She was so deep in her notebook that she jumped when the telephone rang. It was Maria.

"Oh, darling," said Anna.

"Were you asleep, Mom?"

"No, no, just sitting here making notes and remembering."

"I'm not sure it's good for you, all these memories," said Maria in troubled tones. She had been to a conference in Oslo, Anna remembered.

"I came back via Göteborg and went to see Grandfather."

"How kind of you."

But Maria said it was unbearable, both at the old man's house and at the hospital. Intolerable, and impossible to do anything about it.

"I've been thinking a lot about you, how awful and lonely it must be every damned month. I'll come with you next time."

At first, Anna's delight was overwhelming, but then she heard the veiled touch in Maria's voice and realized she had done what Maria most loathed: showered guilt.

Half an hour later, Malin called and said she'd been talking to Maria and they were going to take turns going with her on the visits to Göteborg. As often as they could.

"I think you're mad," said Anna.

Malin was unlike her sister, unlike her mother, as well, for that matter. She was more matter-of-fact, more open, more logical, less emotional. Neither Rickard nor Anna could really grasp that they had a daughter studying theoretical physics.

"I was so pleased I made Maria feel guilty."

"Me, too," said Malin happily. "Listen, Mom, you must know that only monsters manage to escape feeling guilty."

"Salt of the earth," said Anna. That was one of her old nicknames for her remarkable younger daughter.

Johanna wasn't present during Anna's first lonely six months, nor when she moved, nor when she arranged for the children.

During that time Hanna was living with Mother, and then she died. Mother needed a great deal of help. I managed to get there only once.

As Malin said, it's not possible to live without feeling guilty.

She spent all day putting her notes into the third book, the red one with ANNA on the label on the cover. She turned back to the fly-leaf and wrote, "On guilt and gratitude, and on having daughters."

Then she put a question mark beside it.

On Friday morning Rickard was in a bad mood.

"Did you sleep badly?"

"Yes."

As he stood in the hall before going to get the newspaper, he said, "You quoted my letter from Rome."

"But all that's still only notes, Rickard. We'll have to discuss it later . . . when it's really clear it's going to be a book."

"It's not that. What struck me was that you never answered my question."

"What was it?" she said, although she knew.

"Why you never listened to me, never even tried."

"That's just it," she said.

She washed up and cleared away breakfast, her own words ringing in her ears. "That's just it."

Then she sat down to work and wrote.

I want to attempt a fairy tale. Why a fairy tale? I don't know, perhaps because it's true what some people say, that fairy tales can say more than what is called reality.

But it's probably mostly because you don't have to understand fairy tales.

Once upon a time there was a little girl who grew up in a castle. It had three rooms full of secrets, cupboards with wonderful things in them, books with pictures, photographs of dead strangers, though they gazed at her with serious eyes. Around the castle was a large garden, roses and strawberries growing in it, a mountain in one corner, high, halfway to the clouds. One day she climbed it and saw where the blue sea met the sky somewhere far away. After that she made the mountain hers, took herself to the top, and created her own world among the boulders and mountain ledges.

The mountain talked to the sea. She heard it the very first day. After a while, she realized the mountain was also talking to her and to the lilacs flowering at its foot, and to the cat's foot, the houseleek, and the meadow saxifrage growing in the cracks.

It was always summer, the weather always fine, and she was a happy little girl. Her mother loved her, and her father was proud of her, for she was so wise and clever. Her mother also told her almost every day that she was just that, a happy girl. And life was good for her.

If life is good, then you mustn't be sad. That was a great worry to the girl. For sometimes she was incomprehensibly sad. And sometimes she was terribly frightened.

What was she frightened of? Not that her mother would die, well, yes, she probably was. But why?

She would never know.

Once, when she thought she would die of the fright that made her heart beat so it hurt in her chest, she found an invisible stairway leading right into the mountain. Inside was a cave, just big enough for her. She could sit in it and feel all her terrors disappear.

She felt chosen.

How long did she play that game? Was it one summer or was it many? Anyhow, it took years before this happy little girl understood that the game was dangerous, this game that made her invulnerable and invisible. When she finally grasped it, she was grown up and had left home.

What happened was that she took the mountain with her. It was always there, and as soon as she was sad or frightened, she could escape into it. Now she didn't want to any longer. Now she was afraid of the cave that had such thick walls. But the mountain held her in his power.

When the prince came, and love made her even more vulnerable than ever, she found a new use for her secret mountain cave.

The prince thought she was often cold and unreachable. And that was true. It's deathly cold in the the mountain, and anyone sitting in there is turned to stone. She cannot fight for her rights, or burn with jealousy, or scream, ask questions, or accuse.

So without wanting to, the girl went on escaping to her cave and hurting him. But guilt tormented her every time she came out and saw what she had done.

And so they married and lived . . . ever after.

*O*nce Anna had her fairy tale down in her notebook, she started striding around like a captive horse, back and forth, kicking at tables and chairs.

Then she filled a large glass with whiskey and drank it down in one draft. Stubborn and insane she went on, knowing she had nearly found something she'd lost, and it was important. She picked up her pen and turned to a new page.

Then she found it. When Peter died.

When she fell asleep with the dead child in her arms.

And when she found herself in the extreme unreality, when she lost her little boy at the children's clinic.

If you run away, you run the risk of going mad.

She filled her glass again and took it with her into the bedroom. She didn't wake when the telephone rang, nor even when Rickard came home.

He woke her.

"Anna! Are you drunk?"

"Yes. Go away and read it."

When she woke the next time, he was sitting on the edge of the bed with milk and sandwiches.

"I had an inkling," he said.

He said nothing more for a while, then went on.

"I don't think you risk going mad. Nor do you have to feel guilty about me. You learn in time that people have their own characteristics. No, what's dangerous is when the person who has a cave to escape into never learns to fight."

"And I have to do that?"

"Yes."

Saturday arrived, the day for their outing.

Anna woke early, packed some food, and looked out the kitchen window at the gray above the town giving way to the sun.

Of course, the weather had to be fine.

Rickard came out into the kitchen, sleepy, unshaven, and in his awful old bathrobe.

"How's the body feeling?" he said.

"As if I had fizzy lemonade in my veins. They're bubbling."

"An amazing hangover."

"Idiot. I'm happy, lighter in mind than for a long time."

"Catharsis?"

"Precisely."

From the kitchen she could hear him phoning the girls and inviting them out on Sunday, on an outing with a surprise, as he put it. He's so certain, she thought, certain they'll have the time—and the desire. And certain the sale will come off.

When they were on the Roslag road and the traffic had thinned out, he said, "Something occurred to me last night. You've persisted in staying in these damned high-rises because you're afraid of gardens."

"Good God!"

He's right, she thought. Concrete suburbs have no secrets. There's no space for mystery under neon lights, no symbols, no connection to trees and flowers. Or to mountains.

"Good God!" she said again.

"What do you mean?"

"That it's all so sad, Rickard. That we've lived so . . . dismally for all these years. And not really liked it."

They were silent for a long time, and then just as they were passing another vehicle, he said, "There are lots of rocks out there."

"Great!"

An elderly man met them at the turn, and as they bounced along the narrow gravel road, Anna realized it was going to be tougher than she'd thought. In the winter before the snowplow came. In the spring when the snow was melting. But the forest was green along the road, real old-fashioned mixed woodlands with aspens, birches, and maples between the pine trees.

Two squat houses crept along the ground, vacation homes from the 1960s. They had now been linked together with a glassed-in passage that resembled a veranda. They could just glimpse the water between the aspens, not the sea, but a large calm inland lake.

"Gracious!" said Anna, then went on when the man looked at her in surprise. "I just meant I simply can't understand why anyone would want to sell this place."

"My wife died last summer."

There was nothing to say.

The two men started with the well. Anna heard them talking about pressure tanks and how they could be difficult in winter, then she set off on her own across the site. There were lots of rocks, as Rickard had said, flat smooth rocks with polypody growing in the cracks. And plenty of roses, just as she had imagined. Down toward the lake was the old farmhouse, tired and neglected and wonderful.

The garden was in the lee toward land. Two ancient apple trees were still there, laden with red apples. Anna stood with her back against one of the rough trunks and said hello. There was no doubt about it, they had known each for a thousand years.

*T*he next weekend, Anna and Maria went to Göteborg. Maria spent most the time with the old man in the house by the sea, talking, cleaning, and cooking. Anna went to see her mother in the nursing home.

She talked about Hanna.

"I've been living in my head with your mother a long time now. I think I'm beginning to understand her. It's been more difficult to get a picture of you and your life. That's because you're so close to me, I can't see you. It's probably true that we least understand those we love most.

"I know you were a secretive person. So I think you ought to be allowed to speak for yourself in my book. You're a good storyteller, Mother."

In the car on the way back, she told Maria about Hanna and Dalsland.

"Your great-grandmother."

Back at work, she moved from bookshelf to bookshelf, reading the titles, looking things up here and there, finding passages that had once meant so much to her.

Was she looking for prototypes?

No, her thoughts were quite practical, on how everything should be packed and where they would find space in those small houses by the lake. Rickard had said to her what Ragnar had once said to Hanna.

"There's lots of old rubbish you can clear out."

And like Hanna, she wondered how on earth she had collected so much rubbish over the years.

She stopped at the poetry shelf and sat down with Ekelöf, Stagnelius, Martinson, and Boye. That was where it struck her she was searching for a tone of voice, her mother's. She thought everyone had a tone of voice, unique to that person. Of course, she couldn't find it now, not like this. And she knew it was presumptuous to think she could get it to resound as it once did.

But if she was patient, if she waited, then perhaps she would find the right chord. . . .

JOHANNA

BORN 1902,

DIED 1986

*M*y life is divided into two halves. The first half lasted for eight years of childhood, and is the same length as the remaining seventy. When I look back on the second half, I find four events that changed me.

The first was when I was stopped by an invisible hand from opening a door. That was a miracle, and it gave me back the connection.

The next was when I found work I liked, became self-sufficient, and joined the Social Democrat party.

Then there was love and marriage.

The fourth was when I gave birth to a daughter and named her after the old midwife in Norskvattnet. And when my daughter had children and I grandchildren.

What took place between all these events was the ordinary life of most women. A great deal of anxiety, hard work, great joy, many victories, more defeats. And, of course, the sorrow beneath it all.

I have thought a great deal about sorrow. After all, understanding is born from it, as well as reflection and the desire for change. We wouldn't be human if sorrow didn't exist, right down there in the depths of our beings.

I ought to say one more thing before I start my story. I've always tried to tell the truth in the childish belief that it existed and was indivisible. I found it more and more difficult to think when truth fell apart into hundreds of different truths.

I have no words to describe my first eight years in Dalsland. Perhaps I used them up when Anna was small, poured them into her. I did that because it was fun, but also so that she could be at home in the world of a child, the world of stories and nature. Nowadays,

I don't know whether that was any use. Anna did not become a happy person.

Over the years I lost not just the words but also the connection. That was so clear when Anna took me back to Dalsland that time. I recognized everything, the waterfall and the lakes, the trees and paths. But they had forgotten me. That was bitter and I cried a lot.

One should never return to sacred places.

I was Johanna, a city child, born in the pleasant fragrance of new cloth in a corner haberdashery in Haga. The place was as cramped as a dollhouse and had hundreds of drawers full of secrets. Ribbons, elastic, laces—all kinds of wonderful things spread out before me on the polished dark-brown counter. Most of all, I loved the boxes with reels of silk.

"You must keep your fingers clean," said Lisa, and I scrubbed my hands until they were sore.

I always started with the violet box, following the glowing range from pale pinkish blue to faint lilac up to the matte dark blue with the slightest touch of red in it.

"Queen color?"

"I think you're right," said Lisa, smiling.

Lisa rarely laughed, and never exclaimed in surprise or anger. She was quiet and unchanging, and that made me feel safe. When I first minded the shop, she was at her sewing machine in the little room in the back and made me a cotton dress in small gray-and-white check.

"We have to be careful about colors. To consider your mother," she said.

But she made the cuffs, collar, and pocket flaps out of green cotton with pink roses on it.

The moment she put that new dress on me, I began life as someone else, far away from Father and the waterfall. It wasn't easy, and I've thought many a time that if Lisa hadn't existed, I would have gone into the Rosenlund canal.

At first there was the terrible business of words, the old words pouring out of my mouth before I had time to think. I'd been good at school back home, and I was dressed in my best when I went to the city school for the first time. Of course, I was frightened, but all the same . . . I thought I was like everyone else. And perhaps it would have been all right if it hadn't been for the words. Lord, how they laughed at me.

I had to read a bit out of a book. But I never got to the end because of their horrible laughter.

And the teacher said, "Johanna, haven't you ever thought that you speak as you write? The words in your mouth are to be the same as in the book. Go home now and get that into your head."

She wasn't nasty, but she knew nothing about what it was like for me when I got home to those unmade beds, piles of dirty clothes, and stacks of unwashed dishes. And then there were the boys' filthy shoes I had to clean. I had only half an hour before Mother came back from the bakery, bad-tempered as usual when she was exhausted.

"Lazy trollop," she would scold, "spoiled by your father when you was little."

Once she hit me so hard in the face, I couldn't go to school the next day.

After that day, I ran off to Lisa as soon as Mother came home. I could see that saddened her, but she said nothing. Dared not, I suppose, in case I told Ragnar.

In the room behind Lisa's shop, I read aloud, day after day. I soon found that it wasn't at all true what the teacher had said: the words in books weren't at all the words you said, not even in those days. But with Lisa's help I learned to speak properly.

I thought it was proper Swedish, but many years later when I was at a political meeting, a woman said to me, "Your Göteborg dialect is good to hear, but I think you ought to tidy it up a bit."

Oh, how surprised I was.

In time I did well at school, although I never had a friend and my classmates went on laughing at me. Things got worse and worse at home. My brothers gave up working, stayed at home, and drank. While I tried to keep out of the way in the kitchen, I could hear them talking about women, about whores and fucking and pricks and cunts. I washed dishes and listened, and I hated them.

That was when I made my first resolution. I would never get married, never in any way go with a man.

When it got so bad that Ragnar intervened and smashed the furniture and beat up the boys, I stood in a corner and was pleased. Mother screamed with terror, but heaven knows, she deserved it. Then I was allowed to live with Lisa and Ragnar, and a great calm descended on me. I still went back home after school and cleaned up the worst, but I made quite sure I got away before I heard Mother's key in the door.

I had begun to despise her by then.

"She behaves like a gypsy woman," I said to Lisa.

Lisa reprimanded me and gave me a word I've never forgotten.

"Of course, she's a little . . . primitive." she said.

Primitive. Like the natives, I thought. At school I'd read about the savages in Africa, about the time when Stanley met Livingstone.

After that conversation with Lisa, I made my second resolution. I would become a civilized and educated person.

In Lisa's apartment, immediately across the courtyard from ours, there were a great many books. At least ten, maybe fifteen. I read them all. They were love stories, and I found that strange. When I said so to Lisa, she was surprised and thought for a long time before she said anything.

"But that's what it's like, Johanna. For instance, I'm hopelessly in love with Ragnar. It wears me out all the time, but I can't get it out of me."

I must have looked peculiar. I remember sitting down on a chair in the shop and opening my mouth without being able to get a word out. I wanted to tell her that Ragnar was kind, an unusually good man. I wanted to comfort her.

Comfort?

"So that's why you're so sad," I said in the end, surprising even myself that I'd never thought of it before, what now seemed so obvious. That Lisa was sad . . .

I don't remember what she replied. It took me many years before I understood the connection between the talk about Ragnar as a womanizer and my brothers boasting about pricks in the cunts in Järntorget.

Lisa taught me three things of great importance: to understand other people, to endure with patience, and to work in a shop.

*A*nna says I learned the first lesson far too well, the one about understanding people and feeling sorry for them.

My mother never understood. She issued judgments and condemned, and thus avoided a lot of trouble.

But when Lisa started talking about my drunkard brothers, about how scared they'd been in the city and how the sense of alienation was hollowing them out, I recognized something in what she said, like a tune I had once known. It was a long time before I realized what Father had taught me so long ago. I couldn't remember his words, only the feeling, which is always stronger than what is said.

Otherwise I share Anna's opinion that anyone who understands a lot has to endure too much. That's true. What separates us is the actual basic attitude. I think life has to hurt. Anna believes it's to be enjoyed. It's difficult to think about this, because I know who taught her to expect a lot and only the best.

Lisa was an understanding person who had to endure far more than was reasonable. Her father had been an alcoholic and had treated his wife and children very badly. Two brothers had died, one had escaped to America, and Lisa had run away to Göteborg when she was only twelve.

She preferred not to talk about how she made a living, but I realized from the little she told me that she'd begged her way and slept in entrance porches until she got work in the spinning factory, where she ruined her lungs in the dust. It was awful to hear her coughing in the long wet autumns. Ragnar couldn't stand it, and whenever her cough started up, he would slip out through the door and go downtown. I knew what was tormenting him, but it made Lisa even more miserable.

When her mother died out in the country somewhere, her father took his own life. Lisa inherited the whole farm as there were no brothers and sisters to be found. That was when it turned out that she had a good business head. She sold the stock at auction, the fields to the neighboring farmer, the forest to a company, and the house to a merchant wanting a summer place on the Halland coast.

Then she used the money to buy her haberdashery, which was situated on the boundary between working-class Haga and the gentry of Vasastan. She was certainly a free and independent person until the day she met Ragnar and fell hopelessly in love with him.

Was she happy before that? I don't know.

But she did seem happy when she married and became a respectable wife. She said the fact that Ragnar went to the priest with her was due to Hanna Broman, and she would be grateful for that for the rest of her life. I remember wondering what Mother had said to Ragnar. I had never ever seen him take anything she said seriously. He just laughed at her.

I didn't laugh at my mother. I hated her, scolded her, and was ashamed of her.

In the middle of the war when food was at its shortest, my breasts started growing and I had my period. Mother said that now all that wretched business was starting and the shame would afflict me at any moment. I remember quite clearly, because she'd turned as white as a sheet and her eyes looked terrified as she taught me how to fasten the towel.

"Promise me you'll be careful," she said. "And look out for yourself."

I tried to ask her what I had to look out for, but she just snorted, flushed, and said nothing.

As so often when things were difficult, I went to Lisa. But she didn't help me this time. She just looked peculiar, and her voice was odd when she said she had to speak to Ragnar. Then I realized it wasn't just all that horrid blood running out of me. It was something much worse.

The next day Ragnar said rather abruptly and in an embarrassed voice that I must watch out for men. That was all I was told. The rest I put together on my own. I thought about those awful words I'd heard from my brothers, about pricks and cunts. And I got some help from a childhood memory. I remembered when Erik and I were struggling through the forest with one of Mother's cows that was to go to the bull on Grandfather's farm. When we at last got there, we were given cakes and fruit juice by an aunt.

As I watched the bull mounting the cow, I felt sorry for her.

I knew how it was done all right.

Lisa had her first child in the summer, and I had to learn how to mind the shop in all seriousness. It went well. I calculated and measured, cut cloth and talked to customers. Lisa said I was amazingly clever for one so young. She brought the baby in at dinnertime, added up the till, and was delighted.

"Goodness! If only I could afford to pay you more."

The grand ladies from Vasastan said I had good taste. That wasn't true. I laughed in secret at them, for they didn't realize I was only agreeing with them when they said the yellow ribbons suited them best and that blue suited Mrs. Holm.

I soon learned a lot, more about people than materials and ribbons, but most of all, I learned the art of serving in a shop.

Mother was glad of the money I earned. But she didn't like my being alone in the shop.

"As soon as you leaves school, you'll have to go into service," she said. "So I knows where I has you. We'll find you a nice family all right."

"Never!" I shouted at her.

I went on saying no all through my last year at school, but it was no use. Mother was as stubborn as a mule. Lisa tried in vain to persuade her. Not even Ragnar could make her change her mind. Even Erik tried.

"You're stupid, Mom. The girl's much too clever to be a servant."

"She ain't no cleverer than no one else."

I was sent to a family in Viktoriagatan. The master was specially grand, a doctor, and he wrote in the newspapers. Now, afterward, I realize that it was there I became a Social Democrat. They were so colossally superior to me, just like that, as if that was quite self-evident. They simply didn't see me. I didn't exist. They farted, talked over my head, smelled of filth, had disgusting stains on their sheets and peculiar rubber things in bed.

At first I thought they had no shame at all. Then I found out what a fuss they made when they had company coming, and I understood. I was no one. I was like the dog.

They used me like a beast of burden from six in the morning when their children woke up, to late at night when I had to serve at table. They sent my miserable wages to my mother. I had one free afternoon a fortnight. I went to Lisa then, not home. I was there for two years, and no one could ever have been lonelier.

Then there came the night when the doctor was in the dining room, writing an article and drinking cognac. I suddenly heard him staggering through the kitchen to the cubbyhole called the maid's room. He fumbled at the door, and I just managed to get out of bed as he headed straight for me. I kicked him in the crotch. He yelled. The lady of the house came rushing in. While she was shouting and scolding, I grabbed my coat and rushed down the stairs. I pounded my way into Ragnar and Lisa's place, and I don't think I've ever seen him so angry as when he rushed off to Viktoriagatan in the middle of the night.

What he said to them, whether he threatened them with the police or his own fists, I never knew. But he must have frightened them, because when he came back, he had all of fifty kronor for me.

"Hide it away from your mom," he said.

Nor did I ever find out what he said to Mom the next morning. But she fell ill and spent three days in bed with a high temperature. When she finally got up to go to the bakery, because she couldn't call in sick for more than three days, she tried to say something to me. But she couldn't get the words out and I didn't care. I knew I had won.

"You're as thin as a rail," she said when she got back that afternoon.

"Don't go thinking I ever got anything inside me," I said. "Nothing but leftover scraps after they'd eaten. And there wasn't much left over, either."

"There's a shortage of food with the gentry, too," she said.

She made me a sandwich. I threw it straight in her face and went off to Lisa, where I ate my fill. They had plenty of food despite the war. It was whispered that Ragnar did business on the black market, but I didn't know what that meant, and anyhow didn't care. I ate like a maniac and when I wasn't eating, Lisa sent me off on long walks with the children.

They were good children, quiet and affectionate. With them, I discovered Slottsskogen, the large park in Göteborg, which made me feel at home, but was grander, of course, with its grassy slopes and gentle mounds, and amazing trees I didn't recognize. And all those flowers!

In the evenings when I was alone in my sofa bed in Lisa's kitchen, I kept thinking about what had happened that night when the doctor was drunk. At first, I thought most about how frightened I'd been. I really enjoyed the idea that I was a brave person. It took some time for me to realize that I hadn't the wits to be afraid.

That was when I started thinking about the thing I had, the one that ran with blood once a month.

I started investigating it. There was nothing odd about it. It was just a mouth that widened when you stuck a finger up it. What was peculiar was that I liked it so much, got so excited by doing that. Once I'd started, it was hard to stop. I did it every night before I fell asleep.

For six months, I helped Lisa with the children and the shop. Then I got a job with Nisse Nilsson, who had a delicatessen in Saluhallen, the great indoor market hall. He was a friend of Ragnar's. They did business together and went hunting together in the autumn. He was a kind, cheerful man, especially in the afternoons when his bottle of spirits was half empty.

"I need someone I can rely on then," he said.

But he never drank more than he could hold. A bottle lasted for two days.

It was 1918 by then. The bread lines grew shorter, and hunger slowly loosened its grip on the city. But then people started dying of the Spanish flu, which was really just ordinary flu. So they really died of malnutrition—the children in the apartment below, the old woman across the hallway from Lisa, and lots of others.

Spring eventually arrived and we thought that would put an end to the Spanish flu. But the summer seemed to give it new strength, and more and more people died in the wretched basements of Haga. I was always frightened and kept a watchful eye on Lisa's children, and on Mother, who was getting more and more exhausted every day.

But my worries faded away when I went to my new job at eight every morning, walking along the canal and across the bridge into the town center where the market square and Saluhallen were. For the first time, I noticed the city was beautiful, with its glittering waterways and tall trees bowing over the wharfs. And I felt at home there. I was one of many plodding along on my way to work.

We called good morning to each other in Saluhallen as we took down the shutters and put the delicacies of the day on our counters. Greta, who had a cheese booth, was nearly always the first to be ready, calling out that it was time for a coffee.

We drank it standing, munching on hard crispbread with cheese on top, and would just have time to swallow the last gulp of coffee before the great doors were opened and people started pouring in, wanting fresh bread for breakfast, newly churned butter, and sometimes small cakes. I didn't have much to do for the first few hours, but later on in the morning people began thinking about the delicatessen, and by the afternoon there was a line.

I learned a lot—how to cut smoked salmon into paper-thin slices, how to distinguish between the many kinds of marinated herring, how to make delicious sauces, how to know just when the crabs were ready, how to boil shrimp, and how to keep lobsters alive—as well as lots of other useful things such as weighing and calculating. And I got rid of my shyness and learned to talk. To give as good as I got, as Nisse Nilsson said.

"That's the most important of all, Johanna. And don't you forget it."

Nisse was down at the harbor and the smokery in the mornings, and in the afternoon—well, that's what he was like. In the end I did almost everything, the till and the accounts, the invoices and dealings with the bank.

"Christ, what a girl," he said when Ragnar looked in occasionally.

I grew up.

But best of all I had friends, some of them friends for life. Greta at the cheese booth, Aina at the pork butcher's, and Lotta at the confectioner's.

And Stig, of course, the butcher's son. Everyone said he was in love with me, but I pretended to ignore that and in that way we were able to remain friends.

It was there in Saluhallen that I found out I was pretty. "The beauty of the market," Nisse said, though he was always exaggerating. But everywhere I went in the hall the boys whistled at me, however little that meant. As a standing joke they also sang, "Can you whistle, Johanna," that old song.

I'd learned to whistle like that back at the farm, two fingers in my mouth and then a shrill whistle that frightened the cats up into the trees.

I whistled like that in Saluhallen every time I heard that silly song. The boys appreciated it, but Nisse didn't like it.

"Stop that now," he said. "You'll spoil your lovely mouth."

One day quite early on, I caught sight of the doctor from Viktoriagatan. He was heading straight for my counter. My mouth turned dry and my heart started thumping, but the thought of Nisse sitting in the cubbyhole behind me calmed me down.

Anyhow, I needn't have worried. The doctor didn't even recognize me. He wanted two lobsters, twenty thin slices of smoked salmon, a kilo of shrimp, and half a kilo of smoked Baltic herring.

I got them all ready for him and took his money. The total sum was to a krona double the wages he had paid me for a month's work.

He tried to haggle.

"Sorry, but we have fixed prices."

Nisse heard and came out and praised me. "That's as it should be," he said, friendly but firm. Then he said, "How pale you are, girl. Go and have a cup of coffee."

So I sat there in the café and tried to digest what seemed impossible. He hadn't even recognized me, the miserable wretch.

I said before that being in service had turned me into a Social Democrat. But I have a habit of making myself seem better than I am. It was the family in Viktoriagatan that taught me to hate the middle classes.

*I*t happened one stormy April day in 1920, just before the midday rush hour.

I was alone in the stall. The counter was messy because I had just cut up an eel for a customer. He told me there was a hurricane wind blowing outside and the canal had overflowed. After he'd gone, I needed to wipe the counter clean, but I found I didn't have any water left.

We had no running water in the stalls. But in the middle of the hall below the glass cupola was a circular yard with a well and a pump. I asked Greta at the cheese stall to keep an eye on mine for me while I went off with the bucket.

"Hurry on back," she said.

So I rushed. But just as I was about to open the heavy door to the glassed-in yard, I dropped the bucket, and it fell to the stone floor with a clatter. Annoyed, I tried to bend down to pick it up again. But I couldn't bend down.

Then I tried to lift my right hand to open the door. I couldn't do that, either, and I realized I was paralyzed. For a moment, I thought about polio. But I wasn't frightened. It was so quiet all around me. And inside me. Such peace, I could neither think nor feel any fear. It grew strangely light, too. It was somehow . . . solemn.

Several minutes passed and only briefly did it occur to me that I was in a hurry.

Then all at once, the glass cupola gave way in the storm and fell in with a crash that would have woken the dead. The door flew open, struck my head, and hurled me right across the passage into the wall. Splinters of glass flew all over the place and one stuck in my arm, but I covered my eyes with both hands, so my face wasn't affected. People came rushing from all around, crying out, thank heavens, Johanna's here. She'd gone out before . . . but she's bleeding. Telephone! Police! Ambulance!

A nice doctor at the hospital took the glass splinter out of my arm and stitched up the wound.

"Your guardian angel was there with you," he said.

Men from the police and the chief of the fire brigade came to see me. No, I had neither seen nor heard anything unusual.

"I was in such a hurry," I said.

They believed me.

The accident was much talked about, as the crash had been heard all over the city. It was in the newspaper, too, about the crash and me: "The girl with the guardian angel." They teased me at work.

"How's things with your angels today?"

One day it was all too much and I burst into tears. Stig comforted me and wiped my nose, then there was no more about guardian angels.

But Mother read about it in the paper, and she said something strange.

"I hopes you knows it's true."

I didn't answer, but for the first time in many years we looked at each other in agreement. Then she smiled slightly before speaking.

"Were it your father, Johanna?"

"I don't know, Mother."

That was true. I didn't know. I don't know to this day. I didn't want an explanation. Neither then, nor later.

All I knew was a miracle had occurred, and after that I could remember Father and the forests, the roar of the falls, the diver calling at dusk, the stories he told me, the songs we sang. I hadn't dared do that before. Now the images came pouring over me, at first in dreams at night and then in broad daylight. I seemed to have opened a floodgate.

I dreamed we were flying, Father and I, sailing in the upper currents by Wolf Mountain. Night had fallen by the time we got to the peak and sat down to rest. He pointed at the stars and said they were distant alien worlds. When I asked who lived there, he said the houses of the stars were empty and deserted.

We flew over lakes, too, the long lake and the Norwegian lakes and all the thousands of ponds in the forest.

These dreams of flying filled me with an indescribable joy, a feeling of victory. Of power, yes, sheer power.

It was different in the daytime. It all came back to me. Everything, but everything kept reminding me. A bird sang on my way home through the Avenue and I stopped to listen. I knew. It's a chaffinch. I called in on Ernst at his stall and suddenly smelled flour from a barrel and saw the rays of sunlight dancing in the flour dust of the mill back at home. One Sunday, Greta and I walked up to Delsjön Lake, sat down on the promontory where the forest was reflected in the deep lake. On the shore were willows and birches with their perianths and catkins. Then I saw the maples back home, their pale green flowers falling into the Norwegian lakes.

"Can you smell honey?"

No, Greta didn't know that scent.

It was almost as strange with Mother. I'd thought I was free of her. Now she came back with all the power a mother can have. Despite everything, she was the only one who had always been there.

I had long conversations with her, silent conversations, but they were real to me. We were sitting at the dinner table on May Day, after I'd joined the procession, heard the campaign songs and the rattle of the red flags in the wind.

"What's wrong with poor people claiming their rights?" I asked her.

"Things'll go wrong for folk what's no longer humble," she said. "Who's going to do what has to be done if the poor doesn't? Surely you doesn't believe the rich and powerful is going to clean up their own filth?"

"Mother, you must understand that times are different now."

"I has understood. People hate."

"There's something in that, Mother. The hatred is at last beginning to mature and will soon bear fruit."

"And what do that taste like?"

"I think it'll be harsh, like sloes, Mother, which you've always said were so good for us."

"No one can live on sloes."

"No, but honest wages and safe jobs. There's something new, Mother, something you've never thought about."

"And what would that be?"

"Justice, Mother."

"There ain't no justice in this world. God rules just as He's always done."

"Suppose God doesn't exist, that wicked God you believe in. Suppose it's we ourselves who rule?"

"You doesn't know what you're talking about, girl. Some folks is blind, sick, and lame. Innocent children dies. Lots has their life ruined long before they has time to think."

"More would be alive and healthy if people had better food and housing."

"True. But new masters always appear."

"No. We're going to have a world in which people are their own masters. I've just heard the speaker say that."

She shook her head.

"Like Larsson in number three, then," she said. "He's rich, with his workshop, and he don't have to bow to nobody. But he beats the life out of his kids and drinks like a fish. People doesn't get no better from having things better. What about that rich family you worked for? They wasn't no better than the worst of 'em when I were a child."

I thought about that conversation for a long time. Mother's misfortune was not that she was stupid. It was that she hadn't the words.

Then Ragnar had his fortieth birthday. We planned a party with a long table under the big tree in the courtyard. The weather was fine, Lisa baked cakes and buns, and Mother made little cakes. Nisse Nilsson filled a big box with herring and salmon and pâté and all kinds of delicacies.

"Birthday present for your brother," he said. "But tell him he'll have to stand for the beer and spirits himself."

A lot of people were coming, for Ragnar had friends all over town.

We women were proud when the table was ready. It looked beautiful with all the flowers and birch twigs and broad green ribbons. No one minded that the tablecloths were sheets and the plates were of various kinds borrowed from the neighbors.

When Mother and I went back up to the apartment to put on our best clothes, the accordion players came and we could hear them practicing the "Emperor Waltz": "A quadrille into the room does reel, rejoicing with its merry peal."

Mother snorted. Then she took out her old long black woollen dress.

"Can't you put on something a bit more modern? The green one . . ."

But I knew she was implacable. She wanted to look respectable—old and dignified.

The party was a success. People sang and ate, and as the bottles emptied, they grew more and more boisterous. Mother looked worried, but calmed down when Lisa whispered that Ragnar was sober and would make sure there was no fighting or anything unpleasant. Mother left early, saying quietly that she was tired and her back ached. I went up with her, helped her into bed, and covered her with a blanket.

That annoyed her. She could never accept help or friendliness.

"The dancing's starting in the yard now. Go on down and enjoys yourself."

I did a turn with Nisse Nilsson. But I didn't enjoy it at all. I was thinking about Mother the whole time and was angry as well as miserable. Why couldn't she be happy like other people, like all the women sitting there in the evening sun, gossiping and laughing? Many of them were much older than she was. She was only fifty-three.

She was fifty-three!

Something incomprehensible was trying to come out, breaking through my head.

No.

Yes. She was fifty-three and her son was having his fortieth birthday.

She'd given birth at thirteen.

I counted nine months back and came to October.

When she was only twelve.

A child!

It wasn't possible. Perhaps he was a foster son.

No, they're alike.

I had always known Ragnar had a different father from my brothers and me. Who? They said Mother had been in love with a cousin when she was young, but that couldn't be possible, either. A twelve-year-old doesn't fall so madly in love that she goes to bed with a man. Someone had said she had grieved almost to death when the cousin had been accidentally shot while hunting. Who? I must ask Lisa. But what would she know?

I left early, too, telling Lisa I must go up to Mother.

"Is she unwell?"

"I don't know. I'm worried."

I ran up the stairs, knowing I must ask.

"Are you asleep, Mother?"

"No, just resting a bit."

"I've just figured out you were twelve when you got pregnant and hardly thirteen when you gave birth."

She sat up, and despite the gathering dusk, I could see she was scarlet in the face.

In the end she said, "You've always been a clever one. Strange you didn't work it out afore."

"Yes, it is. But someone had told me you were in love with Ragnar's father and you were terribly miserable when he died. So I didn't want to think about it, or ask you."

She started to laugh, a terrible laugh, as if she'd gone out of her mind. When she saw she was frightening me, she clapped her hand over her mouth and fell silent.

Then she said, "Ragnar's father were a rapist and a rogue. When they shot him, it were the best thing to happen in my life. I were always afraid of him. Though there wasn't no need to be, for when I married Broman, he had church papers for the boy."

"How long were you on your own with Ragnar, before you met Father?"

"Four years it were, as a whore and in disgrace."

I didn't dare look at her while we undressed and made up the beds. But I crept down beside her on the kitchen sofa and cried myself to sleep, the accordions playing and the dancing going on around trees and table, privy and shed, down there in the courtyard.

*H*ow I danced that summer when the city was three hundred years old and presented Liseberg to itself. Nowadays people think of it only as an amusement park with carousels and a roller coaster. Though most have to admit it's lovely.

To us living there when it was built, it was like a fairy tale come true, buildings as beautiful as temples in the park, ponds and a water lily pool, streams singing down the slopes, orchestras playing, theater and ballet in the colonnades, and a thousand, no, tens of thousands of flowers.

I wore out three pairs of shoes in a few weeks, and I remember the first half of the 1920s as the best in my life.

Though it wasn't just Liseberg.

We were given an eight-hour workday. That was important to Mother, for her bad back got better. Then we were given holidays, and Aina and Greta and I took the train to Karlstad. From there, we went walking up Fryksdal to Sunne and Mårbacka. The journey alone was an adventure, especially for the people in the villages along the lake. Three young women in long trousers, my goodness, walking on their own, yes, that really was astonishing at the time.

I now realize I've forgotten something important: Selma Lagerlöf. Aina had read about her books in the newspaper and had borrowed one, *The Löwensköld Ring*, from the library. All three of us read it, wearing it out just as we'd worn out our shoes over that jubilee summer. What an impression she made!

Perhaps most of all on me, who recognized it all. There it was, the enchantment of childhood. I read and reread, and again felt the depths of the world. Here was someone telling me that nothing was what it appeared to be, that everything had a hidden meaning. I put away some of my wages every week and bought her books by paying in installments at the bookshop. Handsome half-bound editions. How proud I was as I accumulated them on my little bookshelf.

I don't remember much about Mårbacka, Selma Lagerlöf's hometown, and I think that's because it was a disappointment. Her stories of Gösta Berling and Charlotte Löwensköld, Nils of Skrålycka and the girl from Stormyrtorpet had woven a spell over me. Perhaps I'd imagined the whole place would glow, that there would be a shimmer over all the grounds, that Lagerlöf's characters would be glimpsed among the trees.

It was Selma Lagerlöf who taught me that love was a tremendous force, irresistible, more painful and more wonderful than I could ever have imagined. This length of time afterward, I still wonder what Lagerlöf did to those of us who were young and yearning, who were born under circumstances that scarcely had room for such grandiose emotions.

Anyhow, we all started dreaming about the prince—Aina, Greta, and I.

I mustn't blame just the books. When, one after another, we started aiming for "Mr. Right" and made marriage the goal of our efforts, there were several other driving forces—though we never saw the connection.

At the time, in the late 1920s, Göteborg was beginning to slow down. Money was tighter, two booths in Saluhallen went bankrupt, and men without jobs began to roam the streets.

The Great Depression had begun, but at first we knew neither the name nor what it would mean.

The newspapers said that women were taking the men's jobs. New laws were demanded, prohibiting married women from having jobs. All over town, girls were dismissed and owners themselves ran the shops. I had considered it obvious that I would always earn my own living, so I began to get more and more worried.

It's almost impossible to explain to young women today how the longing for love became interwoven with fear, and eventually led to a desperate hunt. To us, it was a matter of life and death. We were back where Mother had once been, but with the difference that the peasant girl, in the search for a man who could keep her, had the support of her family.

If anyone was receptive to great love, then I was when I met Arne. He was a foreman at one of the large shipyards, and surely the crisis would never reach them. But then I was ashamed of the thought, and later, when Mother said that he was a decent man and would always be able to support a family, I was angry.

"I'd marry him even if he was a street sweeper."

I've said before that I have an unfortunate habit of making myself seem better than I am. Beautifying. The simple truth was that I felt I simply had to be in love, now that Nisse Nilsson sold scarcely enough salmon to cover my wages. Then Greta's cheese stall went bankrupt, and she had to go into service.

But I was in love. Something happened to my body the first time I saw Arne Karlberg. My hands grew sweaty, my heart thumped, and I had a tickling feeling down below. For the first time, I realized there could be a hunger in that place I had, and a hot longing in my blood.

It was at a meeting of the local Social Democratic party. Man after man got up and said the usual things about injustices and that despite the wretched times, we must stand firm with our demands. Toward the end a strapping great fellow went up and said that females were not only taking work from the men, but they also contributed to keeping wages low by doing the same jobs as men, but not having the wits to ask for the same pay.

I was so angry, I forgot to be shy and asked to speak. I asked what they thought all the wives of drunken husbands, all the unmarried women, all the widows and other lone mothers were supposed to do to have a roof over their heads for themselves and their children.

There was a muttering in the audience.

But then Arne went up to the lectern and said that he agreed with the previous speaker, and that the trade unions ought to put all their energies into aligning themselves with the women and making sure they got the same working conditions.

"Equal pay for equal work," he said, and that was the first time I'd ever heard those words.

There was a lot of derisive whistling in the hall.

But I looked at him and all those physical things happened, those I've just described. He was handsome. Tall and fair, his face both sensitive and forceful, with blue eyes and a pugnacious chin.

At last!

After the meeting, he came over to me and asked if I'd like a cup of coffee. We went to a café in Södra Allégatan, but realized that we weren't all that keen on coffee after all. So we walked on past the café, through the Avenue and along the canals. We walked for half the night, taking in the wharfs as well as West and North and East Hamngatan. In the end we sat down on the base of the statue of the hero king in Gustaf Adolfs Square, and Arne said the king was a robber and a miscreant who could well listen to an honest conversation between two modern people.

I laughed. Then I stared at him, remembering what Father had said about King Karl XII—that the bullet that had put an end to that hero was a blessing.

But the night grew colder, and he walked me home. In our entrance, he said he'd never in his life seen anything prettier than the girl who'd stood up at the meeting and been so sparklingly angry.

He had a sailboat he had built himself. On Friday, just as we were shutting up the booth, he appeared in the market hall and asked me if I'd like to go sailing with him on Saturday. We could go north beyond the islands toward Marstrand and look at the fortress.

Then he said tentatively, "Takes a bit of time, a trip like that. So you'll have to plan on sleeping on the boat."

I nodded. I understood. I was prepared.

He had a few instructions, too, about warm clothes and cool

clothes. He would bring eggs and bread and butter and sausage. If I wanted anything else, perhaps I could arrange it.

At noon on Saturday I cleared the booth of all the delicacies left, for I'd noticed his hungry eyes as he'd stood by the counter looking at all the good things we sold.

What did I say to Mother? I've forgotten.

What I remember most of all that weekend is neither Arne nor making love in that cramped boat. No, it's the sea. And the boat.

It's strange. I'd lived in Göteborg for many years. I'd known the city smelled of sea and salt when the wind came from the west. But I'd never seen the sea. All my outings had been to the forests and the mountains inland, not to the coast. Of course I'd roamed around the harbor like everyone else, gazing at foreign ships and taking in the smell of spices and hemp and fruit. And like all Göteborgians, I'd stood on the wharf as the *Kungsholm*, which had just returned home from America, slipped in and moored.

But the Swedish cruise ship with its sloping funnels, so vast and handsome, did not belong in my world. That was for the rich.

Now I was in a boat dancing with full sails across infinity. Blue expanses to the end of the world, the murmur of the wind, the splash of waves, the glitter—so sparkling, it hurt your eyes.

"Borrow my cap," said Arne.

But I didn't want its visor shading my eyes. I wanted my eyes wide open to take in everything, the sea and the sky.

"Put a shirt over your shoulders, or you'll get burned," said Arne.

But neither did I want a shirt. I wanted to receive all that magnificence with my entire body. But Arne insisted when it came to the shirt, and I had to obey. I was grateful later that evening, for I could feel the skin on my face and neck burning.

"That's Böttö lighthouse to port," said Arne. "And right out there is Vinga. When we get there, we'll turn and tack north in the channel between Invinga and Vinga. The boat'll list then, but that's nothing to worry about."

I nodded, and when he tacked and the boat heeled over I screamed, not from fear, but from sheer exhilaration.

"D'you think it fun?"

Fun was not the word, and I laughed like a child.

"It's wonderful," I cried.

We sailed close to the wind beyond the islands, heading north along the coast, the sails singing, the sea roaring and hissing salt water over us.

"I can take in the sail if it frightens you."

I didn't know what he meant, but I laughed again and cried out that I wasn't scared.

"I'll head for Stora Pölsan into the lee below Klåver Island," he yelled. "There's a good harbor called Utkäften."

It all sounded as if he were reading poetry. The wind rose and Arne yelled again.

"We'll have to take down the foresail."

I drew a great question mark in the air, and he burst out laughing.

"You'll have to take the tiller while I go forward," he yelled.

I took the tiller, and he showed me the course. "Due west over there, you see." It took me only a couple of minutes to learn how to keep a straight course.

Once the foresail was down, the boat began to righten and we slowed down. A moment later, we slipped into the lee behind the island, and it was as calm as in the kingdom of heaven.

"You must take the tiller again while I take down the mainsail."

The mainsail fluttered and flapped before it came down on deck. Then it was as quiet as quiet, nothing but a gentle murmur as the boat glided through the water. A gull screamed, and after that the silence was even more intense. Arne flung the anchor into the sea with a huge splash, then ran forward and jumped ashore with a rope.

"This'll do fine," he said when he came back. "Why are you crying?"

"It's all so marvelous."

We stood on deck and kissed and hugged.

"God," he said. "You're the girl I've been waiting for all my life."

Then he showed me around the boat. Steps went down into the cabin, each step a big roomy drawer, in them a whole kitchen, glasses, porcelain, knives, cutlery, saucepans—everything. He had stowed the food under the floor of the cabin, in the keelson, he said. He showed me the paraffin stove and how to keep it out of the draft.

I cooked while he put the sails in order. It smelled divine, salt and seaweed and fried eggs and sausages. We ate as if we were starving.

"The sea gets you."

"What do you mean?"

"The sea makes you hungry."

I remember the island, flowers I'd never seen before, how warm the smooth rocks were to walk on, and the gulls diving down, screaming at us as if they'd gone mad.

"They've got eggs in their nests," said Arne. "We mustn't disturb them."

That's just what Father said whenever we got too close to Wolf Mountain in the spring.

So we returned to the boat and went on kissing, and now I could feel the air between us tingling as if it had become electric, and I felt the blood rushing through my veins.

After that, I remember that it hurt, and then it was all over. Disappointing in a way. Not overwhelming.

Mother and I were living on our own in the apartment now and could keep it clean and tidy. I had been given some leftover pelargoniums by the florist in the market hall, and Mother tended them so that our windows looked lovely. Even in the middle of the week, we used the embroidered tablecloths in the living room.

She was in a better mood these days, not just because we'd become closer and got on so well together, but mostly because things had gone better for my brothers. All three had work and were safely married.

She became quite talkative, and in the evenings we often sat talking about the old days, remembering together. I mostly remembered the forest and the lakes, the peregrine falcons over Wolf Mountain, and the birds singing in the evenings. Mother remembered people—the smith's wife and her evil eye, her husband who tempted Father into drinking, and old Anna, the midwife.

"Surely you remembers her. She lived with us when you was little," she said, and then I remembered the person who taught me everything about food and baking, herbs and medicines.

"She were a great person," Mother said. "And kind, too."

She was an angel, I thought. Whatever had made me forget her?

"You has her cleverness to thank for your life," Mother said, and then I had to hear about that terrible birth "of the babe that didn't wants to come into the world. She hunged on till Anna had to cut me."

I was horrified and didn't dare think about the Saturday on Arne's boat.

We talked a lot about Father and his stories.

"Do you remember the story about Death and the candle he had in his cave for every person?"

"Oh, yes. That were Johannes."

She told me about the healer, about Grandmother's death, and Johannes's prediction about Father.

"Turned out to be right in time."

She talked about Ingegerd, the aunt who'd never married and was a free and independent person although she was a woman. In the middle of that story, she stopped and then said something very strange.

"She had a life that were her own. 'Tis why she could always be true and honest."

I said nothing for a long time. Then I told her about Arne.

She flushed as always when agitated.

"Can he keeps you and the children?"

"Yes."

She thought for a long time, then said, "Do you likes him?"

"I think so."

"It ain't so important at first. If he's a good man, you'll gets fond of him with the years."

This was as far from Selma Lagerlöf as anyone could get, but I didn't laugh, only hoped she was right.

Then the Saturday when Arne was to visit us arrived. I had told him about Dalsland and Father by then, about my brothers who'd had such a bad time at first in the city, and about Ragnar who'd been a father to us.

"He's marvelous and a bit mad but now he's got three vehicles, and as always, things are going well for him."

Arne looked rather dubious at the mention of Ragnar, but when I told him about Mother, that she was kind but let her tongue run away with her like a child, he brightened.

"I like people like that," he said. "They don't lie."

Gracious, I thought. It was true and I'd never thought of it before. Although we were walking along the street, I stopped and gave him a hug. People laughed and Arne was embarrassed.

At home everything was the best, from the most expensive cups on the very best cloth to coffee with seven different kinds of fancy biscuits. Mother was wearing her black dress, her jet necklace, a cross at her throat, and a dazzling white apron.

"We have an apartment just like this, only the other way around, if you understand," said Arne.

Then he noticed the Värmland sofa.

"What a beauty. Such fine craftsmanship."

He ran his hand over the joints and corners, saying no one did that kind of carpentry these days, or such marquetry either.

Neither Mother nor I knew what marquetry was. I was surprised, but Mother almost fainted with delight.

"I'll has you know, Arne, they've all mocked me over the years on account of that there sofa."

Everything went smoothly that afternoon. Arne told us about his job at the Göta works and that he was responsible for the carpentry workshop where they made the interior equipment for the big ships.

Interior equipment, new words for both Mother and me.

"Do you mean the furniture?"

"Yes, but not ordinary furniture. Most of it's built in. Like on my little boat. But better quality, mahogany and walnut, that kind."

"Oh, so grand," said Mother.

Toward the afternoon Ragnar dropped by, and the two men looked each other up and down as if measuring each other's strength before a fight. But they shook hands like decent folk, and in the middle of it all Ragnar started laughing. I've probably not mentioned it before, but somehow no one can ever resist his laughter. It shakes the whole room, the cups, too, and goes right to the heart, making everyone else laugh, as well. At first Arne looked surprised, but then he laughed, and so they laughed together so much the petals started falling off the pelargoniums.

"Can't think what's that funny," said Mother. "But I'll brew some fresh coffee."

Then surprisingly, Arne said, "Maybe only a man can understand what's funny."

I caught a glint of approval in Ragnar's eyes before the laughter started up again and rolled around the apartment. Then the two men started talking about motor vehicles, Ragnar showing off, though it was soon clear Arne knew quite a bit about engines, as well. After a while, they started on boats, and Ragnar gave up.

"I know nothing about them. Landlubber, that's me."

"Come on out for a spin some time."

So it was decided we would go sailing the next day if wind and weather were right. But Mother didn't want to.

"Deadly afeared of the sea, I am."

I had my period the next morning, so I didn't go with them either. But when the men got back in the evening, I could see they'd had a good time. I was pleased, almost as pleased as I was about that blessed period.

Two things of importance were said that evening. First Ragnar said I'd always been a clever girl so of course I'd managed to get hold of a decent man.

Arne was glowing with pride after Ragnar left.

But when Mother heard that Arne still lived at home although he was the eldest of the brothers, she said, "So you's one of them chicks afeared to leave the nest, eh?"

He turned scarlet first, then white. I didn't know at the time that he changed color like that when he was angry. But he was also too embarrassed to shout and bang his fist on the table. So he said nothing.

Many years later, he told me that it was Mother's words that evening that made him decide. For he did in the end. But not until I was pregnant. By then I had met his mother and begun to understand a thing or two.

She was seated in the middle of the sofa, alone, a small person demanding a great deal of space.

She was beautiful, too, rather like the Chinese ivory statuettes sold in grand shops in the Avenue. She had a straight back, long neck, finely drawn features, blue eyes—like her son. But she was colder than him, much colder. I gave a little dip and held out my hand. She didn't take it.

I regretted the curtsy.

Another woman was there, younger and friendlier.

"This is Lotten. She's married to my brother," said Arne.

"Gustav's coming soon," she said. "He had something he had to do."

I liked her at once, and she held my hand firmly for a long time, as if encouraging me.

It was quite a while before I noticed his father, a large man taking up no space at all. He was sitting in a corner behind the kitchen door, reading a newspaper. There was something timid about him, and he didn't look at me as we shook hands. I could see he was afraid.

"So this is Johanna who wants to marry my boy. I suppose you're pregnant," said the Ice Queen.

"No, not as far as I know," I said. "Anyhow, Arne's the one who wants to get married."

The ivory yellow face flushed with anger, then turned white. Like her son's.

"Mother." Arne's voice had appeal in it.

She offered me nothing, not even the simplest cup of coffee. They were all silent. It was ghostly. I looked around. The apartment was older and shabbier than ours, with dark brown wallpaper, and walls covered with photographs and glossy religious prints. The moment I'd stepped over the threshold, I realized it smelled in there, that the people who lived there peed in the kitchen sink. Then Arne's brother came bouncing in and gave me a great hug.

"Lord, what a grand girl you've got hold of," he said to his brother, then turned to me. "Don't let Mother scare you. She's not as fierce as she looks."

The ivory lady clutched at her heart.

Lotten said, "Let's go now. Gustav and Arne are going to try out the new sail."

All four of us ran down the stairs. No one said good-bye, except me, and I shook the old man's hand.

We didn't go to the boat, but instead to Gustav and Lotten's home. They had a fine two-room apartment where the coffee was already on the table. There was even a cream cake to welcome me.

"You weren't scared, were you, girl?" said Gustav.

"A little. But surprised more than anything else."

"So Arne hadn't told you?" Lotten asked, and there was ice in her voice.

"What the hell should I have said?" said Arne. "You can't describe what Mom's like."

"Yes, you can," said Lotten, her voice frosty. "She's selfish and a megalomaniac."

For the second time I saw him turn first red then white. He crashed his clenched fist down on the table and shouted.

"She has only one failing; she's too fond of her children."

"Calm down, now," cried Lotten. "You have to behave in our house."

Gustav tried to mediate.

"It's not easy, Lotten. She was a kind mom until her heart started acting up."

"And that happened conveniently just when her sons started acquiring wives."

"We're leaving, Johanna," said Arne furiously.

"Not me," I said. "I'm not going to be the one to cause trouble between you. You must admit it wasn't nice of her, refusing to shake hands and not even offering us coffee. I've never been received like that before."

I realized then how miserable I was. I swallowed the lump in my throat, but could do nothing about the tears.

Gustav and Lotten comforted me. Arne looked desperate.

"Can't you try to explain without quarreling?"

They couldn't, so it turned quite silent.

"I'm sorry for your father," I said. "So shaming for him. Why didn't he say anything?"

"He got out of the habit of talking years ago," said Gustav. "It's awful."

"But he could stand up to her," said Arne loudly. "Why the hell's he so cowardly, just creeping around saying nothing?"

"He's frightened of her," said Lotten. "So are you. And Gustav."

"I'm damned well not frightened of her."

"Show it then. Don't go home until she's apologized. And marry Johanna."

"I don't know whether I want to any longer," I said, getting up. After thanking them for coffee, I left. As I went out the door I heard Lotten berating Arne, telling him he was letting his mother destroy his life. He ran after me down the stairs, but I turned around and said I wanted to be alone, that I needed to think.

But that didn't go well. My thoughts were whirling around confused in my head.

When I look back at what I've written about that first strange meeting with Arne's mother, I wonder whether I'm telling an untruth. I can't remember word for word what was said. Memory selects and distorts, so perhaps I'm being untruthful without meaning to. What happened was that I detested my mother-in-law as long she lived. Over the years, I came to hate those sides of Arne that reminded me of her, his insistence on always being in the center, on always getting his own way, his rage and fearful short temper.

When I got home to Mother, I told her I'd never met such a difficult person as my future mother-in-law. I cried as I told her about it.

"Is she religious, too?" she said.

"I think so. There were crosses and pictures of Jesus on the walls."

"Lordie me, it's bad," said Mother. "They's the ones what begrudge you your good name."

Arne was waiting for me after work on Monday evening.

"I've left home," he said.

"Where are you living?"

"On the boat. It's fine as long as the summer lasts."

"What did you say to her?"

"Nothing. I just went home and packed my things. She'll have to give in now."

Of course, I was pleased. And yet?

"I need more time to think," I said, and left him.

*B*ut there was no time and I had no choice. Three weeks later, I was clearly pregnant. We exchanged rings, assuring each other that we belonged together, and I convinced myself he was kind and safe.

"You doesn't have to marry," said Mother. "We can manage, you and me."

That was magnificent.

I had to tell her, though, how bad things were for Nisse Nilsson's shop, that we hardly sold more than we bought.

That night I found it hard to sleep. I lay there twisting and turning, trying to get my pictures of Arne to fit together. The young man who'd bravely stood up at the meeting and been mocked for agreeing with justice for women. The sailor who was so bold at sea. The politically clear-sighted, intelligent, and knowledgeable man. The foreman in the carpentry workshop. And then this feeble creature sneaking away from his mother.

I can't deny I thought a bit about Stig, as well, the butcher's son in love with me, a man who would inherit the shop. With him I could keep my job, all my friends, and all my self-confidence. He was a nice person. Considerate. And both his parents liked me.

But he couldn't make my body tingle.

We were going to be married in Copenhagen, to sail there. But first there would be a betrothal party back at home with Mother. She took out her savings and equipped me as if I were gentry, with sheets, pillowcases, handwoven towels, the finest lace for curtains, and two damask tablecloths.

There was a shortage of apartments, but we were relying on Ragnar. He would fix that for us, with all his connections with builders in the city.

Then came that awful Monday. I was three months along, but had peculiar period pains when I went to work in the morning. At Nisse Nilsson's, I collapsed and started bleeding heavily. Aina took me in a taxi to a private maternity clinic where they anesthetized me. When I woke, I was achingly empty inside.

Mother came in the afternoon. She was pale and went on and on about fate. Ragnar and Lisa sent flowers. I was sleepy and sick. I was also homesick, a strange longing for an unknown place I could call home.

They woke me with strong coffee and a sandwich. My head cleared. There were quite a few thoughts in my head and plenty of time to brood on them.

When Arne appeared, I would tell him that he should go back to his mother. Calmly, not angrily or unpleasantly, I would say that would be best for us both. He would have a clear conscience and wouldn't have to be torn between his mother and me. I would be free and feel good about it, because I was a very independent person.

But when he came, he took both my hands in his, and his eyes were moist, his voice wavering.

"Dear girl," he said. "Dear girl."

That was all. It was enough. I knew at once he was a person to be trusted. And I wasn't wrong in my judgment. When things were difficult, when danger or illness arose, or fear threatened, he was the kind of man who became adult, strong and safe as Father had once been.

"It was a little boy," Arne said, and then I saw he was crying, too.

Before they pushed him out, he tried to say that it was an accident and we'd soon have another child. That gave me hope and when I fell asleep that night, I pressed my hands to the aching vacuum down below and whispered, "Come back."

Since then, I've often thought that moment at the clinic sealed my fate. The question of just who Arne was came up again many times over the years. I gradually also learned to ask myself who I was. And what had he meant to me and I to him? What had we had between us apart from our yearning? He was like me, after all, far away from home.

Now that I am old, I realize for the first time that yearning isn't a bad basis for fellowship. It can be both more secure and greater than the reality I desired so ardently when I was young. I don't believe in any reality now, and it is by chasing after it that we kill everything.

Mother gave the betrothal party one sunny summer Sunday, directly after morning service. Arne's mother sat alone on the Värmland sofa, and at last it came into its own right. They suited each other, the ivory lady and the uncomfortable but elegant piece of furniture. She didn't say much but she observed everything very closely. She hadn't brought a wedding present with her, and I don't think it pained her to spend a long time critically examining all Mother's fine linen. Dear kind Lisa devoted herself to Arne's father. They talked about farming, his eyes brightening and a ring coming into his voice.

He had something to say on that, indeed he had.

Then Gustav and Lotten came, bringing with them a coffee service, and both Mother and I noticed that Lotten did not speak to her mother-in-law. Ragnar came last and that was the end of worrying about keeping the conversation going. He brought bubbly white wine with him, opened it with a pop, and proposed a toast to us.

"You've had better luck than you deserve," he said to Arne. "For Johanna isn't only the prettiest girl in town, she's also got the best mind and the kindest heart."

Arne looked proud, and his mother clutched at her heart. When Ragnar noticed, he burst out into his famous laughter. As it spread through the company, the old girl lost her certainty. Her gaze wandered, and the hand holding the glass trembled. For one brief moment, I felt sorry for her.

Ragnar also had a taxi firm, so he drove the old couple home while I helped Mother with the dishes. Arne kept hovering around us as if he wanted to say something. Then he finally got it out.

"She's a bit peculiar, my mother."

Hanna Broman was not a person ever to smooth things over, not this time either.

"To say the least of it. I'm sorry for your dad."

Then Ragnar was back wanting to talk about an idea he'd had. People were building their own houses out toward the sea, small houses around an old fishing village a few miles from town. One of the men had lost his job and gone bankrupt, and a lumberyard Ragnar worked for had taken over the house the man was building. The roof was on and only the indoor carpentry and painting needed to be done. The lumberyard man wanted to sell, quickly and cheaply.

The color rose in Arne's face as Ragnar talked, and his eyes gleamed.

"How much?"

"About twelve thousand, but we can haggle."

The eagerness in Arne's blue eyes faded, and he said, "I've only half that." Ragnar went on, though.

"That's all right. You can borrow the rest from the bank. It'll work out all right. You've got a steady job, and I'll stand as guarantor."

"But I promised Mother I'd never borrow."

"Oh, for Christ's sake," shouted Ragnar, and Arne realized he'd made a fool of himself.

"When can we look at the house?" he said.

"Now. I have a car outside. But maybe you ought to ask Johanna first."

"We can at least go and take a look," I said, but as we ran down the stairs I was dizzy with expectation and squeezed Arne's hand.

There was squelching mud, high hills, and low smooth granite rocks. There was goosefoot and couch grass and a half-finished house, low and long, three rooms and a kitchen, with space for a nursery on the upper floor. We liked it from the very first moment, and I remembered those strange dreams of coming home.

"There's a lot of work to do," said Ragnar.

"Who's afraid of work?" said Arne.

"I want a garden," I said.

"It's windswept here, so that won't be easy," said Arne. "I'll have to build you a wall so it's sheltered."

We took a ladder and climbed up to the floor above, and it was just as Arne had thought. We could see right out to sea, across the harbor where the fishing boats lay that Sunday.

Then we sat all evening in Mother's kitchen working out interest and the mortgage. It was going to be a tight squeeze, but we'd manage.

Nothing came of sailing to Copenhagen. We had a simple wedding at the priest's in Haga, and then we went to work on the house, me outside, Arne inside. That was when I found that Arne had plenty of friends and a surprising ability to organize, lead, and decide. He paid with spirits to go with all the good food I cooked. Sunday evenings were cheerful and not much got done. He himself seldom took a drink.

All around us, young people were working on their half-finished houses. I at once had acquaintances, newly married women with the same expectations as I had.

In October we moved in. We hadn't decorated and we had practically no furniture. But it was fun. And we had a kitchen stove and two fireplaces, so we didn't freeze.

*T*he bad times went on, and things got worse. At the ball-bearing factory where they once had almost five thousand employees, they now employed only three hundred. Others went hungry and froze. Cars were being made in an empty ball-bearing factory in Hisingen, cars called Volvo, and there were people who believed something would come of it.

Even the shipyards were threatened, Arne said. But so far they were getting by on repairs.

I was happy during all this. I had laid out a garden, and I'm not boasting when I say it was wonderful. No one had such glorious apples as I had, and nowhere, not even in the Gardening Society, were there such beautiful roses.

My garden had high mountains behind it, an open slope to the southwest, and a wall facing the sea. Here on the west coast it's amazing; if you have a sunny piece of land sheltered from the wind, your garden becomes almost as lovely as in the Mediterranean. You can grow grapes and peaches on trellises. Not to mention roses.

I never told Arne things were going badly for Nisse Nilsson at his delicatessen. There was no need to, for Arne took it for granted that I would stay at home and he would support the family.

That autumn, it also seemed natural to me, as I had so much to do. All the sewing for our new home, just to mention one thing. Lisa gave me an old treadle sewing machine. It was sluggish and kept jamming, and I swore and argued with the monstrosity. When Arne came home, he laughed at me, took it apart, and oiled it here and there, while I stood admiringly beside him. When he put it together again, it turned good and obedient, and over the years I've tromped a great many miles on it.

Our first bit of furniture was a huge secondhand workbench. For the basement! When Ragnar brought it home, I was angry— buying a workbench when we didn't even have a table to eat at! But I didn't say anything, and I soon understood. Arne disappeared into the basement every evening. Table and chairs, cupboards and shelving soon appeared in a steady stream up the basement stairs.

Fine furniture, oak, mahogany, and teak for the kitchen benches.

"Where do you get this fine lumber from?"

He turned scarlet and said angrily I shouldn't ask so many questions. As usual, I didn't understand why he was so angry.

Most of my time that autumn was taken up keeping an eye on the painter, Andersson. He was one of Arne's innumerable friends, and I had been given explicit instructions: a beer every other hour, no more, because then the wallpaper would be crooked. A cooked meal and a drink before he went home in the evening. No more, for then he wouldn't come back.

I kept Andersson going like that, and our home grew lighter as the evenings grew darker. We had green stripes in the bedroom and pale pink roses on a white background in the front room, where we put the new dark red mahogany furniture. We did the kitchen ourselves, because one Saturday Andersson disappeared with a crate of beer I thought I'd managed to hide in the pantry.

I reproached myself, but Arne laughed at the whole sorry tale.

Christmas came and we invited the family to dinner. Mother balked, for she found the new relatives difficult. But I went to Ragnar and said that if they didn't come, I'd kill him. So they all came, Mother, Lisa, Ragnar, and the children. And two of my other brothers with their wives. We invited Gustav and Lotten, as well, but they said they couldn't come.

The Ice Queen was quiet, not a single unpleasant remark crossing her lips.

"You see," whispered Arne to me. "She's softening."

I couldn't see it. But before we all sat down to dinner, something significant did happen. There was no snow, it was eight degrees above zero, and a soft wind was blowing from the sea as my father-in-law and I walked around outside and I told him about the garden I'd dreamed of having.

The old man was transformed. His voice rang, his step had a spring in it, and he said he would help me.

"It could be a paradise here," he said. "As long as we can fix a wall to the west . . . then the sun and the Gulf Stream will do the rest. A potato patch," he said. "Rutabagas, strawberries."

"Roses," I said.

When he laughed, he was like Arne.

"Rely on me."

After our guests had gone, I did the dishes and Arne took the Christmas food down to the pantry. Then I told him what the old man had said. At first Arne smiled broadly, but then his face clouded.

"It won't work. Mom won't let him."

"Shall we make a bet?" I said. "He'll come no matter what she says."

"You're an amazing person," said Arne, and I flushed with pleasure, but partly because I was not nearly as sure as I sounded. That evening we sat at the kitchen table for a long time, drawing sketches, one after another, of what the garden would be, me talking about roses and violas, Arne about potatoes and vegetables.

"We'll have to save every öre."

"I know, but I want roses along the wall and a big bed in front of the house. Phloxes, pinks, and mallows . . ."

One morning in early January, I told Arne we had to go into town to see his parents that evening.

"We'll take the garden plans with us so we can discuss them with your father."

Arne was scared and pleased at the same time. I could see that, but pretended I hadn't. At this stage, I'd realized he always felt guilty about neglecting his mother. As we arrived at the apartment door in the old building they lived in, she was clearly pleased, and it took her several seconds to stiffen her features.

"Oh, but come on in. I'll make some coffee."

We sat at the kitchen table, and I extracted Father-in-law out of his corner, saying, "Come on now, we have things to discuss."

It worked. Life came back to the old man. He had suggestions. He'd been thinking.

"Arctic pines here by the end of the wall," he said. "The wind doesn't only come from the west. Storms also come from the south, so the wall should be at an angle. You want roses, Johanna, so you'll need a south wall."

The Ice Queen was not the most surprised. Arne was.

And so pleased, so pleased. I took the next step.

"I'll try to get my brother to come, too, so you can come out and go back by car."

"I'll take the bus," said the old man.

"If you get too tired, you can stay overnight," said Arne.

My mother-in-law said nothing.

It was fun that spring when Father-in-law and I laid out the garden. We borrowed a horse and harrow from a farm, and the old man took to it as if he'd never done anything else. We turned the soil, got the potatoes in, and sowed vegetables. We dug flower beds, and I planted flowers. We dup deeper holes and planted apple trees and red and black currant bushes.

Once, when we were having a rest with coffee and a sandwich, he said, "I've got old peasant blood in my veins."

I felt that I had, too.

My father-in-law was not one for words, and yet he taught me such a lot. I learned how to distinguish between fresh and aged manure; how to crumble the soil in my fingers and feel if it needed sand or mulch; that the pretty wild pansies meant a lack of lime; and that I must never let the clay pack the soil solid.

It was knowledge of experience and could be passed on with few words.

But he had ideas, too.

"Roses are all right in summer," he said. "But I should put in a

forsythia by the wall up here by the window. With tulips and cro-
cuses underneath."

I nodded. I could see it in front of me. So we laid out a spring
corner between the wall and the kitchen window. It gladdened me
in March when the days were icy outside and you could hardly stick
your nose out the door for the cold wind. Then I sat with a cup of
coffee by the window, looking out at the golden cloud on the spring
bush.

Father-in-law also tried to teach me patience.

"Growing things means waiting," he said. "You can't do anything about the weather."

That's true, but I never learned patience. I got furious when it
snowed on the tulips in May and when treacherous February drew
out the buds on bushes and trees, only to kill them off with night
frost.

I swore at the peonies, still doing nothing three years later, not
flowering although I manured them and gave them mulch. In the
fourth spring, I didn't even look at them, not until the day I took a
spade and went to dig them up and throw them on the compost
heap.

They were covered with big fat buds. Since then they've flowered every summer for over twenty years.

At this time, only Father-in-law and I worked in the garden.
Arne's brother built the wall, stone by stone, on weekends. Gustav
was a mason, happy as a lark as he and his father argued about
frost-free depths and heights and breadths, or whether he should go
to the expense of a sloping tiled roof. Yes, he should, said the old
man, and he made it sound like an order.

The wall had no sharp corners, but swung around in a curve to
the southwest and joined the hill forming a gentle curve to the
north. So my garden came to be like a round bowl with the house in
the middle.

One day in the middle of all that hard work, Ragnar drove up
with roses in the back of his truck, climbing roses, single roses,

old-fashioned rosebushes. I jumped around him like a delighted child.

"Where did you buy all these? And what did they cost?"

"Nothing to do with you, little sis," he said, looking just like Arne had when I'd asked what he'd paid for all that expensive lumber for our furniture.

I notice I have to be careful not to turn good memories from the past into the only truth. That's easy to do. It's probably a talent we've acquired in order to endure, this blessed ability to remember what was good and forget the bad. But a lot goes wrong if you build on such uncertain ground, as Arne does when he talks about his good mother and happy childhood.

Maybe I'm unjust. For what can anyone know, what does anyone really know about what's a lie and what is truth? About what it was like, and how the child saw it? Nowadays, I'm always uncertain.

Anyhow, I'm sure that our first years out there by the sea were good years. I took the days as they came and accepted my husband for what he was. I don't think young love is as blind as young wives try to persuade themselves.

The first time I saw Arne in an explosion of rage, I was almost as angry as he was. He'd smashed two plates, soup was all over the place, and remains of food and bits of broken china were all over the kitchen floor. I pointed at the door and shouted at him to get out!

After he left, I didn't clean up. I went straight into the bedroom and packed a suitcase. Then I sat on it in the hall and waited. When he came back, he was desperate and full of regrets.

"Johanna. Forgive me."

That frightened me. For the first time I began to think there was something insane about these rapid changes of mood, something sick. I could see he enjoyed the contrition as much as the rage.

"I was going to go back to Mother," I said. "If it happens again, I will."

Then I walked up to the mountains, sat on a rocky ledge for a long time, wept a little, and watched the sun sink into the sea.

When I got back home, the kitchen was clean and tidy, and afterward he was unnaturally kind for a whole week.

The next time Arne lost his temper, he hit me. It was summer. I ran, fled to the bus, to town and Mother. She didn't say much, just bandaged me up and put me to bed. She didn't take it all that seriously. She considered it the kind of thing women had to put up with.

"Do you mean Father hit you?"

"Indeed he did, several times."

I was miserable. I didn't think she was lying, yet I felt as if she was slandering him.

Later on, I realized she had spoken to Ragnar, for when Arne appeared in Haga, all regrets and self-pity, he said my brother had threatened to report him to the police for mistreatment of his wife.

"Good," I said. "If he goes to the police, then a divorce will be easier."

I spent two weeks looking for work in Saluhallen and got an hour or two here and there. A permanent job was out of the question, for booth after booth had closed down. Then I ran into Greta. She had trained as a hairdresser and had opened a little salon in Vasastan, where people could still afford to get their hair done. I could start with her, learn the trade, and gradually earn enough wages to live on. But I had washed only a couple of ladies' heads when I found I was pregnant again. Mother said it was just as she'd thought, fate.

When I went back to our house by the sea, the garden was overgrown with weeds and the currant bushes were almost collapsing with overripe currants. Nevertheless, I was glad to see it all again. I had the courage to admit that I'd been longing to be there all the time . . . longing for the apple trees, the flowers, and the view over the sea.

Arne wept like a child when he came home and found me there. I told him what the situation was, that I'd come back because we were to have a child. He was pleased and his delight was genuine.

But I no longer believed his assurances that he would never again give in to his fearful temper.

Things were a little warmer between us, although I was constantly on my guard. I was really only truly calm when Ragnar came out, and he often did. If Arne was at home, he would ask out loud, "And how's things between you two, little sis?"

It was insulting, and at first I was afraid Arne would be furious, he would vent his anger on me. But he wasn't angry, and I gradually began to realize he liked being put in his place.

I would never understand my husband.

In September, I had another miscarriage. I can't bring myself to describe it.

What I want to remember is the garden, and our long summer sailing trips, just the two of us. They were wonderful. In the boat, Arne was a grown man, never unpredictable. We sailed to Copenhagen and enjoyed ourselves walking the alleys and parks, looking at all the sights.

The next summer we slipped into Oslo fjord to visit my relatives.

All through my childhood, I'd had fantasies about my aunt, my mother's sister, the beautiful Astrid. I had vague memories of something butterfly-like, exciting and wonderful. And I had the letters. Hanna and Astrid corresponded all through the years. Astrid's letters were long, full of amusing things and unusual thoughts. As Mother was a poor hand at writing, I was always the one to write back. Astrid often asked after Ragnar, and I wrote eloquently about how well things were going for him in Göteborg and how happy he was with Lisa and their two sons.

She replied that she'd always known he would get on in life, and that he was a child of the gods with free access to their good gifts.

I loved the astonishing way she put things and the looping handwriting flowing over the pages.

When I wrote and told her I was going to get married, she sent

me a pearl necklace, genuine cultivated pearls that came right down
to my waist.

In all honesty, I have to say that I wrote a lot more in those letters than Mother dictated to me and I never read them out to her.

Henriksen had taken his business to Oslo, and as far as we could
make out, they were doing well there. So on this day in July, when
Arne moored in the handsome guest harbor in the capital of Norway, I was ill at ease.

"I feel like the poor relation from the country."

"Huh, if they're not nice, we'll have a cup of coffee and leave.
But maybe you should phone first."

So I telephoned, and the soft voice on the phone sounded so
pleased that it seemed to warble.

"I'll come. I'll come at once and get you."

She drove her own car and was just as beautiful as in my
dreams. The years didn't seem to have left a trace on her figure or
her character. Flowery organdy floated in clouds around her slim
figure, and she smelled like the peach blossoms on the wall at home.

She hugged me, pushed me away, clapped her hands, and said,
"Lord, how pretty you've become, Johanna."

Then she hugged Arne, who blushed, delighted and appalled.

"Goodness, how alike you are," he said.

"Aren't we, yes," said Astrid, laughing. "It runs in the family.
And I have a double dose of it, like Ragnar, but in another way."

We didn't know what she meant, but she went on, her head
tilted to one side and the corners of her mouth turned down.

"My own sons all take after Henriksen and are as ugly as sin.
Now, I want to see your boat."

She jumped on board, as light as a fairy, admired everything,
then kissed Arne when she was told that he'd built the boat and
equipped it himself.

"Henriksen wants a sailboat, too," she said. "When he sees this,
he'll go mad." She spoke quickly, and I found it difficult to understand her Norwegian, although it sounded familiar.

We had dinner in their large apartment. She and I talked and talked, while Henriksen and Arne discussed Hitler. I suddenly heard Arne say loudly, "Is that true?"

Henriksen did business with Germany, and this was the first time we'd heard about Jews disappearing and the killing of people in asylums.

Henriksen was sure of his facts. A silence fell around the table and it was hard to breathe. Then Astrid said, "German boots will be tromping along Karl Johan in a few years."

It sounded like a prediction. Arne protested.

"England would never allow that."

Henriksen sighed.

"Astrid's been saying that for a long time now," he said. "And she's a great one for seeing into the future."

Henriksen and Arne went out sailing, but the fish merchant was old and heavy, so slow to learn. "He'll never be a sailor," Arne said later. We had dinner with them again in their fine apartment. I met my cousins and for the first time truly did feel like the poor relation from the country.

The most important thing that happened in Oslo was a long conversation when Astrid, Arne, and I were in a café out by the museum with the Oseberg ship. We talked about my father, and Astrid had a lot to say about him and many memories of him.

"He was the kind of person who was quite content simply to be himself," she said. "You know, that kind has no need to assert themselves."

Then she told me how much he had loved me, the little daughter named after a child he'd had by his first marriage, how he'd looked after me when I was small, carrying me in a knapsack on his back and teaching me to listen to all the voices of the forest and to see the water, the skies, and clouds.

"Hanna snorted, of course," said Astrid. "You were only an infant at the time."

I had known all that, because the body and the senses have

memories of their own. But no one in my family had ever said a word about it, only that he'd spoiled me. Now it was all confirmed.

She talked about the stories he told and the songs he sang. Mother had done that, too, so I wasn't all that surprised.

"I've often thought about you, and what a loss it must have been when he died," she said.

Then she said nothing for a while, as if hesitating before going on.

"And yet I didn't begrudge him dying. The last time we met, he said life had always been hard to bear for him. That he'd found it difficult to live, even as a child."

In the winters Arne and I went to party meetings. I read a lot and learned a lot, and we had a lot to talk about.

Arne put a wireless together, a great monster that I loved for the music it broadcast. When he noticed my interest, he came with me to concerts, where he almost at once fell asleep, while I enjoyed myself.

We bought a hand-wound gramophone.

They were good years.

We shared our anxiety about Hitler and the Nazis in Germany. Ragnar was a political idiot, and he said the bastard would at least get the wheels turning again. Arne said that times would improve once rearmament got going, but then there would be war.

He sounded like Astrid, but I refused to let myself be frightened.

I was expecting again. This time it was going to be born. I'd decided. The doctor who'd helped me through my miscarriages had assured me there was nothing wrong with me.

The district nurse came once a week, a good woman, who told Arne he should be confident and take care of me. He did, too, reliable as always in critical situations. She told me to be happy.

I did my best to obey. I thought about my garden and acquired new seed catalogs. I thought about Arne and how much gentler he'd become. I thought about Mother, soon to get a pension and be allowed to rest. Most of all I thought about all those lovely things Astrid had said about Father, and every night before I fell asleep, I promised him I would give him a granddaughter. I was absolutely certain it was a girl. And strangely enough, so was Arne.

I did mention in passing that we had new neighbors out there in the old fishing village, young families like ourselves. They were nice people, the kind you could make friends with, and I was friends with most of them, I think. We had coffee in each other's kitchens and talked and exchanged confidences in the way women do. I was wary of some, the kind that come too close. It was interesting and unpleasant to see the way we reestablished the patterns that had governed life in the old villages where people all had their roots. We observed and were envious, helped and aggravated, soon creating a hierarchy, with the wretches who drank and were unemployed at the bottom, and the good people at the top.

Best of all was the schoolmaster's family. Then came the pilot, the police, and the customs officer. No, Mrs. Gren probably came after the schoolmaster. She kept the shop. Not that she did all that well, but she had power. You had to ask her for credit when things were tight toward the end of the week.

The old people, the fishermen and their families, lived in a world of their own and didn't mix with us. They were Pentecostalists, at least on the weekends.

Their boats came in on Saturday mornings. By then they had already been to the Fisherman's Wharf in town and sold their catches. After they moored their boats, the bachelors, in their best clothes, went in an assembled troop to the pubs in Majorna and started drinking. They came back at night, and there was much singing and merrymaking in the harbor. Sometimes they had women of a familiar kind on board. But on Sunday, once the fishermen had slept it off, their faces dark, they went to the Pentecostal church, where they confessed their sins and were forgiven.

Arne thought it disturbing. I thought it strange, but Mother, who often came to see us on the weekends, found it quite natural, just as things had always been, she said.

Naturally we also had a gossip, the usual kind with eyes that saw no further than the length of her nose, noting just a little bit at a time, but very thoroughly, every tiny detail, and always implying the worst when she put the details together into somewhat dubious patterns.

Arne said Agneta Pettersson knew everything that was in every letter we ever received, even before they'd been written. He detested her.

"You may wonder how the Karlgrens can afford both a grand garden and a boat," she said to Irene, who lived nearest to us and didn't hesitate to tell us.

I laughed. Arne was angry.

That was the spring we got a telephone. Even worse, Arne bought a secondhand car, a ramshackle DKW, from Ragnar. Then he neglected the boat, took the engine apart, put in new parts, and was much praised by Ragnar.

"You could get a job as a mechanic at any time."

But Arne wasn't interested. He was proud of his work at the shipyard, where times were good.

"We're making skis for airplanes," he said. "They've been ordered by the military and are to defend Norrland."

"Good gracious!"

A Jewish family moved right in among us in these colorful little red houses. Agneta Pettersson had a great deal to observe and much to talk about, racing excitedly around with her tongue wagging, as Mother put it.

Rakel Ginfarb looked like a bird and was just as timid. I thought about what I'd heard Henriksen telling us in Oslo. I went to the nursery to buy a flower, then rang the newcomers' bell.

"Just to wish you welcome," I said.

She probably saw how shy I was, for she slowly managed a smile, so I dared to go on.

"If you want any help, or have any questions, I live in the last house down toward the harbor."

"Thank you," she said. "Thank you very much."

That was how a friendship began that was to be of great importance to me.

On Sunday, we asked them to coffee in the garden. We actually asked them on Saturday, but that wasn't possible, Rakel said, as it was the Sabbath.

"We have a few problems," said Simon Ginfarb, after three cups of coffee and trying all my little cookies. "I'm no good at putting up bookshelves."

He didn't ask Arne directly for help, but Arne understood. He disappeared with Simon and was away all afternoon, while Rakel and I talked and her children played in the garden.

She had a son and two girls.

"And another on the way," she said, running her hand over her stomach.

"So have I," I said, surprising myself even. For some superstitious reason, I hadn't told anyone before. Only Arne and Mother knew. We quickly calculated that our children would be born at the same time, and Rakel brightened.

"How wonderful for both to have someone the same age," she said. "Mine's a girl, I know."

"So is mine."

"It must be a sign," she said, and I was suddenly afraid.

"What is it, Johanna?"

For the first time I was able to talk about my miscarriages, how much it had hurt to lose children and how . . . inferior I felt.

"I sort of lost confidence," I said.

She said nothing, but she listened. Afterward, we sat in silence for a long time, a sweeping silence so profound that it had to change something. By the time the children's laughter, the screams of gulls, and the chug of a fishing boat out at sea had broken the stillness, I had acquired new hope.

As she left, she whispered that she would pray for me, and I, who had no God to appeal to, was grateful.

Arne came back and said Simon was just as he'd thought, all thumbs. They'd laughed, and while Arne had sawed and nailed, they'd talked politics.

"It's true what Henriksen told us. Both Rakel and Simon have relatives in Germany and they're damned worried. Always, every day."

Arne's eyes darkened, as always when he was disturbed.

"I was thinking about Astrid's prediction," he said. "Do you think she can see into the future?"

"They say so. There've always been people with second sight in Mother's family."

Arne snorted.

"Superstition!"

But then he said Astrid hadn't said the Germans would march through Göteborg. "Not a word about Sweden," he said, looking relieved.

Before he fell asleep that night, he talked about the Ginfarbs.

"You wouldn't believe how many books they've got. He's a teacher at the college."

That rather worried me. I thought about the new family being the best of all in the village, and about how uneducated I was, and also how much I hated the middle classes, the bourgeoisie.

But most of all I thought about that strange moment when Rakel and I had sat together in silence.

That autumn, I helped Rakel plant roses in her garden. What she liked best was when we went with her children through the high pass in the mountains, or toward the inland meadows, along the shores, or up in the forest. One day I showed her my secret mountain ridge, warm, sheltered from the west wind, and with the most beautiful view out over the sea.

"I'll soon be a real Swedish nature lover," she said.

She had persuaded her husband to buy the house out there in the country, she told me. She didn't like cities and regarded them as military defenses.

"Huge buildings and neat streets," she said. "As if people were trying to find safety by limiting their lives."

I thought about the dirty alleys in Haga, and the vulnerable, constantly threatened life inside those huge apartment blocks. Her city wasn't my city. But I said nothing. I was cowardly, anxious that a chasm would appear between us.

She had a lot to give, primarily confidence, but also knowledge— about children, bringing them up, and how important it was to respect every single little child.

"They're all different, right from the beginning," she said.

She once told me she always knew when a person was lying, and that she'd inherited that quality from her grandmother. When she said she was less sure than usual when it came to me, I knew that was true. I had a habit of lying to myself, although I neither meant to nor even understood why I did.

"You're full of secrets," she said.

Her husband was very elegant and smelled of well-being and cigars. He was religious and as an orthodox Jew regularly attended the synagogue. But his attitude was rational, more marked by respect for ancient rites than religious enthusiasm, he told us. Both Arne and I thought he was rather arrogant, though neither of us ever said so. The new neighbors were Jews, so above all criticism.

Like everything Arne did with his hands, our large wireless that he had put together from various parts was excellent, and we had better reception than anyone else. That made Simon take his evening walk in the direction of our kitchen, to listen to the news from Berlin.

Rakel was never there when we heard Hitler bawling away on the wireless.

"The women can be spared that," said Simon.

But Arne objected.

"I don't think Johanna wants to be kept in ignorance," he said.

Simon laughed. By this time we'd found out that he always laughed when he was unsure of himself.

The autumn storms came, then the winter, and Rakel and I grew in size together. I began to find it difficult to tie my shoelaces, and I thought, now it's a child, a real child that's only got to grow a little more before it comes out.

*T*hen she came, one blue March day, and I would never have believed it could be so difficult. It was like walking a long way through unendurable pain, finally to reach a merciful death when the anesthetic obliterated everything.

It went on for over twenty-four hours.

For many years afterward, I looked at every mother with surprise. You! And you, too, and you, several times!

God, what women have to go through, so rarely talked about, so secret most women keep it to themselves.

But then it was the same for me as for others, an infinite joy, worth any suffering.

When I woke at the clinic, I was given some creamed fruit, then the baby was put in my arms. The next hours are harder to describe than the pain. We looked at each other. She looked steadily at me, and I saw her only through a blur of tears. We were surrounded by light. I recognized it from my walks along the lakes that summer before Father died, and from the miracle in the market hall when I was prevented from opening a door.

There weren't many thoughts in my head that first day. I could only smile like an idiot when Arne came and tried to tell me how pleased he was.

When Mother came the next day, I remembered her description of when I was born.

"Mother," I said. "How strong you were."

She was embarrassed and as usual warded off praise. It wasn't due to her that things had gone well that time, she said, it was the midwife.

Then I remembered Anna, and without thinking I said I wanted to call the child Anna. Mother was pleased, I could see that, but she said I had to speak to Arne first.

He thought the name was old-fashioned and good, and he was also pleased it wasn't already in the family.

"Have you noticed how intelligent she looks?" he said.

Of course, I laughed a little at him, but in secret I agreed. And he turned out to be right.

What a spring it was. And what a summer! As if life wanted to make up for things going so wrong for me before, this time seemed to be blessed. I had plenty of milk, and Anna was healthy, ate, slept, smiled, and gurgled. I told stories to her. Suddenly they were just there, all Father's rhymes and jingles. And I realized now that Arne had listened carefully when we were in Oslo and Astrid had talked about my father. For he did as Father had done, made a bark knapsack and roamed around the mountains with the child. And he sang to her. He had a good singing voice.

My abundance was so great, I was even able to receive my mother-in-law with some warmth.

"Look, Anna, here's your grandmother."

Anna was her first grandchild. She emerged from behind her stony exterior and smiled and prattled to the child. For the first time, I saw a pleading behind the ivory mask. But when she said— and she was the first to say so—that the child resembled her, I was afraid.

And annoyed.

Maybe Arne was also scared, for he laughed scornfully and said that all old women were crazy.

"Johanna's mother was here yesterday," he said. "And she thought Anna was like her and her family."

I looked at him and smiled. We both knew Mother hadn't said a word about any family likeness. He's standing up for himself, I thought. He'd become a father and at last can oppose his mother.

My mother-in-law snorted.

A long time later, I realized she hadn't been entirely wrong.

There's a fragile timidity in Anna, a pride and fear of relaxing or letting anyone in. And she has her grandmother's ivory complexion and finely drawn features.

Only her mouth is mine, large and expressive.

Rakel returned from the hospital a week after me. The little girls were very different, mine fair, strong, and stubborn, hers dark, good, and submissive.

Then it was 1937, and Franco was dropping Hitler's bombs on the towns of Spain. We could no longer close our eyes to the fact that the world was darkening all around us.

I've no intention of describing what the second world war did to us, all of us crouching down like frightened rabbits behind a fragile neutrality.

I made a tremendous effort to build a wall between the world out there and my world with the child. I had seen very early on that she sensed every shift of mood in me, and I made myself not think about the war, not listen to the news, not be frightened, as long as the child was awake.

I sat by the radio in the evenings, as I slept badly at night. I was alone for long periods, for Arne had been called up and was "somewhere in Sweden."

It wasn't easy trying to live in two worlds, but I did my best, and it took some time before I knew I'd failed. When Anna had her first birthday, Hitler marched into Austria. When she was two, he incorporated Czechoslovakia into the Third Reich, and in the autumn it was Poland's turn, and it was world war.

So far, I'd managed to keep my fears at bay. Then came Anna's third birthday, and just after it the invasion of Denmark and Norway.

Swedish antiaircraft guns rattled in the mountains around us, and Anna's eyes darkened with questions. "What are they shooting at?"

I lied and said they were only practicing.

One day a burning plane flew right over our heads, a plane with a swastika on it. It flared up, spun around, and disappeared to the west. I saw the German boy burning like a torch against the sky before being mercifully extinguished in the sea.

We were up on the mountain, Anna in my arms and me trying to hide her face against my shoulder. But she struggled free and stared as if bewitched. Then she turned her eyes to mine, and I knew she could see right into my terror.

She didn't ask anything. I had nothing to say.

Arne came home on leave. Different. Harder. In uniform. He didn't avoid Anna's questions. He sat her on his knee and told her as it was, that there was great evil in the world and every decent person had to resist it. He was a soldier because we had to defend ourselves, the antiaircraft guns fired to keep the enemy outside our borders, and the good would be victorious in the end.

"But they kill . . . ," she said.

"Yes, Anna, they have to."

He told me it was all appalling on the borders, that sometimes they had guns and no ammunition, sometimes ammunition and no guns.

"Are you frightened?"

"No, mostly angry."

He wasn't lying. He was what he was, strong when things were difficult. The next day he phoned his parents.

"Hi, Mom. I'm in a hurry and want to talk to Dad."

Then he spoke for a long time about evacuating us to their old farm out in the forest where there was a cottage.

"You must come out here, Dad. Fix things up with Johanna. She'll help you phone up there and ask them to put the old place in order."

"But what about Mother?" I said after he'd put down the receiver.

"If Ragnar doesn't arrange something for her, then you'll have to take her with you."

But Ragnar had been called up, as well, and all his vehicles had been requisitioned. I thought it would never work with Mother and Mother-in-law in a cramped cottage. Then I was ashamed.

Before Arne left that evening, he stood for a long time with Anna in his arms.

"Now promise me you'll be a good little girl and look after your mother."

The wrong thing to say. I felt in my whole being how wrong it was. But I had no desire to argue at that moment. Then things went as they went, and Anna's unease acquired a definite goal.

"Don't be frightened, Mommy."

"I'm not frightened," I said, then I cried and my three-year-old comforted me.

The war crept closer in other ways, as well. Jewish refugees from Denmark and Norway poured through Rakel's house. They appeared in the dark, in the evenings or at night, slept there, ate their fill, then disappeared. There was still a refugee route open from Torslanda to London.

Most of them were going on to America.

Some of them were Jews of the kind I'd seen only on Nazi posters and in Albert Engström's horrible comic magazine. Like caricatures. I realized then that they really existed, men with peculiar hats and long curly locks. I can admit now, all this time later, that they frightened me.

One of them was a rabbi, and in contrast to the others, he came with his wife and sons one sunny afternoon. Anna was at the Ginfarbs' house. Things had worked out well with the two little girls, just as Rakel had predicted. They were inseparable.

She came running home, her eyes shining.

"Mommy, I've been blessed by God. He put his hand on my head and said lovely things I didn't understand."

Thank God for that, I thought, then smiled wryly at the way I'd put it.

Then came all the questions about God. Anna had a way of asking as if you were being cross-examined in court. Why didn't we pray to God? Who was he? Was he invisible?

I answered as best I could, and I can take some credit for that. I spoke seriously, as if to an adult. She was disappointed that the rabbi wasn't God himself, only his messenger on earth. But he had done something for the child, because she went on glowing long after that Jewish blessing.

"Simon's being very pressing," said Rakel. "He wants us to go, too."

"Where?"

"To America. We have relatives there. I try to resist, but he keeps talking about all those blind and crazy Jews in Germany who stayed until it was too late."

A week later, Swedish Nazis drew swastikas and Stars of David on the windows and doors of the Ginfarbs' house. Crying, I went to help her wash them off, and that morning I was more ashamed than I'd ever been before. A fortnight later, the family was on its way to America. One of Arne's carpenters at the shipyard bought their house cheaply. I told Arne that was shameful.

The contents of the house were all put in storage.

I was lonely.

In the terribly cold winter of 1941, on Christmas Eve itself, I counted the days and became aware I was pregnant again. I don't think I realized from the start that I would lose the child, but by February I had already arranged with Lisa that Anna would stay with her for a week or two in March. Should anything happen.

That was good. Anna never knew. On the fifteenth of March, the first creeping pains started, but I managed to get to Lisa's with Anna just before going into the hospital. When I came around, I thought what a good time Anna was having at the haberdashery with all those lovely reels of silk.

I probably mourned that child, too, but all over the world there were so many dead.

Arne got leave, came and fetched me from the hospital. He was miserable. It had been a boy this time, too. We picked up Anna in Haga.

She had become quite pale, and Arne said, "You can't have become so city pale in only a week, girl."

That was the first time I wondered whether she knew. I

thought, in some way, she knows, though she can't know. I bled a lot and was often in bed. That was the spring Anna started playing up on the mountain, alone, secret games of her own.

"She's missing little Judith just as I miss Rakel," I said to Arne.

Despite everything, he was in a better mood, the defenses at last functioning, but then the Germans invaded Russia.

"Now they're in for it," said Arne, and began going on about King Karl XII and Napoléon.

And just in time for Christmas, the Japanese bombed Pearl Harbor, and America was forced into the war.

"Now you'll see," said Arne. "Things'll be all right now."

And they were.

In 1943, when the German army surrendered at Stalingrad, I had my next and last miscarriage. It came suddenly, and I was already bleeding when I left Anna with Lisa.

I don't want to say anything more about that.

I remember the spring when peace came, the shimmer over the days, a light that gave a sharpness to every detail.

I remember the last day of school in that spring of 1945.

The bus to school was full of boys in white shirts, their hair plastered down, and girls in new light dresses, their hair curled, and the mothers in their best clothes with bunches of flowers in their hands. Anna had a seat opposite me and was as lovely as the apple blossoms in our garden at home, although her hair was dead straight, the kind no curling tongs had any effect on.

I sat there thinking the war had overshadowed her whole childhood, and peace had made it more difficult to hide anything from her. That spring she had bought a newspaper on her way back from school, a foreign paper full of photographs from the recently opened concentration camps.

By the time she got home, her face had turned green. She flung the paper at me and disappeared into the bathroom to be sick.

I had no words to console her. I sat at the kitchen table and looked at the unfathomable photographs, incapable of even crying.

The time of flowering was to come.

Did I imagine it, or was there some hope in those voices singing on that last day of school? No one had yet heard of the bomb or that city with its lovely name.

Hiroshima awaited us that autumn.

Soon the wheel began turning as never before, prosperity increased, and the foundations of the "people's home" were laid. The Social Democrats were in power, and the reforms demanded but restrained by the war now lay in front of the Riksdag. Taxes on businesses and the rich rose, and oh, my goodness, what anger that caused among the bourgeoisie.

Arne and I were jubilant.

Things were good for me. Both Mother and my friends thought things were as good for me as a woman could ask for. Only one child to see to, and a husband who brought money in every week and neither drank nor slept around. Mother didn't even lament my miscarriages. Unchanging, she considered every child not born to be a plus. I didn't have Mother's ability to accept without protest the role imposed on me. Arne's power increased and my ability to object decreased.

I wanted to believe it was the miscarriages that broke me, and it was obvious that the child I did have increased my vulnerability. I evaded Arne, saying nothing in order to protect her. No disputes, no quarrels. All was to be sun, security, and coziness.

If I'd had four children, I'd have probably humbly crawled along the floor.

Or, would I?

What did his power consist of?

Why was I so easily hurt and submissive? For I was. This was when I started appealing for pity. In vain, of course. I became one of those martyrs, the woman who stayed at home, the housewife.

Detestable.

It was a long time before I found an answer to my questions, and that was perhaps because I didn't want to see. It seemed so feeble, for it was all about money.

I don't think anyone who hasn't experienced it understands what it means to have to ask for every öre. He said his money ran through my fingers. That was true, and it wasn't my fault. I was not a bad housewife, but the value of money had gone down in the postwar period, now marked by a belief in the future and inflation.

I tried to think my situation was just. I'd looked for security and had been given it.

* * *

I can see I have underestimated love. For it was there. I was fond of Arne. All through those years, I was in love with him in a way. But I don't believe love would have led to submissiveness if I had kept on working and earned my own money.

One strange thing I shared with many women of my generation was that being in love had little to do with sex. Sex was inevitable, something that came with it, that you had to have. I did not find it repulsive, anyhow not often. But neither did I enjoy it.

Maybe I hurt him? No, I don't think so. I think he would have been shocked and considered me lascivious if I'd liked it.

We were so ignorant. We didn't know how to show tenderness in sex. We closed our eyes and somehow let things go the usual way. We talked about emotions only when we quarreled. He did, too, whenever he got so horribly sentimental in that way.

Once, in bed, afterward, he said his grandparents had been lustful. He flushed scarlet and I was surprised. I had actually never given a thought to what they were like, the ivory lady's mother and father.

"But they were religious," I said.

"That's never stopped anyone being lustful, has it?"

"Was your grandmother like that?" I was so surprised, I sat up.

"No, I don't suppose so. But Grandfather was an old goat and she liked it."

"How do you know that?"

He shouted at me, "Stop nagging!"

I was frightened, as usual when he got angry, and said nothing. I soon heard him sleeping, and I lay awake thinking.

Long afterward, I thought about that strange exchange, about whether it could be true what he'd said and why he had said it. Now, so many years later, I wonder whether he had wanted to apologize for his own attitude to sex. And his mother's.

We didn't have enough words when it came to practical things, or politics.

Nor did I, with Anna. One day when she was about eleven, she came in, white in the face and moving stiffly. She told me what a friend had said about that horrid thing a man has and how he pushes it in and pumps and pumps and how it hurts so you could die. I was ironing towels and was so startled, I burned one. Then I said what Mother, Grandmother, and Great-grandmother had always said over the centuries, that it was something women had to put up with.

"And it doesn't hurt, Anna. A lot of people think it's wonderful."

"Do you?"

"I've nothing against it."

So feeble. But how was I to explain how infinitely complicated love and sex are, with falling in love and desire, how doubly complicated, how multifold?

One day in the autumn when the sky and the sea had merged into a heavy grayness, Nisse Nilsson phoned to say that business was picking up again. Would I consider helping on Friday afternoons and Saturdays? For good wages?

I didn't even consider it. I said yes, just like that.

I sat by the telephone for a long time, realizing there would be a tremendous to-do that evening. I prepared dinner with extra care, and Arne ate it and afterward said, as so often, what a good cook I was.

Anna disappeared up into her room, and Arne went down into the basement as usual, thank goodness. If we were to quarrel, Anna wouldn't hear.

So I went down to him and told him about my conversation with Nisse. He was surprised, then nodded. He said Anna was old enough to look after herself for a few hours. If I wanted to . . .

"I do."

"I've often thought it must be lonely and boring for you here at home."

I was surprised.

"It's not that, I've plenty to do, sewing and all that. But it's like being a servant, always doing things for others and having to ask for money."

He wasn't angry, but dismayed.

"But why didn't you say so?"

It was a strange evening. I was the furious one, not him. For ten minutes at least, it all poured out of me, the boat that cost so much, the rows over money for food, the fact that he simply expected freshly ironed shirts and perfect service at home.

"I'm nothing but a servant!" I shouted at him. "Nothing else."

Then I rushed up the basement stairs.

When he came to bed, he was miserable.

"I didn't know," he said. "You could have said something."

I thought for a long time, then decided he was right.

"You're rather a secretive person," he said.

Just as Rakel had said.

I had to agree with that, too.

Things were better from that day onward. It wasn't just the joy of crossing the bridge with all the others on Saturday morning, nor just friends at work, nor just the chat, the laughter, and taking an interest in every customer, listening and answering back, as Nisse Nilsson said.

It was about self-esteem.

I told Nisse he had saved my life. I told Mother we needed the money, but that wasn't true. I told Anna that I had to get outside our four walls.

She understood. She matured, cooked the dinner on Fridays, cleaned the house on Saturdays, and so learned a lot about running a household, even though she was only twelve.

"She has a sense of responsibility," said Arne.

He didn't complain when the meatballs were too salty and the fish wasn't cooked through. That was just a start. As always, Anna was ambitious and learned things from books. She wore out my old cookbook and got a new and better one from Arne.

When I got home with my first wages, he said he had thought about what I'd said and admitted that he'd been stingy and difficult about money.

"I was afraid of being like Dad," he said. "She took every öre from him, then graciously gave him enough for his snuff. Whenever he asked for it."

I was, thank goodness, so surprised I said nothing about what I was thinking. Arne ran no risk of being like his father, but he had a lot of features in common with his mother.

He now wanted me to take over the family finances and said I was sure to be better at it than he was. From that day on, he handed his wages over to me and finally there was an end to all that talk of "my money you keep spending." And our finances were in much better shape. In the spring, he wanted to order new sails for the boat, but I decided we couldn't afford them. We needed our savings for a new oil-fired central heating system.

At last I'd proved something I'd always known. Women never get any respect until they can stand on their own two feet.

Now, so many years later, I'm not so sure.

Anna has always supported herself and her children. She managed better than I did, even with her divorce. But then, is there something in women, something we don't want to see or admit?

*J*ust a few words about the old people.

With all the strength of my new self-confidence, I set about Mother's housing problem. The apartment in Haga was too large for her, too difficult and old-fashioned to manage. It was heated by wood-burning stoves and was drafty. And there was the privy down in the courtyard and three floors to climb up and down. She wasn't happy there, either, now that so many of her neighbors had moved, and Hulda Andersson across the landing had died.

They were building new blocks with apartments for pensioners, so I got her and Ragnar to come with me to look at a one-room apartment, smaller than the one she had, but with central heating, a bathroom, and hot water.

She thought it was paradise.

Arne helped with all the paperwork. A great deal was required by the authorities, and the red tape took even longer than building the place.

But we signed an agreement and she moved in with her Värmland sofa, which I covered in striped silk and a lot of soft cushions. She sat on it and was happy.

An awful and unexpected thing happened to the two old people in Karl Johansgatan. The ivory lady's heart survived over the years, but one day she stepped straight out into the street in front of a streetcar.

She died in the ambulance on her way to the hospital.

When the message came, I was alone at home. I had time for a lot of thinking before Arne came home, uneasy thoughts as to how I should tell him. And I can't deny feeling considerable relief.

As soon as I heard the car, I went out with my coat over my shoulders.

"Arne, something terrible has happened. We must go to Karl Johansgatan at once."

I told him about the accident. As soon as I saw how relieved he was, I looked down, but he knew I'd noticed and would never forgive me.

"What shall we do about Dad?" he said as we backed out.

"I suppose he'll have to move in with us."

"But your job?"

I was frightened.

"He's sure to be able to manage for a few hours."

He was. He was pleased to live with me, whom he'd always liked, but he wanted to be left to himself. So Anna gave up her room upstairs without complaint. She had always liked her grandfather.

Arne installed water and a WC up there.

I had a lot to do that summer and was very tired. So I was forced to admit I was no longer young.

At first I thought the old man would be relieved when his strange wife died, but I was wrong. He grieved for her, calling out for her when his cough woke him at night, and he wept like a child when she didn't come. He caught one cold after another, and though the doctor came and gave him antibiotics, they were no help. He just grew worse and died that winter from pneumonia. I sat with him and held his hand. That was good for me. Afterward I figured he cured me of the fear of death that had been with me ever since Father coughed his life away in the mill house in Dalsland.

Anna was in high school now. She thinks she remembers some discussion about it, but she's wrong about that. Somehow it had always been obvious from the start to both Arne and me that she should have what we'd never had.

Education was the most important of all.

But there were consequences we hadn't foreseen. Anna had one foot in another world, the world of education, the middle-class world.

She gave a lot of thought to it at first.

"I can't help liking some of my new friends," she said.

"That's good," I said, and I meant it. But she looked at me suspiciously.

"They're childish in a lot of ways," she said. "Just think, they know practically nothing about the war and the extermination of the Jews."

"That's understandable. In their homes, unpleasant things aren't talked about. I know that. I was once in service in that kind of household."

As I said it, I remembered trying to protect Anna from all the horrors of war. I noticed then that I'd become a little middle class myself.

"Were you in service? You never told me that," Anna said.

So I did then, with all the awful details right up to the attempted rape.

Anna cried for me, so then I could cry, too, over those two lost years of my youth.

But she also saw things much more personally than I did, so she was suddenly angry with Mother.

"How could she? . . ."

"Don't you understand? It was expected of her, of everyone in those days. It was the social system."

At first I found it difficult with all those middle-class children flitting in and out of my house and garden. Anna's school friends with all their self-confidence reminded me of the horrid children in that doctor's family. But then I thought of Rakel, that lovely Jewish woman.

We wrote to each other. I remember the first letter I had with American stamps on it and me dancing around my roses as I read it.

Little Judith wrote, too, to Anna. She wrinkled her little nose and said Judith couldn't spell. Both Arne and I laughed at her and said Judith would certainly be able to spell in English, now that she had another mother tongue. A few years later, Anna wrote back to her in English, at first with her teacher's help, then on her own.

In the 1960s, Judith emigrated to Israel, and Anna and Rickard flew to Jerusalem to go to her wedding.

I don't know how Anna managed to juggle her school life with ours. She didn't say much. Like me, she was secretive about anything that was difficult. But I saw the distance increasing between her and Mother, the whole family, actually. She even distanced herself from Ragnar, whom she loved and admired.

She began correcting my speech.

Sometimes she was sharp to Arne, ironic and spiteful.

When she wanted to go on to the university, Arne said he would somehow scrape up the money, though it wouldn't be easy. She said he needn't bother, she'd already gotten a student loan.

She pretended not to notice how hurt he was.

The house felt empty when she moved into a student apartment in Lund, but I can't deny it was also a relief. I didn't have to see the gap between us widening every day, and I no longer had to act as intermediary in the quarrels that had become more and more frequent in recent years.

But I missed our closeness and confidences. Heavens, how I missed them. Every day I said to myself that you can't hang on to your children, you must let them go. Perhaps it's true that confidence isn't possible between people so close to each other. The risk of hurting is too great. How could I tell her I knew all about her unhappy love affair with that foreigner in Lund? And the abortion?

The abortion.

How could I talk about that, I who'd said nothing to her about having had four miscarriages?

When she came back that summer, pale, thin, and grave, I almost cracked with pity for her. We worked side by side in the garden, but she told me nothing and I didn't dare ask. Then she got a temporary job as a proofreader at the newspaper.

And she met Rickard Hård.

I liked him from the very start.

That was due to many things, that his eyes were light gray with such long eyelashes they ought to have been a woman's, and then his mouth. Many people think eyes say the most about a person. But I've never understood that. Gentle brown eyes lie just as well as blue. To me it's always been mouths that reveal character and attitudes. Not from the words pouring out of them, but the actual shape.

I've never seen a more sensitive mouth than Rickard's, large, generous, the corners curling up when he was amused or curious. Although so young, he already had plenty of laughter wrinkles.

He certainly could laugh.

And tell stories, one crazy story after another.

He reminded me of someone, but I couldn't think who at the time, because he was so unlike him. A few weeks later when he was having coffee with us and Ragnar came barging in, then I knew.

So I can't really say I was surprised when Anna phoned one day, and said with panic in her voice, "They say he's a womanizer, Mother."

I don't remember what I answered, just that I sat there by the phone for a long time afterward, thinking Anna is not like Lisa, not in any way.

That year, when Anna was twenty-three and we had to write 1960, I learned that you can do nothing for your adult children.

Rickard had soon charmed his way with the family, friends, and neighbors. Mother was the worst. She literally melted as soon as she saw the boy. It was good to see, as he both liked and respected her. He never laughed at her as my brothers had done. On the contrary, he listened with great interest.

"A book should be written about her," he said to me.

"She hasn't that much to tell."

"She has traditional ideas and values," he said. "Haven't you ever thought about her being one of the last of a dying breed?"

I was surprised, but he was right. Suddenly and without really wanting to, I told him about Ragnar's fortieth birthday and what I'd discovered in the middle of the party.

"Raped at twelve and mother at thirteen," I said.

"Good God!"

I regretted telling him, of course, thinking I'd exposed her, and I made Rickard promise not to tell anyone.

"I don't want Anna to know."

"I can't think why," he said, but he promised.

They got engaged in August before Anna went back to the university and Rickard went to Stockholm to work for a major newspaper.

"So you'll live in Stockholm?"

"I have to go with him. It's also easier for me to get a job there."

She said she was sorry, but I knew that wasn't true. She was pleased to be going to a new life in a large and exciting city. Pleased also to get away from me and my eyes, which saw all too much.

"There are lots of trains, Mother. Fast ones, too. You can be up to see me in a couple of hours."

Arne and I had the fear all native Göteborgians have of that alien city on the wrong side of the country. And we thought Stockholmers were self-important and complaining, both when they spoke on the radio and when they spent their vacations on our islands.

But we had to learn. On our first visit, we overcame our fears, and people in Stockholm turned out to be like most people, nice. And they dressed much more simply and were less arrogant than lots of snooty Göteborgians. The city was beautiful. We'd heard about it, but all the same were much taken by it as we strolled along the beaches with Anna and watched the fishermen with their huge strange seines.

But now I've gone ahead of myself. First we had the wedding at our place by the sea. And that's where I met Signe, Rickard's mother, and began to understand one thing and then another.

*W*e did push the boat out, we really did. As Arne said, we had only one daughter, so . . . But I've forgotten most of it and have only a few scattered memories of cooking food for a whole week and the house full of young people, dancing, and music. What I do remember is Signe.

This time, I knew at once who she was like although she was so dissimilar, smelling of perfume, wearing cosmetics, and talking about everything except what was important. She had the same blue unseeing eyes as the ivory lady.

"Superficial and stupid," Arne said afterward.

Worse than that, I thought. Icy cold.

"The boy's like putty in her hands," said Arne.

"I suppose he must have had a good dad."

Arne looked relieved. Of course, that must be it. We knew the father had died when Rickard was twelve, but not that he had taken his own life.

Before they went off to Paris on their honeymoon, Anna and I had a brief conversation. We were stacking bottles in the dim light of the pantry in the basement.

"What did you think, Mother?" said Anna. "Of Signe?"

For once I spoke straight out.

"She's . . . she's like your father's mother, Anna."

"Then I was right," she said. "Thanks for being so honest."

But I hadn't been. I didn't say a word about Anna also being like her grandmother, not in her character, but in what she gave out. I thought about how incredibly in love Rickard was with her, and how love is often a reflection of an inner longing, a state within the one who loves.

After they'd left, I was uneasy and finally calmed down by

telling myself I was seeing ghosts, that times were new and these two were clear-sighted young people.

And that Signe from Johanneberg was not as mad as my mother-in-law.

I had given it a lot of thought during their engagement. Why didn't Rickard introduce us to his mother? Was he ashamed of us? No, he wasn't like that. His background was nothing special. His father had been a traveling salesman, in paper.

I realized then that it was his mother he was ashamed of. I'd seen it in his eyes at the wedding dinner. He was embarrassed and afraid of what we'd think about her boastful chatter. But I'd also realized he would never admit it. He'd do as Arne had, defend and gild her.

I knew better than most that men who've never managed to overcome their mothers take their revenge on their wives and daughters.

I tried to think about Rickard not being brutal, not like Arne. But I was worried. It was good they were moving to Stockholm.

But not even that consolation held, for a year or two later, Signe moved, exchanging her apartment in Johanneberg for a similar one in the same suburb in north Stockholm where Anna and Rickard had settled.

"He's all I've got," she said, when she phoned to tell me her plans.

"Don't worry, Mother," Anna said. "I can stand up for myself."

A fortnight later, she phoned, jubilant.

"Just think, Rickard's found her a job in a newspaper office in Södertälje. So she's moving there."

"That's good, Anna."

"He understands much more than he cares to admit."

"Don't you go letting on you know that," I said, laughing in that way women have.

Over all the years, Greta, Aina, and I kept contact. Not Lotta, unfortunately, as she married a policeman in England. We others met every other month, at Aina's apartment in Örgryte in winter, in my garden in summer. It was pleasant. We had open sandwiches and competed at finding new and delicious varieties.

Aina was also married and had stayed at home. Her husband was in the post office and didn't want her to work. She didn't say much about it, but it was clear she wasn't happy.

For a while she grew fat. Then she got terribly thin. One July day among the roses by the wall, she told me she had cancer and hadn't long to live. I'm ashamed when I think about how I could find no words to comfort her. All I could do was cry.

We went to see her in the hospital twice that autumn, and she just wasted away.

But Greta and I went on meeting, more often now, as if we needed each other. We talked about getting older and how hard it was to take. Greta had given up her hairdressing salon and was back at the cheese stall in Saluhallen.

"I'm beginning to find the job hard," she said once. "Not physically, but mentally. I get muddled and can't calculate any longer."

I hurried to tell her I was also getting forgetful. It didn't seem to console her. Then six months went by and I couldn't avoid noticing she was getting more and more . . . incoherent. She couldn't even keep up the simplest train of thought. Everything fell apart, and a month or so later she was admitted to a mental hospital.

In August, Anna and Rickard came to stay on vacation. It had been decided we were to sail to Skagen. They were happy, and their happiness glowed from them.

"No wine for me, thanks," said Anna at dinner the first night. "We're going to have a baby."

I was so pleased I cried, and so frightened I almost fainted.

"Mother, dear, what a fuss!"

I looked at Arne and saw that he understood. He was as frightened as I was.

Anna had a temporary job lecturing at the university.

"I won't be able to keep that," she said.

"Are you going to be a stay-at-home housewife?"

I tried to keep my voice steady, but don't know if I succeeded.

"Not on your life!" said Rickard. "Listen now. I don't want a stay-at-home housewife."

Then they both talked at once about the book Anna was going to write, a book people could understand based on her Lund thesis.

"Rickard's going to help me."

"Oh, good," I said, thinking they wouldn't earn much money from that kind of work.

The baby was due at the beginning of March. Anna made me promise I would be with them.

Maria arrived at the right time, and I'm sure it sounds strange when I say I was just as pleased as Rickard and Anna were. The first time I held her in my arms, I seemed to have been given back something very dear I'd long ago lost.

She was a lovely baby, affectionate and sunny. She looked at me with Anna's clear blue eyes and smiled with Rickard's mouth. And yet she was most like . . . it was true, she was like my mother. A little Hanna, I thought, but I was careful not to say so. I knew how Anna had hated people saying she was like her grandmother.

They had moved into a spacious, light, three-room apartment, beautifully appointed, cool and discriminating as Anna liked it. But as soon as I arrived, I could see there was a shadow over both of them, she bitter and he charged with anxiety.

I'd thought they would be jubilant over the success of Anna's book and filled with delight over the baby. But something had happened and I didn't like to ask. Actually, I didn't want to know.

"Things aren't easy," was all she would say.

"I realize that. Do you want to talk about it?"

"Not now. I just want to think about the baby. And know that things are good for her."

So she became as I had been, so preoccupied with the newborn that everything else fell away. I stayed until she had the feeding going properly, then I left without asking what had happened.

"You know where I am," I said when I said good-bye.

"It's all about trust."

"I realize that."

In actual fact I'd understood all along. That first evening in Stockholm, I'd thought about the telephone call she'd made a few years ago, when she'd said, "They say he's a womanizer, Mother."

All the way back on the train, I tried to concentrate on my delight over Maria. I knew we would be the best of friends. I imagined long summers with her by the sea and in my garden, all the things I'd teach her and show her, all the stories I would tell her and the songs I'd sing.

I wasn't all that successful. The train thumped along the rails with its "Devil take all men, devil take all men, devil take all damned men."

My own man was waiting at the central station in Göteborg, bad-tempered because I'd been away so long.

"I've been starving to death," he said.

Devil take you, devil take you.

"So you couldn't find your way to the freezer?"

I had cooked ten dinners for him and all he had to do was heat them up.

"No need to be sarcastic."

I said nothing.

Then he said he'd really meant he'd been so lonely, and I had to clench my teeth in order not to feel sorry for him. At home the forsythia was in bud, a faint golden shimmer.

Mother was often ill that spring. In the end, Ragnar and I had to be tough with her to get her to a doctor.

Heart, he said.

She was given drugs, and that helped after a while.

One evening, when I'd been with her for so long I missed the last bus home, a very unpleasant thing happened. I had phoned Arne and said I'd take the streetcar to Kungsten. He was to meet me there with the car.

It's true I was tired as I sat there right up at the front of the streetcar. I looked up, straight into the driver's rearview mirror. In it was a woman so incredibly like my mother, I started, the same aged face and sorrowful eyes. I turned around to see who she was.

The streetcar was empty. I was the only passenger.

It took me a long time to realize I had seen my own face. I was so miserable, tears started running down that old face in the mirror.

"You look tired," Arne said when I got into the car.

"Yes, more than I realized, I think. I'm getting old, Arne."

"You're not," said Arne. "You're as young and pretty as ever."

I looked searchingly at him in the dim light from the dashboard, and he was just like himself, young and handsome.

The eyes of love tell lies. He was sixty-five and had only three years to go before retirement.

As usual, Arne fell asleep as soon as his head touched the pillow, but I lay awake trying to persuade myself I hadn't seen what I'd seen, that it couldn't be true. Then I crept out to the mirror in the bathroom and stood there for a long time in the cold revealing light.

What I'd seen was true. I had sharp perpendicular wrinkles on my long upper lip, so like Mother's. Flabby jawline, worry lines around my eyes, sorrowful eyes, gray streaks in my pride and joy, my chestnut brown hair. That wasn't really very strange. I would be sixty next year.

The strange thing was that I hadn't noticed, had actually had no idea. Nor felt it. I was as I'd always been, the same childish person. Inside.

But the body ages, and it doesn't lie.

I held firmly on to the basin, and the tears fell, making the face in the mirror older than ever. Can you whistle, Johanna? No, I no longer could.

In the end I crept into bed and cried myself to sleep.

The next morning Arne said I was to stay in bed that day. "To rest. You've got books."

I always had books. I borrowed a pile every week from the library. But on this day, I couldn't read. I lay in bed all morning, trying to comprehend all this about growing old, that I was old, and I had to accept it.

Aging with dignity.

What does that mean? How idiotic. At eleven o'clock, I got up, phoned the hairdresser, and made an appointment to have my hair cut and tinted. I bought an expensive "miracle" cream and the first ever lipstick in my life. I finished the day off with a long walk up the steep mountains.

Exercise is supposed to be good for you.

When Arne came back, he said I was looking marvelous, and that was good because he'd been worried. He never even noticed the miracle cream, or that I now had dark red hair without a gray streak in it.

I hadn't dared use the lipstick.

But all my tricks were useless.

You're old, Johanna.

I tried some joyful thoughts. Things were all right for me. I had a good husband who couldn't live without me, a lovely daughter, a new and beautiful grandchild, the garden, the sea, my mother still alive, friends, family.

But my heart kept objecting. My husband was becoming more like his mother over the years, complaining and demanding. My daughter was unhappy. Mother was sick.

Little Maria!

Yes.

And the garden?

I'd begun to find it rather hard, all the work it required. The sea?

Yes, it still had its strength.

Mother?

It was difficult thinking about her. She'd chosen old age early on, and had never really been young.

Later, when I'd gotten used to the idea of age, I wondered whether the shock that evening in the streetcar was some kind of fear of death. I didn't think so. I'd never thought about aging, but often had about death. I'd always done that. Every day since I was a child.

I wasn't afraid of it any longer, not since my father-in-law died. Fundamentally, I needed to put myself into the position of what it meant not to exist. It was almost a longing to be there sometimes.

Perhaps we learn not to age if we try to get used to death.

Anna phoned at the end of the week. Her voice sounded happier, and she had news. Rickard was to go on a long assignment in America, and she asked whether she and Maria could spend the summer with us.

If she could!

I was so pleased I forgot about getting old.

"Maybe you ought to ask Dad first?"

"But you know he'll be pleased."

"I haven't been all that nice to him."

"Anna, dear . . ."

And Arne was pleased. I made him phone Anna, and I could hear his pleasure when he said he was looking forward to seeing her and it would be great to see the little one.

"We'll go sailing. We'll make her into a real little sailor. It's never too early," he said. "You know, the earlier the better."

I knew Anna must have burst out laughing.

On Saturday, he set about redecorating her old room upstairs. I bought a new bed for Anna, and Arne made a pretty little cradle for Maria. We also got a new rug, and I made some airy white curtains.

"Darned good thing we put in water up there for Dad," said Arne.

They flew down on the last day of April. Arne didn't like the idea. He didn't trust airplanes, and when we went to meet them on Walpurgis Night, the eve of May Day, the weather was bad and stormy as usual.

His fear was infectious, and I also stood holding firmly onto a railing at the terminal as the Stockholm plane danced down and slowed with a screech of tires. It was just as Rickard had said on the phone, as safe as by train and much more comfortable for the baby.

I'd thought Arne would be pleased with the child, but hadn't expected him to be so over the moon about her. He stood there with the baby in his arms as if he were in heaven. When their luggage arrived, Anna and I had to carry everything to the car, because he refused to let go of Maria.

"Aren't you going to say hello to me?" said Anna.

"Haven't time."

We laughed, even more when we got to the car and Arne sat in the back with the baby and told Anna she could do the driving.

It took us longer than expected to get through town because of the carnival celebrating Valborg.

"Let's park somewhere," said Anna. "I'd like to watch the carnival as we used to when I was small. You can stay with the baby in the car, Mother."

"I will," said Arne. "Go on, you two, off you go."

That day was one long party. Anna and I laughed like children at the crazy Chalmers University students, and when we got back home, the table was laid and all Anna's favorite dishes were in the oven.

Anna fed the baby while I heated up the food. The little girl sucked away, burped as she should, then abruptly fell asleep.

Arne asked after Rickard, and I saw a shadow cross her face as she said he'd gone and was sorry to be away from Maria this first summer. He hadn't been able to refuse the assignment. He was to do a whole series of reports on the racial scene in the United States, she said, smiling a sad little smile.

"A few months'll soon pass," Arne said. "Meanwhile you two'll have to put up with us."

"You can't imagine how much we'd like to."

That was the first time she had even considered divorce.

She drank down a glass of red wine in one gulp. I must have looked worried because she said, "There'll only be one, Mother."

On May Day, Arne launched the boat, now scraped and freshly painted. We'd had a long and warm spring, so all the early work in the garden had also been done. Anna had no carriage with her, so I went down into the basement and hunted out her old one. It was old, but not ramshackle, I thought, and once I'd washed it, we put the child to sleep in it under the cherry tree blossoms.

"I couldn't take everything on the plane," Anna said. "A friend of mine, Kristina Lundberg, is bringing everything we need by car next week. She's awfully nice, a social worker. Separated."

She said nothing for a moment, then went on.

"She's bringing her two little boys with her. I hope they can stay overnight here."

I was irritated by her timidity.

"You know perfectly well your friends have always been welcome here."

"I soon won't know anything, Mother. And I find it hard to accept all this kindness, my room that you've made so lovely for us . . . and . . ."

Then she was crying.

"Anna, dear," I said. "Let's leave everything until tomorrow, when we're on our own."

"Yes. Dad needn't know anything. Not yet, anyhow."

"Exactly."

Arne came home and almost had a stroke when he saw the carriage.

"Johanna, for Christ's sake, the pins are all loose and the wheels aren't firm. Have you gone out of your mind?"

He mended the carriage. It took almost an hour and he was really happy as he kept saying, "Ah me, women!"

The kitchen was sunny and warm. We undressed the baby and let her kick naked on a blanket on the kitchen table. When Arne came back, he sat on the kitchen sofa for ages, bouncing the baby and prattling.

"What a miracle."

Then she peed on him and smiled with relief.

"She's like Johanna. And Hanna. Have you noticed?"

"Yes," said Anna. "I'm glad she is."

The good weather lasted all week. On Monday, Anna and I were sitting under the cherry tree again, and at last she told me. It was worse than I'd thought.

I had no words to comfort her.

In the afternoon, we walked with Maria in the mountains, and I told her about Ragnar. And Lisa.

Anna listened wide-eyed. She hadn't know all that.

"They're two of a kind, those two men," I said. "The same warmth, humor, and . . . lightheartedness."

Her eyes were large and dark blue when she answered.

"You're right. The worst of it is that I'm not like Lisa."

I'd thought that myself.

It was all miserable.

But at the end of the week, the first letter from America came, and when I saw how eagerly she tore it open and how she glowed as she read it, I knew she'd never escape.

We talked a lot about men that summer, how mysterious they were. I told her Arne had hit me when we were first married, and how I'd gone back to Mother and she'd taken it all with a shrug.

"Then I found out that Father, my wonderful father, had hit her quite hard, several times."

"That was in the old days," said Anna. "Why did you go back to Arne?"

"I like him," I said.

"Did it ever happen again?"

"No."

I told her about Ragnar, how he'd watched over me like a hawk.

"I think he threatened Arne with the police, as well as a beating. You know, he's much bigger and stronger."

We sat in silence for a long time, no doubt both of us thinking violence was a language men understood.

Then Anna said, "I've seen over the years the way he slowly strangled you with his power games. I'd already noticed when I was only twelve, when you started working part-time."

You can't hide things from children. I should have known that. And yet it still hurt.

"A lot of it had to do with money," I said. I told her about how I was the servant, and how I'd had to ask for every öre. I didn't say I was heading back into the same situation, because I didn't want to worry her. Maybe she understood. And she also realized what I meant with my story, because she said she managed her own finances, had a good income from her book, and the publishers wanted another from her.

"I also write articles for various magazines and journals."

* * *

We talked about our in-laws.

"Have you ever thought that Dad's mother was sick, mentally ill?"

I suppose I had occasionally, but reluctantly. I didn't like the modern way of explaining away evil as illness. As we walked back along the shore, I asked her if she thought illness of that kind could be inherited. No, she didn't.

"Otherwise I wouldn't have wanted a child descended from Grandmother. Imagine a little thing like this deprived of grace and favor."

She was carrying Maria in a pouch in front of her, the kangaroo bag, as Arne called it.

Then she said slightly miserably, "That applies to Rickard, too, and his damned ice-cold mother."

She was a more uncertain mother than I was, more afraid and clumsier. Not all that strange, considering I was thirty-five when I had a child and Anna was only twenty-four. It didn't worry me, for she showered love and affection on the child. One afternoon, Maria had a stomachache. Anna walked her to and fro, but she screamed as soon as we put her back to bed. I relieved her, while she called around for a children's doctor and finally got hold of one who said what I'd already said, that it was normal and nothing to worry about.

Anna was almost frantic with anxiety.

In the middle of it all, Arne came home, and with his large calm hands took over the child, put her against his shoulder, and started walking to and fro, as well.

"Now, now, just you calm down, little 'un."

In two minutes, Maria was quite calm and sound asleep.

Anna wept in Arne's arms with relief and said she remembered, she'd suddenly remembered what it felt like when he'd held her when she was small and frightened.

Then she cried even more, until Arne said, "That's just the way to frighten the baby. Just calm down."

But I knew why she was crying, and said nothing.

* * *

Kristina Lundberg came by car with all Anna's clothes, a large, rather plain girl with a beaky peasant nose, heavy eyelids, and an ironic mouth. She had her two small boys with her, and they raced around the house and garden like hooligans, and worst of all along the wharfs in the harbor.

Wonderful kids.

We liked their mother, too. She was the kind you can rely on. Politically, she was much more to the left than we were, a communist. In the evenings, she argued with Arne in the kitchen about social reforms and the dictatorship of the proletariat, often very loudly, and they both unabashedly enjoyed themselves. On the weekend, Arne and she went sailing with the little boys, and calm descended on Anna, Maria, and me.

When they came back on Sunday, Kristina packed. They were going on to relatives on a farm in Västergötland.

"It would've been nice if you could have stayed a little longer," I said, and I meant it.

"I'd like to," she said. "But I mustn't rub the relations the wrong way."

She looked downcast but decisive.

"It'll be good for the boys," she went on. "And not much hard work. My mother's got lots of staff. She's already found a nursemaid, because the children are to stay all summer and my mother doesn't want the bother."

She must have seen my surprise.

"Didn't Anna tell you?" she went on. "My father's a count and has an estate, blue blood and all that, arrogant and generally somewhat limited."

I remember that moment so clearly, for it was the first time I understood that we see only according to our own prejudices. The peasant girl in front of me was transformed, the long curved nose and the heavy eyelids becoming aristocratic.

How handsome she was!

* * *

The letters from America arrived in a steady stream, answers were sent, Anna seemed in a better mood, and I felt things were improving. July came with rain, as usual. I was often alone with Maria, for Anna was working on her book. I sang to the child and listened to the even clatter of the typewriter upstairs. I went for long walks with the carriage, in all weather. That was good for me and I became healthier.

Anna didn't think I'd grown old.

I have suddenly had another clear memory. It was a gray afternoon, rain streaming down the windowpanes, and Anna said, "Can we have a look at the jewelry?"

I see I've omitted an awful lot in this description of my life, such as my Norwegian relatives. Aunt Astrid died suddenly, without being ill, at the time when German boots were tromping at their worst down Karl Johan and outside Møllergatan 19, where Henriksen the fish merchant had vanished. Mother had a short letter from one of the sons, and I had a longer one from his wife Ninne, the only contact I had from our visit to Oslo. We were sad, but Mother wasn't surprised. She'd always known Astrid would leave life when it no longer suited her.

Some time after that, I had a telephone message from a lawyer in Oslo. He said there was a will and that Astrid Henriksen had left her jewelry to me. He also said that it was probably not worth very much, but the Norwegian relatives wanted to keep it for sentimental reasons.

I was angry and said curtly that this concerned my mother's family jewelry and, of course, I would have it. Then I rushed off to Mother, who was still living in Haga at the time. She was so furious she screamed to high heaven, then got on the phone to Ragnar, who came and was just as angry. As he had acquaintances absolutely everywhere, it wasn't long before I was closeted in an office with a nice elderly lawyer.

I'd written down the name of the Norwegian who had phoned

me, and the lawyer in Göteborg soon acquired a copy of the will and an inventory of the jewelry.

"The Norwegian lawyer was an honest man, thank goodness," he said.

I went on sending food packages to the Norwegian cousins, but I stopped writing to them.

I'd almost forgotten all about it, as it was a minor detail in comparison with everything else that was happening during those years. But in the summer of 1945, my lawyer went to Oslo and came back with a large brown package, which Arne and I fetched from his office. Arne hadn't taken the matter very seriously, either, until that autumn evening when in Mother's and Ragnar's presence, we took off the brown paper, found the blue jewel case, and opened it with its gilt key.

There were brooches, rings, necklaces of sparkling red stones, bracelets, earrings, and many old-fashioned buckles and clasps in various shapes. Were they pewter? Or could they be silver? Anna was dumbstruck and wide-eyed. Mother said there was much more than just the family jewelry there, some that Astrid must have either bought herself or been given by Henriksen over the years. Ragnar said, "We must get it all valued," and Arne said, "Where the hell shall we hide it?"

There were two heavy gold rings.

"Men's rings," said Ragnar.

He told us about a farmer in the family who'd once found a gigantic gold coin when he'd been digging holes for new fence posts. King Karl XII himself had dropped the ducat when he had stopped for a rest there at some time. That's what the farmer thought. He had the coin melted down, and there was enough gold for two wedding rings, which had then been passed down through the family.

"Can I feel?"

Anna weighed the two royal rings in her hand, her eyes gleaming like the gold.

Ragnar smiled at her and told her about all the treasures that had been hidden in the soil of this poor country. When they'd finally built a road between Ed and Nössemark, they'd found a great hoard of silver with coins from the eighteenth century.

Anna looked at him in surprise, and he went on to explain.

"There was unrest in the neighboring area," he said. "Sometimes the land on the west of the long lake was Norwegian, sometimes Swedish. When King Karl XII lived in Ed and was planning his invasion of Norway, rich people buried their treasures."

Mother picked up one of the finely worked buckles and told us the strange story about the Norwegian goldsmith who had fled from Bergen and been given a small farm below Framgården.

"Nothing but wilderness," Mother said.

He lived there for many years with his wife and children, had his workshop in the front room, and made brooches, pendants, and buckles out of silver. It was called royal silver.

"You can sees for yourselves how he mixed it with cheap metals," Mother said. "It's quite gray."

I remember I wanted to give one of the royal rings to Lisa. But Ragnar said no, the family jewelry shouldn't be dispersed, and if Lisa wanted a gold ring, he was man enough to get her one.

Arne pondered all weekend on how to solve the problem of where to keep the jewelry. Then he bought a fireproof safe and made a secret compartment under the floor in the basement pantry. We never bothered to get the jewelry valued, as if we didn't want to know. We wanted to think of the hidden treasure as an extra insurance, a security should something happen.

Now, sixteen years later, Anna wanted to see the jewelry, and I said that was no more than right, as she would have it one day.

"But you must wait until your father comes back because I'm not going to burgle his secret compartment."

"Where *your* jewelry is," said Anna.

"I don't want to hurt him unnecessarily," I said. "Anyhow, I've no idea how to open it."

"But, Mother . . ."

It was a festive evening as we stood around Arne in the basement, Anna with Maria in her arms, while Arne showed us the secret way to the safe.

"So now you know, should anything happen to me."

Then we sat there as before, gaping at all the glitter, Maria's eyes as wide as Anna's had been that time, though she was probably most affected by the solemn atmosphere. Anna took out a pendant in pale green enamel, partly gilded and richly decorated with small glittering stones.

"It's art nouveau," she said. "And I wouldn't be surprised if the stones were diamonds."

"You're mad," said Arne. "She was only a fish merchant's wife."

"Take it, if you like it so much," I said.

Then Anna said what Ragnar had once said.

"No, family jewelry shouldn't be split up."

At the end of July, the sun came back, and at the end of August, Rickard returned from America. He had matured, deep lines of pain around his mouth and a dark sorrow in his eyes.

We spoke to each other alone only once.

"You don't understand me, do you, Johanna?"

It was more of a statement than a question, so I had no need to answer.

He tilted his head to one side, and then I saw for the first time that he was like a cat, a supple tomcat, sure of his worth and his beauty. But also the kind that slinks around corners and howls for love on March nights.

I've always kept cats. Neutered tomcats.

I flushed and my heart thumped.

This man had all his sensuality intact, and I just touched on the thought that perhaps it was possible to understand him. Then I snorted at myself. Nonsense.

After they'd left, it was very empty everywhere. I missed Maria. I thought a lot about Anna and what she risked losing, something I didn't understand because I'd never had it. But something that perhaps meant more than security.

We did a lot to our house over those years. It was shabby and needed repairs. As usual, Arne did almost everything himself in the evenings and on weekends, with cheap assistance from friends of his, a metalworker and an electrician.

As soon as he retired, he made another room upstairs. In the daytime, I made curtains for our newly painted windows. Now influenced by Anna, I bought only white material.

It is the dreams I had that I remember from this time, particularly the first one. In it, I found a door in the wall of the new upstairs room and opened it into a long corridor, narrow and scary. I fumbled my way along it in the dark, and the passage grew narrower, but eventually I saw a strip of light far ahead, where there was another door, just ajar. I hesitated for a long time before knocking.

The voice calling "Come in" was familiar, as if I'd heard it every day for thousands of years. I went in and there was Father, sitting looking in a book. The whole room was full of books, bulging on shelves and in piles on the floor. He had a yellow pencil behind his ear and a large notebook beside him. A small girl was sitting in the corner looking at me with radiant brown eyes.

"Good that you came, Johanna. You can help me look."

"What are you looking for, Father?"

I woke, so I never heard the answer. When I sat up in bed, rather scared but mostly pleased, I remembered the great library had no ceiling and was open to the sky. There was nothing surprising about the dream, nothing I hadn't always known.

The dream recurred, changing shape, but the message was the same and the feeling quite familiar. Once the corridor was a steep staircase and the room Father was in was a laboratory. He lived there, he said, doing chemistry experiments. It smelled acrid and bracing. Again he was pleased I'd come, and asked me to help.

These dreams made me tidy up. On mornings when the dream seemed particularly vivid, I went so far as taking out the rugs and cleaning the windows.

My house was never just as I wanted it, never finished. The best of it was the roar of the sea beyond the wall. I was notorious in the village for my walks along the shore, every day and in all weather. These roamings over the years taught me a great deal about the sea, what it sounds like and how it smells in storms or calm, in dull weather, sun or mist. But I know nothing of its intentions, anyhow nothing I can put into words, though occasionally I think it is all-embracing like the presence of God.

Sofia Johansson was the person to induce such thoughts in me. She was a new friend, and unlike Rakel as anyone could be, a fisherman's wife from the old village.

As I said before, the original villagers didn't mix with us newcomers. But Sofia had a lovely garden, and one day I'd stopped by her fence to look at her anemones, large deep blue flowers with black centers.

"I was just admiring them," I said.

She'd smiled warmly.

"Yes, aren't they lovely? I could dig up a few tubers for you, if you like."

I'd flushed with pleasure and said I'd look after them well.

"I know you will," she said. "I've seen your garden."

She came the next morning with the knobbly brown tubers and helped me find a suitable place for them. We had coffee together and sat out of the wind below the wall. I had a low-growing, old-fashioned rose she liked, and we agreed I'd dig it up and give it to her in the autumn.

"My name's Johanna," I said.

She smiled again in that warm way, and we agreed to use Christian names. From then on we often met in her garden or mine. As women do, we talked about many things. She had two sons on one of the fishing boats, but the sea had taken her husband many years ago.

"That must have been hard," I said. "How old were the children?"

The boys had already left school, and the boat lost with her husband had been their own. When they'd received the insurance, they'd bought another boat.

"They don't like life ashore," she said.

She had a daughter, too. She sold fish in Saluhallen.

That interested me, so I told her I'd worked there for many years, indeed, right up to last year.

"Though only on Saturdays."

She knew that. Her daughter had often seen me there and had been surprised.

"Why?"

"Your family's rather grand, aren't they?" said Sofia.

"No, now listen," I said, and before I could think, I'd told her about growing up in Haga, about Mother and my brothers, and my father who'd died when I was a child. She liked the story, and told me her own, her childhood in the Bohuslän fishing village, where her father and brothers, cousins and neighbors labored at sea for a living. A world of men, she said, dependent on the men, their strength and knowledge. But I realized she had never felt inferior or angry.

"Then I was saved," she said, her eyes glowing.

I was embarrassed and didn't dare ask, thinking she was too intelligent for the rather naive Pentecostalist faith.

Talk about prejudices.

Now I've forgotten which year it was when the spring storm grew into a hurricane and the sea came up over the wharves and houses, smashing boats and ripping loose moorings. Fortunately, we hadn't launched our double-ender. It was propped up firmly in the shelter between the house and the mountain. But the tarpaulin broke loose and vanished inland like a gigantic bird.

The hurricane lasted for three days, and when it eventually moved on, I walked around the garden with dismay. The old apple tree had snapped off, and my roses were standing in the salt water the sea had poured over the wall. Then a neighbor appeared.

"Have you heard? One of the boats from here has gone down," she said. "Crew and all."

I shook all over as I switched on the radio, only to hear what I'd feared most. Sofia's sons were missing. I dug up my best Christmas roses, went down to the fishing village, and knocked on Sofia's door.

There were lots of women there, all praying for her sons' souls.

Sofia was very pale, white and fragile. She wasn't crying, but I was as I handed her the Christmas roses.

"Let me know if there's anything I can do," I whispered.

"They're with God now," she said.

As I walked home, I cried even more, thinking God was just as cruel as Mother had always said, if he existed at all. But I was solemn in some way.

I never was any help to Sofia. If she hadn't been there, though, that year when Mother was living with me and lay dying, I don't think I could have coped.

Every summer, Arne and I looked after Maria, and it became as I had dreamed between the child and me. We had the same slow pace. We roamed about discovering new and amazing things in the mountains and along the shore. What a lot there was to stop and wonder at, driftwood, strange stones, flowers we'd not seen before. We picked them and looked them up in the flora book at home. And worms. And insects. And a tadpole we put in a bowl. It disappeared and I said nothing about the cat perhaps having eaten it.

Maria loved the cat.

We often spent Christmas in Stockholm. Things were better for

Rickard and Anna, and they were both calmer. But I didn't dare ask any questions. Anna was expecting again.

"We're having another girl in May," said Rickard.

"How do you know it's not a boy?" said Arne.

"Anna's sure. They've got that mysterious gift, this Dalsland family."

Arne shook his head. Then he told Rickard what Astrid had said about the Nazis marching in Oslo. In the mid-1930s!

We agreed Maria should come to us in the spring. I was to take the train to pick her up.

That didn't happen, for in March, Mother moved in with me and was dying.

"It won't be long now," she said.

But it was. She wanted to die, but her body refused, and it was stronger than she.

*I*t was difficult. My friend the district nurse came three times a week, tended Mother's bedsores, and helped me remake the bed. I borrowed a wheelchair and a bedpan. The doctor came and we were given sleeping pills, so it was easier once I could get some sleep at night. As usual when things were difficult, Arne was strong and patient. There wasn't much he could do, for Mother was dreadfully embarrassed as soon as he appeared to help me lift her.

That was the worst, that she was so desperately ashamed and afraid of being a nuisance.

"You has to be wishing me gone," she said.

It wasn't true. Not even when things were at their worst was it true. I felt great tenderness for her, a tenderness I couldn't express and she couldn't accept. In me was also a dark and angry sorrow over her poor lonely life.

The only person to provide Mother with some joy in her last days was Sofia Johansson. She came every day, sat by Mother's bed, and talked about her God. Mother had always been a believer, but her image of God was dark. She listened to this talk about this other God now and found consolation.

"You has to believe her," she said. "God's taken husband and sons from her. She says He's called them home."

Sofia said she hadn't come to save her soul. She wanted me to take a walk in the middle of the day, and perhaps rest a bit after a bad night.

At the end of May, Anna came with her new baby. Malin was different, not so affectionate as Maria, more serious, more observant. Like Anna when she was little.

On the very first evening, Anna told us she was getting a divorce. Nothing could be hidden from either Maria or Arne any longer. He nearly went mad when she told us briefly about the other woman, a journalist Rickard had lived with when Anna was pregnant and in the hospital. Anna had had preeclampsia and a complicated delivery.

Arne wanted to go to Stockholm to teach Rickard a lesson.

"Then you'll have to go to Hong Kong. That's where he's working at the moment," Anna said.

"Poor Daddy," said Maria. My heart ached for her.

There was nothing we could do to help, not even obvious things like looking after Maria. When Anna went back with the children to move to a smaller apartment and find a permanent job, I phoned Kristina Lundberg and asked her to keep in contact with me.

"Anna's so proud. And reticent," I said.

"I know. I'll phone you once a week and not tell her. But don't worry. She's strong, as well."

Arne went up in June and helped Anna move. She'd found a two-bedroom apartment, and places at day care for both children.

He said what Kristina had.

"She's strong. She'll manage."

Mother died in October. It was difficult. She was in terrible pain to the very last and cried out a lot.

I slept for two days. Arne arranged everything for the funeral, and when I returned to everyday life again, I felt relieved, for her sake as well as for mine. She was buried on a Friday. Ragnar made a speech.

On the next Sunday, he was dead, accidentally shot while hunting. I fell ill and vomited all day and night. I had already been bleeding internally for some time and felt very weak. Now I couldn't even stand up. We had to get the doctor, and a week or so later I was admitted to the hospital.

Stomach ulcer. Operation.

Sometimes I think I was never the same again after that autumn.

But I'm exaggerating.

What I mean is that after Mother's and Ragnar's deaths, I grew old, finally old. And I didn't mind.

Nor does telling this story make things any better. That's because I can't bring myself to make the story feel true. I've read a lot of memoirs in my day and always found them unbelievable. I seem to see quite quickly that the writers were selecting from among their memories, illuminating bits—but why just those? Once you discover that, then you begin to have an inkling of what they had allowed to vanish into the darkness.

What have I been doing? I don't think I've been selecting, not consciously. Memory has struck me here and there as if it had a will of its own.

I think I have a lot of secrets left, but I don't really know which they are. Probably things that were so difficult I didn't dare look at them.

I remember now the day Lisa came to see me in the hospital.

*I*t must have been about a week after the operation. The unpleasant sore in my stomach had begun to heal, and I had less pain, but was so tired I slept all day and night.

I had dreaded Lisa coming. I didn't want to see her grief. Now I'm letting the truth slide again. I didn't want to see the person with the right to such great grief over Ragnar.

She was pale but calm and normal. I wept.

"It was so unfair," I said. "Ragnar should've been immortal."

She laughed at me, and when she said, "That's childish, Johanna," I hated her. But she went on.

"I don't think you ever grew up in relation to your big brother. You just closed your eyes and worshipped him."

I closed my eyes quite literally then. She was right. I've never grown up when it comes to men. First Father, then Ragnar. Then Arne, who could treat me like a senseless child. Why had I allowed it? And then I brooded on my humiliation as if on something bittersweet.

"But Ragnar was a wonderful person," I said in the end.

"Oh, yes," said Lisa. "He's left a big gap behind him, too. But that's being filled now. With relief."

When she saw my horror, she became more voluble than usual.

"Don't you see? I need never again lie awake at night waiting for him, never wonder where he is or who he's with, never smell things on him. I've washed his damned stained underwear for the last time."

"Lisa, my dear . . ."

"Yes, yes," she said. "We'll calm down."

She spent half an hour talking about the future. She had bought a large apartment in a stone building diagonally across from her shop. She was going to move in there and use one of the rooms as a workshop.

"I'm going to expand," she said. "The boys and I will sell the transport firm, and I'm thinking of buying the big shop on the corner, where Nilsson used to be with those old-fashioned clothes. We'll do it up and make it smart. Anita is already designing new clothes. She and I are going to Paris next week to see the new fashions."

I listened. This was a new and strong Lisa sitting by my bed. I detested her at that moment. She was spitting on my brother. Worst of all, she was free and I was stuck.

"I remember when Anna phoned me and told me about her divorce," she said. "I congratulated her from my heart. Rickard Hård is a sorcerer, too. Like Ragnar. Oh, Johanna, if only I'd had the strength to do the same when I was still young."

That was the only time I ever saw her downhearted.

Just as she about to leave, she said, "The police are investigating the accident. Most people say the friend who shot him is innocent. Ragnar had left his place and come out of the forest just behind the elk. That was careless."

After she'd left, I tried to protect myself with horrible thoughts. About Anita, for instance, Lisa's daughter-in-law, whom I disliked. She had been properly trained at the Handcraft Association. She made pretty clothes and was pretty herself. She took on life without hesitation, almost insolently. I knew who would be mistress of Lisa's new business, and I hoped it would go wrong.

Then I was ashamed and remembered what Ragnar had said. "Anita reminds me of you, when you were young and ran Nisse Nilsson's shop."

That afternoon, my temperature went up and I was given drugs. I slept through the evening meal and all night until four in the morning. When I woke I was cool and my head had cleared, so I had plenty of time to think about what Lisa had said. Mostly about myself, my dependence on men. About sorcerers like Ragnar and Rickard. About Arne, who wasn't a sorcerer, and was in many ways more childish than I was. About how I knew that, and yet made him out to be a forceful man and gave him power.

About Ragnar again. Had he committed suicide?

Arne came during visiting hours, pleased. He'd talked to the doctor and had been told I could go home next week.

"It's damned lonely without you," he said.

Anna had phoned and asked him whether he thought I would be strong enough to have the children next summer.

"I'll do what I can to help," he said, and I was able to smile at him and say what I felt, that, of course, we'd have them. And it would be nice.

I told him about Lisa's visit and what great plans she and her family had. And what she'd said about the police investigation. He knew all about it. There'd been something in the papers and wild rumors had gone around about Ragnar's firm being bankrupt. Then the gossip ceased, for the firm was solvent and his widow got a good price for it.

"Do you think Ragnar . . . killed himself?"

"No. If Ragnar wanted to do himself in, he'd never choose a way that'd put a friend in a difficult position. I think he was tired, and confused with grief over Hanna."

That was a great relief, for I saw at once Arne was right. Afterward I thought for a long time about how strong the ties were between Ragnar and Mother, and that no one had understood that.

*T*he years came and went, the children came and left. The worst of getting old is not tiredness and aches and pains, but that time rushes on, so quickly that in the end it doesn't seem to exist. It's Christmas and then it's Easter. It's a clear winter's day and then a hot summer's day. In between is a vacuum.

The girls grew and developed. The divorce didn't seem to have done them any harm, and they didn't have to miss their father. He lived at the top of the same building as they did and took responsibility for them as well as taking part in their lives.

"What about your mother?" I asked them.

"She seems all right. There are lots of children of divorced parents where we live, but our parents are different. They never speak ill of each other."

Then Rickard came back, to Anna and to us. They married again. I grieved. I didn't understand. Anna sounded like a lark in spring when she rang and told me they were coming on Pentecost Sunday, Rickard from Italy and the children and she from Stockholm. It was strange to see him again, older but more handsome than ever. Even more like a cat.

It was worse for Arne. They had a long talk down in the basement, he and Rickard, and afterward Arne said he understood more now. Just what, I was never told, but I remember thinking the sorcerer had been waving his magic wand again.

Then Anna had another baby, a tiny boy who died. I could still help then.

The girls were grown up by the time illness crept up on me.

Perhaps you think it begins with forgetfulness, with something like going out into the kitchen to get something and then forgetting what. That happened more and more often. I fought against it by acquiring definite routines for everyday tasks. First this, then that, then . . . They became rituals and worked quite well. I looked after the house and myself, keeping my fears at bay.

For a few years.

But my illness had begun earlier, when I no longer had any . . . any connections. When someone spoke to me, I didn't hear what was being said, just saw the mouth moving. And when I spoke, there was no longer anyone listening.

I was alone.

Arne explained and explained. Anna was busy running around. Mother was dead. Ragnar was dead. Sofia was with God. Greta was in an asylum, and I didn't want to see Lisa.

The only people who had time and could listen were the grandchildren. I'll never understand why Anna had children who were so much nicer than mine was.

Then the conversations with Maria and Malin also ceased. By then I had been alone for so many years, no one could know where I was.

The last thing I remember is that they were suddenly all standing around me, all of them, their eyes large, dark with anxiety, and I wanted to comfort them with words that still existed but couldn't get as far as my mouth. Then there was a hospital bed with high bars and a terrible fear of being shut in. I shook those bars all night, trying to break out and be free. At first, Anna sat beside me, all day long. She wept. She'd stopped running around. Now that a connection at last had become possible, I had lost any ability to do anything.

It was too late.

ANNA

CONCLUSION

Outside was raw cold March, pop music and drunken young people shrieking in the square below, car tires screeching on the wet asphalt by the kiosk. Not even the suburbs slept at night these days.

As Anna drew the curtains, she stopped for a moment to look over at the city glittering on the horizon, menacingly, she thought. A few weeks ago, someone over there had assassinated the prime minister.

She had no desire to think about Olof Palme, the former head of state.

She set about Johanna's manuscript once again. She had read it over and over again, gripped and grateful she had found the right tone, and yet disappointed, as if she had wanted something else. I've always wanted something else, she thought. In my idiotic way, I wanted . . . well, what?

To solve a mystery.

How naive. A life can't be deciphered. You map it out as best you can and then there you are, more uneasy than ever. So much has been stirred up and messed about. I was always aware you were secretive; that does come through in your story. Only a brief glimpse, soon vanished, like in a dream. Then you again take on the role of a caring person, orderly and comprehensible.

I have to start now with what is simple. I think I know that, she thought. I'll write a letter.

She keyed in the date.

Stockholm, March 1986.

Dear Mother,
I'm going to write you a letter tonight, say things I would never dare say if you were able to read it.

I have told your story, thoroughly. In a way you have come down from heaven and taken your place in an ordinary worldly existence.

There was nothing worldly in your life.

Naturally, neither were you the person I tried to trample on when I was young, scolding you for your lack of education and dead certainty. You say nothing about that time, as if it had passed without hurting you. Maybe you understood that I needed that idiotic academic defense that insecure young people from my social-climbing generation took to in order to overcome their parents and deny their origins.

For a while, I thought I had taken away your power with my superior education. Then when I became a mother, you recaptured your place. Do you remember when Maria was crying with hunger in her cradle? It was awful, but I had learned, from a book, of course, that infants should be fed at definite times. And you said, "But, Anna, dear . . ."

That was enough.

It's late at night and I am writing in tumult. I am alone and upset. Oh, Mother, how healthy you were and how sick you became. So strong and so crushed.

I remember trying to protect you by drawing Father's rage onto me. As children do. Did you let it happen? Or didn't you see it? He said I was like his mother, proud and fair-haired. Did that maybe add to transferring the weight from you to me?

I challenged him. I was much angrier than you, too, more like him. And when I was in my teens and school had its effect, I was quicker to answer back and had many more words than he did.

Was I contemptuous? Yes. Was it a class matter? Yes, that, too. It was unendurable for him, who couldn't bear the slightest criticism. If he was offended, and that easily happened, he had to get it out of him. On to others. On to us.

He had had many a beating as a child and, like most of his

generation, he talked about beatings with pride. He had strange sadistic fantasies. As neither he nor anyone else acknowledged they were sexual, he was able to give free rein to them.

Did he hate me? God, he's alive—does he hate me? Is all his furious rage directed at me now? Is that why it's so hard for me to call him? And go home to see him?

I'm simplifying. He had many good sides. He was security when things were difficult. He didn't let us down. Did you give Father the right to insult you because he reminded you of your own father? And what do you know about your father, the miller from Värmland, about his dark spells and drinking? As far as I know, he was all you had. A child probably grows anxious in that kind of relationship. Was that the terror you passed on to Arne?

And me? I do as you did, submit, let things happen. Rickard is in London now on a three-month job as a correspondent. There's a woman there and he sleeps with her. He thinks that it's me he wants to reach, my "untouchableness," but it's always his mother, that banal ice-cold Signe from Johanneberg.

She's been dead for five years. But what does death mean to the person with no feet on the ground? And what happens to the child if the very first reality, the mother, lets it down?

Rickard soars, Mother, that's what makes him irresistible.

While I've been working, I've thought Hanna was the strongest of the three of us. She had sense and continuity. She was a realist. When I think of her, I am astonished at her boldness, stubbornly taking a stand of her own. And she lived as she believed. As your father says somewhere, she counted on injustices, so didn't collect them.

As you and I do.

She was angry because she couldn't cry. We've both cried as if we had oceans of tears to pour out.

Not that it helped.

I don't hesitate for one moment to say you're a better person than I am, much better. But I am stronger. I have not been bowed into total dependence. Of course, that's due to the spirit of the day, education, and that I can support myself and the children. It's also because I acquired my strength from a mother, not a father.

How surprised I was when I realized you envied me my divorce. I had no idea. As you say, it didn't remain a victory. I fell back like a damned clinging vine.

Perhaps there is no independence.

When you tell me about sexuality, I am miserable on your behalf. Sensuality is nonetheless so wonderful. So magnificent, in some way all-embracing.

That's why Rickard's infidelities are so unbearable.

Tomorrow I'll write a letter to London. "I'm not going to take you back. . . ."

Shall I?

Mother, it's morning. I've slept for a few hours and am calmer. But am I less clear-sighted? I have something simple and important to tell you. What you got from your father, I got from you. To some extent, I have passed it on to Maria and Malin, and sometimes I dare to think they have more self-respect than you and I have. Perhaps they are not happy, whatever that is, but they have their children and their self-respect. You never met Stefan, Malin's fellow and Lena's father. He was like Rickard. And Uncle Ragnar.

I'm reading your story again, in the sober light of dawn. How strange it is that a child can know without knowing. For in some way I knew there were, had been, siblings.

Dear Lord, how did you bear it! I know what it feels like.

I've lost a child and I nearly went mad. Literally. I didn't tell you how far out into border country I was. I didn't want to frighten you.

The war is even more remarkable. I've never thought about how it left its mark on my childhood, how much of my fear has its origins there. Yet I remember the German pilot burning in the air above us, and Father coming and going, in uniform and talking about evil. Most of all, I'll never forget that foreign newspaper I bought at the kiosk with money Ragnar had given me.

There are things you've not seen, things about your brothers. You just see them as male chauvinist pigs. You had a need there for revenge when you had to put up with their drunkenness, clean their shoes, and listen to their foolish sexual boasts. They were jealous of the girl who was the best looking and the most talented, the one who got all their father's attention.

I know that, because Uncle August told me once. "She was Father's doll. He would do anything for her. He never even looked at us."

They had their mother's interest, you may protest. I don't think that was worth much, partly because as soon as you all came to town, she became an anachronism, uneducated, a bumpkin. Also because her love for them was suffocating.

I don't know. I'm fumbling my way through a jungle of prejudice and psychological public property. This morning I woke in a dream about a train. I was alone in a passenger car that was standing still somewhere in a yard. It had been uncoupled by mistake. Forgotten. But it wasn't horrible, nothing to worry about. On the contrary, I'd been given time to think in a forgotten space.

It strikes me now that perhaps there's a main line we've missed.

Love.

Perhaps we're prisoners of it, both you and me.

I suddenly remember an event some years ago. You were confused but hadn't entirely disappeared. You still had words and were pleased when I came to see you. You recognized me. Then Father fell ill and had to have an operation. I was alone in the house and went every day to see him in the hospital and then on to the nursing home where you were.

Every day, he said, "You don't have time to sit here. Go on now, see Mother."

I said, "Okay, I'll go."

He smiled and waved as I left.

A week or two later he was discharged. I fetched him and drove him straight to you. When you caught sight of him, you flung your arms out like a bird about to fly away.

You called out, "Oh, there you are." Then you turned to the girl pushing the wheelchair, and said, "Things'll be all right now, you'll see."

I remember being jealous.

Why do men make it so difficult to love them?

Another thought: I said before that I was angrier than you. The strange thing is that I'm never angry with Rickard. It was the opposite for you. You directed all your aggression at Arne. Was that because you failed in the sexual arena? That your love was never given any outlet?

What did I want with this journey through the lives of three women? Was it to find my way home?

In that case, I've failed. There was no home. Or it couldn't be found again, anyhow not in the way I'd chosen. Everything was much more structured and full of contradictions, larger, darker than the child had ever had an inkling of.

I don't even know whether I understand much more now.

I've learned a great deal, though, and I'm damn well not going to do what you did, Mother, give up when the truth collapses into a thousand truths.

Anna was just about to finish off the letter when the telephone rang. She looked at the time in surprise, scarcely seven. Who would be phoning at this time on a Sunday morning?

As she reached out and picked up the receiver, she was frightened. So she wasn't surprised when the agitated home aide at Father's in Göteborg cried out, "We found him unconscious, and an ambulance has just taken him to the hospital."

Anna dressed, packed a case with the barest necessities, and phoned the hospital. It took a while to get through to emergency in Göteborg, and a tired doctor said, "Coronary. You'd better come at once. He hasn't long to go."

She managed to get a call to Maria, as well. "So you know where I've gone."

She took a taxi, managed to get a stand-by ticket at Arlanda airport in Stockholm and another taxi at Landvetter airport in Göteborg.

She was sitting at his bedside by just before ten. He was in a general ward, unconscious, a drip in his hand.

"Isn't there a private ward?"

Yes, they were just getting one ready. They would give her a chair and a bunk to rest on.

The doctor with the tired voice came shortly afterward and listened to his heart and lungs.

"Pneumonia has set in."

There was a question in his voice, and she understood.

"Can he get better?"

"No. His heart's giving out."

"No antibiotics."

He nodded and told her they would see to it that the old man would not be in any pain.

So Anna sat there, the hours passing, her mind vacant. She was drained of emotion, too, strangely unmoved. The ward sister came in during the afternoon and said they would send someone in so that she could go and get something to eat. There was a café in the entrance hall and she should stay there so that they would know where she was.

For the first time, Anna realized how hungry she was.

She had hash with two fried eggs and beets and had time to phone the nursing home to tell them that she would be unable to visit Johanna today. Nothing had changed when she went back to the ward and took his old hand in hers again. A sister came in around seven to say there was a call for her from London.

She was unreasonably relieved.

"How are things, Anna?"

"Strangely enough . . . it's rather boring," she said, then was ashamed.

"I'll get an early plane tomorrow. I'll be with you at about twelve."

"Thanks."

"I've spoken to Maria. She's going to try to come tomorrow, but she's having trouble getting a sitter. We haven't gotten hold of Malin yet. She's in Denmark at some seminar."

Once back with the old man, she started crying, the emptiness giving way and feeling returning. She took his hand again.

"You've been a good father," she whispered.

It was true, she thought. He was always there and he always cared for me.

It was his rage that got in the way. Anger, not hatred.

At half past two in the morning, he moved uneasily. She was about to ring for the night sister when she saw he was trying to say something. His dry lips were moving but no words came.

She stroked his cheek and whispered that she understood.

He looked straight at her, then he heaved a great sigh and stopped breathing. It happened quickly, almost unnoticeably, as easily as if it had never happened.

She pressed the bell, and when the night sister came and looked grave, Anna realized he had died. A quiet, impotent pain filled her, and she knew it was grief, a grief she would long have to live with.

Some long silent minutes later, the sister whispered that there was hot coffee in the office, and Anna should go there while they made the necessary arrangements. She obeyed like a child, drank the coffee, and ate half a sandwich. Finally, she was allowed back into the room, now neat and tidy. They had lit a candle on each side of the old man and placed a bouquet of flowers on his chest.

She sat there for an hour, trying to fathom what had happened. At five in the morning, she phoned Maria and told her, saying she needn't come now. She would call again when she had arranged for the funeral.

Silvery mist lay over the town as she took a taxi to the house by the sea, the fog horns sounding over rock and island.

The home aides had cleared away all traces of the night before when they had found him. She went from room to room, thinking as so many times before that the place had lost all personality since her mother had gone. No house plants, no tablecloths or cushions. Only orderliness and the kind of bleak matter-of-factness men often surrounded themselves with.

It was cold, too. She went down into the basement to adjust the oil heating, then went back upstairs to her room and took the quilt out of the cupboard. Once in bed, she thought about practical matters and found that helped.

She woke at eleven. The heating was roaring away in the basement, and it was almost unbearably hot. She didn't turn it down, just opened all the windows and aired all the rooms. Her back and arms ached with fatigue after the long sleep, but she stubbornly continued considering practicalities: I must leave a message at Landvetter so Rickard knows to come here, not to the hospital. I need a hot bath. Was there any food in the house? I must go shopping.

She made the decision as she lay in the hot water feeling the ache leave her body. She would stay. She would live here. For the spring, perhaps for always. She went out into the garden. My garden, she thought for the first time, and was dismayed to see how neglected it was. The sun emerged through the mist, and in the cold March light she saw the overgrown roses that hadn't flowered for many years, the lawn that was mostly moss, and last year's tall weeds in the flower beds.

She heard the car and it was him, then she was in his arms.

"Out in the cold in nothing but a bathrobe! And pretty well barefoot," he said as he let her go.

"It was so hot indoors," she said.

"Have you had anything to eat?"

"No, there's no food here."

"You crazy girl," he said. Then without her understanding how it had come about, they were in the narrow bed upstairs and he was kissing her eyes and breasts, her grief obliterated, and she knew that this was where she belonged.

The main line?

Later, after he had found a jar of old coffee and given her some, she thought that nothing was ever simple except just this, what Hanna called the bedding.

Rickard didn't ask about the death and Anna was grateful.

"We must go to Mother," she said.

He had hired a car at Landvetter, which was good. They made out a shopping list, and Anna said he could go and get the things while she was at the nursing home. They could have lunch in town before going to the undertaker's.

"You're busy arranging things, as you always do when you're scared," he said in a warm voice.

He was about to drop her off in front of the nursing home, when she suddenly panicked.

"What should I say to her?"

"Tell her as it is."

"Rickard, please come with me."

"Of course," he said, and went and parked the car.

He waited while she spoke to the ward nurse, who also told Anna she should tell her mother.

"We'll see if she understands."

Johanna was far away as always, a long long way away.

They sat looking at her for a while. Rickard took her hand, and Anna leaned over her and spoke very clearly.

"Mother, listen to me. Arne died in the night."

Did she start? Had she understood? No, I'm imagining things.

But when they left her, Rickard said he was sure her hand had reacted.

They had an early dinner in a new seafood restaurant, then bought supplies and went to the undertaker's, such a lot of decisions to be made. Anna said yes to an oak coffin, no to a cross in the newspaper announcement, yes to an urn. She suddenly understood what they meant when people said funeral arrangements kept grief at bay for the first week.

On their way home, she went shopping at Mother's old co-op. Then they went to the garden market, and Anna bought flowers for the house. When they at last got home, they found Malin sitting on the steps. Anna smiled and Rickard laughed with delight. Maria had gotten hold of her in Copenhagen the previous night, and a friend had driven her to Helsingør, where she'd gotten a seat on the ferry.

"Mother, you've gone and shut yourself in again. What about having a good cry?"

"I can't."

*A*nna lay on her back in bed, holding Rickard's hand, a cold hand fumbling for a warm one. She was too tired to sleep.

He was worried, she could sense that.

"A sleeping pill?"

"No."

"What about a whiskey?"

"Okay."

She drank like a child drinking water and was surprised how quickly it calmed her down. Just before she fell asleep, she said she could easily become an alcoholic. She woke to the smell of coffee coming up the stairs and heard Rickard and Malin talking in the kitchen. It was fine outside.

I must tell them, she thought as she went downstairs. She was given a large cup of coffee at the kitchen table, added some milk, and drank it down.

"I've thought of staying here . . . for a while. Someone has to visit Mother."

"That suits me," said Rickard. "It's actually easier to get to Göteborg than Stockholm from London."

"You'll be lonely," said Malin. "But we'll come down as often as possible."

"I thought I'd call Maria and ask her to drive my car down. And bring the computer and printer and all my notes with her. And my clothes."

Then she said, "I might just as well stay here and work."

The words hung below the kitchen light. The same words her father had said so many times before.

She lowered her head to the table, gave in, and wept.

"I'll go back to bed for a while," she said. "I need to be alone." She took a box of tissues and went upstairs.

Then she lay there in her old room until the tears finally dried and she began to shake with cold.

God, how cold she was.

She woke again to a good aroma. Food. Fried bacon, potatoes, onions. Her legs felt weak as she went to the bathroom, washed her face in cold water, and thought she looked old and ravaged.

But when she went into the kitchen, Rickard said, "Wonderful, your eyes have come back again."

"No longer empty wells," said Malin, smiling at her. Anna felt her answering smile truly came from within her.

"It was good he was allowed to die," she said.

"Yes, good for him and good for us. I think you should think about what an unusually long and full life he had."

There was nothing remarkable about what Rickard said, but Anna had been in meaninglessness for so long, words again acquired some weight. Every word.

"How long can you two stay?"

"Until after the funeral," they both said.

"Do you think you could take on selling the boat, Rickard? It'd be good to get rid of it. And we need some cash."

It didn't take him long to write out an advertisement and contact the *Göteborg Posten*. He disappeared down to the boatyard and came back with a man who tapped all around the hull, examined the interior, and suggested a reasonable price.

"Talking about cash, shouldn't we perhaps go through his accounts and bankbooks?" Rickard said.

"Yes. I'll show you his hiding place."

They found the secret box built into the wall behind the old man's underclothes in the wardrobe.

"Cunning," said Rickard with admiration. "Why are you looking so strange?"

"I happened to think of something. Malin, where are my flowers?"

"In the basement. You took them down there yesterday afternoon."

In the basement! Anna said to herself.

Malin and Anna cleaned all the windows, washed and ironed the curtains, and bought some more pelargoniums for the empty windowsills. Rickard sold the boat, went to the bank, and fetched a calm woman who came to do the inventory. She went through the whole house and put the lowest of prices on everything.

"Considering inheritance tax," she said.

On Thursday afternoon, Maria came with the car and the children. Anna nearly hugged the air out of the little girls. After dinner, Rickard brought in the computer and printer.

"We'll have to fix up a proper place for you to work after the funeral."

A lot of people came, many more than they had expected, friends from work, party members, sailing friends, and the last remnants of the old family. The ceremony in the church and the reception afterward both vanished into unreality for Anna.

She was lonely. Days came and went.

She spent every morning on her book. It was going sluggishly, nothing but scattered thoughts. She could sit there for long spells thinking about Hanna's mother, who had seen four children die of starvation. Then she brooded over Johanna and her miscarriages, and over how strange it was that they, too, were four. She herself had lost only one child and that was quite enough.

Two children. The abortion. How had Mother found out about that? What kind of child was it that she had not allowed to be born? Boy? Girl?

"Pull yourself together," she said aloud to herself. "It's not good to weep into the keyboard."

Then she wrote, "To think that I've never known I grieved for the child."

She thought about the ivory woman, Arne's mother and her grandmother, and that Johanna had made no attempt to understand her. That was unusual. Mother had always tried hard to understand and excuse. She must have hated her mother-in-law, blaming her for everything that had been difficult and incomprehensible in Father.

"He's getting more and more like his mother," she used to say in her last years. I couldn't bring myself to listen, Anna thought. I just ran away.

Was there a dark secret in Grandmother's life, a shame that had to be kept out of sight with all that suppressed pride?

She ate her yogurt and corn flakes and went to the nursing home to feed her mother. The old people in the ward no longer frightened her. Just like everything that becomes ordinary, there was something natural about them. She got to know other visitors, the tired little woman who came every day to feed her brother, the old man who made his way through town with his bad leg to visit his wife.

Daughters, many her age.

They greeted each other, exchanged a few words about the sick relatives and the weather, this fine spring, sighing when they discussed how much longer the old one in number five had left.

Anna told Johanna about the garden, how she worked in it every afternoon to revive it. She no longer thought about whether Johanna understood.

"The lawn's the worst," she would say. "I've got all the moss out and bought some soil improver. As soon as it rains I'll sow some seed."

Next day.

"The currant bushes are improving. I've cut them back fiercely, dug around them, and manured them."

One day she had some good news.

"The roses are in bud. Just imagine! It helped to prune them and add some new soil and manure.

"Everything'll be as it was before, Mother," she would say. "I'm sowing annuals because only one perennial has survived. The peonies, those dark red ones, you know."

In the end she was able to tell her more.

"It's almost done, Mother. And it'll look great."

When the garden was ready, Johanna died, one night, in her sleep. Anna sat there as she had with her father, holding her hand.

When she got back home in the morning and walked around the garden, she felt no misery, only a great melancholy.

The family came and helped her arrange the funeral, and more people than they had expected came this time, too.

"I'll stay on for a while," said Anna.

"Anna!"

"Mother!"

Rickard's job in London was over, and he was back at the office. He was miserable, and she could see it.

"How long?"

"Until the dead are cold in their graves."

He looked alarmed, and she realized what she had said had been insanely put. Their bodies had been cremated. Together, Rickard and she had put the urns into Hanna's grave. Hanna was the only one to have prepared herself for death by buying a burial patch in Göteborg with the money from the mill.

"That was an odd expression," said Rickard.

"Yes," she said, nodding. "But right in all its absurdity."

She tried to explain.

"I had a vague idea I might learn . . . not to worry. To get used to the idea that things would be as they would be, with everything."

"With what, for instance?"

With your woman in London, to mention just one. I don't care who she is or what she looks like, or what she does in your life. Anna didn't say it, but laughed aloud with joy when she sensed it might be true.

"But we must be realistic. I've put down the deposit on the houses in Roslagen."

She nodded, but was surprised. He hadn't mentioned the purchase since he'd gone to England. Perhaps there was no woman in London.

"You'll have to give me time."

Malin settled the matter.

"I think that's sensible. You're not finished with this house yet. I don't think you will be until that book is finished."

*T*here was a wordless joy in being alone.

After she had raked up the dead leaves and rubbish from last year into a pile and set fire to it, she stood looking at the bonfire for a long time, solemnly, far away in time. She roamed along the shores, sometimes running, climbing the steep hills, rolling small stones over the precipice down into the sea.

"You seem happy," said Rickard as she picked him up at the airport late on Friday evening. It was a question. She thought for quite a while.

"No," she said finally, not really knowing what she meant. "I have no expectations," she said.

Happy? The question preoccupied her after he left to go back to Stockholm. It annoyed her. No more happiness, she thought. No more of what was lovely—instead fragile and anguished, condemned to be crushed, the fragments always hurting. Bleeding, a bandage applied, an aspirin taken, hoping it will all heal.

But as Mother says, everything leaves traces.

And all old scars ache when there's bad weather ahead.

Maria came and went. She got nearer the truth when she said to Anna that she, Anna, had become childish.

"Yes."

Malin came, too.

"Free at last, are you, Mother?"

There was something in that, yes.

"Maybe on my way," said Anna with a slight laugh. "At the moment I'm in limbo. You can see there without words. Best of all, there are no labels. I haven't seen for many years, neither the trees nor the sea, nor even you and Maria and the children. Those damned labels constantly get in the way."

Eventually Anna would find what existed in limbo. She hoped so, but she was in no hurry. She was cautious. Not inquisitive. She would take her time before asking any questions. For the time being, she was content to stop at interesting details.

Faces. Her own in the mirror. The postmistress's, the postman's, and the grave face of the child next door. And Birgir's, her father's neighbor, the only person to come to see her. His bright smile occupied her, the strange darkness in his eyes no longer frightening her. She paid a lot of attention to her whims. There weren't many. They came and went. But they surprised and pleased her, like the buds on the old rosebushes.

When the apple trees blossomed and were buzzing with bees, she made a new discovery. She could stop thinking and the eternal chatter in her mind fell silent. Suddenly she reached the place she had striven toward for years for with her meditations.

Objects fascinated her. Driftwood along the shore. Stones. Again she found constant delight in stones. One day she found a polished stone with strange veins through it, softly shaped like a fetus. She sat still there for a long time, weeping. For a while she thought of taking it back with her, but she changed her mind and threw it back into the waves.

Nothing's ever comprehensible, she thought to herself. But in small things, we can have an inkling.

*W*hen she got home, a man and a woman were standing at her gate with a heavy pot of Christmas roses, the flowers spilling over. There was something familiar about the woman with her broad face and open blue gaze.

"We met a long time ago," she said. "I'm Ingeborg, Sofia's daughter. We came to offer our condolences and return the Christmas roses your mother gave my mother when my brothers were lost at sea."

"This is my husband, Rune," she went on, and Anna shook a strong male hand.

When Anna tried to thank her, she found herself crying.

"How kind of you," she whispered, fumbling for a handkerchief, finding one, then stopping.

"I've become a real crybaby," she said. "Please come in and have a cup of coffee."

They sat in the kitchen while Anna brewed coffee and thawed out cinnamon buns.

"If anyone knows what grief is," she said, "then you must, Ingeborg."

"Yes, that's true. Worst was when Father was lost. I was so small, I couldn't understand."

"Your mother was an angel. You know, she came here every day when Grandmother was dying."

"Yes. She was pleased to be able to help."

"When my mother grew old, she often listed all her dead. This one was dead, and this one, and Sofia was with God, she used to say."

Then it was Ingeborg's turn to take out a handkerchief, and

Rune began to look uneasy. He shifted on the kitchen sofa and cleared his throat.

"To tell the truth, we didn't just come to offer our condolences," he said. "We have something to ask you, too."

"Rune!"

Ingeborg managed to stop him, and over their coffee, the two women spoke about how they'd never known each other.

"There were ten years between us, and that's a lot when you're a child."

"I thought you were so big and good-looking. And you had a job in Saluhallen. Like Mother."

"You were rather impressive with all your education."

They could laugh now. Then they went out into the garden and planted the Christmas roses in their old patch of soil on the south slope.

"You've done a fine job here."

"I managed to get the garden in order before Mother died."

"Did she know that your father . . . had gone before her?"

"I think so."

They went all over the house, and Rune praised it, again saying they must get down to what they wanted to say.

"The thing is, we'd like to buy it."

Anna's head spun.

"And one day reality knocked at her door," she whispered, then she laughed with relief and said aloud, "I can think of no better solution than that Sofia's daughter . . . and husband should take over Mother's house and garden."

Rune talked about market prices and told her that they had the money. Anna shook her head and said what was important to her was that they didn't alter the house with all those cutesy nouveau-riche things. Rune said he was a carpenter and was good at old houses.

Anna smiled and said, "How you remind me of my father. I think you'll be happy here."

Ingeborg said she had always dreamed of this place ever since she was small, that it had been a kind of image of happiness with its young family and pretty little daughter.

I suppose it could have seemed like that, Anna thought with surprise. She said she had to talk to her husband and children first. Rune looked worried.

Anna said that Rickard would be pleased and so would the girls.

"They want me back home. Rickard's coming on the weekend. Then we can meet again and settle the details. I'm worried about the furniture . . ."

"The fine mahogany furniture?"

"That Father made, yes. I don't want to throw it out . . ."

"Throw it out?" said Rune. "That'd be mad."

"Would you take over anything we haven't room for?"

"The lot," said Rune, and Anna laughed.

"It belongs in this house, doesn't it?"

Then she said there was only one hitch; she had to finish her book.

"Three weeks," she said. "I promise I'll get it done in three weeks."

After they left, she sat and stared at the computer. She hadn't written a word since Mother had died.

"The time has come," she said aloud to herself. "What I've found out, I won't forget."

She phoned Rickard. She'd expected him to be pleased but not that he would be so loud in his delight.

"My God, how I miss you."

"See you on Saturday. You must settle things with this Rune."

"I'll call a Göteborg real estate agent to find out what current prices are. How's the writing going?"

"It'll be all right now."

She stood by the phone for a long time after putting down the receiver. At last she understood. There was no woman in London.

If I hadn't had these weeks to myself, I might have become paranoid, she thought.

At seven the next morning, she was at her computer, thinking with astonishment that it was all going to have a happy ending. Despite everything.

The decision to sell forced her into the long postponed clearing of the house, sorting and arranging. She spent the afternoons doing it, starting on the top floor.

After a while she realized the house had more to reveal than just Johanna's story, like all those books in the north attic. They were in an old seaman's chest and were all tattered, read to pieces. Had Mother saved them because she hadn't the heart to throw out books? Had she thought of mending them? Some had their spines taped.

All her life, Johanna had devoured books. All that reading must have left some traces, and yet she had scarcely mentioned it, only the author Selma Lagerlöf at the beginning and then, somewhere in passing, that every week she borrowed a stack of books from the library.

Here was Strindberg, all his books as far as Anna could make out, in cheap unbound editions, some falling apart, some pages missing. Underlinings everywhere, angry exclamation marks here and there. What made the greatest impression on Anna was Dostoyevsky's *Idiot*, a bundle with notes in the margins. At first Anna couldn't read what had been written, but when she took the book out into the daylight, she found that Johanna had written "How true!" alongside every underlining.

Hjalmar Bergman's *Grandmother and Our Lord* was there, too, with Karin Boye's *Kallocain* and the poems of Harald Foss and Moa Martinson, all unbound and tattered.

Strange!

The famous proletarian writers Ivar Lo-Johansson, Harry Martinson, and Vilhelm Moberg were all on the shelves in the living room in finely bound editions.

Why did we never talk about books? It had been a common interest, after all.

Because you didn't dare.

No, it can't be that.

Because I didn't listen? Yes.

I wasn't interested in you as a person, only as my mother. Not until you fell ill, disappeared and it was too late, had all the questions come.

The next afternoon, she went through all her mother's clothes, good clothes, well cut and of good quality. Like Johanna herself. There was a jewelry case containing nothing but junk. She didn't like decking herself out, making herself visible, challenging.

Though you were so beautiful, Mother.

She found an unfamiliar box of old photographs. How pretty you were. That must be Astrid on a wharf in Oslo. Anna's heart beat faster as she took the photographs down to the sofa in the living room. There was one of Astrid and Johanna together. Arne must have taken it. How alike they were.

So unlike Hanna, both of them. Here it was, in the break between the heavily earthbound and the butterfly-light—this was where the secret lay. The . . . supernatural.

Anna hesitated for a long time over the word.

Found no better one.

It was something you knew, both of you.

Far in by the roof ridge was a huge great parcel, gigantic, wrapped firmly in an old sail. Anna hauled and tugged at it. It was heavy but she finally managed to get it out and loosen the ropes.

There it was! Hanna's Värmland sofa!

*W*hen Rickard came on Friday, he looked ten years younger. He raced through the house exclaiming at everything she had done.

They hardly slept at all the first night. For the first time Anna thought, here it is, the land without thoughts.

Then they became strictly practical, sorting, going to the dump—an impressive new installation, designed to accept most things, special cupboards for clothes, great boxes for books, paper there, metal here.

At midday, Rune and Ingeborg appeared as they had agreed. They were shyer now, as if Rickard frightened them. He was also uncertain.

"I'm no businessman," he said. "But I called a real estate agent here in town, and he gave me a price that seems to me a pure swindle. Around about a million, he said."

"That's about right," said Rune.

"No!" cried Anna. "That's shameless, Rickard."

"Yes, that's what I said."

"It's the location," said Rune. "View over the sea and large garden."

"Eight hundred thousand at the most," said Anna.

Rune's shyness vanished.

"I'm damned well not going to exploit the fact that we are dealing with financial idiots," he said, and suddenly all four of them began to laugh.

"We have some capital, Anna," said Ingeborg. "You see, we saved the insurance money from the boat that went down."

Rickard and Anna lowered their eyes.

"Let's seal it with a drink," said Rickard, unable to bear it any longer. "We can settle the rest at the bank on Monday."

"That's fine," said Rune, and when Rickard brought the whiskey, he added, "Not bad at all."

"Rickard!" said Anna, after their guests had left. "Why didn't you tell me anything about the value yesterday? Or last night? Or this morning?"

"Things were so great for us, Anna. I didn't want a fight."

"Are you afraid of me?"

"Yes, of your seriousness."

Anna felt those idiotic tears coming again, but Rickard was angry, and shouted, "Why can't we ever be like other people? Why don't we cheer because we've suddenly become rich? Why don't we sit down and plan everything we can do to the houses by Lake Risjön?"

Anna started laughing, and said, "You're absolutely right. Having money is wonderful. And there won't be any inheritance tax because the house has been mine for years, but we still owe about a hundred thousand on it."

"As you're for once willing to discuss the realities of life, then I can tell you I got ninety thousand for the boat. And there's over fifty in his savings account."

Anna gaped.

"And the way he complained about never having enough money. Why didn't you tell me?"

"Anna, my dear, why didn't you ask me?"

He's right, she thought. Any normal person would have been interested. I must get out into reality.

"There's another garden waiting for me," she said.

"Exactly."

They sat at the kitchen table all evening, sketching and planning. Anna realized at once that he had been thinking a great deal about it.

"We'll build a new large kitchen in the north angle. In a new house, you see? We'll have room for a bathroom and a laundry room there, too. And closets and other storage space."

"But what about water and drainage?"

"I've talked to a builder out there. They've got technical solutions to that kind of thing nowadays. Then we have the glassed-in corridor between the houses. I'd like to widen it, here, in the middle. It could be like a conservatory, you see?"

Anna nodded eagerly.

"I'll put Grandmother's Värmland sofa in there," she said.

They were so involved, they found it hard to sleep, which was just as well, as at midnight the phone rang.

Anna went rigid with fear. Rickard leapt up to answer.

"Hi. Have you no shame? Do you know what time it is?"

Who is it, thought Anna, calm now. He sounded pleased.

"Yes, that'll be all right. But wait a moment while I talk to my wife."

He called up the stairs that it was Sofie Rieslyn on her way home from London and she wanted to come and show him her photographs.

"She's welcome," called Anna, as surprised as anyone could be.

"I've quite forgotten to ask about your book," she said when he came back. "It's dreadful how peculiar I've been."

"It's finished now, Anna, but I need your help with the arrangement and with . . . the language. I'd like to make it into something more than just reporting. Anyway, we can leave that until tomorrow."

Thank goodness my manuscript's complete, Anna thought as Rickard fell asleep. Still, how odd that I forgot the reason he'd taken time off to go to London: to write a book about the city.

Together with Sofie Rieslyn.

On the borders of sleep, she realized it was the famous photographer she'd been afraid of. Paranoia, she thought. Watch your step, Anna.

"She looks like a crow," said Rickard at morning coffee. As usual when nervous, Anna was busy organizing things.

"I'll clean up Father's room and make a bed up for her. I'll pack away my papers so you can use the desk and the dining room to work in. Make a detour, will you, and get some fresh turbot."

"Will do."

She did not look like a crow, but more like a raven. Small, intense eyes, observant. Sharp lines in her face, white streaks in her dark hair.

"You're not a bit like the photographs Rickard showed me," Sofie said to Anna. "I'll take some better ones."

"Watch it, Anna," said Rickard. "Her top speed when it comes to portraits is four hours."

"I'd like that," said Anna. "I'd like to know at last what I really look like."

"Whoever you are," said the photographer, "you get interested when you're grieving."

It became a long lazy Sunday lunch, and then Sofie said she needed to rest.

"Not surprised," said Rickard. "After being up so late last night."

Anna usually found journalist's jargon difficult and their humor crude. But not today. She laughed and was able to share the joke.

In the afternoon, Sofie unpacked her photographs, and Rickard whistled loudly with delight, and groaned, "How the hell can I write captions to photos like these?"

Anna walked around the tables, and some time went by before they saw she had turned quite white and rigid.

Here's someone who knows, she thought. Who always focuses on the details, on the little things that could say everything.

"What's the matter, Anna?"

She didn't reply, but turned to Sofie.

"Have you always known?" she whispered.

"I think so."

"I've just learned to. For three weeks here on the shore, I've learned—about really seeing."

"Good, Anna. You won't lose it. You know, once seen . . ."

"I know."

After a long silence, Rickard said he realized a simple hack like him shouldn't ask questions.

"Exactly," Sofie and Anna agreed with a laugh.

"Horrible women," said Rickard.

Anna hurried to say, as usual, in consolation, "I'll explain later, Rickard."

"Hello there," said Sofie, and Anna flushed.

Sofie left that same evening for her neglected studio in Stockholm, as she put it. "We'll meet again," she said, and Anna knew it was true, the two of them would meet again.

On Monday they met Rune and Ingeborg at the bank as agreed.

On Tuesday the children came from Stockholm. Together they cleared the house and cleaned it. Malin wanted a bureau and two armchairs. Maria had never been able to resist books and packed the contents of the bookcases into her car. Both wanted the old porcelain, and Rickard took some of the tools from Arne's basement.

"What about you, Mother? Don't you want anything?"

"Yes, I'm taking the Värmland sofa that's in the attic."

"Heavens!"

"Out of sentiment?"

"You could say that."

They finished by Wednesday. Early Thursday morning Ingeborg and Rune were coming to fetch the keys. Then the laden cars were to drive west and then on the E4 highway northward.

The long journey home, thought Anna.

After a light dinner of cold cuts and salmon, she said, "Now listen to me, all of you. I'm going to tell you a fairy story."

Her granddaughters' eyes glowed. The little girls loved Anna's stories, though Malin was uneasy.

"I can't bear it if you get sentimental, Mom."

"Just sit still and listen," said Anna.

She told them about the old place on the Norwegian border, the waterfall and the mill, and the miller who came from Värmland and proposed to Hanna.

"Your great-great-grandmother," she said to the children.

She went on to tell them about the rich farm Hanna's ancestor had once been given by the king himself. Then she went on about the famine years, the children who had died of starvation, and the farm that had been divided up into smaller and smaller lots.

"When the last big farmer died, the big farm was still worth quite a lot," she said. "His daughter changed the inheritance. Hanna was given the deeds of the mill and all the stock on the farm, and her brothers the smaller farms.

"There was another sister, an elflike girl who married in Norway. She was left all the family jewels. It was said they were just as valuable as the other shares."

Anna showed them the photograph of Astrid, and the younger girl spoke.

"She's like Grandmother Johanna."

"So, you saw that, did you?" said Anna.

"According to tradition, the jewelry was to go from daughter to daughter in the family," she went on, and now they could all feel the tension. "But Astrid had no daughters so she decided my mother should have it. Norway was at war when she died, but in the summer of 1945, a lawyer came here.

"I'll never forget that day.

"And now, Rickard, you must get yourself a suitable tool. For we're going to bring the treasure up from the basement."

The children were pale with excitement, Maria's eyes wide

open and dark, and Malin had to make an effort to keep up her skeptical expression as they went down the basement stairs.

"You must count now, little one," said Anna. "Sixteen stones from the north wall."

"Here," said the girl.

"Good. Stay there now. Lena, you count four stones from the west wall."

"There's a beer crate there," said the girl.

"Then we'll move it."

The stone floor was clean and untouched under the crate, but Anna went on, "Now, Rickard, get your chisel into the cracks just where Lena's standing."

"It's mortar."

"No, it's modeling clay."

"Darn it, so it is."

He raised the first stone, the second, then another.

"A safe!" he cried.

"Where's the key?" cried Malin.

"I've got it. Let's take the case up to the kitchen."

They sat there staring at the glitter on the kitchen table, and Malin gasped and said, "Whatever is it all worth?"

Anna said it had never been valued, but she thought the big red stones in the necklace were probably rubies and the glittering stones in the brooches diamonds.

"The most valuable jewels don't really belong in the old inheritance. They're the ones Astrid was given or bought in Oslo. Her husband grew wealthy over the years."

Then she lifted up the two heavy gold rings and told them the story of the warrior king who had dropped the gold coin and how the farmer who had found it had melted down the gold into rings for his daughters.

Then she started laughing and said, "The fairy tale is over. Only one thing remains. I've had an extra key to the safe cut, so now I'm giving my daughters one each."

They accepted the keys, but were quite incapable of thanking her.

"I think you've been struck dumb," said Anna, still laughing.

Finally, Rickard said he wasn't surprised. He'd always known he'd married into a family full of secrets.

At dawn the next morning, they drove away from the house. Ingeborg said they were always welcome to come back to visit them, and Anna thanked her, but had the same thought that Hanna had that day when she had left the mill house.

I'll never return here again.

Hanna's Daughters

Marianne Fredriksson

A Reader's Guide

A Conversation with Marianne Fredriksson

Q: **Why do you think a story that is so deeply rooted in Scandinavian history found such huge appeal in the international community?**

MF: I received an answer to that question from a Korean publisher. He said that the issues and conflicts addressed in *Hanna's Daughters* were, to a wide extent, of current interest in his country—in particular the development from a primitive farming society to an industrial society and then to an information-based society. As far as I know, both research and literary works that examine what this "revolution" has meant for women have been scarce.

Q: **Is it your aim, then, to address women's place in this societal evolution?**

MF: I view all of my books as a kind of voyage of discovery. With *Hanna's Daughters*, I wanted to investigate why women in our western society aren't able to help themselves to the rights they have received. Women today have the same educational opportunities as men. Most have their own jobs, make their own money, and have legal rights their grandmothers didn't even dream about. Yet, most of them continue the tradition of thousands of years of humble serving: taking care of their homes, putting their children first, loving their husbands as well as possible, doing the dishes and the laundry, caring for everything and everybody.

With *Hanna's Daughters*, I wanted to examine the possibility that this was a social inheritance, a pattern that is passed on from generation to generation.

That was the starting point. The answer I thought I could sniff out during the course of the journey was that women are so incredibly dedicated in their love. That was a bit sad, I thought, because what the world needs most of all is precisely that—love.

And then we come to the question of where the line between real love and self-obliteration begins. I should mention that I've written another book with the title *If Women Were Wise, the World Would Stop*.

Q: **For you as a woman writing at the close of the twentieth century, it must have been a challenge to tell Hanna's story. How did** you become that character—this woman of such a dramatically different era and mind-set?

MF: Working with Hanna wasn't hard at all. Since her life and experiences were the most distant from mine, she gave me the greatest freedom to invent.

Q: Hanna's story is narrated in the third person, while Johanna's is told in the first. This shift in narration seems very natural as the story progresses through time and history. Although each woman has her own story, there is a subtle sense of a collective voice speaking. When the narrative moves from third to first person, it's as if that collective voice grows louder and surer of itself as it traverses the generations. Can you share your insights regarding this?

MF: I am happy with the way you put it: "a subtle sense of a collective voice speaking." That's exactly what I wanted to achieve by changing storytellers; sometimes in the first person, sometimes in the form of a diary, and so on. I should also mention that the similarity of the women's names is an expression of the collective voice as well. In the Swedish, Finnish, Norwegian, and Dutch editions the title is *Anna, Hanna and Johanna.*

Q: In many ways, Johanna seemed to be the most objective of all the women regarding her feelings toward her mother, her children, and her spouse. Is this, perhaps, a result of her growing up during such a pivotal period in history, in the flux between the old world and the new? Did she gain a keener sense of empathy because of this?

MF: That's an interesting observation. I haven't seen this phenomenon myself. Perhaps there's some truth to what you say—that people in a time of flux become more objective. And maybe the spirit of the time matters. The time after the war gave birth to a strong belief in the future and a conviction about social improvements.

Q: Can you talk a bit about the element of magic and mysticism in the novel? Does any of this derive from Scandinavian folklore? What about the recurring theme of extraordinary "coincidence"? For example, both Broman and Ragnar died within a week of their mothers, and Ragnar died in the same way as his father. Likewise, Sophia's husband and sons also died under similarly tragic circumstances. **What is symbolized by these uncanny occurrences? Is this something you have experienced in your own life?**

MF: Naturally, I read most of the research in Sweden on the subject of ethnology (a science that deals with the division of human beings into races and their origin, distribution, relations, and characteristics). This knowledge was put to great use in *Hanna's Daughters*—in addressing the idea of magic (what we call superstition) and in the patterns of expulsion in what are called cultures of shame, which still exist in smaller communities. In the modern anonymous society, we are kept on a leash out of guilt, not out of shame.

The second part of your question is more interesting, regarding that which you call "extraordinary coincidence." I don't believe in chance. I'm actually childish enough to believe there is a reason for whatever happens to us, that there are connections we can never perceive. You call it mysticism. That's okay by me; I believe life is mystical, filled with riddles science can never explain. You mention that Ragnar's death resembles his father's. One can imagine that Ragnar, like many happy and easygoing people, was carrying a great melancholy. And because of that sorrow he unconsciously chose to get in the way of his friend's bullet when his mother died. His tie to his mother was also extremely strong. But these are psychological explanations, and what good are they?

Q: **Hanna's beloved Varmland sofa seems to be a metaphor for Hanna herself, as it travels through generations and homes, always intact, and is incorporated into each new environment. Does Anna's nostalgia for the sofa symbolize an acknowledgment of her grandmother's strength and adaptability, despite her "old" ways and ideas?**

MF: The Varmland sofa is a symbol of immense importance to Hanna. It represents the advancement of the poor people from living in cottages to achieving gentry status—in other words, a journey in class. Anna suspected this, and perhaps her decision to keep the old couch was an expression of tenderness and understanding of her grandmother's struggles.

Q: **In the Dutch newspaper *De Telegraaf*, you stated that you studied your family origins to get to know yourself better. By delv-**

ing into her family's past, Anna says she was looking for home and didn't find it. How does your experience differ from Anna's, and how is it similar?

MF: I haven't read *De Telegraaf*, since I can't read Dutch, but obviously I didn't make myself clear. What I meant is that every human being eventually reaches a point where he or she wants to know more about his or her childhood: How did I think? What did I grieve? Why was I afraid, angry, happy? What shaped me? This has nothing to do with my personal background.

Q: **Do you think that this kind of psychological probe into family history speaks more to women than men? Why or why not?**

MF: I don't know. If you visit one of the big family archives in Sweden—as a lot of Americans who originally emigrated from Sweden do—you find just as many men as women there. But if you look at the psychological aspects, it seems to me that women are more interested in the private, the personal, the relationships. Are these patterns that are inherited related to the biology of the woman? I'm not sure.

Q: **While we're on this subject, did you discover any interesting stories or facts in your own family history?**

MF: In fact, I have a book being published in the United States next year that has autobiographical elements. It's titled *Simon's Family*.

Q: **Broman had an extraordinary love for Ragnar. How was Broman able to rise above the rigid morality of his time and love and embrace Ragnar, a bastard child, as his own?**

MF: Broman was a man breaking with a conservative farming society. He did the impossible: as a sole heir he left a big family estate. In other words, he was an exceptionally free person in his time—also free to love a child that wasn't his.

Q: **Broman, Arne, and Rickard all ponder the "mystery" of their wives, believing them to be full of secrets that they will never understand. Why do you think these women were so mysterious to their husbands?**

MF: But that was the way it was—and is—in our culture. The woman is either a whore or a madonna; she is a riddle that can never be solved; she is seductive and dangerous—the witch and the great good mother.

It's true that it's getting better; today there are some female life partners.

Beneath everything it's probably about sexual fear, the man's fear of being absorbed. Personally, I sometimes find it's the other way around—in my world it's the men who are mysterious (laughs).

Q: **Was Johanna and Hanna's lack of true enthusiasm for sex simply a product of the times, or did they not, perhaps, find the true loves of their life?**

MF: Sure, it's a question of the times. Women's sexual desire was often shameful. True love seldom reached down to the depths of the people and was probably rare in the upper classes, too. It existed in songs or plays.

Did it have its breakthrough with the movie, the movie kiss? I don't know.

And has this domineering myth made marriages any happier? Is it perhaps even a projection, a dream about him or her filling all my needs, giving me what I never had? I'm sorry, I keep asking questions. I haven't got any answers.

Q: **Anna writes that her mother and grandmother had no "language" to free themselves. Aside from financial independence, in what ways do you feel Anna's relationship with Rickard reflects a freedom that was missing in Hanna and Johanna's marriages?**

MF: Your question about Anna's relationship to Rickard is interesting. Despite professional and economic independence, intelligence and good education, she's not much freer than her mother and grandmother. If her lack of freedom is a result of her love for Rickard, maybe I was right with my earlier conclusion: Women love too much.

Q: **Your honest, unsentimental prose has a beautiful quality of restraint. Was this a conscious attempt to mirror, through language, the mystery and reserve of these three women?**

MF: Thank you. I don't know how I do it. I don't work consciously on my language. But I have received many letters from my readers saying the same thing—that there's something in the language that takes them to another world.

Q: **Is there any anxiety and expectation surrounding the translation of one of your novels into languages that you do not speak fluently?**

MF: I'm not anxious about the translations. You have to rely on translators and publishers to do their best. I stare in surprise at Hanna when she performs in Turkish and Hebrew, and still more when she appears in Chinese and Japanese.

Q: **Since *Hanna's Daughters* is such a worldwide success, do you think that in the future you will write with an international audience in mind?**

MF: I don't write for the audience. Maybe it sounds terrible, but I write for the sake of my own joy. And because of my agony. And because of my curiosity about life and the human being.

Q: **Do you have any favorite American novels or authors?**

MF: Oh, I have many. You have a wealth of good authors. For example, Kurt Vonnegut and Toni Morrison, to mention just a few. Right now I've fallen in love with James Salter's books.

Reading Group Questions and Topics for Discussion

1. Regarding the notion of psychological inheritance, the author states in the foreword that "we inherit patterns, behavior, and ways of reacting to a much greater extent than we like to admit. It has not been easy to take this on; so much was 'forgotten,' disappearing into the subconscious when grandparents left farms and countryside where the family had lived for generations." In your opinion, and drawing from your own experiences, what is the "forgotten" that the author speaks about?

2. What are some psychological patterns and behaviors that women of your generation have "inherited"? Are they at odds with your ambitions and desires? Why or why not?

3. Which of the main female and male characters did you most easily identify with? Why?

4. Have your ever traced your family history before, or had a friend or relative who has? Share the experience.

5. John Broman describes Hanna as "heathen and witchlike." Do you think that her superstitious nature is just about her fears and insecurities, or does she, like her daughter and granddaughter, have a special sense of things? Is it possible that, because she wasn't educated, her intuitiveness just expresses itself in this way? In that vein, what kind of woman do you think Hanna would have become had she been a part of Johanna's or Anna's generation?

6. Do you feel that any of the women achieved genuine fulfillment in their marriages? Why or why not?

7. In Anna's cathartic letter to her mother, she writes that Hanna was the strongest of the three women, that she had "sense and continuity" and was a "realist," who "lived as she believed." Do you agree with Anna's assessment? In what respects was Hanna more of a realist than her daughters? If you were to write this kind of letter to your mother, what would you tell her?

8. In the last line of this letter, Anna writes, "I've learned a great deal, though, and I'm damn well not going to do what you did, Mother, give up when the truth collapses into a thousand truths." What do you think Anna means by this? How has Johanna given up? What is the truth Anna speaks of?

9. In Johanna's story, we learn that Hanna offered to help Johanna raise her daughter and assured her that she didn't need to marry Arne. Does this seem an uncharacteristically modern attitude for Hanna, especially for a woman who suffered firsthand the shame of having a child out of wedlock? Why do you think she so adamantly maintains that Johanna doesn't need a husband, despite her own experience?

10. Anna believes that she is much stronger than her mother and has not "been bowed into total dependence." Has Anna really achieved emotional independence? Why or why not?

11. Consider this passage at the end of the novel when Anna meets Sofie—the photographer working with Rickard.

> Anna walked around the tables, and some time went by before they saw she had turned quite white and rigid.
> Here's someone who knows, she thought. Who always focuses on the details, on the little things that could say everything.
> "What's the matter, Anna?"
> She didn't reply, but turned to Sofie.
> "Have you always known?" she whispered.
> "I think so."
> "I've just learned to. For three weeks here on the shore, I've learned—about really seeing."
> "Good, Anna. You won't lose it. You know, once seen . . ."
> "I know."

What does this exchange mean to you? Why did these two strangers have such an intense connection?

12. Johanna mentions that the writer Selma Lagerlof had a huge impact on her and her girlfriends in the 1920s—that she dangerously shaped their expectations of love and happiness. Is there a particular book, movie, or figure that affected you—or your generation—in this way?

13. Aside from the great influence of family, each of these women has been significantly shaped by the spirit of her time and generation. Which do you think shapes us more—our personal, family history or the generation to which we belong? Why?

About the Author

Marianne Fredriksson's novels have sold more than two million copies in her native Sweden. *Hanna's Daughters* is her first U.S. publication.

The following is an excerpt from Marianne Fredriksson's
novel *Simon's Family*, now available in a
bookstore near you.

T W O

*S*imon's mother was a good woman.

That could never be forgotten, for her goodness was somehow always present. It shaped the world in which the boy grew up.

She was also beautiful, tall, and blond, with a large sensitive mouth and startlingly brown eyes.

Her goodness was not the cloying kind. She was strong in herself, not threatened by growth in other people. Karin was one of those rare people who know that love cannot be cultivated simply with nourishment and water.

She also understood that almost nothing could be done about the fear running through people's lives and that no one can help another person internally. And that makes the need for consolation endless.

So she became the person everyone turned to. There was no ill-treated woman or man not given coffee and comfort in her kitchen, not to mention all the children who were allowed to cry it out and then given cocoa.

She neither dried their tears nor found any solutions.

But she could listen.

She wasn't a woman to get satisfaction from other people's sorrow. Her patience and great heart gave her little joy. In fact, all the misery in life she confronted in her kitchen only increased her own sorrow. But from it she found new fuel for her socialist convictions. She avowed that people treat each other like animals because *they* are treated like animals.

Like all good people, she did not believe in evil. It existed, but not in itself, and was only an outgrowth of injustice and unhappiness.

Now it was the evening after the day Simon had decided to be grown up. The fog had lifted toward afternoon, and the light May sky dyed pink by the red-and-white-checked cloth on the kitchen sofa as he lay there thinking about his decision.

He had done it for his mother's sake, that was clear. But he hadn't found the words that would explain it to her. So he had lost his reward, that of seeing the sorrow disappearing from her brown eyes.

That sorrow was the only truly alarming thing in the boy's life, the only unbearable thing. He would not understand until much later, when he was an adult and she was dead, that her sorrow had little to do with him.

He could make her happy. Over the years he had thought up a great many tricks to get that laughing glint in her brown eyes. Subsequently, he always thought he was the cause of both her happiness and her sadness.

A few days earlier, they had learned that Simon had gotten into high school, the first in the family to be allowed to study. Although only eleven, he had filled in the application form himself and cycled alone on the long road to that stuck-up school, as his parents called it, when the time came for the entrance test.

The boy had seen the glint in his mother's eye when he had returned with the news that he had passed.

The light went out the moment his father spoke.

"So you're going to be something, are you? And I'll have to pay, of course. Are you sure we can afford it?"

"We'll handle the money," his mother said. "But the rest you'll have to do yourself, Simon. It was your idea."

A few years later, in puberty, he would hate them for the words spoken in the kitchen that evening, and for the loneliness that followed. But later in life, he came to understand his parents, understand their ambivalence toward the middle-class school that devoured the bookish children and ate at the working classes from within. Later he would also have some idea of their feelings as they sat over dinner and wondered if the boy would now outgrow them.

But on the other hand they wanted their child to have the very best.

So one night, when Karin cleared the table and wiped the oilcloth clean, Erik took out his account book and, looking worried, asked about school fees, calculating the cost of books and tram money. But that was all largely for show, as there was no real shortage of money.

Only the eternal terror of poverty.

His mother hardly gave money a thought, but she was not in a good mood and her eyes darkened with the weight of her words. "Then all these dreams'll have to come to an end."

Perhaps her anxiety had nothing to do with whether Simon could cope with school. Perhaps she was worried her boy would now become one of the kind who was neither one thing nor the other, one of those people who were always searching for something in themselves.

But Simon only heard their words, and he lay there on the kitchen sofa thinking how pleased she would be if he could somehow tell her that he would be like the other children, but more so and better. For he had noticed she was proud of his good marks and the teacher's words at the end of term last year.

"Simon is very gifted," his teacher had said.

His father had grunted, suspecting the very word, then had been embarrassed for the teacher. Saying things like that when the boy could hear, that was crazy.

"The lad could get uppish," he said as they walked slowly home. "Gifted," he went on, savoring the word, spitting it out.

"He's clever," said Karin.

"Of course he's clever," said Erik. "He takes after us."

"And you talk about being uppish," his wife said, but her laugh was happy.

The boy had always been bookish, as they say. It was a quality that was accepted, like his smallness and his black hair.

Simon had devoured all the books in the house that first summer holiday. He remembered when one woman found him on the sofa in the parlor with *Gösta Berling's Saga*.

"Is the lad reading Lagerlöf?" she said in a disapproving voice.

"You can't stop him," said Karin.

"But he can't understand a book like that."

"He must understand something or he'd stop reading it."

His mother hadn't sounded apologetic, but nevertheless the woman had the last word.

"Believe you me, nothing good can come of it."

Did a shadow of unease come over Karin? Perhaps, for she must have told his father.

"Don't you go thinking the world consists of upper-class misses and mad priests," he said. "Read Jack London."

Simon read the collected works of Jack London, brown marbled editions with red borders on the spines. He would remember these characters and images for some time—Wolf Larsen, a priest who ate human flesh, the mad violin player, that long leafy lake in the sun, and the East End slums.

The rest sank into his subconscious and flourished there.

At the age of eleven, he had found his way to the public library in Majorna, his thirst less urgent now, as happens in someone who knows he always has access to water. He had also become more cautious, seeing the anxiety flitting over his mother's face as she asked herself whether there might be something seriously different about her boy.

"Get on outside and run around before the blood rots in your veins," she would say. It was a joke, but beneath it lay an unease.

She once found him in the attic, deep in Joan Grant's book on the Queen of Egypt. He stared at Karin from Pharaonic heights, not even hearing what she had said. Not until she shook him back through the centuries did he see she was frightened.

"You mustn't lose your grasp on life like that," she said.

It still hurt whenever he remembered that.

That evening on the kitchen sofa, he questioned himself: Was there something seriously wrong with him?